"The thing is, Mr. Valenti, I'm pregnant."

Renzo Valenti, heir to the Valenti family real estate fortune, known womanizer and chronic over-indulger, stared down at the stranger standing in his entryway.

He had never seen the woman before in his life. Of that he was one hundred percent certain.

He did not associate with women like this. Women who looked like they had spent an afternoon traipsing through the streets of Rome, rather than an afternoon tangled in silk sheets.

Esther was red-cheeked and disheveled, her face void of make-up, long dark hair half falling out of a bun that looked like an afterthought.

Had she been walking by him outside he would never have paid her any notice. Except she was in his home. And she had just said words to him no woman had spoken to him since he was sixteen years old.

But they meant nothing. As she meant nothing.

"Congratulations. Or condolences," he said. "Depending."

"You don't understand—"

"No," he said, his voice cutting through the relative silence of the grand antechamber. "I don't. You practically burst into my home, telling my housekeeper you had to see me, and now here you are, having pushed you~~~~ not drawing this out a~~~~ no patience for either.~~~~

"It's *your* baby."

THE ITALIAN'S PREGNANT VIRGIN

BY
MAISEY YATES

First Published in Great Britain 2016
By Mills & Boon, an imprint of HarperCollins*Publishers*
1 London Bridge Street, London, SE1 9GF

© 2016 Maisey Yates

ISBN: 978-0-263-92505-0

Printed and bound in Spain
by CPI, Barcelona

Maisey Yates is a *New York Times* bestselling author of more than thirty romance novels. She has a coffee habit she has no interest in kicking, and a slight Pinterest addiction. She lives with her husband and children in the Pacific Northwest. When Maisey isn't writing she can be found singing in the grocery store, shopping for shoes online and probably not doing dishes. Check out her website: maiseyyates.com.

Books by Maisey Yates

Mills & Boon Modern Romance

Carides's Forgotten Wife
Bound to the Warrior King
Married for Amari's Heir
His Diamond of Convenience
To Defy a Sheikh
One Night to Risk it All

Heirs Before Vows

The Prince's Pregnant Mistress
The Spaniard's Pregnant Bride

The Chatsfield

Sheikh's Desert Duty

One Night With Consequences

The Greek's Nine-Month Redemption
Married for Amari's Heir

Princes of Petras

A Christmas Vow of Seduction
The Queen's New Year Secret

Secret Heirs of Powerful Men

Heir to a Desert Legacy
Heir to a Dark Inheritance

Visit the Author Profile page at
millsandboon.co.uk for more titles.

To my parents, who actually are great
and have always supported me. In spite of
what 90% of my characters' parents might suggest.

CHAPTER ONE

"THE THING IS, Mr. Valenti, I'm pregnant."

Renzo Valenti, heir to the Valenti family real estate fortune, known womanizer and chronic overindulger, stared down at the stranger standing in his entryway.

He had never seen the woman before in his life. Of that he was nearly one hundred percent certain.

He did not associate with women like this. Women who looked like they had spent a hot, sweaty afternoon traipsing through the streets of Rome, rather than a hot, sweaty afternoon tangled in silk sheets.

She was red-cheeked and disheveled, her face void of makeup, long dark hair half falling out of a bun that looked like an afterthought.

She was dressed the same as many American college students who flooded the city in the summer. She was wearing a form-fitting black tank top and a long, ankle-length skirt that nearly covered her dusty feet and flat, unremarkable sandals that appeared to be falling apart.

Had she been walking by him outside, he would never have paid her any notice. Except she was in his home. And she had just said words to him no woman had said to him since he was sixteen years old.

But they meant nothing, as she meant nothing.

"Congratulations. Or condolences," he said. "Depending."

"You don't understand."

"No," he said, his voice cutting through the relative silence of the grand antechamber. "I don't. You practically burst into my home telling my housekeeper you had to see me, and now here you are, having pushed your way in."

"I didn't push my way in. Luciana was more than happy to *let* me in."

He would never fire his housekeeper. And the unfortunate thing was, the older woman knew it. So when she had let a hysterical girl into his home, he had a feeling she considered it punishment for his notorious behavior with the opposite sex.

Which was not fair. This little *creature*—who looked as though she would be most at home sitting on a sidewalk in the vicinity of Haight-Ashbury, playing an acoustic guitar for coins—might well be some man's unholy punishment. But she wasn't his.

"Regardless, you're not drawing this out and making a show, and I have no patience for either."

"It's *your* baby."

He laughed. There was absolutely no other response for such an outrageous statement. And there was no other way to remove the strange weight, the strange tension that gripped him when she spoke the words.

He knew why it affected him. But it should not.

He could imagine no circumstance under which he would touch such a ridiculous little hippie. And even so, he had just spent the past six months devoted to the world's most obscene farce of a marriage.

And though Ashley had been devoted to the pleasure of both herself—and other men—during their union, he had been faithful.

A woman with a small baby bump, barely showing

beneath that skin-tight top, claiming to be carrying his child could be absolutely nothing but ridiculous to him.

He'd had nothing at all but six months of fights, dodging vases flung in a rage by his crazy wife—who seemed to do her best to demolish the stereotype that Canadians were a nice and polite people—and then days on end of ridiculous cooing like he was some kind of pet she was trying to tame again after a sound beating.

Little realizing that he was not a man to be tamed, and never had been. He had married Ashley to make a point to his parents, and for no other reason. As of yesterday, he was divorced and free again.

Free to take this little backpacker in any way he wanted to, if he so chose.

Though, she would find the only place he wanted to take her was out the front door, and back onto the streets she had come from.

"That, you will find, is impossible, *cara mia*." Her eyes went round, liquid, shock and pain visible. What had she imagined would happen? That he would fall for this ruse? That she would find her salvation in him? "I can see how you would build some strange fantasy around the idea I might be your best bet for help," he said, attempting to keep his tone calm. "I have a reputation with women. But I have also been married for the past six months. So whatever man is responsible for knocking you up in a bar crawling with tourists and never calling again? He is not me, nor will you ever con me into believing it is. I am divorced now, but in the time I was married I was faithful to my wife."

"Ashley," she said, blinking rapidly. "Ashley Bettencourt."

He was stunned, but only momentarily, by her usage of his wife's name. It was common knowledge, so of course if she knew about him, she would know about Ashley. But if she knew he was married, why not choose an easier target?

"Yes. Very good," he said. "You're up on your tabloid reading, I see."

"No, I *know* Ashley. She's actually the person I met in a bar crawling with tourists. *She's* the one who knocked me up."

Renzo felt like he'd been punched in the chest. "Excuse me? None of what you're saying makes sense."

The little woman growled, lifting her hands and gripping her head for a moment before throwing them back down at her sides, curling her fingers into fists. "I am… I am trying. But I thought you would know who I was!"

"Why would I know who you are?" he asked, feeling at a loss.

"I just… Oh, I should never have listened to her. But I was… I am just as stupid as my dad thinks I am!" She was practically wailing now, and he had to admit, this farce was inventive even if it was damned disruptive to his day.

"Right at this moment I'm on your father's side, *cara*, and I will remain so until you have offered me an explanation that falls somewhere short of being as stupid as my *ex-wife* getting you pregnant."

"Ashley hired me. I was working at a bar down by the Colosseum, and she and I started talking. She was telling me about the issues in your marriage and the trouble you were having conceiving…"

The words made his gut twist. He and Ashley had never attempted to conceive. By the time they'd gotten to a place where they might discuss giving him an heir to his empire, he'd already decided that no amount of shock value made her worth it as a wife.

"I thought it was weird, her talking to me like that. But she came back the next night, and the next. We talked about how I ended up in Italy and how I had no money…" She blinked. "And then she asked me if I would consider being her surrogate."

Pressure built in Renzo's chest until it exploded. English deserted him entirely, a string of vulgar Italian flowing from his lips like a foul river. "I don't believe it. This is some trick that bitch has put you up to."

"It's not. I promise you it isn't. I had no idea that you didn't know. No idea at all. It was all very… What she said… It made sense. And…and she said it would be easy. Just a quick trip to Santa Firenze, where the procedure is legal, and then I just have to…be the oven. I was supposed to get paid to make the bread, so to speak, and then… well, give it to the person I…baked it for. Someone who wanted the baby desperately enough to ask for help from a stranger."

Panic tore through Renzo like a wild beast, savaging his chest, his throat. Making it impossible to breathe. What she was saying was impossible. It had to be. Mostly.

Ashley was…unpredictable. And God knew how that might manifest. Especially since she'd been enraged by the divorce—made simple because of their marriage in Canada, which she had felt was calculated on his part. It was, of course.

But she wouldn't have done this. She couldn't have. Still, he pressed.

"It made sense to you that a woman pursued surrogacy, and claimed to have a husband whom you never saw?"

"She said that it would be impossible for you to come to the clinic. She could only do it because she wore large sunglasses and a hat. She said that you were far too recognizable. She said you were very tall." She swept her hand up and down. "You are. Obviously. You don't blend. Not even sunglasses would disguise… You know what I mean."

"I know nothing. It has become apparent to me over the past few minutes that I know less than I thought. That snake talked you into this. How much did she pay you?"

"Well, she hasn't given me everything yet."

He laughed, the sound bitter. "Is that so? I hope that final price is a high one."

"Well, the problem is that Ashley said she doesn't want the baby anymore. Because of the problems that you're having."

"Problems?" The question was incredulous. "Does she mean our divorce?"

"I…I guess."

"So, you did some cursory research on us, and then no more?"

"I don't have internet at the hostel," she said flatly.

"You live in a hostel?"

"Yes," she said, her cheeks turning a darker shade of pink. "I was just passing through. And I ran out of money. Took a job at a bar, and I've been here longer than I anticipated. Then I met Ashley about three months ago."

"How far along are you?"

"Only about eight weeks. I just… Ashley decided she didn't want the baby anymore. And I don't want to…I don't want to end the pregnancy. And I thought that even though she said you didn't want to handle any of this, because it damaged your view of the whole thing…I wanted to come to you. I needed to make sure."

"Why is that? Because you fancy that you will raise the baby if I don't want it?"

It was her turn to laugh. There was no humor in it, only hysteria. "No! I'm not going to raise a baby. Not now. Not *ever*. I don't want children. I don't want a husband. But I was involved in this. I agreed to it. And I feel like…I don't know. How can I not feel responsible? She became a friend to me almost. I mean, she was one of the first people in forever who talked to me, told me about her life. She made sure I knew how much she wanted this baby and…now she doesn't. She might have changed her mind, but I can't change my feelings about it."

"What will you do?" he asked. "What will you do if I tell you I don't want the baby?"

"I'll give it up for adoption," she said, as though it were the most obvious thing. "I was going to give birth anyway. That was part of the agreement."

"I see." His thoughts were racing, trying to catch up with everything that the woman in front of him—the woman whose name he still didn't know—was saying to him. "And was Ashley planning on paying you the rest of the fee if you continued with the pregnancy?"

The woman looked down. "No."

"So, you had to make sure that you could still collect your fee? Is that why you came to speak to me?"

"No. I came to speak to you because it seemed like the right thing to do. Because I was becoming concerned about your lack of involvement in the whole thing."

Anger built inside him, reaching its boiling point and bubbling over. "Allow me to paint a clear picture for you of what exactly happened. My ex-wife went behind my back to hire you. I still don't understand how this happened. I don't understand how she was able to manipulate both you and the doctor. I don't understand how she was able to accomplish this without my knowing. I don't understand what her endgame was, as she is now clearly backing out. Perhaps now that she has seen she will get no money from me, and I'm not worth the effort anyway, she does not wish to be saddled with my child for the rest of her shallow existence. Or, perhaps it is simply Ashley. Who decided to do something on a whim, thinking that something of this magnitude would be a delightful surprise she would drop in my lap like the purchase of a new handbag. And much like my ex feels about handbags, she has decided she is bored of this one and moved on to the next shiny thing. Regardless of her motivation, the end result is the same. I didn't know. I did not want this baby."

At that, she seemed to deflate. Her shoulders shrunk inward, some of her defiant posture diminishing. "Okay." She blinked rapidly, lifting her chin and staring him down. "If you change your mind, I'm at the hostel Americana. You can find me there. Unless I'm working at the bar across the street." She turned on her heel and began to walk away from him, toward the front door. Then she paused. "You claim you've been in the dark this whole time. I just didn't want you to have that excuse anymore."

Then she walked out of his house. And just like his ex-wife, he determined that he would think about her no more.

It nagged at him. There was no escaping it. For three days he'd attempted to ignore and dismiss the events that had occurred earlier. He did not know the woman's name. He didn't even really know if she was telling the truth. Or if she was another of his ex-wife's games.

Knowing Ashley, that was it. Just a game. A weird attempt to try to draw him back into her web. She had been far too content with the dissolution of their union. Particularly after she had been so bitter about it in the first place. She had claimed he had always known it would end this way. Which was why they had sought marriage outside the country. Divorce in Italy was far too complicated. And, he supposed, the fact that he had covered his bases in such a manner was in some ways indicative of his commitment. Or at least, his faith in the mercurial Ashley.

But then, he imagined Ashley had gotten her revenge. Surrogacy was not legal in Italy. Undoubtedly why she had sought to have the procedure done in neighboring Santa Firenze.

More the pity that his sister, Allegra, had dissolved her agreement with the prince of that country and married Renzo's friend—Spanish duke Cristian Acosta, who would be no help to him in this situation—instead.

He should let it go. Likely the woman was lying. Even if she weren't…what should it matter to him?

A sharp pang in the vicinity of his heart told him he clearly hadn't had enough to drink. So, he set out to remedy that. But for some reason, grabbing a hold of the bottle of Scotch reminded him of what the stranger had said before she'd left.

She worked at a bar. She worked at a bar near the Colosseum, and if he wanted to find her he could look there.

He took the stopper out of the Scotch bottle. That would all be very well and good if he in fact wanted to find her. He did not. There was no point in searching for a woman who was—in point of fact—probably only attempting to scam money out of him.

But the possibility lingered. It lingered inside him like an acrid smell that he couldn't shake. One that remained long after the source of the odor was removed. He couldn't let it go because of Jillian. Because of everything that had happened with her.

He gritted his teeth, setting the bottle back down. Then, he strode toward his closet, grabbing a pair of shoes and putting them on quickly. He would get his car, he would go down to the bar, and he would confront this woman. Then, he would be able to come back home and go to bed, sleeping well, knowing with full confidence that she was a liar and that there was no baby.

He paused for a moment, taking a deep breath. Perhaps he was being overly cautious. But given his history, he felt he had to be. He had lost one child, and he would not lose another one.

CHAPTER TWO

ESTHER ABBOTT TOOK a deep breath as she cleared off the last table of her shift. Hopefully, she would have a decent amount of money in tips when she counted everything up, then, she would finally be able to rest easy. Her feet hurt. And she imagined that as early on as she was in the pregnancy, she couldn't exactly blame it on that.

It was just the fact that she had been working for ten hours. But what other choice did she have? Renzo Valenti had sent her away. Ashley Bettencourt wanted nothing to do with her or the baby. And if Esther had any sense in her head she would probably have complied with the other woman's wishes and pursued a termination. But she just couldn't do it.

Apparently, she had no sense in her head. She had a lot of feelings inside her chest, though. Feelings that made all of this seem impossible, and painful, and just a bit too much.

She had come to Europe to pursue independence. To see something of the world. To try to gain perspective on life away from the iron fist of her father. That brick wall that she could no more reason with than she could break apart.

In her father's world, a woman didn't need an education that extended beyond homemaking. In her father's world, a woman didn't need to drive, not when her husband should accompany her everywhere at all times. In her father's world a woman could have no free thought or independence. Esther had always longed for both.

And it was that longing that had gotten her into trouble. That had caused her father to kick her out of the commune. Oh, she'd had options, she supposed. To give up the "sinful" items she'd been collecting. Books, music. But she'd refused.

It had been so hard. To make that choice to leave. In many ways it had been her choice, even if it was an ultimatum. But the commune had been home, even if it had been oppressive.

A place filled with like-minded people who clung to their version of old ways and traditions they had twisted to suit them. If she had stayed any longer, her family would have married her off. Actually, they would have done it a long time ago if she hadn't been such a problem. The kind of daughter nobody wanted their son to marry.

The kind of daughter her father eventually had to excommunicate to set an example to the others. His version of love. Which was really just control.

She huffed out a laugh. If they could see her now. Pregnant, alone, working in a den of sin and wearing a tank top that exposed a slim stretch of midriff whenever she bent over. All of those things would be deeply frowned upon.

She wasn't sure if she approved of her situation either. But it was what it was.

Why had she ever listened to Ashley? Well, she *knew* why. Because she had been tempted by the money. Because she wanted to go to college. Because she wanted to extend her time in Europe, and because she found that waiting tables really was kind of awful.

There was nothing all that romantic about backpacking. About staying in grimy hostels.

It was more than that, though. Ashley had seemed so vulnerable when they'd met. And she had painted a picture of a desperate couple in a rocky place in their marriage, who needed a child to ease the pain that was slowly breaking them apart.

The child would be so loved. Ashley had been adamant about that. She had told Esther about all her plans for the baby. Esther hadn't been loved like that. Not a day in her life.

She had wanted to be part of that. Even in just a small way.

Finding out that was a lie—the happy-family picture Ashley had painted—was the most wrenching part of it all.

She laughed and shook her head. Her father would say this was her punishment for being greedy. For being disobedient and headstrong.

Of course, he would probably also expect this would send her running back home. She wouldn't do that. Not ever.

She looked up, looked at the view in front of her. Looked around her at the incredible clash of chaos that was Rome. How could she be regretful? It might be difficult to carry the baby to term with no help. But she would. And then after that she would make sure that the child found a suitable home.

Not one with her. But then, it wasn't her baby, after all. It was Renzo's. Renzo and Ashley's. Her responsibilities did not extend beyond gestation. She felt pretty strongly about that.

The hair on the back of her neck seemed to stand on end, a rush of prickles moving down her spine. She straightened, then slowly turned. And through the crowd, across the bar that was teeming with people, tables crammed together, the dark lighting providing a sense of anonymity, he seemed to stand out like a beacon.

Tall, his dark hair combed back off his forehead, custom suit tailored perfectly to his physique. His hands were shoved in his pockets, his dark eyes searching. Renzo Valenti.

The father of this baby. The man who had so callously sent her away three days earlier. She hadn't expected to see him again. Not when he had been so adamant about the fact that he would have nothing to do with the child. That he didn't even believe her story.

But here he was.

A surge of hope went through her. Hope for the child. And—she had to confess internally, with no small amount of guilt—hope for her. Hope that she would be compensated for the surrogacy, as she had been promised.

She wiped her hands on her apron, stuffing a bar towel in the front pocket and striding across the room. She waved a hand, and the quick movement must have caught his attention, because just then, his gaze locked on to hers.

And everything slowed.

Something happened to her. A rush of heat flowed down through her body, pooling in her stomach, and slightly lower. Suddenly, her breasts felt heavy, her breath coming in short, harsh bursts. She was immobilized by that stare. By the fathomless, black depths that seemed to pin her there, like a butterfly in one of the collections her brothers had had.

She was trembling. And she had no idea why. Very few things intimidated her. Since she had stood there in front of her father—in front of the whole commune, like a bad movie or something—refusing to recant the "evil" things she had brought in from the outside, there wasn't much that bothered her. She had clung to what she wanted, defying everything she had been taught, defying her father, leading to her expulsion from the only home she'd ever known. That moment made everything else seem mundane in many ways.

Perhaps, she had imagined, the world would turn out to be every bit as scary and dangerous as her mother and father had promised her it would be. But once she had purposed in herself that she was willing to take that chance to discover herself, to discover her freedom, she had made peace with it. With whatever might happen.

But she was shaking now. Was intimidated. Was maybe even a little bit afraid.

And then he began to close the space between them. And it felt as though there was a connection between the two of them. As though there was a string tied around her waist, one he was holding in his hands. And even though he was the one drawing nearer to her, she felt the pull to him.

It was loud in the bar, but when he spoke it cut through like a knife. Effortless, sharp and exceedingly clear. "I think you and I need to have a little chat."

"We tried that," she said, shocked at how foreign her voice sounded. How breathless. "It didn't exactly go like I planned on it going."

"Well, you walked into my home and dropped a bombshell on me. So, I'm not entirely certain how you expected it to go."

"Well, I didn't know it was a bombshell. I thought we were just going to discuss something you already knew. A bombshell you were complicit in."

"Sadly for you, I was not complicit. But if what you're saying is true, we definitely need to come to an agreement of some kind."

"What I'm saying is absolutely true. I have the documentation back at the hostel."

He narrowed his eyes. "And I'm supposed to believe that this documentation is factual?"

She laughed. "I wouldn't know where to begin forging medical paperwork like that."

"That means nothing to me. Your word means nothing to me. I don't know who you are. I don't know anything about you. All I know is that you showed up at my house earlier and are now asking me to believe the most fantastical of tales. Why should I?"

"Well," she said, looking down at her sandaled feet, "I suppose because you're here." She looked back up at him, her breath catching in her throat when she met with his furious gaze. "That means you must think it could be true. And if it could be true, why wouldn't it be? Why would I target you? Why would I…I don't know. It's just… Trust me. I would never have cooked this up on my own."

"Take me back to your hostel."

"I'm just off shift. I need to go write down my time."

He reached out, grabbing hold of her bare arm. The contact between his fingers and her skin sent an electric crackle down through her body. She had to think. Really think if she had ever been touched like this by a man. Other than a doctor or her family members, she'd had very little physical contact with anyone. And this seemed… It seemed more than significant. It burned her all the way down to the soles of her feet. Made her feel like her shoes might melt.

Like *she* might melt.

"I will speak to your boss later if need be. But you're coming with me now."

"I shouldn't."

A smile curved his lips. It was not kind. It did nothing to dispel any of the tension in her chest. If anything, it made everything feel heavier. Tighter. "But you will, *cara mia*. You will."

After that statement of declaration, she found herself being propelled out of the open-air bar and onto the busy street. It was still teeming with people, humidity hanging in the overly warm air. Her hair was sticking to the back of her neck, her tank top sticking to her skin, and his body was like a furnace beside her as they strode purposefully down the street.

"You don't know where I live."

"Yes I do. I am fully capable of looking up the name of a hostel and finding the directions. And I know the streets well."

"This isn't the way back," she said, feeling the need to try to find some power in the situation. She despised feeling helpless. Despised feeling controlled.

"Yes," he said, "it is."

Much to her dismay, this alternate route seemed to put them back at the front door of the hostel much more quickly than the one she typically took. She pursed her lips together, frowning deeply.

"You're welcome," he said, pushing the door open, his entire posture and tone radiating a kind of arrogance she had never before come into contact with.

"For what?"

"I have just showed you a better route home. Likely I will save you time in the future. You're welcome."

She scowled, ducking her head and walking past him into the narrow hallway. She led him down the hall, to the small room that she had in the back. There were four bunk beds in it, with two other women currently occupying the space. It was fairly private, all things considered. Though, as Esther began to feel more symptomatic of her pregnancy, it began to feel more and more crowded.

She kicked her sandals off, making her way across the pale, uneven stone floor, and headed to the bottom bunk, where all of her things were kept when she wasn't sleeping. Her backpack was shoved into the corner by the wall, and she grabbed hold of it, dragging it toward her.

When she didn't hear footsteps following her, she turned to see Renzo standing in the doorway. His frame filled the space, and when he took that first step inside, he seemed to bring something with him. Tension. A presence that filled not only the room, but any empty space in her chest.

"Welcome," she said, her tone flat.

"Thank you," he responded, his words carrying a level of disdain that was almost comical. Except, it was difficult to find much of anything funny at the moment.

She tugged on the drawstring that kept her backpack cinched shut, then hunted around for the tightly folded papers that were down in the bottom. "This is it." She held it out to him and he took it. His fingertips didn't brush hers, and she found herself preoccupied by the realization that she had almost hoped they would.

"What is all of this?" he asked, unfolding the documents.

"Medical records of everything and the signed agreement. With both mine and Ashley's signature. I suppose you would know if it looked different from your wife's actual signature. And I think we can both agree that the likelihood of me randomly being able to forge it is slim."

He frowned, deep lines forming between his dark brows. "This seems… It seems like perhaps there could be some truth."

"Call Ashley. Call her. She's mad at me. I'm sure she'll be more than happy to yell at you, too."

"Ashley wants you to end the pregnancy?"

Esther nodded, swallowing hard. "I can't. I agreed to

this. And even though the baby isn't mine, without me, maybe it wouldn't exist. And I just… I can't."

"Well, if this is in fact my child, that isn't what I want either."

"You want the baby?"

She tried to read his expression, but she found it impossible. Not that she was exceptionally adept at decoding what people were thinking. She had spent so many years growing up in a closed community. Seeing any faces at all that were unfamiliar was a shock. Going out into the wide world after an entire life being cloistered was… There were so many sights. So many sounds and smells. Different voices, different accents. Different ways of expressing happiness, sadness.

While she often felt at a disadvantage, sometimes she wondered if she actually read people a bit better than those who didn't have to look as closely at the people around them. She always felt that if she released hold on her vigilance—even for a second—she would find herself lost in this endless sea of humanity.

But there were no clues at all on Renzo's face. It was as though he were carved from granite. His lips pressed into a firm line, his black eyes flat. Endless.

"I will take responsibility for my child," he said, which was not the same as wanting the child. But she supposed, it didn't matter.

"Well…I suppose that's…" She didn't want to ask about payment. Except, she desperately wanted to ask about payment.

"But the first thing we must do is get you out of this…" He looked around the room, his lip curling slightly. "This place. You cannot stay here. Not while you are carrying the heir to the Valenti fortune."

She blinked rapidly. The baby that she was carrying

was the heir to a fortune? She knew that Renzo was rich. Of course she did. She had seen the way that Ashley was accustomed to living after their stay at the lavish hotel the other woman had insisted they stay in when they'd gone across the border for the procedure.

Still. This revelation seemed different. "But we've been fine for the past couple of months," she said.

"Perhaps. Though, I imagine our definition of 'fine' may be sharply different from one another's. You are not to work at that bar, not anymore. And you will come with me. Back to my villa."

Esther felt like she had been punched in the chest. She found that she couldn't breathe. She felt immobilized. Utterly and completely weighted down by that dark, uncompromising gaze.

"But what if I... What if I don't want to?"

"You don't have a choice," he returned. "There is a clause in this agreement that says Ashley can choose to terminate it should she decide she no longer wants the pregnancy carried to term. That has happened. That means unless you comply with my demands, with my word, you will get nothing. And you will have no recourse. Not—I assure you—in Italy. I will pay you more than the sum my wife agreed on, but only if you do exactly as I say."

Her head was spinning. She felt like she needed to sit down or she was going to fall down. She found herself doing exactly that before she even realized it, her weak legs folding, plopping her down roughly onto the edge of the thin mattress, the wood frame digging sharply into her thighs.

The noise from outside filtered through the single-pane windows, joining the thoughts in her head, swirling around, making her feel dizzy. "Okay," she said, only because she could think of no discernible reason to refuse him.

She knew there were other consequences to consider. Concerns for her safety, perhaps? She didn't know him. Didn't know him in any way beyond a brief understanding of his reputation as a businessman.

She also knew that he had been married to Ashley. Ashley, who had proved to be untrustworthy. Manipulative and—if Renzo was to be believed—a liar.

So, she imagined that said something about his character.

But she didn't see another option. Not one beyond putting herself through something that would undoubtedly be both physically and emotionally demanding without any kind of recourse. Not for the first time, she felt a deep sense of guilt and regret.

She tried not to traffic too much in guilt. Mostly because she had spent so much of her life neck deep in it. Every time she found a book at the local book exchange and slipped it into her bag—one she knew she shouldn't have. Every time she figured out a way to smuggle in a CD she shouldn't have had.

When she'd been kicked out after the discovery of her smuggled items, she'd become determined to live life on her own terms. To shamelessly adore pop music, and sugared cereal and movies. To read all the books she wanted, including books with dirty words and dirty scenes. And to feel not even a hint of shame.

But on this score, it was difficult for her to feel anything but a creeping sense of shame. She had seized this opportunity because it had seemed like a chance for her to make her dreams come true. To go to school. To continue to travel. To start a life that would remain completely separate from where she had come from.

She had been so single-minded, so focused, so determined to keep herself from ever returning to her family, to that small, claustrophobic existence, that she had ignored any and all twinges of discomfort over this arrangement.

But now, it was impossible to ignore. Impossible to wave her hand over the fact that she was carrying a baby. That she had some kind of responsibility in all of this. That it would be incredibly hard on her body. That it would likely wreck her emotionally. And that if she didn't comply with what Renzo was asking her to do…

There was a very good chance she would come out of it diminished. That the strength she had gained, strength enough to strike out on her own, would be gone. And for what? For money she wouldn't even be able to get.

So, she found herself cinching her backpack back up. Slipping her feet into her sandals, and turning to face Renzo.

"Okay," she said, her lips feeling slightly numb. "I'm going with you."

CHAPTER THREE

ADRENALINE AND ANGER coursed through Renzo in equal measure on the car ride back to his villa. It did not escape him that the woman—whose name he had read in the documents, but whom he had yet to be formally introduced to—was looking around the Italian-made vehicle with an expression akin to a country mouse. But he found he could spare little thought to it.

Not when the reality of the situation was so sharp. When his pulse was beating a steady tattoo in his throat, when his blood was running hot and fast beneath his skin. A baby. Esther Abbott, this American backpacker, was pregnant with his baby. Yes, he would have to verify all of this with Ashley, but he was forced to believe Esther. Though he had no real reason to.

Nothing beyond gut instinct. The idea of trusting his gut nearly made him laugh. But then, he rarely trusted his gut. Usually, he trusted in parts lower. And his own quick intellect, which he often allowed himself to imagine was above reproach.

In matters of business, it was. When he was consulted on where a certain business should be built, when he was tasked with seeing to a major bit of real estate development, he never failed. Instincts, inherited from his father, drove him in that arena.

Apparently, in other matters he was not quite so discerning. Or so unerring. His ex-wife was one of the very prominent examples of that truth.

Jillian being another.

Women. It seemed he had a tendency to be a fool for women. No matter that he kept his heart out of any such entanglements, he seemed to have a knack for finding women who got him in other ways.

He looked sideways at Esther, then quickly turned his focus back to the road. He would have no such issues with her. She was plain. Pretty, he supposed. But her wide brown eyes were unlined, unenhanced in any way. Her dark eyebrows a bit heavier than he typically liked on a woman. There were vague bruised-looking circles beneath her eyes, and he couldn't work out if that was because of exhaustion, or if it was simply part of her coloring.

He was so accustomed to seeing women with a full face of makeup that was near enough to airbrushing in real life that he found it very hard to say.

Her lips were full, dusky, and he thought probably the most attractive thing about her. Though, her body was also nice enough. Her breasts weren't large, but they were beautiful shaped, and it was clear she wasn't wearing a bra beneath that black tank top of hers.

But her breasts were immaterial. The only thing that mattered was her womb. And whether or not his child currently resided inside it.

He turned sharply into his driveway, leaving the gate wide open, and not particularly caring. Then, he got out of the car, rounding it and jerking open the passenger door. "Welcome to your new home," he said, knowing that his tone sounded anything but welcoming.

She bit her bottom lip, gathering her backpack from the floor of the car, and getting out, holding the offensive canvas bag to her chest. She looked around, eyes wide, a sort of sickly pallor appearing beneath her tan skin.

"You were just here a couple of days ago," he said. "You can stop looking so intimidated."

"Well," she said, directing her focus to him, "you're intimidating. A house like this… One that is practically a castle… That's intimidating." She took a deep breath. "And I know I was here earlier. But this is different. I was focused on telling you about the baby. I wasn't thinking I would stay here."

"Are you going to pretend that you would prefer the hostel? There is no need to pretend with me. You agreed to carry a child for money. It isn't as though you can suddenly make believe you have no interest in material things."

She shook her head. "I don't. I mean, not the way that you think. I want to go to college."

He frowned. "How old are you?"

"Twenty-three."

He held back a curse. She was the same age as his sister, Allegra. Possibly a bit younger. Had he been the sort of man who possessed the ability to feel sympathy for strangers, he thought he might feel some for her. But those softer feelings had been bled from him long ago, empathy replaced by a vague sense of concern.

"And you couldn't access any scholarships?"

"No. I had to pay to take the SATs. I didn't exactly go to high school. But my scores are good enough to get into a few places. I think. I just need to get my financial ducks in a row."

"You didn't go to high school?"

She pursed her lips together. "I was homeschooled. Kind of. Anyway, it isn't like I was trying to get myself a yacht. And even if I was, nobody does surrogacy for free for a stranger."

He lifted a shoulder. "I suppose not. Come this way."

He led the way into the villa, suddenly completely at a loss. His housekeeper had already retired to her quarters, and here he was with an urchin whom he suddenly had to manage. "I imagine you're tired," he said.

"Hungry," she replied.

He gritted his teeth. "The kitchen is this way."

He led her through the expensive house, listening to the sound of her shuffling footsteps behind him as they made their way to the kitchen. The house itself was old. Stonework dating back centuries. But inside, all of the modern conveniences had been supplied. He made his way to the large stainless steel fridge and opened it. "You may have your pick of what's inside."

As soon as he said that, he realized that most of the food was still ingredients, and not exactly a meal. But surely, there would be something. Then he remembered that his housekeeper often left portions in the freezer for him just in case.

He didn't often eat at home, and he would just as soon go out if there was no staff on hand to make him something. But he was not going back out tonight.

He looked until he found what looked to be a container of pasta. "Here you go," he said, setting it down in front of a wide-eyed Esther.

He didn't stay to see what she did after that. Instead, he strode from the room, taking the stairs two at a time and heading toward his office. He paced the length of the room for a moment, then turned to his desk, taking hold of his phone and dialing his ex-wife.

It took only two rings for Ashley to answer. That didn't surprise him. If she was going to answer, of course she would do it quickly. Otherwise, had she intended to ignore him, she would have done so steadfastly. She was nothing if not extreme.

"Renzo," she said, sounding bored. "To what do I owe the pleasure?"

"You may not find it such a pleasure to speak to me, Ashley. Not when you hear what I have to say."

"I have not actually found it a pleasure to speak to you for quite a few months."

"We were only married for six months, so I hope that's an exaggeration."

"It isn't. Why do you think I had to find other men to satisfy me?"

"If you are talking about emotional satisfaction, I have several answers for that. However, if you mean to imply that I did not satisfy you physically, then I'm going to have to call you a liar."

Ashley huffed. "There's more to life than sex."

"Yes indeed. There is, in fact, the small matter of the woman who is currently downstairs in my kitchen."

"We're divorced now," Ashley said, her voice so sharp it could cut glass. "Who is or is not in your kitchen—or bed—is none of my concern."

"It is when it's Esther Abbott. A woman who claims that she had an agreement with you. For her to carry *our* child."

There was a pause. He was almost satisfied that he had clearly succeeded in rendering Ashley speechless. It was such a difficult thing to do. Even when she had been caught in bed with someone else, she had done her best to talk, scream and cry her way out of it. She was not one to let it rest. She was never one to let someone else have the last word.

Her silence now was telling. Though, of her absolute surprise, or of her chagrin at being found out, he didn't know.

"I thought it might save us. But that was before…

Before the divorce was final. Before you found out about the others."

"Right. The five other men that you were with during the course of our marriage?"

Ashley laughed. "Seven, I think."

It didn't matter to him. Five, seven or only the one he had actually witnessed. He had a feeling the truth didn't matter to Ashley either. It was all about scoring points.

"So this is true," he said, his tone harsh.

"Yes," she replied, her voice tight.

"How?" he bit out.

She huffed out an impatient-sounding laugh. "Well, darling, the last time we were intimate you used a condom. I just…made use of it after you discarded it. It was enough for the doctor."

He swore. At her. At himself. At his body. "Is there nothing too low for you?"

"I guess that remains to be seen," she said, her tone brittle like glass. "I have a lot of living left to do, but don't worry, Renzo, you won't be part of it. My depths will not be of any concern to you."

"This woman is pregnant with *our* child," he said, trying to bring it back around to the topic at hand. To the reason he had some creature-ish backpacker in his home.

"Because she is stubborn. I told her she didn't have to continue with it. In fact, I told her I refused to pay the remainder of the fee."

"Yes," he bit out. "I have had a discussion with her. I was only calling you to confirm."

"What are you going to do?"

That was a good question. An excellent question. He was going to raise the child, naturally. But how was he going to explain it? To his parents. To the media. These would be headlines his child would read. Either he would have to be honest about Ashley's deception, or he would have to concoct a story about a mother abandoning her child.

That would not do.

But surrogacy was not legal in Italy. No agreement would be binding within these borders. And he would use that to his advantage.

"There is nothing to be done," he said, his tone swift, decisive. "Esther Abbott is pregnant with my child. And I will do the responsible thing."

"Renzo," she said, her voice fierce, "what do you intend to do?"

He knew. There was no question. He had been in a situation similar to this before. Only then, he had had no power. The woman involved, her husband, his parents, had all made the decisions around him. His ill-advised affair with Jillian costing much more than his virginity.

At sixteen, he had become a father for the first time. But he had been barred from having anything to do with the child. A story carefully constructed to protect her marriage, her family, that child and his reputation had been agreed on by all.

All except for Renzo.

He would not allow such a thing to happen again. He would not allow himself to be sidelined. He would not put him, or his child, in such a precarious position. There was only one thing to do. And he would see it done.

"I shall do what any responsible man would do in this situation. I intend to marry Esther Abbott."

Esther had never seen anything quite like Renzo's kitchen. It had taken her more than ten minutes to figure out how to use the microwave. And even then, the pasta had ended up having cold spots and spots that scalded her tongue. Still, it was one of the best things she had ever tasted.

That probably had more to do with exhaustion and how long she'd gone without eating than anything else. Pasta was one of her favorite newly discovered foods, though. Not that she'd never had noodles in some form. It was just that her mother typically made them for soups, and not the way she'd had it served in Italy.

Discovering new foods had been her favorite part of travel so far. Scones in England with clotted cream, macarons in France. She had greatly enjoyed the culinary adventure, nearly as much as the rest of it.

Though, sometimes she missed brown bread and stew. The kinds of simple foods her mother made from scratch at home.

A swift kick of loneliness, of homesickness, punched her low in the stomach. It was unusual, but it did happen sometimes. Most of her home life had been difficult. Had been nothing at all like the way she wanted to live. But it had been safe. And for most of her life, it had been the only thing she'd known.

She blinked, taking another bite of her pasta, and allowing the present moment to wash away the slow-burning ache of nostalgia.

She heard footsteps and looked up. Renzo strode into the kitchen, and that dark black gaze burned away the remaining bit of homesickness. There was no room for anything inside her, nothing beyond that sharp, cutting intensity.

"I just spoke to Ashley."

Suddenly, the pasta felt like sawdust in Esther's mouth. "I imagine she told you the thing you didn't want to hear."

"You are correct in your assessment."

"I'm sorry. But it's true. I really didn't come here to take advantage of you, or to lie to you. And I really couldn't have forged any kind of medical documents. I had never even been to a doctor until Ashley took me for the procedure."

He frowned. She could tell that she had said something that had revealed her as being different. She did that a lot. Mostly because she didn't exactly know the line. Cultures were different, after all, and sometimes she thought people might assume she was different only because she was American.

But she was different from typical Americans, too.

"I lived in a small town," she said, the lie rolling off her tongue easily. She had always been a liar. Because if ever her parents asked her if she was content, if ever her mother had asked her about her plans for the future, she'd had to lie.

And so, covering up the extent of just how strange she was became easier and easier as she talked to more people and picked up more of what was expected.

"A town so small you did not have doctors?"

"He made house calls." That part was true. There had been a physician in the commune.

"Regardless of your past history, it seems that you were telling the truth."

"I said I was."

"Yes, you did. It is an unenviable position you find yourself in—or perhaps it is enviable, depending on your perspective. Tell me, Esther, what are your goals in life?"

It was a strange question. And never once had she been asked. Not really. Her parents had spoken to her about what she would do. About what her duty was, about the purposes of women and what they had to do to be fulfilled. But no one had ever asked her if it would fulfill her. No one had ever asked her anything at all.

But he was asking. And that made something warm glow inside her.

It made her want to tell him.

"I want to travel. And I want to go to school. I want to get an education."

"To what end?" he asked.

"What do you mean?"

"What do you wish to major in? Business? History? Art?"

"Everything." She shrugged. "I just want to know things."

"What do you want to know?"

"Everything I didn't before."

"That is an incredibly tall order. But one that is certainly possible. Is there a better city in the world to learn about history? Rome."

"Paris and London might have differing opinions. But I definitely take your point. And yes, I agree I can get quite an education here simply by being here. But I want more."

He began to pace, and there was something in that stride, attention, a purpose, that made her feel a bit like a small, twitchy little field mouse standing in front of a big cat. "Why shouldn't you have more? Why shouldn't you have everything? Look around you," he said, sweeping his hand in a broad gesture. "I am a man in possession of most everything. For what reason? Simply because I was born into it. And yes, I have done all that I can to ensure I am worthy of the position. I assumed the helm of the family business and have continued to navigate it with proficiency."

"That's very nice for you," she said, mostly because she had no idea what else she was supposed to say.

"It could be very nice for you," he said, leveling his eyes on her. Her skin prickled, somewhere beneath the surface, where she couldn't tamp it down, not even by grabbing hold of her elbows and rubbing her forearms vigorously.

"Could it?"

"I am not going to be coy. I am a billionaire, Ms. Abbott. A man with a limitless supply of resources. Ashley was not as generous with you as she might have been. But I intend to give you the world."

She felt her face growing warm. She cleared her throat, reaching up and tucking a strand of hair behind her ear, just so she had something to do with the reckless energy surging through her. "That's very nice. But I only have the one backpack. I'm not sure the world would fit inside it."

"That is the catch," he said.

"What is?"

"You will have to give up the backpack."

She blinked. "I'm not sure I understand."

"I am a man with a great deal of power—that, I should think, is obvious. However, there are a few things I am bound by. Public perception is one of them. The extremely conservative ideals of my parents are another. My parents have gone to great lengths in my life to ensure that I became the man that I am today." His jaw seemed to tighten when he said that, a muscle there twitching slightly. "And while I was certainly pushing the edges of propriety by marrying Ashley, I did marry her. Marriage, children, that is what is expected of me. What is not expected? To have a surrogacy scandal. To have it leak out to the public that my wife conspired against me. I will not be made a fool of, Esther," he said, using her first name for the first time. "I will not have the Valenti name made foolish by my mistake."

"I don't understand what that has to do with me. You're going to have to be very direct, because sometimes I'm a little bit slow with shorthand."

He frowned. "Just how small is that town you're from?"

"Very small. Very, very small."

"Perhaps the size of the town makes no difference. Admittedly, we are in a bit of an unprecedented situation. Still, my course is clear."

"Please do enlighten me."

He paused, looking at her. Which shouldn't have been significant. He had looked at her before. Lots of times. People looked at each other when they talked. Except, this time when he looked at her it felt different.

But this was different. Whether or not that made any sense, it was different. His gaze was assessing now, in a different way from what it had been before. As though he were looking deeper. Beneath her clothes, the thought of which made her feel hot all over, down beneath her skin. As though he were trying to see exactly what her substance was.

He looked over her entire body, and she felt herself begin to burn everywhere his gaze made contact. That strange, restless feeling was back between her thighs, an intense heaviness in her breasts.

She sucked in a sharp breath, trying to combat the sting of tears that were beginning to burn there. She didn't know why she wanted to cry. Except that this felt big, new and completely unfamiliar. Whatever this was.

"Esther Abbott," he said, his words sliding over her name like silk, "you are going to be my wife."

CHAPTER FOUR

ESTHER FELT LIKE she was dreaming. She had a strange sense of being detached from her body, of looking down on the scene below her, like it was happening to somebody else and not her. Because there was no way she was standing in the middle of a historic mansion, looking at the most beautiful man she had ever seen in her entire life, his proposal still ringing in her ears.

Beautiful was the wrong word for Renzo, she decided. He was too hard cut. His cheekbones sharp, his jaw like a blade. His dark eyes weren't any softer. Just like the rest of him, they were enticing, but deadly. Like broken edges of obsidian. So tempting to run your fingers over the seemingly smooth surface, until you caught an edge and sliced into your own flesh.

It struck her just how ridiculous it was, fixating on her mental use of the word *beautiful*. Fixating on his appearance at all. He had just stated his intention to make her his wife. *His wife.*

That was her worst nightmare. Being owned by a man again. She couldn't stand it. Never. Yes, Renzo was different from her father. Certainly this was a different situation. But it felt the same. It made her feel like her throat was closing up, like the walls were closing in around her.

"No," she said, panic a clawing beast scurrying inside

her. "That's impossible. I can't do that. I have goals. Goals that do not include being your... No."

"There is not a single goal that you possess that I cannot enable you to meet with greater ease and better style."

She shook her head. "But don't you see? That isn't the point. I don't want to stay here in Rome. I want to see the world."

"You have been seeing the world, have you not? Hostels, and dirty bars. How very romantic. I imagine it is difficult to do much sightseeing when you are tethered to whatever table you are waiting at any given time."

"I have time off. I'm living in the city. I have what I want. Maybe you don't understand, but as you said, you had very much of what you possess given to you. Inherited. My legacy is nothing. A tiny little house with absolutely no frills in the middle of the mountain range. And that's not even mine. It's just my father's. And it never would've passed to me. It would've gone to one of my six brothers. Yes, *six* brothers. But not to any of my three sisters. You heard that number right, too. Because there was nothing for us. Nothing at all for women. Though, I'm not entirely certain that in that scenario the boys have it much better." She took a deep breath. "I'm proud of this. Of what I have. I'm not going to allow you to make me feel like it's lacking."

"But it is lacking, *cara*." The words cut her like a knife. "If it were not lacking, you would not have goals to transcend it. You wish to go to school. You wish to learn things. You wish to see the world. Come into my world. I guarantee you it is much more expansive than any that you might hope to enter on your own."

The words reverberated through her, an echo. A promise. One that almost every fiber of her being wanted to run from. Almost. There must have been some part of her that was intrigued. That wanted to stay. Because there she was, as rooted to the spot as she had been when he entered the bar earlier that night. There was something about him that did that to her, and it seemed to be more powerful than every terrified, screaming cell in her brain that told her she should run.

"That's insanity. I don't need you, I just need the payment that was agreed upon, and then I can better my circumstances."

"But why have a portion of my fortune when you can have access to the entire thing?"

"I wouldn't have the first idea what to do with that. Frankly, having anything to call mine is something of a new experience. What you're talking about seems a little bit beyond my scope."

"Ah, but it does not have to be." His words were like velvet, his voice wrapping itself around her. Her mother had been right. The devil wasn't ugly. That wouldn't work when it came to doling out temptation. The devil was beautiful. The devil—she was becoming more and more certain—was Renzo Valenti.

"I think you might be crazy. I think that I understand now why your wife left you."

He chuckled. "Is that what she told you? One of her many lies. I was the one who threw that grasping, greedy shrew out onto the streets, after I caught her in bed with another man."

Esther tried not to look shocked. She tried not to look as innocent and gauche as she was. The idea that somebody would violate their marriage vows so easily was foreign to her. Marriage was sacred, in her upbringing. Another reason that what Renzo was suggesting was completely beyond the pale for her.

"She cheated on you?"

"Yes, she did. As I said to you earlier, I, for my part, was faithful to my wife. I will not lie and say that I chose Ashley out of any deep love for her, but initially our connection was fun at least."

Esther turned that over for a moment. "Fun?"

"In some rooms, yes."

The exact meaning of what he was saying slipped past her slightly, but she knew that he was implying something lascivious, and it made her face get hot. "Well, that is…I don't…I'm not the wife for you," she finished. Because if she couldn't exactly form a picture to go with what he was trying to imply here, she knew—beyond a shadow of a doubt—that she could never be in that kind of relationship with him.

She had never even been kissed. Being a wife… Well, she had no experience in that area. Not only that, she had no desire to be. Oh, probably eventually she would want to be with someone. It was on the list. Way far down.

Sex was a curiosity to her. She'd read love scenes in books, seen them in movies. But she knew she wasn't ready for it herself, not so much because of the physical part, but the connecting-to-another-person part.

And for now, she was too busy exploring who she was. What she wanted from life. She had never seen a marriage where the man was not unquestionably in control. Had no experience of male and female relationships where the husband did not rule the wife with an iron fist.

She would never subject herself to that. Never.

"Why is that? Because you harbor some kind of childish fantasy of marrying for love?"

"No. Not at all. I harbor fantasies of never marrying, actually. And as for love? I have never seen it. Not the way that you're talking about it. What I have seen is possession and control. And I have no interest in that."

"I see. So, you are everything that you appear to be. Someone who changes with the wind and moves at will."

He spoke with such disdain, and it rankled. "Yes. And I never pretended to be anything else. Why should I? I don't have any obligation to you. I don't have any obligation to anyone, and that's how I like it. But I got myself into this situation, and I do intend to act with integrity. At least, as I see it. I wanted to make sure you knew about the baby, I wanted to make sure that your wishes were being met."

"And yet, you saw no point in checking in with me in the first place?"

She let out a long, slow breath. "I know. I should have. But that was part of why I came to find you after Ashley said she no longer wanted the baby. Because she had made it so clear that you wanted a child desperately in the first place, and I could not believe that you would suddenly change your mind. Not based on everything she had said."

"A convincing liar, is my ex-wife."

"Clearly. But I don't want to be tangled up in any of this. I just want to have the baby and go on my way."

"That… That can be discussed. But for all intents and purposes, we are going to present you to the world as my lover. What happens after the birth of the child can be negotiated, but we will conduct ourselves as an engaged couple until then."

"I don't understand… I don't want…"

"I am a very powerful man. The fact that I'm not throwing you over my shoulder and carrying you off to the nearest church, where I have no doubt I could bring the clergy around to my way of thinking, shows that I'm being somewhat magnanimous with you. I am also not overly enticed to jump back into marriage, not after what I have just been through. So, it is decided. You will play the part of my fiancée, at least until the birth of the child, at which point your freedom—and the parting price—can be negotiated."

"We will be in the news?" The idea of her parents seeing her with him… It terrified her.

"Tabloids most likely. Perhaps some lifestyle sections of respectable papers. But that will mostly be contained to Europe."

She let out a slow breath, releasing some of the tension that had built in her chest. "Okay. Maybe that isn't so bad."

He frowned. "Are you hiding from someone? Because I need to know. I need to know what might put my child in danger, *cara*."

"I'm not hiding from anyone. And, trust me, I'm not in danger. I mean, I'm kind of hiding. But not because I'm afraid somebody will come after me. My parents were… strict. And they don't approve of what I'm doing. I just don't want them to see me written about in the paper, with a man. Pregnant. Not married." In spite of the fact that she had long since given up hope of pleasing her parents—in fact, she had come to terms with the fact that her leaving home would mean cutting ties with them forever—she felt sick shame settle in her stomach.

"They are traditional then."

"You have no idea." The shame lingered, wouldn't leave. "They never even wanted me to wear makeup or anything."

"Well, I fear you will be defying that rule, as well."

"Why?" She had the freedom to wear whatever she wanted now, but she hadn't bought makeup yet. There had not been an occasion to.

"Because my women look a certain way."

That forced a very specific image into her head. A *certain* kind of woman. The kind of woman her mother often talked about. Fallen, scarlet.

She had a difficult time wrapping her head around the

idea that she would be presented to the world like that. Not because she felt ashamed, but because it just never occurred to her. The idea that she might be made up, and dressed up, on the arm of a man like Renzo Valenti.

"You go to… You go to a lot of events, don't you?"

"A great many. As I said to you before, the world that I will show you is far beyond anything you could access on your own. If you want to experience, I can give you experiences you didn't know to dream of."

Those words made something hot take root at the base of her spine, wrap around low and tight inside her, making her feel both hot and empty somehow.

"All right," she said, the words rushed, because they had to be. If she thought about it any longer, she would run away. "I'll do it."

"Do what exactly?" he said, his eyes hard on hers.

"I will play the part of your fiancée for as long as you want me to. And then after that… After the baby is born… I go."

He took a step forward, reaching out and taking hold of her chin between his thumb and forefinger. His touch burned. Caught hold of her like a wildfire and raged straight through her body. "Excellent. Esther," he said, her name like a caress on his lips, "you have yourself a fiancé."

Renzo knew that he was going to have to tread extremely carefully over the next few weeks. That was one of the few things he knew. Everything else in his life was upended. He had a disheveled little street urchin staying in one of his spare rooms, and he had to present her to the world as his chosen bride soon. Very soon. The sooner the better. Before Ashley got a chance to drop any poison into the ear of the media.

He had already set a plan in motion to ensure she would

not. A very generous payout that his lawyer would be offering to hers by the time the sun rose in Canada. She would not want to defy him. Not when—without this—she would be getting nothing from him due to the ironclad prenuptial agreement they had entered into before the marriage.

Ashley liked attention, that much was true. But she liked money even more. That would take care of her.

But then there was the small matter of his parents. And his parents were never actually a small matter.

He imagined that—regardless of the circumstances— they would be thrilled to learn that they were expecting a grandchild. Really, they would only be all the happier knowing that Ashley was out of the picture.

But Esther was most certainly a problem he would have to solve.

With great reluctance, he picked up his phone and dialed his mother's number. She picked up on the first ring. "Renzo. You don't call me enough."

"Yes, so I hear. Every time I call."

"And it is true every time. So, tell me, what is on your agenda? Because you never call just to make small talk."

He couldn't help but laugh at that. His mother knew him far too well. "Yes, as it happens, I was wondering if you had any plans for dinner."

"Why yes, Renzo. I in fact have dinner plans every day. Tonight, we are having lamb, vegetables and a risotto."

"Excellent, Mother. But do you have room at your table?"

"For?"

"Myself," he said, amused at his mother's obstinance. "And a date."

"Dating already. So soon after your divorce." His mother said that word as though it were anathema. But then, he supposed that was because for her it was.

"Yes, Mother. Actually, more than dating. I intend to introduce you to my fiancée, Esther Abbott."

The line went silent. That concerned him much more than a tirade of angry Italian ever could. Then, his mother spoke. "Abbott? Who are her people?"

He thought of what she'd said about the mountain cabin her rather larger-than-usual family lived in, and he was tempted to laugh. "No one you would know."

"Please tell me you have not chosen another Canadian, Renzo."

"No, on that score you can relax. She is an American."

The choking sound he heard on the other end of the line was not altogether unexpected. "That," she said finally, "is even worse."

"Even so, the decision is made." He considered telling her about the pregnancy over the phone, but decided that it was one of those things his mother would insist on hearing about in person. She did like to divide her news into priorities like that. She had never gotten over Allegra's pregnancy news filtering back to her through the gossip chain.

"So very typical of you." There was no real condemnation or venom in her tone. Though, the simple statement forced him to think back to a time when it had not been true. When he had allowed other people to force his hand when it came to decision making. He tried very hard not to think about Jillian. About the daughter who was being raised by another man. A daughter he sometimes caught glimpses of at various functions.

Just one of the many reasons he worked so hard to keep his alcohol intake healthy at such things. It was much better to remember very little of it the next day, he found.

He had been sixteen when his parents had encouraged him to make that decision. And since then, he had changed the way he operated. Completely, utterly. He was not bitter at his mother and father. They had pushed him into making the best decision they could see.

And hell, it had been the best decision. He had proved that fifty times over in the years since. He had not been ready to be a father. But he was ready now.

"Yes, I am typical as ever. But will we be welcome at your table tonight, or not?"

"It will be an ordeal. We will have to purchase more ingredients."

"When you say 'we,' you mean your staff, whom you pay handsomely. I imagine it can all be arranged?"

"Of course it will be. You will be there at eight. Do not be late. Because I will not wait, and the one thing you do not want, Renzo, is for me to be one glass of wine ahead of you."

He felt his mouth turn upward. "That," he said, "is very true, Mother, I have no doubt."

He disconnected the call. Then, he made another call to the personal stylist his mother had used for years, asking that she clear her schedule and bring along a team of hair and makeup artists.

He was not sure if Esther had enough raw material to be salvageable. It was very difficult to say. The women whom he involved himself with tended to be either classic, polished pieces of architecture, or new constructions, as it were. He had no experience with full renovations.

Still, she was not unattractive. So, it seemed as though he should be able to fashion her into something that looked believable. The thought nearly made him laugh. She was pregnant. She was pregnant with his child. And while it may take a paternity test on his end to prove that to the world—or his parents—they would never ask for a test to prove maternity.

Therefore, by that very logic, people would believe their connection. But he would like to make it slightly easier.

When he went downstairs and found her sitting in the dining area, on the floor by the floor-to-ceiling windows, her face tilted up toward the sun, a bowl of cereal clutched tightly in her hands, he knew that he had made the right decision in bringing in an entire team.

"What are you doing?"

She squeaked, startling and sloshing a bit of milk over the edge of her bowl, onto the tile floor. "I was enjoying the morning," she said.

"There is a table for you to sit at." He gestured to the long, banquet-style piece of furniture, which had been carved from solid wood and was older than either of them, and was certainly more than good enough for this little hippie to sit and eat her cereal at.

"I know. But I wanted to sit by the window. And I could have moved a chair, but they're very heavy. And I didn't want to scuff the tile. And anyway, the floor is fine. It's warm from the sun."

"We are going to my parents' house for dinner tonight," he said, because it was as good a time as any to broach that subject. "And I trust you will not sit yourself on the floor then." The image of her crouched in a corner gnawing on a lamb shank was nearly comical. That would upset his mother. Though, seeing as she had been prewarned that Esther was an American, she might not find the behavior all that strange.

He regarded her for a moment. Her hair was caught up in that same messy bun she'd had it in yesterday, and she had traded her black tank top for a brown one, and yesterday's long, flowing skirt for one in a brighter color.

She frowned, her dark brows locking together. "Of course not." He had thought her face plain yesterday, and now, for some reason, he thought of it as freshly scrubbed. Clean. There was something… Not wholesome, for this exotic creature could never be called something so mundane, but something natural. Organic. As if she had materialized in a garden somewhere rather than being born.

Which was a much more fanciful thought than he had ever had about a woman before. Typically, his thoughts were limited to whether or not he thought they would look good naked, whether or not they would like to get naked with him, and then, after they had, how he might get rid of them.

"Good. My parents are not flexible people. Neither are they overly friendly. They are extremely old, Italian money. They are very proud of their lineage, and of our name. I told them that we are getting married. And that you're American. They are amused by neither. Or rather, my mother is amused by neither, and my father will follow suit."

Her dark eyes went round, the expression on her face worried. It was comical to him that she might be concerned over what his parents thought. Someone like her didn't seem as though she would concern herself with what other people thought.

"That doesn't sound like a very pleasant evening," she said, after a long pause.

"Oh, evenings with my parents are never what I would call pleasant. However, they are not fatal."

"I have an aversion to being judged," she said, her tone stiff.

"Oh, I quite enjoy it. I find it very liberating to lower people's expectations."

"You do not," she said, "nobody does. Everybody cares about pleasing their parents." She frowned. "Or, if not their parents, at least somebody."

"You said yourself, you left your parents. And that they weren't happy with you. Obviously, you don't worry overly much about pleasing your parents."

"But I did. For a long time. And the only reason I don't now is out of necessity. I mean, I would've never had any freedom if I hadn't let go of it."

There was a strange feeling in his chest, her words catching hold of something that seemed to tug on him, down deep.

About freedom. About letting go.

"Well, on that same subject, there is some work to be done if we are going to present you at dinner tonight."

"What sort of work?" She looked genuinely mystified at that statement, as though she had no idea what he might be referring to.

As he stood before her in his perfectly pressed custom suit, and she sat cross-legged on the floor looking like she would be more at home at a Renaissance fair than in his home, it occurred to him that she really was a strange creature. The differences between the two of them should be obvious, and yet, she did not seem to pick up on them on her own. Or rather, she didn't seem to care.

"You, Esther."

"What's wrong with me?"

"What did you plan on wearing to dinner tonight?"

She looked down. "This, I suppose."

"You do not see perhaps a small difference in the way that you are dressed, compared with the way that I am dressed?"

"Did you want me to wear a tux?"

"This is not a tux. It's a suit. There is a difference."

"Interesting. And good to know."

He had a feeling she did not find it interesting at all. "I have taken the liberty of having some clothing ordered for you." He lifted his hand and looked at his watch. "It should be here any moment."

Just then, his housekeeper came walking into the room, a concerned expression on her face. "Mr. Valenti, Tierra is here."

His stylist went by only one name. "Excellent."

"Should I have her meet you upstairs with all of her items?"

"Yes. But in Esther's room, if you don't mind."

Esther's eyes widened. "What exactly are you providing me with?"

"Something that doesn't look like it came out of the bottom of a bargain bin at some sort of rummage sale for mismatched fabrics."

She frowned. "Is that your way of saying there's something wrong with what I'm wearing?"

"No. My way of saying that is to say what you're wearing isn't suitable. Actually, it's perfectly suitable if you intend to continue to wait tables at a dusty bar crawling with tourists. However, it is not acceptable if you wish to be presented to the world as my fiancée, and neither is it acceptable for you to wear on the night you are to meet my parents."

At that, his housekeeper's face contorted. She began to speak at him in angry, rapid Italian that he was only grateful Esther likely wouldn't be able to decode. "She is pregnant with my child," he said. "There is nothing else to be done."

She shook her head. "You have become a bad man," she huffed, walking out of the room. That last part she had said in English.

"Why is she mad at you?"

"Well, likely because she thinks I impregnated some

poor American tourist while I was still married. You can see how she would find that upsetting."

"I suppose." She blinked. "But doesn't *she* work for *you*?"

"Luciana practically came with the house, which I purchased more than a decade ago. It's difficult to say sometimes who exactly works for whom."

She frowned. "And now what? You're going to...buy me new clothes?"

"Exactly. And take your old clothes and burn them."

"That isn't very nice."

He raised his brows, affecting his expression into one of mock surprise. "Is it not? That is regrettable. I do so strive to be nice."

"I doubt it."

"Don't snarl at me," he said. "And, remember, you have to pretend to be my fiancée. In front of Luciana, and in front of Tierra."

She scowled, but allowed him to direct her up the stairs, depositing her cereal bowl on the dining room table as she went. He watched the gentle sway of her hips as she began to ascend the staircase. When she was in motion, her clothing seemed less ridiculous. In fact, the effect was rather graceful.

There was an otherworldly quality to her that he couldn't quite pin down. Something that he had difficulty describing, even to himself. She was very young, and simultaneously sometimes seemed quite old. Like a being who had been dropped down to earth, knowing very little about the customs of those around her, and yet, somehow knowing more than any human could in a lifetime.

And that was fanciful thinking that he never normally allowed himself.

So instead of that, he focused on the rounded curve of her rear. Because that, at least, he understood.

When they reached the bedroom, the stylist had already unveiled a rack of clothing. She was fussing around with the hanging garments, smoothing pleats and adjusting the long, complicated skirts on the various gowns.

"Oh, my," she said, turning and getting her first look at Esther. "We do have our work cut out for us."

CHAPTER FIVE

FOR THE NEXT two hours, Esther was pulled, prodded, poked with pins and clucked at. Well and truly clucked at. As though this woman, Renzo's stylist, was a chicken. And as though Esther was a naughty chick rather than a woman.

Renzo had left them to it, and she was thankful. Since the moment he had walked out, the other woman had begun stripping Esther's clothes off her body and forcing new undergarments, new dresses and new shoes onto her.

Esther had never felt fabrics like this. She had never seen styles like this on her spare curves. She had been all about experiencing new things since she had left her home, but she hadn't gotten around to the clothing and makeup. Or hair. That all required a disposable income that she simply didn't possess. She was more concerned with keeping food in her belly. And clothing herself in the basics, rather than exploring the world of fashion.

But now she felt as though she had been well and truly educated in which colors looked best on her, which shapes best suited her figure. Of course, most of it had happened in abrupt Italian that Esther could understand only parts of, but still. She could see herself.

In fact, right at the moment, she couldn't take her eyes off herself. She was wearing a dark green gown that had little cap sleeves and a plunging V neckline that showed off acres of skin around her neck and down farther. The kind of daring look that would never have been allowed in her family home.

The skirt was long, falling all the way down to the tops of the most beautiful pair of shoes Esther had ever seen. Of course, they were also the tallest pair of shoes she had ever worn, and she had serious doubts about her ability to walk in them.

Somewhere in the middle of the clothing frenzy, two men had arrived to work on her hair and makeup. And work they had. Her hair was tamed into a sleek, black curtain, a good half a foot cut off the near-unmanageable length.

Her eyes, which she had always thought were almost comically large, didn't look comical now. Though, they still looked large. They had been rimmed with black liner, the corners of her eyes highlighted with gold. They had brushed something onto her cheeks, too, making them glow. And her lips… A bit of pale, burnished orange gloss colored them, just slightly, highlighting them, just enough.

She looked like a stranger. She couldn't see so many of the defining features of her face, not the way she usually did. Those dark circles that had permanent residence beneath her eyes were diminished, her nose somehow appearing more narrow, her cheeks a bit more hollow, thanks to a technique they had called contouring.

And then there was her body. She had never thought much about it. She didn't have overly large breasts, and for convenience, she typically opted not to wear a bra, sticking to plain, high-necked tops in dark colors that she always hoped concealed enough.

Even though this gown still didn't allow for a bra, it created an entirely different effect on her bustline than the simple cotton tank tops she preferred. Her breasts looked rounder, fuller, her waist a bit more dramatically curved, rather than straight up and down. The shape of the skirt enhanced the appearance of her hips, making her look like she almost had an hourglass figure.

It was strange to see herself this way. With all her attributes enhanced, rather than downplayed.

The bedroom door opened and she froze when Renzo walked in. She felt hideously exposed in a way that she never had before. Because for the first time in her life she was aware that she might look beautiful, and that there was a man who was most certainly beautiful looking her over. Appraising her as he might a work of art.

"Well," he said, turning his focus to the team of people who had accomplished the effect, and away from her, "this is a very pleasant surprise."

"She is a dream to dress," Tierra said. "Everything fits so nicely. And that golden skin of hers allows her to pull off some very difficult colors."

"You know all of that is lost on me," he said. "However, I can see that she is beautiful."

Warmth flooded her. Such a stupid thing. To feel affected by this charade. But she wasn't entirely sure if she cared at all that it was a charade. What did it matter, really? Even playing a game like this was new. Feeling like she was the center—the focus—of male attention was something that she had scarcely gotten around to dreaming about.

She had been grappling with freedom. Both the cost of it and the gains. With who she wanted to be, apart from everything she'd been taught. Apart from the small rebellions she'd waged hidden in the mountains behind her house, listening to contraband music while reading forbidden books.

To find it especially appealing to link herself up to a

man, even in a temporary way. But now, beneath Renzo's black gaze, she found something deliciously enticing in it.

A swift, low kick of temptation hit her hard, making it difficult for her to breathe. And she couldn't even quite work out what the temptation was. It reminded her of walking past the bakery down in the town she'd grown up adjacent to, and seeing a row of sweets that looked delicious. Treats she knew she wouldn't be allowed to have.

That same feeling. Of wanting, feeling empty. Of that intense, unfair sense of deprivation that always followed.

Except, no one controlled her life now. If she wanted a cake, she could buy it and then she could eat it.

Which made her deeply conscious of the fact that if she wanted Renzo, she supposed she could have him, too.

But for the love of cake, she didn't know what she would do with him. Or what he would do with her if she reached out and tried to get a taste.

She took a deep breath, craning her neck, straightening her shoulders and doing her best to make herself look even more statuesque. She didn't know why. Maybe to inject herself with a little bit more pride, so she wasn't just standing there being subjected to the judgment of every person in the room.

It was so strange being the center of attention like this. She wasn't entirely certain she disliked it.

"That dress is spectacular. However, it is a bit too formal for dinner," Renzo said, sitting down in one of the armchairs that were placed up against the back wall. "What else is there?"

"Oh," Tierra said, turning around and facing the rack, pulling out a short, coral-colored dress that Esther had tried on earlier. "How about this?"

Renzo settled even deeper into the chair, his posture like that of a particularly jaded monarch. "Let's see it."

"Of course."

Esther found herself being turned so that she was facing away from Renzo, and then she felt the zipper on the gown give. She gasped, then froze, not quite sure what she was supposed to do next. If she should protest the fact that she was being undressed in front of a man who was a stranger to her, or if that would ruin the charade.

And then it didn't matter, because the green dress was pulling down at her feet, and her bare back and barely covered bottom were now fully exposed to Renzo.

"Very nice," he said, his voice rough. "Part of the new wardrobe?"

She knew he meant the black pair of lace panties she was wearing, and she wanted to turn around and tell him off for making this even more uncomfortable. Except, then she would have to turn around. And expose herself even further, and she wasn't going to do that. Instead, she decided that she would do her best to show him that she wasn't so easily toyed with.

"Yes," she said simply.

A few moments later the next dress was on and firmly in place. Then, she turned back to face Renzo, and her heart crawled up into her throat. Because as intense as he always looked, as much impact as those dark eyes always had on her, it was magnified now.

"Come closer," he said, his tone hard-edged, the command clearly nonnegotiable.

She swallowed hard, taking one unsteady step toward where Renzo was sitting. His dark gaze flicked away from Esther, landing on the style team. "Leave us," he said.

They did so, quickly and without a word. And when they were gone, it felt as though they had taken all the air out of the room with them.

"Do people always do what you ask?"

"Always," he said. "Closer."

She took another step toward him, trying to disguise the fact that her legs were shaking and that she had no idea how she was supposed to walk in heels that were tantamount to stilts.

He rested his elbow on the arm of the chair, propping his chin on his knuckles. "Of course, some people obey more quickly than others."

"Did you want me to break an ankle? Because I guarantee you if I walk any faster I'm going to."

He moved swiftly, his movements liquid, his grace making a mockery of her own uncertain clumsiness. He stood, reaching across the space between them and sweeping her up into his arms. Then he turned, depositing her in the chair he had occupied only a moment ago.

She pressed her hand to her heart, feeling the rapid flutter beneath her palm. Her throat was dry, her head feeling dizzy. Her body felt warm. As though she had been burned all over. His arms had been wrapped around her, her shoulder blades pressed up against that hard, broad expanse of his chest.

That was what stunned her most of all. Just how hard he was. There was no give in him at all. His body was as unbending as the rest of him.

He turned away from her, facing the rack of clothing and the stack of shoes that was beneath it. "If you cannot walk then you will not present a very convincing picture. We don't want you to look as though you were only polished today."

"Why? Why does it matter?"

"Because I associate with a very particular kind of woman. I do not need my parents thinking that I swooped in and corrupted some innocent, naive backpacker."

It took her a moment to process that. She wondered if

he really believed that she was naive and innocent. She was. It was just that he had never seemed particularly sold on that version of her.

"They would believe that?"

He laughed, not turning to look at her. "Oh, yes. Easily." Then he bent, picking up a pair of bejeweled, flat shoes before facing her again. He moved back to where she was sitting, dropping to his knees before her and making a seeming mockery of her earlier thought that he was unbending.

"What are you—"

He said nothing. Instead, he reached out, curling his fingers around the back of her knee. The warmth shocked her. Flooded her. He let his fingertips drift all the way down the length of her calf, the touch slow, much too slow. Something about it, about that methodical movement, seemed to catch her at the site of their contact and spark through the rest of her. Reckless. Uncontrollable.

She fought the urge to squirm in her seat. To do something to diffuse the strange energy that she was infused with. But she didn't want to betray herself. To betray that his touch made her feel anything.

He grabbed hold of the heel on her shoe and pulled it off slowly, those searching fingertips dragging along the bottom of her foot then as he removed the shoe.

She shivered. She couldn't help it.

He looked up then and a strange, knowing smile tilted the corner of his lips upward. It was the knowing that bothered her more than anything else. Because she was confused. Lost in a sea of swirling doubts and uncertainty, and he seemed to know exactly what she was feeling.

You do, too. You aren't stupid.

She gritted her teeth. Maybe. She really wished she were a little bit more stupid. She had tried to be. From the first moment she had laid eyes on him, and he had looked back at her, she had done her very best to be mystified by what all of the feelings inside her meant.

She wasn't going to give a name to them now. Not right now. Not when he was still touching her. Slipping the ornate flat shoe onto her foot, then moving on to the next. He repeated those same motions there. His fingertips hot and certain on her skin as he traced a line down to her ankle, removing the next stiletto and setting it aside.

"A little bit like Cinderella," she said, forcing the words through her dry throat.

Not that she'd been allowed to read fairy tales growing up, but a volume of them had been one of her very first smuggled titles.

"Except," he said, putting the second shoe in place, then straightening, "I am not Prince Charming."

"I didn't think you were."

"Good," he returned. "As long as you don't begin believing that I might be something I'm not."

"Why would I? I'm actually not just a stupid backpacker. I already told you that my family situation was difficult." She took a deep breath, trying to open up her lungs, trying to ease the tension in her chest. She wasn't bringing up her family for him. She was bringing them up for her. To remind her exactly why being bound to someone—anyone—was exactly what she didn't want.

She wanted freedom. She needed it. And this was a detour. She wouldn't allow herself to become convinced it was anything else.

She would enjoy this. The beautiful clothes, the expertly styled hair. She would enjoy his home. And maybe she would even allow herself to enjoy the strange twisting sensation that appeared in her stomach whenever he walked into a room. Because it was new. Because it was different. Because it was something so far removed from where she had come from.

But that was all it was. It was all it would ever be.

"But now," he said, looking down at her feet, "you will be able to walk into my parents' home tonight without falling on your face. That, I think, will be a much nicer effect."

He stood completely and held his hand out. She hesitated, because she knew that touching him again would reignite that burning sensation in the pit of her stomach she had when he'd touched her leg. But resisting would only reveal herself more. And she didn't want to do that.

And—she had to admit—she had perversely enjoyed it. Even though she knew it could never come to anything. Even though she knew there was nothing she could do beyond enjoying it as it was, as the start of a flame and nothing more, she sort of wanted to.

And so, she reached out, her fingertips brushing his palm. Then, his hand enveloped hers completely, and she found herself being pulled to her feet with shocking ease. In fact, he pulled her to her feet with such ease that she lost her footing, tipping forward and moving her hands up to brace herself, her palms pressing flat against that rock-hard chest.

He was so… He was so hot. And she could feel his heartbeat thundering beneath her touch. She hadn't expected that. She wondered if it was normal for him. For his heart to beat so fast. For it to feel so pronounced.

And then she had to wonder if it was related to her. Because her own heartbeat was thundering out of control, like a boulder rolling down a hill. It wasn't normal for her. It was because of him. And she couldn't pretend otherwise, not even to herself.

Was that why? Was that why his heart was beating so

fast? Because she was touching him? And if so, what did that mean?

It was that last question that had her pulling away from him as quickly as possible. She smoothed the front of her dress, doing her best to take care of any imaginary wrinkles that might be there, pouring her focus into that, because the alternative was looking at him.

"Yes," he said, his voice hard, rough, infused with much less ease than seemed typical for him. "Tonight will go very well, I think." And then he reached out, taking hold of her chin with his thumb and forefinger. He forced her to look at him, stealing that small respite she had attempted to take for herself. His eyes burned, and she wasn't sure if she could still somehow sense his heartbeat, or if it was just her own, pounding heavily in her ears. "But you will have to find a way to keep yourself from flinching every time I touch you."

Then, he dropped his hand, turning away from her and walking out of the room, leaving her alone. Leaving her to wonder if she had imagined that response in him because of the strength of her own reaction, or if—somehow—she had created movement in the mountain.

CHAPTER SIX

DINNER AT HIS parents was always infused with a bit of dramatic flair. Tonight was no exception. They were greeted by his parents' housekeeper, their coats taken by another member of staff and then led into the sitting room by yet another.

Of course, his mother would not make an appearance until it was time to sit down at the table. He had a feeling it was calculated this time, even more than usual. That she was preparing herself for the unveiling of Renzo's new fiancée.

His father would go along with his mother's plan. Mostly because he had no desire to have something thrown at his head. Not that his mother had behaved with such hysterics for a great many years. But everyone knew she possessed the capacity for such things, and so they tended to behave with a bit of deference for it.

He turned to look at Esther, who was regarding the massive, Baroque setting with unconcealed awe. "You will have to look a bit more inured to your surroundings. As far as my parents know you have been with me for at least a couple of months, which means you will have been at events like this with me before."

"This place is like a museum," she said, keeping her tone hushed, her dark eyes glittering with wonder. It did something to him. Something to his chest. Unlike earlier, when she had done something to him in parts much lower.

"Yes," he said, "it is, really. A museum of my family's achievements. Of all of the things they have managed to collect over the centuries. I told you, my parents were very proud of our name and our heritage. Of what it means to be Valentis." He gritted his teeth. "Blood is everything to them."

It was why they would accept Esther. Why they would accept the situation. Because except in extreme circumstances, they valued their bloodline in their heritage.

He deliberately kept himself from thinking of the one time they had not.

"Renzo." He turned at the sound of his sister's voice, surprised to see her standing there with her husband, Cristian, at her side, Renzo's niece held securely in her father's arms.

"Allegra," he said, standing and walking across the room to drop a kiss on his younger sister's cheek. He extended his hand for Cristian, shaking it firmly before touching his niece's cheek. "I did not know you would be here."

"Neither did we."

"Did you fly from Spain for dinner?"

Cristian lifted a shoulder. "When your mother demands an audience, it is best not to refuse, as I'm sure you know."

"Indeed."

He turned and looked at Esther, who was still sitting on the settee, her hands folded in her lap, her shoulders curved inward, as though she were trying to disappear. "Allegra, Cristian, this is my fiancée, Esther Abbott."

His words seemed to jolt Esther out of her internal reclusion.

"Hello," she said, getting to her feet, stumbling slightly as she did. "You must be… Well, I'm not really sure."

Allegra shot him a questioning glance. "Allegra Acosta. Formerly Valenti. I'm Renzo's younger sister. This is my husband, Cristian."

"Nice to meet you," she said, keeping her hands folded firmly in front of her but nodding her head. He was hardly going to correct her, or direct her to do something different from what she had done, but he could see that coaching would be required in the future.

"It seems the family will all be here," he said. "Such a surprise."

"Engaged. You're engaged. That's why Mother called us and told us to get on Cristian's private jet, I imagine."

"Most definitely," Renzo returned.

"You didn't tell me," Allegra said.

"In fairness to me, you did not tell me that you were expecting my best friend's baby until it became unavoidable. You can hardly lecture me on not serving up a particular piece of news immediately."

His sister's face turned scarlet, and he looked back at Esther, who was watching the exchange with rapt attention. "Don't pay attention to him," Allegra said to Esther. "He very much likes to be shocking. And he likes to make me mad."

"That seems in keeping with what I know about him," Esther said.

Cristian laughed at that. "You two can't have been together very long," he said. "But it does seem you have a handle on him."

Esther looked down. "I wouldn't say that."

Renzo poured himself a drink, feeling slightly sorry for Esther that he could not offer her the same. Especially given what he was about to do. "Since Mother didn't tell you the great news of my engagement, I imagine she didn't tell you I have other news."

"No," Allegra and Cristian said together.

"Esther and I are expecting a baby." He reached out, putting his arm around Esther's shoulders, rubbing his thumb up and down her arm when he felt her go stiff. That didn't help, but he knew that it needled her. So, he would have to take that as consolation.

Allegra said nothing, Cristian's expression one of almost comedic stillness. Finally, it was Cristian who spoke. "Congratulations. Start catching up on your sleep now."

Allegra still said nothing.

"I can see you're completely stunned by the good news," he said.

"Well, yes. I know you've made many declarations to me about how you intend to be shocking at all times, so I don't know why I'm surprised. Actually, I heavily resent my surprise. I should be immune to any sort of shock where you're concerned."

Of course, she wasn't. Being his younger sister, Allegra always seemed to want to believe the best of him. Which was a very nice thing, in its way. But he was a constant disappointment to her. He knew that his marriage to Ashley had been something more than a shock. Although, why, he didn't know. He had told her, in no uncertain terms, that he intended to marry the most unsuitable, shocking woman that he could find.

That was one that had backfired on him.

"Truly, little sister, you should know me better than that by now. Anyway, let us refrain from speaking of the other ways in which I've shocked you in front of Esther. She's still under the illusion that I'm something of a gentleman."

Esther looked at him, her expression bland. "I can assure you I'm not."

Cristian and Allegra seemed to find that riotously amusing. Mostly, he imagined, because they thought she was being dry. In fact, he had a feeling Esther was being perfectly sincere. She was sincere. That was something he was grappling with. Because he didn't know very many sincere people.

He was much more accustomed to those who were cynical. Who approached the world with a healthy bit of opportunism. It was the sincere people who dumbfounded him. Mostly, because he couldn't figure out a way to relate to them. He couldn't anticipate them.

Seeing her earlier today trying on all of those clothes, the way she had looked at him when he had touched her leg, when he had bent down to change her shoes, had been something of a revelation. Until then he had still been skeptical of her. Of her story, of who she claimed to be.

But who she seemed to present was exactly who she was. A somewhat naive creature who was from a world entirely apart from the one she was in now. Her reaction to his parents' house only reinforced that. He had watched her closely upon entry. If she were a gold digger, he felt he would have seen a moment—even if it was only a moment—where she had looked triumphant. Where she had fully understood the prize that she was inheriting.

Frankly, the position he had put her in gave her quite a bit of leverage for taking advantage. Yes, DNA tests would prove that the child wasn't hers, but who knew how a ruling might go in Italy where there were no laws to support surrogacy. She was the woman who carried the child, and she would give birth to the child. He imagined that legally there was no way she would walk away with nothing.

And he had offered to marry her. Another way in which she could take advantage of him and his money. And yet she had not seemed excited by that either.

That didn't mean things wouldn't change, but for now,

he was forced to reconcile with the fact that she might be the rarest of all creatures. Someone who was what she said.

"Excellent," Allegra said to Esther. "I would hate for you to marry my brother while thinking he was well behaved."

Spurred on by his earlier ruminations, he turned his head, nuzzling the tender skin on Esther's neck, just beneath her jawline. "Of course," he said, allowing his lips to brush against her, "Esther is well aware of how wicked I can be."

He looked up, trying to gauge her response. Her burnished skin was dark pink beneath, a wild, fevered look in her eye. "Yes," she said, her voice higher than usual. "We do know each other. Quite well. We are… We're having a baby. So…"

"Right," Allegra said.

Just then, a servant came in, interrupting the awkward exchange. "Excuse me," the man said. "Your mother has asked me to 'come and fetch you for dinner.'"

Likely, those were his mother's exact words.

Keeping his hand on Esther's lower back, he led the charge out of the room and toward the dining hall. He could feel her growing stiffer and stiffer beneath his touch the closer they got, almost as if she could sense his mother. He wouldn't be surprised. His mother radiated ice, and openly telegraphed her difficulty to be pleased.

"Take a breath," he whispered in her ear just before they walked in. She complied, her shoulders lifting with a great gasp. "See that you don't die before dessert."

And then he propelled her inside.

His mother was there, dressed in sequins, looking far too young to have two grown children, one grandchild and another on the way. His father was there, looking every bit his age, stern-faced and distinguished, and likely a portrait of Renzo's own fate in thirty years.

"Hello," his mother said, not standing, which Renzo knew was calculated in some way or another. "So nice to meet you, Esther," his mother said, using Esther's first name, which he had no doubt was as calculated as the rest. "Allegra, Cristian, so glad you could come. And that you brought my favorite grandchild."

"Your only grandchild," Allegra said, taking her seat while Cristian set about to setting their daughter in a booster seat that had already been put in place for her.

All of this was like salt in a wound. He loved his niece, but there was a particular kind of pain that always came when he was around small children. And when his parents said things like this…about their only grandchild… that pain seemed insurmountable.

"Not for long, though," Allegra continued. "Unless Renzo hasn't told you?"

"He has not. Good. Well, at least now we're all up to speed." His mother gave Renzo a very pointed look. "Do you have any other surprises for us?"

"Not at the moment," he said.

Dinner went on smoothly, their mother and father filling up most of the conversation, and Renzo allowing his brother-in-law to take any of the gaps that appeared. Cristian was a duke, and his title made him extremely interesting to Renzo and Allegra's parents.

Then suddenly, his father's focus turned to Renzo. "I suppose we will see both you and Esther at the charity art exhibit in New York in two weeks?"

Damn. He had forgotten about that. His father was a big one for philanthropy, and he insisted that Renzo make appearances at these types of events. Not because his father believed firmly in charity in a philosophical sense, but because he believed in being seen as someone who did. Oh, he wasn't completely cold-blooded, and truly, it didn't matter either way. A good amount of money made it into needy hands regardless.

But bringing Esther to New York, having her prepared to attend such a land mine–laden event with very little preparation was… Well, just thinking about it was difficult.

More than just the Esther complication, there was always the Jillian complication. Or worse, Samantha. They split their time between Italy and the States, so the probability of seeing them was…high.

But he'd weathered that countless times. Esther was his chief concern. She would probably end up hiding under one of the buffet tables, or perhaps eating a bowl of chocolate mousse on the floor. Thankfully, it would be at night, so there would be no sunbeams for her to warm herself beneath.

"Of course," he said, answering as quickly as possible, before Esther opened her mouth. He had to make it seem as though they had discussed this. That he had not in fact forgotten about the existence of this event—one that he attended every year—due to the fact that he had been shocked by the news of a stranger carrying his child.

"Excellent," his father said. "I do find that it's much better for a man such as yourself to attend with a date."

"Why is that?"

"So you aren't on the prowl for women when you should be on the prowl for business connections."

That shot from his father surprised him. Especially in front of Esther. His father was typically the more restrained of his two parents. Still, he was hardly going to let the old man see that it had surprised him. "You live in the Dark Ages, Father," he said. "Sometimes, women are in high-powered positions of business, in which case, my being single helps quite a bit. However, Esther will not be an impediment, on that you are correct."

"Certainly not," his father said. "If anything, she will be something of an attraction to those jaded big fish you intend to catch."

"Are you going to be there, Father?"

"No. When I said I hoped to see you there, I meant only that I hope to see your photograph in the newspaper."

Renzo couldn't help but laugh at that. And after that, conversation went smoothly through dessert. At least, until they were getting ready to go. A staff member waylaid Esther, a maneuver that Renzo fully took notice of only when his father cornered him near the front door.

"I do hope this isn't some sort of elaborate joke like your last relationship seems to have been," his father said.

"Why would it be?"

"She is a lovely girl. She's a far cry from the usual vacuous model types you choose to associate yourself with. I had to cut ties with one of my grandchildren already, Renzo, lest you forget."

"You didn't have to. You felt it was necessary at the time and you convinced me the same was true. Don't pretend that you have regrets now, old man," Renzo said, his tone hard. "Not when you were so emphatic about the need for it all those years ago."

"What I'm saying is that you best marry this girl. And that marriage best stick. A divorce, Renzo. You had a divorce. And a child outside of wedlock that none of us can ever acknowledge."

"What will you do if I disappoint you again, Father? Find the secret to immortality and deny me my inheritance?"

"Your brother-in-law is more than able to take over the

remainder of the business that is not yet under your control. If you don't want to lose dominion over the Valenti Empire upon the event of my death, I suggest you don't disappoint me."

His father moved away from him swiftly then, and Esther came to join him standing by the door. She looked like a deer caught in the headlights, blindsided completely by the entire evening.

And he knew he now had no choice in the matter. This farce would not be enough. It had to be more. His father was threatening his future, and not just his, that of his child.

Esther Abbott was going to have to become his wife, whether she wanted to or not.

And he knew exactly how to accomplish it. He had seen the way she had reacted to his touch back at his villa. He knew that she wasn't immune to him. And a woman like her, naive, vulnerable, would not be immune to the emotions that would come with the physical seduction.

It was ruthless, even for him. He preferred honesty. Preferred to let the women he got involved with know exactly what they were in for. Preferred to let them know that emotion was never going to be on the table. That love was never going to be a factor.

But he would offer her marriage, and she could hardly ask for more than that. In this instance, what would the harm be?

There was no other option. He was going to have to make Esther Abbott fall in love with him. And the only way to accomplish that would be seduction.

"Come on, Esther," he said, holding out his arm, "it is time for us to go home."

CHAPTER SEVEN

ESTHER WAS USED to the breakneck pace of working in the bar. Going out every night and working until closing time was demanding. But the routine of getting ready, polishing herself from head to toe, so that she could go out with Renzo for a dinner in Rome, was something else entirely. And it was almost no less exhausting.

Being on show was such a strange thing. She was used to being ignored. Invisible.

But two nights ago they had gone to his parents' house, and the scrutiny she had been put under there had been unlike anything she'd experienced since she'd lived at home and it had always seemed as though her father was trying to look beneath her skin for evidence of defiance, sin or vice.

Then, last night they had gone out again to a very nice restaurant, and Renzo had explained to her exactly what the charity event in New York was, and how she would be accompanying him.

Tonight, they were going to another dinner, though Renzo had not explained the purpose of this one. And it made her slightly nervous. He had also made her a doctor's appointment at a private clinic, not the one that Ashley had used. But one that he had chosen himself. Based on, he claimed, the doctor's reputation for discretion.

It seemed ridiculous to have to get dressed up for a doctor's appointment, but Renzo had explained that they would be going out afterward, so she would have to dress appropriately for dinner beforehand.

So, here she was now, sitting in the back of a limousine, being driven out to her appointment where Renzo was supposed to meet her. She was wearing lipstick.

The limo came to a stop, and she was deposited in front of a building that seemed far too polished to be a simple medical clinic. But then, Ashley had been aiming for a different kind of discretion when they had gone to the surrogacy clinic.

The driver opened the door for her, and she realized that she had to get out. Even though she just wanted to keep sitting there. For one horrifying second she wondered if she was going to go into the clinic, lie down on the doctor's table, and he was going to tell her the baby was gone.

For some reason, in that moment, the thought made her feel bereft. She wasn't sure why it should. Maybe for Renzo? Because he was rearranging his life for this child?

Or maybe, it's because you aren't ready to let go of the baby?

No, that was unthinkable. She wasn't attached to this. She just felt natural protectiveness. It was a hormone thing. She was sure of that. But she couldn't remember feeling sick for the last couple of days, not even a little bit of nausea, and she wondered if that was indicative of something bad. She wondered that even while she spoke to the woman at the front desk and was ushered into a private waiting room.

She wrung her hands, jiggling her leg, barely able to enjoy the opulence of the surroundings. She tried. She really did. Because she had purposed to be on this journey.

To enjoy this little window into something that would always and forever be outside her daily experiences.

She didn't know when she had started to care. At least not in a way that extended beyond the philosophical. That extended past her feeling like she had to preserve the life inside her out of a sense of duty. She only knew that it had.

Thankfully, she didn't have a whole lot of time to ruminate on that, because just then, Renzo entered the room. There was something wild and stormy in his gaze that she couldn't guess at. But then, that was nothing new. She didn't feel like she could ever guess what he was thinking.

"Where is the doctor?" He didn't waste any time assessing the situation and deciding it was lacking.

"I don't know. But I imagine it won't be much longer."

"It is a crime that you have been kept waiting at all," he said, his tone terse.

She hugged herself just a little bit more tightly, anxiety winding itself around her stomach. "You weren't here anyway. It didn't matter particularly whether or not the doctor materialized before you, did it?"

"You could have been preparing for the exam."

Esther didn't say anything. She could only wonder if Renzo was experiencing similar feelings to hers. It seemed strange to think that he would, but then, also not so strange. It was his baby. It actually made more sense than her being nervous.

"Ms. Abbott," a woman said, sticking her head through the door. "The doctor is ready to see you now."

Esther took a deep breath, pushing herself into a standing position. She was aware of walking toward the door on unsteady legs, and then hyperaware of Renzo reaching out and cupping her elbow, steadying her. "I'm fine," she said.

"You look like a very light breeze could knock you over."

"I'm *fine*," she reiterated. Even though she wasn't certain if she was.

Renzo let the line of conversation go, but he did not let go of her arm. Instead, he held on to her all the way down the private hallway and into the exam room.

"Remove your clothing and put on this gown," the nurse said. "The doctor will be in in just a few moments."

Esther looked at Renzo, her gaze pointed. But he didn't seem to take the hint.

"Can you leave?" she asked, the moment the nurse was out of sight.

"Why should I leave? You are my fiancée, after all."

"Your fiancée in name only. You and I both know that this child was not conceived in the…in the…the usual way that children are conceived. You don't have any right to look at me while I'm undressing. I couldn't say that in front of the stylist the other day, but I will say it now."

"I will turn," he said, his tone dry. And he did.

She took a deep breath, her eyes glued to his broad back, and she began to remove her clothing. It didn't matter that he couldn't *see* her. The feeling of undressing in the same room as a man was so shockingly intimate.

Everything had happened so quickly during her little makeover the other day. And while she had been embarrassed that he was looking at her body, she hadn't fully processed all of her feelings. Right now, she could process them all a bit too well.

From the dull thud of her heart, to the fluttering of her pulse at the base of her throat. The way that her fingers felt clumsy, numb, but everything else on her body felt hypersensitive and so very warm, tingly.

She could sense him. More than just seeing him standing in front of her, he felt all around her. As though he took up every corner of the room, even though she knew such a thing wasn't possible.

Finally, she got all of her clothes off, and stood there for a moment. Just a moment. Long enough to process the fact that she was standing naked in a room with this powerful man, who was dressed in a perfectly tailored suit.

It was such a strange contrast. She had never felt more vulnerable, more exposed or…stronger, than she did in that moment. And she could not understand all of those contrasting things coming together to create *one* feeling.

She picked up the hospital gown and slipped it onto her shoulders, then got up onto the plush table that was so very different from the other table she had been on just a few months ago. "This is different," she said. "From the clinic in Santa Firenze."

He turned then, not asking if he could. But she had a feeling that Renzo was not a man accustomed to asking for much. "In what way?"

"Well, I get the feeling that Ashley was doing her best to keep all of this from getting back to you. So, she opted for discreet. But not like this. It was…rustic?"

His lip curled. "Excellent. She took you to a bargain fertility clinic." His hands curled into fists. "If I ever get my hands on her…"

"Don't. The fact that she is who she is is punishment enough, isn't it?"

He laughed. "I suppose it is."

There was a firm knock on the door, followed by the door opening quickly. Then, the doctor—a small woman with her hair pulled back into a tight bun—walked into the room. "Ms. Abbott, Mr. Valenti, it's very nice to meet you. I'm very pleased to be helping you along with your pregnancy."

After introductions were made, and Esther's vitals were

taken, the woman had Esther lie down on the table, then she placed a towel over Esther's lap and pushed the hospital gown up to the bottom of her rib cage.

"We're going to do an ultrasound. To establish viability, listen to the heartbeat and get a look at the baby."

Anxiety gripped her. This was the moment of truth, she supposed. The moment where she found out if those prickling fears she'd had in the waiting room were in any way factual. Or if they were just vague waves of anxiety, connected to nothing more but her general distrust of the situation.

She really hoped it was the second.

The doctor squirted some warm gel onto her stomach, then placed the Doppler on her skin. She moved the wand around until Esther caught sight of a vague fluttering on the monitor next to her. Her breath left her body in a great gust, relief washing over her. "That's the heart," she asked, "isn't it?"

"Yes," the doctor said, flipping a switch and letting a steady thumping sound fill the room. "There it is."

It was strange, like a rhythmic swishing, combined with a watery sound in the back. The Doppler moved, and the sound faded slightly.

"I'm just trying to get a good look." She kept on moving the Doppler around, and new images flashed onto the screen, new angles of the baby that she carried. But Esther couldn't make heads or tails of any of it. She had no experience with ultrasounds.

"Do either of you have a history of twins in your family?"

The question hit Esther square in the chest, and she struggled to come up with any response that wasn't simply *why*.

She didn't. But she knew that the question didn't actually pertain to her, since the child she was carrying wasn't hers. "I…"

"No," Renzo said, his tone definitive. "However… The baby was conceived elsewhere through artificial means. If that has any impact on what you're about to say."

"Well, that does increase the odds of such things," the doctor said. "And that is in fact what it looks like here. Twins."

All of the relief that had just washed through Esther was gone now, replaced by wave after wave of thundering terror. Twins? There was no way she could be carrying twins. That was absurd.

Here she had been worried that she had lost one baby, that they would look inside her womb and see nothing, when they had actually found an extra baby.

"I don't understand," Esther said. "I don't understand at all. I don't understand how it could be twins. I've been to the doctor before to have the pregnancy checked on…"

"These things are easy to miss early on. Especially if they were just looking at heartbeats with the Doppler."

She felt heat rush through her face. "Yes," she confirmed.

"I understand that it's a bit of a shock."

"It's fine," Renzo said, his tone hard, belying that calm statement. "I have more than enough means to handle such things. I'm not at all concerned. Of course we are able to care for twins."

"Everything looks good," the doctor said, pulling the Doppler off Esther's stomach and wiping her skin free of gel. "Of course, we will want to monitor you closely as twins are considered a more high-risk pregnancy. You're young. And all of your vitals look good. I don't see why you shouldn't have a very successful pregnancy."

Esther was vaguely aware of nodding, while Renzo

simply stood there. Like a statue straight from a Roman temple.

Seeing that neither of them had anything to say, the doctor nodded. "I'll leave you two to discuss."

As soon as the doctor left, Esther sagged back onto the table, flattening herself entirely, going utterly limp. "I can't believe it."

"You can't believe it? You're the one who intends to leave. Why would it concern you?"

"*I'm* the one who has to carry a litter," she shot back.

"Twins are hardly a litter."

"Well, that's easy for you to say. You're not the one gestating them."

He looked stunned. Pale beneath his burnished skin. "Indeed not." He turned away from her. "Get dressed. We have reservations."

"I know I do. I have several reservations!"

"For dinner."

"You're not seriously suggesting that we just go out to dinner as though nothing's happened?"

"I am suggesting exactly that," he said through gritted teeth. "Get dressed. We are leaving to go to dinner."

She growled and got off the table, moving back over to her clothes on unsteady legs. She picked up the lacy underwear that had been provided by Renzo's stylist and slipped them up her legs, not even bothering to enjoy the lush feel of the fabric as she had been doing every other time before.

There was no pausing for lushness when you'd just found out you were carrying not one, but *two* babies.

She made quick work of the rest of her clothes. At least, as quick work as she could possibly make of them with her trembling fingers. "I'm ready," she snapped.

"Very good. Now, let us cease with the dramatics and go to dinner."

He all but hauled her out of the office, taking her to his sports car, where he yanked open the passenger-side door and held it for her.

She looked up at him, at his inscrutable face that was very much like a cloudy sky. She could tell a storm was gathering there, but she couldn't quite make out why. Then, she jerked her focus away from him and got into the car, clasping her hands tightly in her lap and staring straight ahead.

He closed the door, then got in on his side, bringing the engine to life with an angry roar and tearing out of the parking lot like the hounds of hell were on his heels.

"You dare call me dramatic?" she asked. "If this isn't dramatic, I don't know what is."

"I only just found out that I'm having two children, not one. If any of us is entitled to a bit of drama…"

"You seem to discount my role in this," she fired back. "At every turn, in fact, you treat me as nothing more than a vessel. Not understanding at all that there is a bit of work that goes into this. Some labor, if you will."

"Modern medicine makes it all quite simple."

"That is…well and truly spoken only like a man. What about what this is going to do to my body? It's going to leave me with stretch marks and then some." She didn't actually care about that, but she felt like poking him. Goading him. She wanted to make him feel something. Because for whatever reason this revelation had rocked her entire world, made her feel as though she herself had been tilted on her very axis. She didn't think he had a right to be more upset than she was. And maybe that wasn't fair. Maybe it was hormones. But she didn't particularly care.

"I will get you whatever surgery you want in order to return your body to its former glory. If you're concerned about what lovers will be able to get afterward, don't be."

That statement was almost laughable.

"I am not concerned about lovers," she said. "My life is not dependent on what other people think. Been there, done that, got rid of the overly starched ankle-length dresses. But what about what *I* think?"

"You are *impossible*. And a contradiction."

He drove on with a bit too much fervor through the narrow streets, practically careening around every corner, forcing her to grip the door handle as they made their way through town.

They stopped in front of a small café, and he got out, handing the keys to a valet in front of the door. It took her a moment to realize that he was not coming around to open the door for her. She huffed, doing it herself and getting out, gathering the fabric of her skirt and getting herself in order once she was fully straightened.

"That was not very gentlemanly," she said, rounding the front of the car and taking as big a step as her skirt would allow.

"I am very sorry. It has been said that I am perhaps not very gentlemanly. In fact, I believe it was said recently by you."

"Perhaps you should listen to the feedback."

He wrapped his arm around her waist, the heat from his hand shocking. His fingertips rested just beneath the curve of her breast, making her heart beat faster, stronger.

"I'm *very* sorry," he said, his voice husky. "Please say you'll forgive me. At least in time for the paparazzi to catch up with us. I would not want pictures of our dinner to go into the paper with you looking stormy."

"Oh, perish the thought. We cannot have anything damaging your precious reputation."

"Our association is entirely for my reputation. You will not ruin this. If you do, I promise I will make you pay. I will take money out of our agreement so quickly it will make your head spin. You do not want to play games with me, Esther."

He whispered those words in her ear, and for all the world he would look like a lover telling secrets. They would never guess that it was a man on the brink issuing threats.

It galled her that they worked.

He walked them inside, without being stopped by anyone, and went to a table that he had undoubtedly sat at many times before. He did pull her chair out for her, making a gentlemanly show there as he had failed to do at the car.

"Sparkling water," he said to the waiter when he came by.

"What if I wanted something else?" she asked, just to continue prodding at him.

"Your options are limited, as you cannot drink alcohol."

"Still. Maybe I wanted juice."

"Did you want juice?" he asked, his tone inflexible.

"No," she said, feeling defeated by that.

"Then behave yourself."

He took control like that with the rest of the dinner, proceeding to order her food—because he knew what the best dishes were at the restaurant—and not listening to any of her protestations.

She didn't know why she should find that particularly surprising. He had done that from the beginning. She had tried to come to him, had tried to do things on her own terms, but he had taken the reins at almost every turn.

Suddenly, sitting there in this restaurant that was so far outside her experience—would have been outside her scope for imagination only a few weeks earlier—she had the sensation that she was being pulled down beneath the surface. That she was out in the middle of the sea, unable to grab hold of anything that might anchor her.

She was afraid she might drown.

She took a deep breath, tried to disguise the fact that it was just short of a gasp.

Finally, their dessert plates were cleared, and Esther felt like she might be able to approach breathing normally again. Soon, they would be back at the villa. And while she still found his palatial home overwhelming, it was at least a familiar sort of overwhelming. Or rather, it had become so over the past few days.

Then, she looked up at him, and that brief moment of sanity melted into nothing. There was a strange look in his eye, one of purpose and determination. And if there was one thing she knew about Renzo it was that he was immovable at the best of times. Infused with an extra sense of purpose and he would be all-consuming.

She didn't want to be consumed by him. Not in any capacity. Looking into his dark eyes now, an answering twist low in her stomach, she wasn't certain she could avoid it.

He reached into the interior pocket of his jacket then, his dark eyes never wavering from hers, and then he got out of his chair, kneeling in front of her. She couldn't breathe. If she had had the sensation of drowning before, it had become something even more profound now. Like being swept up in a tide that she couldn't swim against. The effect those eyes always had on her.

The effect he seemed to have on her.

She was supposed to be stronger than this. Smarter than this. Immune to the charms of men. Especially men like him. Men who sought to control the world around them, from the people who populated their surroundings, to the homes they lived in, all the way down to the elements. She imagined that if a weather report disagreed with Renzo, he would rail at that until it changed its mind.

She knew all about men like that. Knew all about the importance of staying away from them.

Her mother had been normal once. That was something Esther wasn't supposed to know. But she had found the pictures. Had seen photographs of her mother as a young girl, dressed in the trends of the day, looking very much like any average girl might have.

She had never been able to reconcile those photographs of the past with the woman she had grown up with. Quiet. Dowdy. So firmly under the command of her husband that she never dared to oppose him in any way at all.

It had been a mystery both to her father and her mother that Esther had possessed any bit of rebelliousness at all. But she had. She did. And if there was one thing Esther feared at all in the world, it was losing that. Becoming that drawn, colorless woman who had raised her.

Love had done it to her. Or more truthfully, control carefully disguised as love.

It was so easy to confuse the two, she knew. She knew because she'd done it. Because she'd imagined her father had been overbearing out of a sense of protectiveness.

Those thoughts flashed through her mind like a strobe light. Fast, confusing, blinding, obscuring what was happening in front of her.

She blinked, trying to get a grip on herself. Trying to get a grip on the moment. It wouldn't benefit her at all to lose it now.

"Esther," he said, his voice transforming itself into something velvet, softening the command that had been in it only moments before. Brushing itself against her skin, a lush seduction rather than a hard demand.

He was dangerous. Looking at him now, she was reminded of that. She told herself over and over again as he opened the box he had taken out of his coat pocket and held it out to her. As he revealed the diamond ring inside.

He was dangerous. This wasn't real. This was something else. A window into a life she would never have. This was experience. Experience without consequence. She was pregnant. She was having twins. And she was playing at being rich and fancy with the father of those twins. But they weren't her babies. Not really. And he wasn't her fiancé. Wasn't her man at all.

That was a good thing. A very good thing. She didn't want anything else. Not from him. Not from anyone. She couldn't sustain this.

But she had to go along with this. And she had to remember exactly what it was, all the while smiling and doing nothing to disrupt the facade. Which, he had reminded her, was the most important thing. She could understand it. On a surface level, she could understand. But right now, she felt jumbled up. And she hated it.

Still, when he took the ring out of the box and then took her hand in his, sliding the piece of jewelry onto her fourth finger, she felt breathless. Felt like it was something more than a show, which proved all the weakness inside her. All the weakness she had long been afraid was there.

"Will you marry me?" he finished finally, those last words the darkest, the softest of all.

This was a moment she had never even fantasized about. Ever. She had never seen marriage or relationships as anything to aspire to. But this felt… This felt like nothing she had ever known before. And the question Renzo was asking seemed to be completely different from the one her father had undoubtedly asked her mother more than twenty years ago.

Of course it was. Because it was a ruse. But more than

that, this whole world might as well exist on another planet entirely.

But that doesn't make him less dangerous. It doesn't make him a different creature. He's still controlling. Still hard.

And he doesn't love you.

Her heart slammed hard against her rib cage. "Yes," she said, both to him and to the voice inside her.

She knew Renzo didn't love her. She didn't want Renzo to love her. Not like that. Love like that wasn't freedom. It was oppression.

She was confused. All messed up because of the doctor's appointment today. Because of the revelations that had resulted. Because of her hormones and because she was—frankly—in over her head.

That was the truth of it. She, Esther Abbott, long-cloistered weirdo who knew very little about the outside world and a very definite virgin, had no business being here with a man like Renzo. She had absolutely no business being pregnant at all, and she really shouldn't be on the receiving end of a proposal.

It was no great mystery that she felt like a jumble of feelings and pain while her head logically knew exactly what was happening. Her brain wasn't confused at all. Not at all.

But there was something weighty about the diamond on her finger. Something substantial about her yes that she couldn't quite quantify, and didn't especially want to.

It was the confusion inside her, tumbling around like clothes in that rickety old dryer at the hostel, that kept her from preparing herself for what happened next. At least, that was what she told herself later.

Because before she could react, before she could catch her breath, move or prepare herself in any way, Renzo brought his hand up and cupped her cheek, sliding his thumb over her cheekbone. It was like putting a lit match up against a pool of gasoline. It set off a trail of fire from that point of contact down to the center of her body.

And while she was grappling with that, added to everything else, he closed the distance between them and his mouth met hers.

Everything burned to ash then, bright white and cleansing. Every concern, every thought, everything gone from her mind in a flash as his lips moved over hers. That was what surprised her the most. The movement.

She hadn't imagined there was quite so much activity to being kissed. But there was. The shift of his hand against her face, sliding back to her hair, his lips learning the shape of hers and giving to accommodate that.

Then, his lips, lips she had never imagined could soften, did. And after that they parted, the shocking, wet slide of his tongue at the seam of her mouth undoing her completely. It set off an earthquake in her midsection that battled through her, leaving her devastated, hollowed out, an aching sense of being unfulfilled making her feel scraped raw.

She didn't know what to do. And so, she did the one thing she had always feared she might do when facing down a man like this. She gave. She allowed him to part her lips, allowed him to take it deeper.

Another tremor shook her, skating down her spine and rattling her frame. She didn't even fight it. She didn't even hate it.

When she had left home, when she had decided that she was going to go out into the world and see everything that was there for her to take. When she had decided finally to sort through what her parents had taught her and what was true, when she had decided to find out who she was, not who she had been commanded to be, this had never factored in.

She had never imagined herself in a situation like this. In the back of her mind she had imagined that someday she would want to explore physical desire. But it had been shoved way, way to the back of her mind. It had been a priority. Because so much of her life had been about being bound to a group of people. Being underneath the authority of someone else.

So, she had wanted to remain solitary. And at some point, she had imagined she might make a group of friends. When she decided to settle. At some point, she had imagined she might want to find a man for a romance. But it had been so far out ahead of what she had wanted in the immediate.

Freedom. A taste of the world that had always been hidden from her. Strange food and strange air. Strange sun on skin that had always been covered before.

Suddenly, all of that was obscured. Suddenly, all of it paled in comparison to this. Which was hotter than any sun, more powerful than any air she'd ever tasted—from the salted tang of the Mediterranean to the damp grit of London—and brighter than any flavor she'd ever had on her tongue.

It was Renzo. Pure, undiluted. Everything that gaze had promised her from the moment she had first seen him. The way he had immobilized her with just a glance had been only a hint. Like when a sliver of sun was just barely visible behind a dark cloud.

The cloud had just moved. Revealing all of the brilliance behind it. Brilliance that, she had a feeling, would be permanently damaging if she allowed herself to linger in it for too long.

But just a little while longer. Just a moment. One more

breath. She could skip one more breath for another taste of Renzo's mouth.

He pulled back then, dropping one more kiss on her lips before separating from her completely. And then he curled his fingers around hers, pulling her from her chair and up against his chest. "I think," he said, a roughness in his voice that had been absent only a moment ago, "that it is time for us to go home, don't you?"

"Yes," she said. Because there was nothing else to say. Because anything more intelligent would require three times the brain cells than she currently possessed.

And then he took her hand and led her from the restaurant. The car was waiting against the curb when they got back, and she didn't even ask how he had made sure they wouldn't have to wait.

He hadn't made a phone call. She hadn't caught any sort of signal between himself and a member of the restaurant staff. It looked like magic. More of the magic that seemed to shimmer from Renzo, that seemed to have a way of obscuring things. At least, as she saw them.

She had to get herself together. She told herself that, all the way home from the restaurant, and as she stepped into the house. And then she told herself that again when she realized that she had just referred to Renzo's home as her own in her mind.

She wanted to look at the ring on her finger. To examine the way the landscape of her own body had changed since he had put it on. She had never owned a piece of jewelry like that. She had bought a few fake, funky pieces when she had left home. Because she liked the way they jingled, and she liked the little bit of flash. Something to remind her of her freedom.

But diamonds had been a bit outside her purview.

She stole a quick glance down, the gem glittering in the light.

Then, it was as though a bucket of water had been dumped over her head. Suddenly, the haze that she had been under diminished. And once it did, she was angry.

"What were you thinking? Why didn't you warn me?"

CHAPTER EIGHT

RENZO DID NOT have the patience to deal with Esther and her pique right at the moment. His world felt like it had been completely turned on end. He was not having one child, but two. He could hardly sort through that.

He had opted to carry on with his plan, as though there had been no surprises at the doctor's today. He had continued on with his plan to propose to her at one of the more high-profile restaurants in Rome, where they would be sure to have their picture taken, so they could be splashed out on the tabloids. The same tabloids that had covered his incredibly public divorce from Ashley just recently.

It had been calculated. Very specifically. To set the stage so the people would believe this relationship was real. So that they would believe this pregnancy had come about in a natural way.

What he had not counted on was the kiss. Or more specifically, how it had affected him. Yes, he had known that Esther was beautiful. He had also known that he was not immune to that beauty. When he had watched Tierra dress her just the other day, he had been captivated by the smooth curve of her waist, her hip, the way that black lace underwear had barely covered her shapely rear.

But that big attraction still hadn't prepared him for what had transpired in the restaurant. She was unpracticed. Much less experienced than he had even imagined, judging by that kiss. She had barely moved.

But somehow, she had lit him on fire inside. He had tasted every female delicacy the world had to offer. Had delighted himself in feminine company after his first heartbreak. Seeing no reason he could not satisfy his body since he was bound and determined never to involve his heart again.

But she had broken through that jaded wall that surrounded him. She had done something to him. And now, she was yelling at him.

"I could not warn you, *cara*," he said. "That would have spoiled the surprise."

"I didn't like the surprise," she said.

"Still, I needed you to look surprised. You are aware that most women do not know when they're going to be proposed to, are you not?"

She sniffed audibly. "Maybe I'm not."

"I think you are. I needed it to look real."

"Is that why you…pawed at me afterward?"

"That's a very elegant way to describe what transpired between us. Though I do believe, you did some pawing of your own."

She huffed. "I did not. Like I said, you surprised me. I feel as though you could have warned me. About all of it. And you would not have lost the element of surprise. I could have acted."

"Sadly, you're a terrible actress. I hate to be insulting, but it's true. You have no artifice." As he said it, he realized how very true it was.

"You were trying to control me," she said, her tone hard, the anger behind it indicative of a deeper wound. One that had existed long before he'd arrived in her life.

"That wasn't it," he said, although he imagined it was

semantics at this point. "You have no… You're very soft. You seem to have no way of protecting yourself from any of this at all. You sit in sunbeams with bowls of cereal. And I do not know what to do with you. I do not know what you might do next. I do not like it."

She breathed in deeply, and if a breath could be called triumphant, then this one certainly was. "Good. I don't live my life to please people anymore. I am my own person."

"Yes. So you've said."

"It's the truth. I know that I told you my parents were difficult. But you have no idea."

"Well, you have met my parents. Assume I have some idea of difficult parents."

She snorted. "Trust me. Your parents seemed delightful to me."

"Your frame of reference is off."

"Undoubtedly." He began to pace the length of the room, all of the unquenched fire and unspent energy inside him threatening to boil over. "You must remember that you are not in charge here. This thing that we're doing is important only to me. Therefore, I will direct all actions. If I decided that this was the best way to go about confirming our engagement for the public, then you must accept that my way is law."

"You keep saying this is only important to you. But that isn't the case. I care. You may not understand it—I don't even understand it. But it matters. I'm linked to it. Physically. I know that these babies aren't mine, but it's all jumbled up. Biology and ownership, what it means… I don't know. I just know that I don't feel like a womb for rent. I feel like a person, a person who is going through something big and terrifying. A person who is carrying a baby. *Babies*, even. There is no divorcing my emotions from it. There is no detaching myself, not completely."

He regarded her closely. "Have you changed your mind about leaving?" She would. He would make sure of it. But if she was leaning toward a change of heart now, that would make his job all the easier.

Her reaction to that kiss would seal things completely.

"No," she said, her tone muted. She looked away, biting that lush lower lip that he had tasted less than an hour ago. "I can't. I have too much to do. I know that…I know that. But stop telling me that what I want doesn't matter. That what I feel isn't like what you feel."

"But," he said, unable to let that comment slide, even if he should for the sake of harmony. For the sake of manipulation. "It is the truth. I'm going to be a father to these babies. To these children. I'm going to be the one who raises them. I know what that entails. It is going to require sacrifice. Change." Until he spoke those words he had not realized that he intended to change it all. Somewhere in the back of his mind he had imagined that he would throw the raising of these children over to nannies. But now, he realized that was not the case.

He thought of his daughter. The daughter whose name he could barely stand to think, even after all these years. The daughter he sometimes saw across the room, through crowds of people, growing from a child into a young woman. Without him. Without ever knowing.

The idea of being a distant father again, even if his children were in the nursery and he was downstairs seeing to his routine while they were cared for by others, was too much.

"My life will change." He reiterated that, as much for himself as for her.

"I have a feeling mine will, too."

"Yes. Because of all the money that I will pay you."

"No," she said, her tone fierce now. "Because I was

naive. Because I was foolish to think that I could do this and feel nothing. That I could do this and simply walk away with a check at the end. This experience is never going to go away. I... I'm going to be changed," she said, sounding sad now, broken. "I thought that everything would be fine because I was committed to having this life or I didn't have ties and strings and any of those things that I was trying to avoid. But that's not true. Everything has consequences." She laughed. "I think I pushed that out of my mind. Because it was something that my father used to talk about. Consequences for actions. How everything you do will come back to you. How distressing to find out that not everything my parents taught me is wrong."

"That is usually the case," he said, her words hitting him in an uncomfortable place yet again. "Tragic though it may seem, no matter how difficult the situation, no matter how unreasonable your parents can be at times, they are often not entirely incorrect."

She shook her head. "I'm going to bed."

She turned away from him, and he reached out, grabbing hold of her arm and stopping her from going. "Remember," he said, not quite sure what he was going to say. For a moment, he just stood there holding on to her, not certain of why he had prevented her from leaving. "Remember that we have to go to New York in two weeks. If you thought tonight was public, then what you encounter there will surprise you. If you need any kind of preparation in advance, I suggest you speak to me about it. Otherwise, I will assume that you know what you're getting yourself into and I will expect you to behave accordingly."

He released his hold on her. He knew he was being an ass, but he couldn't quite bring himself to correct the behavior. Why should he?

Seduction, perhaps?

He gritted his teeth. Yes, that might have been the better path. To kiss her again, to soften her fears while he claimed that soft mouth of hers. And yet, he found he needed more distance from that initial kiss than another. More than he would like to admit.

"I think I can figure it out," she said, her tone soft.

"See that you do."

There were only a couple of weeks left until he would present her to the world as his fiancée. And at that point—his father was correct—it needed to be permanent. But Esther was hungry for experience. To see the world, to see all that life had to offer. And if there was anything that he possessed, it was access to what she craved.

He could give her glamour. He could give her excitement. He could—quite literally—show her the world.

And there was one more thing. Yet another that she would get from no other man, not in the way that he could give it. Passion. The two of them were combustible, there was no denying that after the kiss they had shared tonight. It was not a common kind of chemistry. He was a connoisseur of such things, and he should know.

Yes. New York would be the perfect place to spring his trap.

He would take her to the finest hotel, show her the finest art, take her to unsurpassed restaurants. And then when he took her back to that plush hotel and laid her on that big bed… He would make her his.

In the weeks since their engagement, they had settled into an odd sort of routine. They ate meals together—and she had none of them on the floor—and they shared polite conversation where he never once tried to kiss her.

He was interesting, and that was perplexing, because

she found herself seeking him out in the evenings just so she could talk to him.

Then there were the books. Every day after work he brought her a new one. Small, hardbound travel guides. Paperback novels. Extremely strange history books that focused on odd subjects such as uniforms for different armies and the types of women's clothing through the ages.

She'd asked him why, and he'd responded that it was so she could learn all the things she didn't know. Just as she'd said she wanted to.

It made her feel…soft. She wasn't sure she wanted that. She also wanted things to stay the same. In this strange, quiet lull where she felt like they were poised on the brink of something.

She liked being on the brink. It felt safe. Nothing too big, or too outside her experience.

Of course, it had to end. And she got her big shove over the brink when he came home from his office one day and swept her and all of her clothing up in a whirlwind of commands, packed her into his car and then summarily unpacked her on his private plane.

A private plane. Now, that she had not managed to imagine with any kind of accuracy. The horrors of traveling economy over the Atlantic had been something she hadn't quite anticipated, but on the opposite end of the spectrum.

The long flight to New York seemed to pass quickly with her enveloped in the butter-soft leather of the recliner in the living area of Renzo's plane. There was food that bore absolutely no resemblance to the meal she had been served on her crossing from the United States, and all manner of fresh juice and sparkling water.

Then, there was some kind of light, sweet cream cake that she could have eaten her weight in if she hadn't been stopped by the landing preparation.

Renzo had spent the entire flight buried in work. That was neither completely surprising nor unwelcome. At least, it shouldn't have been unwelcome. Except she had craved conversation but had instead settled for reading the book he'd gotten her for the flight, which strangely felt like him talking to her in some way.

She didn't know why she was being weird about it. They were connected by the babies she was carrying, and that was it. They didn't need to form more of a personal connection than they already had. More than that, it was probably best if they didn't.

She did her best not to think about that kiss. She did her best not to think of it as she was ushered off the plane and into another limousine. She did her best not to think of it as they made their way down the freeway, the famous Manhattan skyline coming into view.

That helped take her focus off Renzo and the strange ache in her chest.

New York. She had never been to New York. She had hoped to make it there someday, but her first inclination had been to get as far away from her parents as she possibly could, and that had meant taking a little sojourn around Europe.

But this was amazing. The kind of amazing that she hadn't imagined she would experience in her lifetime. At least, not when you combined it with the flight over. In some ways it was a relief to see that Renzo was making good on his promise. To show her a part of the world that she couldn't have seen without him. The way that people with money lived. The way that they traveled, the sorts of sights and foods that they saw and ate.

In another way, it was disquieting.

Because it was just another way Renzo might have

changed her. What if she got used to this? What if she missed it? She didn't want that.

She shook that thought off immediately as the city drew closer.

This was what mattered. The experience. Not the lushness of the car. But where she was. She wasn't going to change in that regard. Not that much. She had been sort of distressed when she had realized fully that her parents might have had some points when they'd lectured her about consequences.

And what she had already known was that the way they had instilled the lack of materialism in her really had mattered. It really had made a difference. And it made it a lot easier for her to pick up and travel around. While a lot of her various roommates in the different hostels had been dismayed by conditions, she had been grateful for a space of her own.

Independence was the luxury. She would remember that.

She and Renzo completed the ride down into Manhattan in silence. She remained silent all through their arrival at the hotel. It was incredible, with broad stone steps leading up to the entry. The lobby was tiled in a caramel-color stone, shot through with veins of deeper gold. It wasn't a large room. In fact, the hotel itself had a small, exclusive quality to it. But it was made to feel even more special as a result.

As though only a handful of people could ever hope to experience it.

The room, however, that had been reserved for herself and Renzo was not small. It took up the entire top of the building, bedrooms on one end and a large common living area in the center. The windows looked out over Central Park, and she stood there transfixed, gazing at the green square surrounded by all of the man-made grit and gray.

"This is amazing," she said, turning back to face him, her throat constricting when she saw him.

He was standing there, deft fingers loosening the knot on his black tie. He pulled it through his shirt collar, then undid the top button. And she found herself more transfixed by the view before her than by the one that was now behind her.

The city. She was supposed to be focusing on the city. On the hotel. On the fact that it was a new experience. She was not supposed to be obsessing on the man before her. She was not supposed to be transfixed by the strong, bronzed column of his throat. By the wedge of golden skin he revealed when he undid that top button. And not just skin. Hair. Dark chest hair that was just barely visible and captured her imagination in a way that stunned her.

It was just very male. And she knew from experience that so was he. His kiss had been like that. Very like a man. So different to her. Conquering, hard. While she had softened, yielded.

No. She would not think about that. She wouldn't think about yielding to him.

"What do you think of your first sight of New York?"

"Amazing," she said, grateful that he was asking about the city and not about his chest. "Like I said. It's big and busy like London, but different, too. The energy is different."

He frowned slightly, tilting his head to the side. "The energy is different." He nodded slowly. "I suppose that's true. Though, I had never thought of it quite that way."

"Well, you've never sat on the floor and eaten your cereal in a sunbeam either."

"Correct."

"Noticing energy is more the sort of thing someone who'd eat their cereal on the floor in a sunbeam would do."

"I would imagine that's true."

"You're too busy to notice things like that. The real estate development business is…busy, I guess."

"Yes. Even during slow times in the economy, it's comparably busy if you've already got a massive empire."

"And you do," she said.

"I would think that was obvious by now."

"Yes. Pretty obvious." She forced herself to turn away from him, forced herself to look back at the view again. "I find cities so very interesting. The anonymity of them. You can be surrounded by people and still be completely alone. Where I grew up, there were less people. By far there were less people. But it felt like you were never alone. And not just because I lived in the house with so many other people. But because every time you stepped outside you would meet somebody you knew. You could never just have a bad day."

He lifted a shoulder. "I am rarely anonymous when I go out."

She frowned. "I suppose you aren't. I mean, I would never have known who you were. I'm not metropolitan enough."

"You're certainly working on it."

She looked down at the outfit that had been chosen for her to travel in. Dark jeans and a white top. She supposed she looked much more metropolitan than she had only a few weeks ago. But it wasn't her. And none of this belonged to her either.

"The appearance of it at least." She regarded him more closely. "I suppose you can't exactly have a public bad day either."

He chuckled, the sound dark, rolling over her like a

thick summer night. "Of course I can. I can do whatever I like, behave as badly as I like. I'm Renzo Valenti, and no one is going to lecture me on decorum."

"Except maybe your mother."

He laughed again. "Oh, yes, she most definitely would. But there is nothing my parents can do to me." He looked past her, at the city visible through the large windows. "They gave me too much freedom for too long, and now I have too much power. All they can do is direct their disapproval at me with as much fervor as humanly possible. A pity for them, but rather a win for me, don't you think?"

"In some ways approval and disapproval is power, isn't it?" She thought of her own family. Of the fact that what had kept her rooted in her childhood home for so long was the knowledge that if she should ever leave she would never be able to go back. That if she ever stepped foot out of line her father would disown her. Would turn all of her siblings against her, would forbid her mother from having any contact with her. It was the knowledge that the disapproval would carry so much weight she would be cut off completely, and in order to make even one decision of her own she would have to be willing to accept that as a consequence.

"I suppose."

"You don't believe me. But that just means that your parents' approval doesn't come with strings."

That made him laugh again, and he wandered over to the bar, taking out a bottle of Scotch and pouring himself a drink. She wouldn't have known what the amber-colored alcohol was only a few months ago, but waiting tables had educated her.

"Now, that isn't true. It's only that I possess a certain amount of string-pulling power myself. So what you have is a power struggle more than a fait accompli."

"That's what I needed," she said, "strings."

Of course, that was what actually hurt, she concluded, standing there and turning over what he said. The fact that she wasn't a string. Her presence in their life wasn't a string. Control mattered to her father, not love. And he couldn't have anyone around to challenge that control because it might inspire the other people in his household to do the same.

Parental love wasn't strong enough to combat that. If there was any parental love coming from his direction at all.

"You should probably get some rest. You will have to start getting ready for the gala tonight as soon as possible. So a short nap might be in your best interest."

She wasn't exactly sure what had inspired the abrupt comment, but she would be grateful for some distance. Grateful for a little bit of time away from Renzo and his magnetic presence, and all of the feelings and emotions he stirred up inside her.

"I think I will have a nap. Is… Is someone going to come and help with my makeup and hair?"

"Of course. I'm hardly going to leave that to chance on the night of the most important professional event of the year."

"Good. I'm too relieved to be offended." And then she turned and walked away from him, heading into the first bedroom that she saw. Without another thought, she threw herself across the plush mattress and closed her eyes.

And if it was Renzo she saw behind her closed lids rather than the brilliant city skyline, she chose to ignore that.

Renzo had a plan. And he had a feeling it would be one that was quite simple to complete. He was intent on seducing Esther tonight. Judging by the way she had looked at him this afternoon, the seduction was halfway complete. He was not a vain man, but he was also not a man given to false modesty.

Esther was attracted to him. She had been affected by that kiss, and he would be able to overtake her senses yet again when he touched her tonight. More than that, she was affected by all of this. By the luxury of the travel, by the places in the world that he brought to her fingertips by virtue of his money and connections.

He wasn't angry that she had an interest in these things; rather, he found it to be a boon to his cause.

If she had been as unaffected by these things as she had claimed that she would be, then he would have lost some leverage. But she wanted to go to school, she wanted to see the world, and whether she knew it or not, she craved his touch. He could give her all of those things. He could satisfy her in a way that no other man could, in a way no other man had.

All she would have to do was agree to marry him. Beyond that, she would have to present a respectable front in public. But that was it. He could see no reason she would find that objectionable.

He had lied to her, of course, when he said that his parents had no leverage with him. His father had presented incredibly hard leverage at his home only two weeks ago. And dammit all, Renzo was not immune. He would not have control in his stake of the family business given up to his brother-in-law. He would not have it given to anyone. He had given up enough.

In order to maintain the status quo, he had already given up a child. He would not lose anything more.

Rage burned in his chest, the kind of rage he had not felt for years. He hadn't realized it was quite so strong still. He had thought he had accepted that decision. His parents had been acting in his best interest. But it burned. In fact, the more the years passed, it seemed to burn even brighter.

The older he got, the more control he assumed of his life, the angrier he was about the lack of control he'd had at sixteen.

His line of thinking was cut off completely when the door to Esther's room opened and a flash of slender leg caught his gaze. He turned his focus to her, a hot slug of lead landing in his gut and making his body feel heavy.

Her dark hair was hanging loose, in glossy waves around her shoulders. The bright blue dress she had in place showed off her curves, enhancing her modest bust with the heart-shaped line.

The shimmering, fluttering fabric hung loose over her stomach, a stomach that was showing subtle changes brought about by the pregnancy.

Gold shadow enhanced her eyes, and her cheeks were the color of poppies, matching her full lips.

She was an explosion of color, of shimmering light, and he could not take his eyes off her. Not for the first time, he wondered who might be seducing whom. Perhaps the idea of staying with him was in her plans already. Perhaps all of this was an elaborate ruse to gain access to his wealth and power.

Looking at her now, combined with the incontrovertible evidence of her pregnancy from the scan, he wasn't sure if it mattered. If she was every bit as innocent as she claimed, and appeared to be, or if she was calculating.

He should care. He just found that he didn't.

"You look amazing," he said, closing the space between them and curving his arm around her waist. The stylist he had hired was behind her in the room, and he knew that he could use that as an excuse later for what he was about to do.

He leaned in, brushing his lips against hers. A taste, a tease for them both.

It became apparent immediately that he had not imagined the heat and fire between them. In fact, just that brief touch ignited something inside him that was hotter than anything he'd felt in his memory.

It was nothing. Just lips. Just a hand on the curve of her waist.

And it left him shaken.

"Come," he said, his voice rough, "*cara*, let us go to the ball."

CHAPTER NINE

THE VENUE WAS packed full of people, lavish and expensive, money dripping from every corner of the place. From the diamonds that hung in women's ears, to the chandelier that hung overhead. It was the perfect example of the kind of opulent lifestyle that Renzo could offer her if she chose to stay with him. The perfect piece of manipulation, and one he had not even planned for.

But it would do. It would do nicely. Esther clung to his side, her delicate fingers curved around his biceps. And even though there were layers between them—his coat and his shirt—he could still feel the heat from her skin.

Yes, this was a very nice diversion, and one that would work to his advantage, but he couldn't wait till after. Till he would finally strip her bare and hold her in his arms. It had become a madness over the past few weeks. To resist her, to wait.

To speak to her over dinner when he'd wanted to pull her over the table and have her there. To bring her books to read in bed, when he wanted to keep her occupied with other things in bed.

He had thought so many times of going into her room and breaking the door down, laying his body over hers and kissing her until neither of them could breathe.

Of taking full possession of her without any of this

pretense. Without any of this delicacy. Because he had a feeling that it wasn't needed. He had a feeling that the fire burned as hot in her as it did in him. And he desperately wanted to find out if that was true.

However, he could not afford to allow impetuousness to make his decisions for him. He could not afford to make a wrong move simply because his libido was ratcheted up several notches.

He shifted, her hip brushing against him. The reaction was immediate. Primal.

He wanted to hold on to those hips, hold her steady as he thrust into her. As he made her cry out. Thankfully, he had thought to call the doctor before they left Rome. Under the guise of discussing safe travel. And he had of course asked her about what sort of intimacy would be all right, given that the pregnancy was considered a slightly higher risk.

She said that normal intercourse would be fine.

A smile curved his lips. Yes, he was going to have her. Tonight.

"There are so many people here," Esther said, "and they all seem to know you."

"Yes, but I do not know them."

"What must that be like?" she asked, as though he hadn't spoken. "To be…famous."

"*Infamous*, more like. I'm not going to lie to you, I'm mostly well-known because men know they have to watch their women around me." Now she stiffened, and he was pleased with himself for that well-timed comment. It was a risk, but there was no hiding his reputation from her. However, using it to fire up a little jealousy in her couldn't hurt, certainly.

"Is that so?" she asked.

"Yes," he said. "I was single for a very long time, Esther. And I didn't see any point in living with restraint. As I told you earlier, I don't have to watch the way that I behave. I have a certain amount of immunity granted to me because I am both male and very rich."

"That must be nice."

"I don't know any differently."

"My father was big on the men-having-whatever-they-wanted thing," she said, the tone of her voice disinterested, casual, but he sensed something deep beneath the surface.

"Traditional, was he?"

She shook her head. "I don't know. Maybe that's one word for it. One of the things I've been working on is recognizing that whatever my father and the other men like him believed, it isn't necessarily connected to anything real. It's not about other people who believe similarly to them. They took something that was all right and twisted it to suit their own ends. And I do understand that."

"You had…a religious upbringing?"

She shrugged. "I'm hesitant to call it that. I'm not going to put the blame on religion. Just the people involved."

"Very progressive of you."

She shrugged both shoulders this time. "Isn't that the point of life? To progress? That's what I'm trying to do. Move forward. Not live underneath the cloud of all of that." She looked up, refracted light shimmering across her face from the chandelier above them as she did. "I'm not under a cloud at all right now." She smiled then, and all of the thoughts he had earlier about her potentially calculated behavior faded. It was difficult for him to imagine somebody who was simply genuine. Because it was outside his experience. Yet, Esther seemed to be, and if he looked at her from that angle, if you looked at her now, he felt slightly guilty about what he intended to do. Because that really did make it a manipulation, rather than a simple seduction.

But still, she would get everything that she wanted in the end, just in a slightly different format. So, he should not feel guilt.

He turned, and suddenly it felt as though the chandelier had detached from the ceiling and come crashing down around him. It was everything he'd been afraid of, and yet no amount of forward thinking could ever prepare him for it.

There she was.

Samantha.

His daughter.

Seeing her like this, closer to being a woman than a girl, always shocked him. But then, everything about this had always been shocking, horrifying. Seeing her was always something like having his guts torn out straight through his stomach. Having his heart pulled out of his mouth.

It was a pain that never healed, and for a man who avoided strong emotion at all cost it was anathema. He controlled the world. He controlled more money than most people could fathom. He had more—would have more—than many small countries ever would. And yet he did not have her, and there was nothing he could do about it. Nothing he could do short of destroying what she thought her life was. Who she thought she was.

In this, he was helpless. And he despised it.

But there was very little that could be done. In order to be a good man in this situation, in order to be a controlled man, he had to go against everything his instincts told him to do. He had to honor the life that he had chosen to give to his daughter. Even if he had been coerced into it, the ultimate result was the same. There were things she believed about herself and her parents that he could not shake, not now.

He knew it. He knew it, but he despised it.

Fire burned inside him, rage, intensity. He couldn't go to her. All he could do was hold even more tightly to Esther. And as he did, he held even more tightly to his conviction. He had to make her his. At all costs. Because he would never take a chance that he might lose his children, not again.

He had lost one daughter. And the pain never faded. He doubted it ever would. There was nothing that could be done about it. It was a red slash across his life that could never heal. A mistake that would not be undone.

Oh, her existence wasn't a mistake. It never could be. The mixture of grief and pride that filled him when he saw Samantha was something that defied description. It was all-encompassing, overwhelming. She was not a mistake. She was destined for a life that was better than the one he could have given her at the time. Than the one she would have had if she had been raised by an angry, bitter woman whose marriage was destroyed because of her existence and a sixteen-year-old boy who could scarcely take care of himself, let alone a little girl.

Yes, there was no doubt she was living a better life than he could have given at the time.

But now… Now he had no excuses. Now he had resources, he had experience, maturity. He had already lived an entire existence trying to prove that he was unsuitable to raise the child he'd had at far too young an age.

Now he was going to have to fashion a new existence. One where he became everything these children would need.

He would give them everything. Starting with a family. One with no room for Ashley, who had engineered their existence for the sole purpose of manipulating him. One that consisted of a mother and a father. Esther. She was the one. She was going to give birth to them. She was the one the public would consider theirs, and so, too, would they.

He was renewed in his purpose. As he stood there, his insides being torn to shreds piece by piece as he looked at the beautiful young woman whom he would never know, who shared his DNA but would always remain a stranger, his purpose was renewed.

He turned away from Samantha. He turned back to Esther. "Dance with me," he said.

She blinked. "I don't know how to dance."

"Don't tell me, dancing was forbidden?"

She laughed, but the sound was uncomfortable, and it made him feel guilty. "Yes," she said. "Dancing was definitely something that was off the table. But…I did a lot of things I wasn't supposed to."

Something about that admission made his stomach tight, made his blood run hotter. "Is that right?"

"Yes," she said, her cheeks turning pink. "But I didn't dance. I might embarrass you."

"You're the most beautiful woman in the room. Even if you step all over my feet I will not be embarrassed to be seen with you."

A warm flush of color spread up her cheeks, her dark eyes bright. She liked that. This attention, the compliments. He reached out, sliding his thumb over her cheekbone, tracing that wash of color that had appeared there. "Do you know that you're beautiful?"

"It's nothing that I ever gave much thought to. I mean, I've probably given it much more thought ever since I met you."

He drew her close to him, guiding her to the dance floor, curving his arm around her waist and taking her hand in his. "In a good way, I hope?"

She looked down. "Meeting you has made me think a lot about people."

"I'm not sure I follow you."

She moved easily along with him as he guided her in time with the music. But she kept her eyes downcast. "Just…people. Men, women." She looked up then, something open and naked in her gaze. It held him fast, hit him square in the chest. "How different we are. What it means. Why it matters. My beauty never mattered until I wanted you to see it. And then, well, since then I've wondered about it. If I had it, and if I did, if it was the kind that you noticed. It's a weird way to think about it, maybe. But I never spent much of my life thinking about how I looked except in the context that being vain about it was wrong." She shook her head, her dark hair rippling over her shoulders. "That's quite liberating in a way. If vanity is wrong, then you simply push thoughts of your appearance out of your mind. You don't worry about it, and neither does anyone around you. But that isn't the way the rest of the world works."

"Sadly not."

"I guess that's another thing about how I was raised that maybe isn't so bad. Because now I have worried about it. How my dresses fit, how they look, what you think. But then… Feeling beautiful isn't so bad. And when you tell me that I am…"

"You like it," he said.

"I do."

His stomach tightened, and a smile curved his lips, a feeling of anticipation lancing him. He was very close to having her in the palm of his hand. To having all that glorious skin under his hands. "Vain creature," he said, injecting a note of levity into his voice.

"Is that a bad thing?" she asked, her tone tentative.

"I find it somewhat charming. Though, I have to ask you now… What have you been thinking about me? You said you had been thinking about our differences."

The undertone of pink in her cheeks turned scarlet. "That's silly. Juvenile. You don't want to hear about that."

"Oh, I assure you I do."

He examined the lush curve of her mouth, the dramatic high cheekbones and her dark lashes. She was the epitome of glorious feminine beauty, but there was an innocence there, and part of him wondered just how much.

"You're just very…" Her lashes fluttered "…big. I'm small. I feel like you could overpower me if you wanted to, and yet, you never have. There's something incredibly powerful about that. It feels dangerous to be near you sometimes, and yet I know you won't hurt me. I don't how to describe that. But sometimes the realization washes over me and it makes me shiver."

He did something then that he could not quite fully reason out. He released his hold on her hand, sliding his fingertips up her arm and resting his thumb against the hollow at the base of her throat as he curved his fingers around the back of her neck. Demonstrating that power, perhaps.

He could feel her pulse beginning to throb faster beneath his touch, and he felt an answering pounding within his own body.

"What else?" he asked, keeping his tone soft and his touch firm.

"You're very…hard."

"Am I?" he asked, lowering his voice further.

She had no idea. He was getting harder by the second. This little flirtation, something he hadn't quite anticipated enjoying, was adding fuel to the fire of his determination.

"Yes," she said, doing something completely unexpected, taking her free hand and pressing it against his chest, sliding her palm down to his stomach. "Much harder than I am."

"You seem like you would benefit from the chance to explore that."

Her breath caught in her throat. "I don't…"

He reached down, catching hold of her wrist and pressing her hand more firmly against his chest. "I want you."

He wanted her. Needed her. And not just because he needed her to marry him, because he needed to ensure that she was bound to him. But because he needed something to blot out the unending pain that was coursing through him—had been coursing through him for sixteen years.

Her eyes widened, an innocent stain spreading across her cheeks. "Want me to…what?"

He pulled her even closer, pressing his lips against her ear. "I want you naked," he said, feeling her shiver against him. "I want to lay you down in my bed and strip that dress from your body. Then I want to touch every inch of you. And then I want to taste you."

He barely recognized his own voice. It was rough, hard. And he was somewhere past control.

Esther trembled, and he could feel her shaking her head. "No, you don't."

"Of course I do. I said you were beautiful. I meant it."

"But that doesn't mean…" Her cheeks looked like they were on fire beneath her golden skin. "There are plenty of other women you could have. You don't have an obligation to me. We might be engaged publicly, but we both know that privately…"

"Of course I can be seen with no other woman but you," he said, "but that is beside the point. You're the one that I want. You, Esther Abbott. Not anyone else."

"But I'm not…I don't know… You can't. Not me."

The fire in him burned even hotter, and he was surprised by the strength of his conviction. Yes, it was all tangled up in the need to keep possession of his children, the need to give them the best life possible, and he believed he needed Esther for that, but there was more. In this moment, there was more. It would not be a hardship to convince her that he wanted her. Because he did.

"Yes," he returned, "you. I love your skin. I want to know if it's smooth like this all over." He moved a fingertip over her arm, relishing the tremor that racked her frame. "Your lips." He moved his fingertip around the lush line of her mouth then, that softness doing something to all of the hard, jagged places inside him. The seduction working better on him than he had intended. This was supposed to be about an end goal, one that extended far beyond finding himself between her beautiful thighs tonight. But it was difficult to remember that with lust pounding through him like a drumbeat.

"Your hands," he said, moving to curve his fingers around her wrist, caressing her palm slowly. "I want to feel them all over my body. And yes, I could have another woman. I have had them. More than I can count, I won't lie to you. But I don't want them now. I couldn't." It was the truth in his words that surprised him more than anything else. The fact that this wasn't simply a calculated statement. The fact that the strange creature in front of him had bewitched him in some way.

That she had compelled him to give her books, of all the ridiculous things. A new one every day because he passed a shop on his way home from work, and he thought of her every time he did. Because she wanted to learn and he wanted her to.

And, *Dio*, what he would teach her tonight.

"You haunt me," he ground out, losing hold of the carefully scripted line of compliments that he had put together moments before, going off into the dark parts of himself, where he could scarcely see an inch in front of him, much less guess at what might come out of his mouth next. "My dreams," he said, the words rough, "and every moment I lay in bed not dreaming because I'm thinking about you."

Her entire body was shaking like a leaf in a storm, and he felt nothing but triumph. His vision was a blur, a haze of everything but Esther. His mind blank of everything except what would happen in the moments immediately following this one.

She would say yes. She had to.

She pulled away slightly, and he wondered if he had gone too far. If he had been too intense, if he had been too honest.

He made a decision then.

He took firm hold of her arms and dragged her forward, closing the distance between them and claiming her mouth with his own. He wrapped her up in him then, folding her in his arms, gripping her chin tightly as he braced her firmly against him and forged a new, intimate territory between them.

He had kissed her before. But not like this. This wasn't a show for the people around them. It was not designed for cameras. And it wasn't designed to end here.

It was a beginning. A promise. A precursor of what was to come. An echo of the act that he intended to follow.

As he thrust his tongue in and out of the sweet, hot depths, as he felt her moan and shake beneath him, he knew that he had won. Because if he could reduce her to this—reduce them both to this—here in the presence of all these other people, then there would be no resisting him once he had her alone.

His father would be angry. Because Renzo had not taken this opportunity to forge new business deals as he had promised. But his father had no idea about the other war that was being raged. The war to keep Esther close, the war to defend the family that was growing inside her even now.

It took all the strength that he possessed to pull away from her. To keep himself from pushing her into the nearest alcove, shoving her dress up her hips and taking her then and there. Claiming her. But that would only further the cause of satisfying his desire. It would not further the cause of seduction.

He doubted if Esther had ever been taken up against a wall in a public place. And he also doubted if she would find that overly romantic.

As much as his body didn't care, the rest of him had to. He managed to find his focus in that. And when he turned back around and saw his daughter standing at the back of the room chatting with friends and taking no notice of what had been happening with him—why would she? She had no idea who he even was—it brought him crashing down to reality with an extreme sense of purpose.

"Come," he said.

She blinked. "We haven't been here that long. We came all the way to New York for this."

He laughed, every jagged thing inside him brought to the surface because of what had happened tonight stabbing through him. "No, *cara*. I came all the way to New York for you. To seduce you. To have you."

She looked shaken by that, her dark eyes filled with confusion. "You could have had me in Rome," she said finally, her tone muted.

"But I will have you here," he said, smoothing his thumb over her swollen lower lip. "With this city in the background, on that big bed in a beautiful hotel. In this place that you've never been before, where no other man has ever had you. And I swear to you, you will never forget it."

She looked away from him, hesitating for a moment as though she were about to say something. But then, she didn't. Instead, she simply nodded and took his hand.

CHAPTER TEN

THERE WAS A wild thing inside Esther. She had always been afraid of it. From the moment she had first suspected that it was there. Of course, it was that very wild thing that had inspired her to rebel against her family in the first place. That had inspired her to break the strict code she'd been raised in to seek out other things.

That had gotten her thrown out of the only home she'd ever known.

But even when she'd left, she'd hoped to control it in some way. Had never imagined she would give it free rein.

She had told herself that she wasn't going to find a man, because she needed freedom. She had told herself she didn't care about making herself look more beautiful, because she had a world to see, and who cared what it saw when it looked back at her.

But there was more to it than that. This was what she had always been afraid of. That the moment she met a beautiful man, the moment that he touched her, she would be lost. Because that wild thing inside her wasn't simply hungry for the beauty of the world, wasn't simply hungry for a taste of food.

It was hungry for the carnal things. For the sensual things. For the touch of a man's hands on her bare skin.

For the hot press of his lips against hers, and on her neck, and down lower.

Renzo had ripped the cover off all her pretense. He had exposed her. Not to him—she had a feeling she had been exposed to him from the moment she'd seen him. It was the fact he had exposed her so effectively to herself that had her shaken.

But she wasn't turning back. Not now. There was no way. Not now that she knew. Not now that she wanted. With such a sharp keenness that it could not be denied.

She didn't want to deny it.

There was a conversation they would have to have. After this. They would have it after. She didn't want to say anything that would make him stop now. She had a feeling that he had some suspicions about her lack of experience, but what he had said just a few moments earlier about having her in the city where no other man had ever been with her before made her think that he perhaps didn't know just how inexperienced she was.

That he hadn't guessed yet that he was the first man to kiss her. That he would most certainly be the first man to...

She shivered as the limousine pulled up in front of the hotel. She could tell him no. She knew she could. And he would stop.

She thought back to the fierce way he had taken her mouth in that room full of people. It had been something more than a kiss, something so intimate it made her catch fire inside to think about other people seeing it.

He had been beyond himself then, all of that icy control that she had witnessed in him from the first time she'd seen him burned away. Scorched by the fire of the attraction between them.

She swallowed hard, looking over at him, at the hard carved lines of his face that seemed to look even more intimidating now than they ever had. She was fairly certain that he would stop if she asked him to.

Yes, of course he would. He was a man, not a monster. Even if he was a man she could scarcely recognize now. There was an intensity to him that she had never witnessed before. A desperation, a hunger. It mirrored her own and stoked the flames inside her so that they burned brighter, hotter.

He didn't touch her during the elevator ride up to the penthouse. She was afraid, for a moment, that it might give her too much time to think. That it might allow the heated passion inside her to begin to cool.

But once the doors closed behind them and they were ensconced in the tight space, she found it to be entirely the opposite. She could scarcely breathe for wanting him. For needing him.

The seconds in the elevator stretched between them tight and thick, wrapping around her neck, constricting her throat. By the time the doors opened into the hall, she let out a great gasp, a sigh of relief that she knew he had heard.

He still didn't touch her as they approached the door and he used the key card to undo the lock. But then he placed his palm on her lower back, ushering her in, the contact burning through the thin fabric of her dress.

And when he closed the door behind them, she was the one who closed the remaining distance between them. She was the one to kiss him. Because she didn't want him to change his mind. Didn't want whatever madness he was beholden to to fade. She kissed him with all of that desperation. That need for satisfaction.

She began to frantically work at the knot on his tie, clumsy fingers then moving to the buttons on his shirt.

"Slow down," he said, his voice a low, gravelly command.

"No," she said, between kisses, between desperate grabs for his shirt fabric. "No," she said again, "I can't."

He reached up, taking hold of her wrists, his hold on her like irons. "There is no rush," he said, leaning in slowly, brushing his cheek against hers. It was much more innocuous contact than the kiss from before, and yet it affected her no less profoundly. "Some things are best when they're taken slowly."

Taken slowly? She felt like there was a wild creature inside her trying to break out, desperate for release, and he wanted to talk about taking it slowly? She had waited twenty-three years for this moment. To be with a man. To want a man like this. And now, with satisfaction so close, he wanted to take it slowly.

She wanted it done now.

That certainty surprised her, especially after the small attack of nerves that she'd had right before coming into the hotel. There were no nerves now, not in here.

What she said to him out on the dance floor, it had been true. His strength, the way that he kept it leashed, all the while with her totally conscious of how easily he could overpower her, was a powerful aphrodisiac.

"I don't want slow," she said, leaning back into him.

And now, he used that strength against her, holding her fast, not allowing her to kiss him again. "Wait," he said, his tone firm.

He shifted his hold, gathering both of her wrists into one hand, then lowering his free hand to her back, grabbing hold of her dress's zipper tab and pulling it down slowly. The filmy fabric fell away from her curves, leaving her standing there in nothing more than a pair of lace panties.

It was similar to what had happened that day he'd come to her fitting. But also, like something completely different. She had been facing away from him then, and though she had been able to feel his eyes on her, she had not seen the expression on his face. She could see it now.

All of that lean hunger directed at her, the intensity of a predator gleaming in those dark eyes. He looked her over slowly, making no effort to hide his appreciation for her breasts as he allowed himself a long moment to stare openly at them.

They felt heavier all of a sudden. Her nipples tightening beneath his close inspection. An answering ache started between her thighs, and she felt herself getting slicker, felt her need ratcheting up several notches without him putting a hand on her.

"See?" he asked, the knowing look in his eye borderline humiliating. "Slow is good. It will be better for you. I don't know what kind of experiences you've had before, but I can guess at the sort of men a woman traveling alone and staying in hostels meets. I can guess the sort of sex those kinds of semipublic quarters necessitate. But we have all night, and we have this room, we have a very big bed. And you have me. I am not a man who rushes his vices, *cara*. Rather, I prefer to linger over them."

"Am I a vice?" she asked, her voice trembling.

"The very best kind."

He leaned in, scraping his teeth across her chin before moving upward, kissing her mouth lightly before catching her lip in a sharp bite. The sensation hit her low and deep, unexpected and sharp, and not unpleasant at all.

He tightened his hold on her, reinforcing his control as he angled his head and kissed her neck, tracing a line down her vulnerable skin with the tip of his tongue. Her nipples grew even tighter, begging for his attention. She knew what she wanted, but she was much too embarrassed to say. She didn't even know enough to know for sure if it was a reasonable thing to want.

But, thankfully, he seemed to be able to read her mind.

He moved his attentions lower then, tracing the outline of one tightened bud before sucking her in deep, the sensation sending sparks down low in her midsection that radiated outward. She struggled against his hold, because she needed to grab on to something, rather than simply stand there helpless, with her wrists captured by him.

If he noticed, he didn't respond. If he cared, he didn't show it. Instead, he continued on his exploration of her body. Turning his attention to her other breast and repeating the motion there. She seemed to feel it everywhere, over every inch of her skin. It made everything far too sensitive, made everything far too real. And not real enough all at the same time.

Part of her felt like she was hovering above the scene, watching it happen to someone else, because this couldn't be happening to her. It was safe, though, to view it that way. Because the alternative was to exist in her skin all while feeling it was far too tight for her body.

Then, he released his hold on her, planting his hands tightly on her hips and pulling her up against him before sliding them around to her rear and letting his fingertips slip beneath the lace fabric of her panties, cupping her bare flesh.

And then she wasn't divided at all. Then, she wasn't hovering over the scene. She was in it, and everything was far too sharp, far too close. She felt too much, wanted too much. The hollow ache inside her was as intense as a knife's cut, slicing unerringly beneath her skin and releasing a hemorrhage of need.

He squeezed her, pulling her more tightly against his body, allowing her to feel the evidence of his need for her. He was so big, so hard, everything she had never known to fantasize about. And yet, it was terrifying, too, even as it was the fulfillment of her every need.

Because she didn't know what to do with this. Didn't know what to do with a man such as him. But she had a feeling she was about to find out.

Slowly, so very slowly, he pushed her panties down her legs and slipped them over her feet—still clad in the jeweled flats she'd put on earlier. Then, he knelt before her, removing her shoes as he had done that day in her room.

Only this time, when he was finished and he looked up at her, she knew that there was no barrier between her body and his gaze. She shivered, relishing being his focus, wanting to hide herself from him, as well.

He gripped hold of her legs, sliding his hands firmly up the length of them, to her thighs, where he paused in front of her, looking his fill at her exposed body. She pressed her knees tightly together, as though that would do something to hide her from him. As if it would do something to stop the pounding ache.

He looked up at her, a smile curving his lips. Instinctively, she struggled to get away from him, but he held her fast. And then he leaned in, the hot press of his lips against her hip bone making her jerk with surprise.

"Don't worry, *cara*," he said, tracing a faint line inward with the tip of his tongue. "I'm going to take care of you."

Surely this was wicked. That was the predominant thought she had when he moved unerringly to her center, his tongue hot and wet at the source of her need for him. Surely this was the height of her rebellion. The furthest that she could fall.

He tightened his hold on her, the blunt tips of his fingers digging into the soft skin on her rear as he took his sampling of her body deeper, as he slid his tongue all the way through her slick folds and back again, a rumbling sound of approval vibrating through his massive frame.

And then she simply didn't care. If it was wrong, if they were wrong. She didn't care about anything, anything at all except for the exquisite sensations he was lavishing her body with. She shivered as his tongue passed over the sensitive bundle of nerves again and again, establishing a rhythm that she thought might crack her into tiny pieces.

She planted her hands on his shoulders, and she didn't push him away. Instead, she braced herself as he stole her control with each pass of his tongue. As he worked to reduce her to a puddle of nothing more than shock and need. Oh, but the need won out. And if it was shocking, if she felt scandalized, it only made all of it that much more delicious.

Because this was the dark secret thing inside her allowed to out and play. This was the piece of herself she had most feared, and here she was living it. She had always been afraid that she was wrong. That she could never, ever be the person her parents wanted her to be, no matter how her dad yelled at her. No matter how they tried to control her. She was proving it right. She had started on this journey more than a year ago, and this was the logical end.

But it didn't feel like a disaster. If anything, it felt like a triumph.

Suddenly, he shifted positions, taking hold of one thigh and draping it over his hip before he wrapped an arm around her waist, keeping the other firmly planted on her rear as he stood, bracing her body against his as he walked them through the main room of the penthouse toward one of the bedrooms.

She clung to his shoulders, shivering as his hot breath fanned over her flesh, as shock and anticipation continued to fire through her with a strength that seemed beyond reality.

When they came into the bedroom, he moved to the end of the bed, setting her down on the edge before going to his knees again, gripping her hips and bringing her to his mouth. He settled her legs over his shoulders, her heels pressed against his shoulder blades as he tasted her deeper, adding his fingers now, pressing one deep inside her. The unfamiliar invasion making her gasp.

But any discomfort was erased as he moved the flat of his tongue over her again and again in time with that finger, before adding a second, pushing her higher, harder than she had imagined it was possible to go. She was moving toward a goal she didn't even recognize. All she knew was need, but she didn't know what it was she needed.

He increased the pace, the pressure, and she forgot to breathe, forgot to think. She threw one arm over her eyes, moving her hips in time with him, not caring if that was wrong. Not caring if she should be embarrassed. She didn't care about anything but satisfying that need. And she knew this was it, she knew that he possessed the power to do it, and she would give him anything, allow him any liberty, in order to see it done.

Then suddenly it all broke apart, the tension that was screaming inside her bursting into shards of glass, shimmering inside her, bright and deadly and much more acute than anything she'd ever known before.

He continued to trace the shape of her with his tongue as aftershocks rolled through her, taking his time, satisfying himself even as she lay there assaulted by the shock of her own satisfaction.

"Renzo," she said, feeling unsteady, trembling all the way through. "I need…"

"I'll give you what you need," he said. "Patience."

She didn't even know what she needed. She shouldn't need anything more than what he'd already given. And yet, she could sense that something was missing. That she wouldn't be fully satisfied until she had him—all of him—inside her.

But then he moved away from her, standing and picking up where she had left off with his shirt, undoing each button slowly, revealing more and more golden skin, hard-packed muscles and the perfect amount of dark hair sprinkled over them.

She ached to touch him. To taste him. But she was boneless, and she found that she couldn't move. Her throat went dry as she watched his slow removal of clothing, the maddeningly methodical reveal of his body. And when his hands went to his silver belt buckle, everything in her froze.

She had never seen a naked man before. She wasn't sure if she was glad then, or if she regretted that she had no other experience to fall back on.

She licked her lips as he lowered that zipper, slowly, everything so very slow, her attention undivided. And then he pushed them down his lean hips—taking his underwear along with them—revealing every inch of his masculinity to her hungry gaze.

Her stomach clenched tight, seizing with desire and no small amount of virginal fear when she saw him.

In the back of her mind she tried to placate herself, tried to say things about new experiences and all of that. Except, it didn't work. It didn't work because he was more than just a new experience. Because she wasn't just having sex with him for the sake of experiencing sex. She wanted him. She wanted him in spite of her nerves, she wanted him more than she could ever remember wanting anything.

It was terrifying in its way. You want someone so much, in spite of any and all hints of fear or doubt. To know that it might end badly and to not care at all. It was also fascinating and about the best reason to do something that she could even think of. Because she couldn't help herself. Because she felt there was no other option.

"You don't have to worry about me. My health," he clarified. "I was extensively tested post-Ashley. And I haven't been with anyone else since."

"I'm good," she said, before she could even fully sort through what he was saying.

"Good," he said.

He joined her on the bed, placing his hand on her head and moving his palm down her thigh, then back up again, to the indent of her waist, to her breast. He cupped her, moving his thumb over her nipple. She gasped, arching against him, shocked at the ferocity with which she wanted him so soon after that soul-shattering release.

He kissed her, and as he did he settled between her thighs, the blunt head of his arousal pressing against her slick entrance. She let her head fall back, everything in her sighing *yes*. She wanted him. There was no doubt now. None at all.

And if there was fear? It was all part of it. All sacrificed on this altar. She was giving him her fear, her body, her virginity. It was what made it matter. It was what made it feel so immense. And that immensity was what made her embrace it so completely.

She would never be the same after this. Her eyes met his as the thought clicked into place, as he began to press inside her. The enormity of that filled her as he did, blotting out the brief, sharp pain that accompanied his invasion.

She reached up, touching his face, not able to tear her gaze away from him. He was… He was inside her. Part of her. They were joined together. And she knew that changed everything. She knew that—for her—there was no experiencing this on a casual level. That for her sex would always be deep like this, something that echoed inside her and resonated through to her soul.

He flexed his hips forward, and she saw stars as he moved even deeper, as he butted up against that sensitive bundle of nerves there. She clutched his shoulders as he established a steady rhythm, pushing them both to the brink, his rough, uneven breathing the soundtrack of her desire.

Knowing that he was so close to the edge, knowing that he was as affected as she was, only pushed her arousal to an even higher place. Impossible. It was impossible to think she could contain so much. So much need, so much of him. She would break apart completely if she didn't find release soon, and yet, she almost didn't want to come. Almost wanted to stay like this, poised on the brink of pain, and closer to anyone than she had ever been in her life.

She moved her hands down from his shoulders, her fingertips skimming over his muscles, feeling his strength as he braced himself above her, as he thrust into her harder and harder. She loved that. This feeling that consumed all of her, that was too much and not enough.

This was life. Life unfiltered, unprotected. Raw and intense, and no doubt every bit as dangerous as she had always been taught.

But it was real. Real in a way nothing else had ever been.

He growled, and it was that sound, that show of intensity, that sent her over the edge. Orgasm rocked her, this release going deeper, hitting her harder than the one that had come before it.

She clung to him long after the release passed, held him while he tensed, and then shattered, his muscles trembling as he gave in to his own pleasure. As powerful as it had been to find climax with him, it was his that undid her. To have him shake and shudder over her body, in her body, this man who was so much more experienced than she was, who was larger than life and seemed to be built out of stone… To have him lose his control because of her was altering in every way.

In a way it never could have been if he weren't the man he was. If he were an easy man, one who gave easily to the environment around him, then she would have simply been one more element that changed the shape of him.

Instead, this made her different. It made her matter. She had moved a mountain, and only a few hours ago she would have said that wasn't possible.

He was different from her father. Who controlled her because he was afraid of what she could be. That wasn't Renzo. It made her wonder if Renzo controlled everything around him because he was afraid of himself.

And that, she supposed, was the difference between a man who acted from a place of weakness and a man such as Renzo, who was coming from a place of damaged strength.

She didn't know why she thought that, why she imagined he was anything other than perfect and beautiful and whole as he presented himself.

Maybe it was because she had seen him in pieces just now. Just like her.

He moved away from her then, levering himself into a sitting position and pushing his hand through his dark hair. "You could have told me you were a virgin."

CHAPTER ELEVEN

"I GENUINELY THOUGHT it was self-evident," she said, not sure how she felt that he was leading with that. "And I kind of thought that after the procedures at the fertility clinic it might not be obvious. I do think that it would be obvious given the fact that I clearly don't know how to kiss."

He shook his head. "A lot of people have sex without knowing what they're doing, Esther. A lack of skill can speak to the fact you've been with men who didn't handle you correctly."

"Well, there were none. I dropped enough hints about my childhood that… Anyway. It doesn't matter. Are you saying you wouldn't have slept with me if you'd known?"

"No," he returned, his voice rough.

"Well, then I suppose this is a fight that isn't worth having."

"I might have been a little bit gentler with you."

"All the more reason for me to not tell you. Because… I liked how you did it."

He treated her to a hard look. "You don't know better."

She shrugged, suddenly feeling small and naked. "That's true of me and a lot of things."

"Explain yourself to me."

She scrambled into a sitting position, grabbing the blankets and holding them over her chest. "That doesn't exactly make me feel inspired to share."

"I want to understand you," he said, clearly deciding that there had to be a better way to approach this. "Tell me about yourself. Everything."

"I feel like if you had been paying closer attention you would have deduced the fact that I hadn't been with anybody."

"I assumed you would have found somebody as part of your world travel. Backpacking and staying in hostels generally lends itself to casual hookups."

She drew her knees up to her chest. "You know that from your time spent backpacking?"

"*Everyone* knows that," he said, his tone definitive.

"Okay. Well, I guess this is where I tell you that I'm not like other girls." She laughed. "I mean, obviously. I wasn't raised in a small town. That was misleading. Not entirely a lie, but not entirely the truth. I was raised in a commune."

That was met with nothing but silence.

"You see," she said, "I've learned not to lead with that."

"Do you mean you were raised in a cult?"

"Kind of. I guess. We weren't allowed to watch TV, I wasn't allowed to listen to the radio. I wasn't exposed to any pop culture, any popular music. Nothing. I didn't know anything my family, or the leaders in the community, didn't want us to know."

"That…strangely makes you make more sense." The way he spoke, slowly, as though he were putting all the pieces together and finding out that they did in fact fit, would have been funny if it didn't make her feel like such an oddity.

"I imagine it does." She took a deep breath. "But I never fit. I started…rebelling. Secretly, though, when I was a child."

He stared at her. "When you're raised in one way, believing one thing, exposed to nothing else, what makes you question your surroundings?"

No one had ever asked her that before. Most people didn't want to talk about her past because they found it uncomfortable. Or, they wanted to ask her if she had been a child bride or if she had shaved her head.

"I don't know. I just know that it never felt right. So I started…collecting things. There was a book exchange in the little town we lived near. A wooden kind of mailbox that had free books. And I used to stick them in my bag and sneak them back home when my mom was distracted with her grocery shopping. Then I would take them home and hide them in the woods. I did the same later, with music. But that was harder because I never had much in the way of money. But between rummage sales and the library, I managed to get a portable CD player and some CDs."

"Not a huge rebellion," he said.

"Well, maybe not for everyone. But for me it was. For… for my father it was. My youngest brother is the one who told on me. I know he didn't mean for it to be as bad as it was. I know he didn't mean to… He was just being a brat." She laughed, shaking her head and trying to hold back tears. "He found my books and my music, and he showed my mom. Who in turn showed…my dad. He said I had one chance to say I would never read or listen to anything unapproved again or I…I would have to go."

"And you didn't?" he prompted.

"I wouldn't. So there was a meeting. A meeting with everyone, and I thought…my father loved me. I asked him, I asked him then in front of everyone. If he loved me, how could he send me away just because I liked different books and different music? Just because I was different."

She pressed her hand to her chest, trying to ease the ache. "But he said…he said that if I wouldn't change I couldn't be his daughter anymore. He said it in front of everyone. He said that it was for the good of everyone else. That it was real love to require that I change and…and I don't think it is. It's control. And if he couldn't control me, he didn't want me."

Even though she would never go back, even though she would never make a different decision, it hurt all the same. Her life had changed for the better because she'd left, but she could still never give her father credit for that.

Not when the rejection hurt so much.

"That must have been hard," he said, his voice rough.

"It was," she said. "I felt sorry for myself for a while, then I got a job at a diner in town. Saved up my money for a year. I took the SATs. I got a passport. I went to Europe and started working wherever I could and…"

"And you met Ashley."

"And you," she said, the words settling strangely in the air, tasting strange on her tongue. Settling strangely in her chest. It felt so significant, meeting him. Being here with him. Even though she had decided to have sex with him, knowing that it wasn't about simply experiencing sex, she was still processing the implications of that.

"Yes," he said, something strange coloring his tone. "You got a bit more than you bargained for with all of this, didn't you?" There was something soft in his voice now, and she was suspicious of it. Mostly because there was nothing soft about him.

"You are a lot," she remarked. "A lot of a lot."

"We get along well, don't we?"

"I'm not sure what context you mean that in. You mean, when you're calling me strange and commenting on my habit of eating cereal on the floor?"

"Mostly I mean in bed," he said, "but that is the place I most often try to relate to women."

She frowned. "I'm not sure that was the most flattering thing for you to say."

"I am divorced. You have to consider that there may be a reason for that."

"Well, I met the other half of your marriage. So, I am not terribly mystified as to why that didn't work out. However, I have asked myself a few times why you ended up with her."

"Because she was unsuitable. Because she was a nightmare. And I knew it."

"I don't understand."

"I imagine growing up in a strict household, you received quite a bit of punishment when you did things wrong, or things that your parents thought were wrong."

"Yes," she said, "of course."

"Ashley was my punishment." He laughed, the sound containing no humor at all.

"For what?"

He shook his head. "It doesn't matter." Except, she had a feeling that it mattered more than just about anything else. "But I knew it was doomed. Somewhere, part of me always knew. But you… I feel like with you perhaps things might not be so hopeless."

It felt, very suddenly, as though her stomach had been hollowed out. "What?"

"What if we tried, Esther?"

"Tried what?" She wasn't thinking straight. It was impossible to think straight right now, with their lovemaking still buzzing through her system, with her heart pounding so hard she could scarcely hear her own brain over it.

"Us. Why do we need to separate at the end of this?" He moved closer to her, touching her face, that simple gesture warming her in a way that nothing else ever had. That connection, so desperately needed after being so intimate with him.

"Because," she said, no conviction behind that word whatsoever, "you didn't choose this. Neither did I. We just… We're making the best out of this. And of course we are attracted to each other, but it doesn't make any sense to start in a way that we can't go on."

"That's what doesn't make sense to me. Why can't we go on?"

"You know why. Because I just got away from a restrictive existence. One that made it so I couldn't decide who I was or what I wanted. I can't do that to myself," she said, but still not even she could believe the words coming out of her mouth. She knew in her head that she should, knew that there was truth in them, and that there was importance and weight to what she was doing. Finding herself out here in the real world when before she had been so isolated from it.

And that it was dangerous to feel that everything of importance had shrunk down to this hotel room. To the space between their naked bodies, and the need for there to be less of it.

That her anticipation of what was to come had become small, focused. On where his hand might travel next, what point on her body his fingertips might make contact with next.

So dangerous. So very dangerous.

"Has anything about your life with me been restricting? I have taken you more places than you could have gone on your own. You're not bound to waiting tables in order to stay alive. You have days you could devote to studying, and there is no reason you can't be with me and go to school."

What he was saying… It was so tempting. So bizarrely

clear and easy in appearance in that moment. A life with him, where they could travel at will, where she could still get the schooling that she wanted. It was just that she would be with him. And she couldn't even see that as a negative. Not now, not while her entire being was still humming from his touch.

"But we can't start something that we can't...keep going. I know these babies aren't mine. I went into this knowing that I would give them up. Things are getting muddled, and I don't know if it's hormones or what. I just know that as it gets more real, it gets more difficult. And I just keep telling myself that I can't do it. But do you know what I really can't do? I can't be their mother for a little while and then walk away. I have to either stay as I am, with absolutely no intention of raising them, or I have to have them forever." The very idea made her stomach seize tight with a strange kind of longing.

It was as though a dam had been destroyed and a flood of emotions was suddenly washing forward. Things she hadn't allowed herself to imagine pushing forward in her mind. What it would be like to see the babies once they were born. If she would hold them. And what it would feel like when she did. When they were in her arms rather than in her womb.

What it would feel like to hand them to Renzo and then walk away forever.

Or, even more insidious, what it would feel like to hold them forever. To become a mother.

That thought made her feel like she was being torn in two. Part of her was desperately afraid of having another human life under her care. What did she know? She was practically a child herself, still learning about the world, discovering all of these things that had been hidden from her for so long.

But there was another part of her... Another part of her that craved it in some ways. That craved real connection. Love. In a way she had never before received it in her life. It would be a chance to love someone unconditionally. A chance at having that love returned.

She looked up at Renzo. And that made her feel like she had been shot straight through the heart. Because there was another person involved in all of this, someone other than the children.

She realized then that she wasn't entirely sure what he was suggesting. "Are you suggesting that I stay as the... the nanny? Your mistress? Or..."

"Of course you will be my wife, Esther."

Her stomach tightened painfully. "You want to marry me?"

"We can give our children a family. We can be a family. I made a terrible mistake when I married Ashley. I was angry at the world, I cannot lie to you about that. I was trying to prove something. To prove my lack of worth. But the reality that I am having two children makes me want to do just the opposite. I want to take this situation and turn it into something that could be wonderful for everyone."

This was the first she had heard him express a sentiment like this. But then, this was also the first time they had ever made love. Maybe it had changed things for him, too. She knew that she felt altered. Utterly and completely. Why wouldn't it be the same for him?

But there was one thing she couldn't overlook. She had lived in a household where there was no love, and she knew beyond a shadow of a doubt that she could never do it again. He was promising her things. Promising her freedom, promising her that she could still see to her dreams.

But she needed to know if there was something behind it. If there was insurance. Something to ensure that it wouldn't all break apart, the way that things had broken apart with Ashley and him. Sure, there was the fact that she was not Ashley, but he was still himself. And even though she had feelings for him, deep feelings, there was so much about him she didn't know.

What she felt was much more instinctual than it was logical. There had been something about him, something electric from the moment she had first laid eyes on him. Maybe it was biology. Maybe it had something to do with the fact that she was pregnant with his babies.

But she had a feeling it was deeper.

She wished it weren't deeper. It would make all of this so much simpler. She could evaluate it a bit more coldly. With the sort of distance that it required.

She had no distance.

And she needed to know something, one thing. Because she had learned something important once already. That control was destructive. It had destroyed her mother. Broken her down from the normal woman she'd once been—vibrant and full of life—into a gray and colorless creature. It had very nearly broken her, too. But she'd found the strength to stand.

If she found herself in the same situation again...would she be able to stand strong? Or would she be too damaged, too broken down this time?

No. She couldn't let it. So she had to know.

"Renzo," she said, speaking the words as soon as she could form them in her mind. "I need to know something. I mean, I need to tell you something. I feel like...I've been happy with you these past few weeks. And I didn't expect to be. I didn't even want to be. Because I wanted to feel nothing for you, to feel nothing about this pregnancy. I wanted to be able to walk away. I don't think I can do that now. Not easily. Not the way that I intended. No matter what my intentions were, I know that something has been building between us. That there's a connection there that wasn't before. I think…I think I might love you. And that's why I'm hesitating to say yes to you now. I've lived in a home where I wasn't loved, and I can't do that again. So I need to know. Do you love me? Do you think you could at least grow to love me?"

There was no hesitation. Instead, he leaned forward, kissing her deeply, with all of the lingering passion that still existed between them even after their crashing releases earlier.

"Of course I love you," he said when they parted, his dark gaze intense, as affecting as it had been from the very first moment they'd met. "I want to spend my life with you. Say yes, Esther. Please, say yes."

She looked at him, and she realized that there was only one answer she'd ever given to Renzo, and that would remain true now, too. "Yes," she said, "yes, Renzo. I'll marry you."

CHAPTER TWELVE

RENZO TOOK A drink and looked out the door of his office, down the darkened hall. He was engaged to Esther now. For real.

And he had lied to her.

There were a great many occasions where he had employed creative truths in order to get his way. It was a necessity in business, and as everyone did it, it seemed as acceptable as anything else. He had done the same with Ashley. From marrying her in Canada to the way he had executed their prenuptial agreement.

He had never felt even the smallest bit of guilt for it. Perhaps because honesty had never gotten him much of anything. Whatever the reasoning, he felt guilty now. He felt guilty lying to Esther.

But would it matter if she never knew? It had cost him nothing to tell her that he loved her. It wouldn't matter one bit that he didn't. She needed to hear it, and that was what mattered.

Except she had told him about her father. About the way he'd controlled her.

He had to wonder how the hell he was any different.

He thought back to the hope shining in her dark eyes, and he crushed the surge of emotion with another slug of alcohol.

They had flown home from New York this morning, and he had done his best to keep his hands off her out of deference to her inexperience. And also, because even he had his limits. He had thought he might keep her mindless and loved up in order to keep her compliance, but that had seemed...distasteful even to him.

However, she seemed happy. She seemed settled in her decision.

And every time she had looked over at him with softness evident in her expression, he had forced himself to continue looking. Had prevented himself from looking away.

And so the guilt had taken even deeper root.

He had lied about a lot of things. But he had never lied about love. He had never once told Ashley that he had feelings for her he didn't have. Not ever.

It shouldn't matter. Because love meant nothing. It had been yanked from his heart by the roots sixteen years ago when his rights to his child had been signed away.

He had forfeited everything then. His right to love. His right to happiness. Even his right to anger. He took another drink.

He set his glass down on the bar with a clink, and then began to walk out of the room, his legs carrying him down the hall and toward Esther. He should stay away from her. He had no right to touch her again. And yet, he was going to.

Of all the things he could not regret that were part and parcel to this deception, it was the fact that he would have possession of her that stood out most. He wanted her. He wanted to keep her near him. Wanted her to live life under his protection, under his care.

And how are you different from the family she ran away from?

He was different. He would give her everything she needed. Everything she wanted. In return they would present a compelling picture of family unity to the world, and his children would have a sense of stability. He would inherit the Valenti family company, and as a result, so would the children. Doing anything less would rob them all of that.

There was nothing wrong with that. She would be happy with him.

Everyone would be happier for this decision having been made.

He curled his hand into a fist as he walked down the hall, trying to ignore the intense pressure in his chest.

He remembered her saying something earlier about letting it go. About how she'd had to let go of her past in order to move forward. He didn't know why it echoed in his mind now as he made his way into her bedroom. Perhaps it was because he was longing for her again. Perhaps it was because right now he could feel the weight of it all pressing down on him. All the things that he couldn't bring himself to release his hold on.

Because if he did, what was his life? If he forgot what had created him, then what would fuel him?

He pushed all of that aside, and he embraced the darkness. The darkness that was around him, the darkness that was in him. And he asked himself, not for the first time, what benefit it would be to his children to be raised in such a place, with such a man.

He put his hand to his forehead, pushing back against the tension that was overtaking him. He'd had too much to drink, maybe. That was the only explanation. For both the attack of conscience and the oppressive weight that seemed to assault him now.

"Renzo?"

Esther's voice cut through the darkness. He knew he must look like quite the looming villain, standing in the doorway dimly backlit by the hall. "Yes?"

"Come to bed with me."

That simple offer, so sweet and void of any underlying request, or motive, struck him even harder than it might have considering how deeply he was pondering his own ulterior motives. But he cast them aside now. As he began to cast aside his clothes. He had done the best he could. Keeping his hands off her as though that made him honorable, somehow, when he was manipulating her with his words already.

He had no honor here. He might as well embrace it. He had forgotten why he was even doing this.

He swallowed hard, pulling his shirt over his head then moving his hands to his belt.

"I love you," she said, shifting beneath the blankets and pushing herself into a sitting position. He clenched his teeth, shoving his pants and underwear down and leaving them on the floor. He felt…cold. His chest felt as though it had been wrapped in ice, his heart barely beating now.

He moved slowly to the bed, pressing his knee down on the mattress. Then he leaned forward, his palms flat on each side of her, caging her in. "I love you, too," he said, feeling nothing around his heart when he spoke the words.

He kissed her then, and everything seemed to come to life. All of the ice melting away beneath the heat of the fire that existed between them.

There were a few things that he was certain of in this moment. That she was an innocent. That she deserved better than him. That he was lying. And that he was going to have her anyway.

She moved her hands over his skin, the joy that she seemed to find in exploring his body stoking the flames of his libido and his guilt all at once. All of this was new for her. She'd never had a lover before. Had never even kissed a man before him, and he was going to be the only lover she ever had. Her sexuality would be completely owned by him, utterly shaped by him.

When it came to technique and skill, he supposed she could do worse. He knew that he satisfied her. He knew that he could give her what she wanted. Physically. Emotionally, the exchange would always be empty on his side.

He pushed the thought away. It didn't matter. She would never know. She pushed her fingertips through his hair, clutching his head as he deepened the kiss, as he flattened her against the mattress. She arched against him, a sound of desperation keening through her.

He despised himself then. He was all inside. Thinking all of these things, calculating his every move. And she was honest. Giving. Generous with her body, with her touch. She wiggled beneath him, managing to slip away and push him on to his back at the same time.

"Esther…"

She put her hand at the center of his chest, making a shushing sound as she leaned in and kissed him gently, right against his frozen heart. "Just let me."

She moved lower, blazing a trail down the center of his stomach, farther still until her soft lips brushed up against the head of his arousal.

"Esther," he said, his voice harder than he intended. But he didn't deserve this. Couldn't accept it from her. She was giving him her body this way because she believed there was an emotion that existed between them when it didn't. He was a relatively cold-blooded bastard, but even he had his limits.

Or maybe he didn't.

Because when she parted her lips and enveloped him

in the velvet heat of her mouth, he found he couldn't protest. Not again.

She tasted him as though he were a new delicacy for her to discover. Savored him. Lingered over him in a way that no other woman ever had. She seemed to draw pleasure from his, and that was a new experience. It was strange, to feel this intense, profound attempt at connection coming from someone when he was so accustomed to keeping his walls up at all times.

They were still up. Firmly. But she was testing them.

He wanted to pull away, but he couldn't. Not just because he had to continue on with this pretense, but because he was incapable. Because she held him in thrall, and he could do nothing but submit to the soft, beautiful torture she was lavishing him with.

Fire gathered low in his stomach, and he felt himself nearing the brink of completion. "No," he said, his breath coming out in hard gasps. "Not like that."

He was breathing hard, scarcely in control of his actions, scarcely in control of anything. Trying desperately hard to keep everything together. He was playing a dangerous game with her. And the worst thing he could possibly do was find himself in a position where he began forgetting exactly what he was doing. Exactly what he was trying to accomplish. This wasn't about them. It never had been.

Of course, he wanted her to be happy. But that was incidental. As was she. The only thing that mattered was keeping his children with him. Keeping their family together, keeping Ashley away. The only thing that mattered was building a solid foundation for the rest of his life.

It could be her, it could be any woman. Any woman whom Ashley had chosen, and he would be doing the same thing. He had to remember that. He had to.

On a growl, he pressed her back against the mattress,

claiming her mouth as he tested the entrance to her body with his hard length. She squirmed beneath him, arching into the invasion. And then he thrust deep inside her, all the way home.

His mind went blank then, of everything. Everything but this. This need for release. This need to be as close to her as possible. Everything he had just been telling himself burned away in the white-hot conflagration of need. He gripped her hips as he moved more deeply within her, as he changed the angle and made them both gasp with pleasure.

And then he lost his control completely, and he could only give his thanks when she cried out her release, her internal muscles pulsing around him, because he had lost any and all ability to hold his own at bay. And when it overtook him, it was like a hurricane, pounding over him, consuming him completely, leaving him spent and breathless in the aftermath.

And as he lay there, turmoil and the aftereffects of pleasure chasing each other through his veins, he knew that he was simply in the eye of the storm. It wasn't over.

He moved away from her, shame lashing at him. He hadn't felt quite so remorseful of his actions in a little over sixteen years. Everything was jumbling together. The past, the present, his future. And the reasons for his behavior.

"I'm so happy," Esther said, the bone-deep satisfaction in her voice scraping him raw. So now, she was peaceful, satisfied, and he was... Well, he was nothing of the kind. He felt utterly destroyed. And he couldn't quite figure out why. He had accomplished everything he had set out to accomplish. He had secured a future just like he had set out to do.

Had ensured that he would retain custody of his children, and that they would grow up with the family that they deserved. With the inheritance they deserved, because he was not going to allow his father to divide up Valenti to spite Renzo.

He was confident in these things. Confident that they were right. And she was happy. So nothing else mattered.

"Good," he said.

"But something's bothering me."

"Something is still bothering you? After that orgasm, if anything is still bothering you then I'm going to have to revise my opinion of you. You're a very greedy woman, Esther Abbott."

"I am," she said, nodding slowly, the gesture visible in the darkly lit room. "I want to experience the whole world. And I want to have you while I do it. That's pretty greedy, you have to admit."

"I have offered you both things. So there's no reason you shouldn't want and expect them."

"I want more now."

A surge of anger rocked him. "What exactly would you like, *cara*? The crown jewels, perhaps? What is it that I have denied you exactly that you feel you should have?"

"You," she said simply.

"You just had me. In fact, I find I am spent due to the fact that you had me so well."

"That isn't what I mean. I have a feeling you could share your body endlessly. It's the rest of you that you find difficult."

His chest, frozen before, burned now. "I told you that I loved you," he said, confident those words would end the discussion. "What more could you possibly need?"

"It's really great to hear those words. And I wish that they could be all that I needed. I wish that this could be everything that I needed. But unless I know what's behind it, unless I know what love means to you, how am I supposed to feel? How am I supposed to feel secure in this?

And what we have? We've only known each other for a few weeks. And I feel… I feel so much for you. It's real. But you know where I come from. I feel like I don't know half as much about you."

"You have had dinner with my family. Met my niece. Met my sister. What else do you need to know?"

"Something. Something about you. You said that you married Ashley because you were punishing yourself. To prove something… To prove that you were…bad in some way. I want to understand that. You're angry, Renzo. And I've done my best to ignore that because you've never been angry with me. But I want to know. I want to know what you're angry at. I want to know why you married her. Why marrying me will be different. Why you feel differently about me. I have to. I have to or…"

"You want to know whom I'm angry at?" He pushed himself off the bed, forking his fingers through his hair. "Well, *cara*, there is a very simple answer to that question."

"Give it to me. Give me something."

"Me. I'm angry at me."

CHAPTER THIRTEEN

ESTHER'S HEART RATE was still normalizing, and hearing those words come out of Renzo's mouth made it tumble over into a strange gear again. She wasn't sure what she had expected when she had demanded that he share something of himself.

Denial, she supposed. Because he was such a closed door she imagined she would have to kick at it more than once in order to get it open.

And so, she was suspicious. She had been growing more and more suspicious ever since their time together in New York. That there was more than he was saying. But he wasn't being as honest or as open as he appeared to be.

She was naive. She knew that. She didn't have experience with men or with romantic relationships, and she knew that it was entirely possible some of her feelings were heightened because of the fact that they were sleeping together.

Except, he hadn't touched her between that first night and tonight. He had been much more careful than she would have liked him to be. Giving her more space than she ever would have asked for.

And in that time all of the tender feelings around her heart hadn't eased. In fact, they had only grown more intense. She knew that there were all kinds of reasons that she might feel something for him that wasn't strictly real.

But with just as much certainty, she knew it was real.

She just wanted it to be real for him, too. She needed to be sure. She had to know. And in order to know, she had to know him.

"Why?" she asked. "Why are you angry at yourself?"

"I wasn't born a debauched playboy. I think that's the place to begin. I was once very sincere, and I believed deeply in love. Though, I perhaps did so in a misguided fashion. But I want to say that so you know I didn't toy with another man's wife as a matter of my own amusement."

Her heart squeezed tight. Another man's wife. If there was a more serious offense she'd heard of in all her growing-up years, she could hardly remember it. Marriage was meant to be sacred. And a man's wife was his. Logically, she knew now that women weren't property, even if they were married. But still, marriage vows were sacred.

"Oh, Renzo… You…"

"It isn't a good story. But then, most origin stories aren't. The man you know isn't one of honor, so you must know that my beginnings were never going to be honorable."

"Don't say things like that. You have honor. Of course you do. Look at everything you're doing to make a life for your children."

"Yes," he said, his tone going utterly flat. "But you have to understand that that need doesn't come from a void. It was born of something. Everything is created. Everyone is created by a defining event. Something that changes you just enough, twists you in your own particular way. You know something about that."

"Yes," she said, thinking of her family.

"My parents care about me. I grew up in privilege. But I made a mistake. I fell in love with the wrong woman. A married woman. She was…my first. My first lover. My first love." He paused, swallowing hard, a muscle in his jaw jumping. "The mother of my child."

Esther felt as though the bottom had fallen away from the bed. She felt as though the bottom had fallen away from the world. She couldn't fathom what he was saying. What he meant. "Your child? But you don't have…"

"Not legally. No. I signed away my parental rights. I have no child. Not as far as the court systems are concerned. Genetically, however, is another matter."

She put her hand to her chest, as if that might do something to still her shattering heartbeat. "Tell me," she said, "tell me everything. How old were you?"

"I was sixteen. And it was agreed there was absolutely no point in a man like me—a boy like me—breaking up a family so that I could… Raise a child? How could I do such a thing? I was nothing more than a child myself. It would be laughable to even think it."

Slowly, realization dawned on her. "That's what you meant. Proving that you were bad. That's why."

"A bit melodramatic, perhaps. But since self-destruction is so much fun, how can I pass up the chance to prove I had no other option? And really, if you look at all of my exploits, how could you possibly believe that I would make a good father?"

"But you will," she said, her tone fierce. "Look at everything you're doing for these children."

He laughed, a bitter sound. "Yes. I'm willing to do anything for these children. Because it is a wound…" His voice broke. "I did what I had to do. I did what I had to do," he said again, as though he were reinforcing it even to himself. "You do not heal from this. You can't. Especially not when…I see her."

"Your ex?"

"No," he said, "I have no lingering feelings for that woman. No attachment to her. I could see her every day and it would make absolutely no difference. But Samantha… My daughter. To watch her grow up across ballrooms, knowing that I can never make contact with her… It is like being stabbed in the same place repeatedly. With no end in sight. The pain never goes away, the wound never heals. There is no chance."

Pain lanced her, for him, for all that he'd been through. For what he still continued to go through, this man who would so obviously sacrifice everything for the love of the children she carried. This man who was already a father, and unable to be with his daughter.

"How old is she?"

"Sixteen," he said. "The same age I was when she was born."

"So," she said, "she's nearly an adult. If you wanted to…"

"And destroy her life? Her view of herself? Her father, her mother, everything? Revealing that she's my child would decimate her entire existence. She has siblings."

"Does her… Does the man who raised her know that she isn't his?"

"I would be surprised if he didn't. I doubt very much he and his wife were ever faithful to each other."

"How did she know it was yours?"

"Jillian had a test done. Mostly because she wanted to make sure it was something I wouldn't contest later. She wanted to know everything. Wanted to make sure that she could protect her marriage. Protect her existing children."

It all made a horrible kind of sense. That it was a situation bound to create casualties. And the solution they had come up with perhaps left the least amount of destruction in its wake. Except when it came to Renzo. As he spoke about it she could see that he had been destroyed entirely over it. That he continued to be destroyed daily.

"You're her father," she said.

He began to pace the length of the room, all restless muscle in the dim light, leashed strength. And she realized it was him all over. Power that he could not wield to its fullest degree. Strength that was impotent in the face of the situation that had been created.

He was a powerful man. He was a wealthy man. But agreements aside, he couldn't go bursting into his daughter's life without destroying the balance. And it was more loving, more gracious, more everything for him to simply stand back and allow himself to bleed so that she never would.

If she hadn't been absolutely certain that she loved him before, this confirmed it. All of her earlier bad feelings about him being with a married woman sort of evaporated. Because he'd made a mistake, but it wasn't who he was.

Except, it had come to define him. Because the consequence was so permanent.

She couldn't continue to punish him by holding it against him. She couldn't hold any of this against him. She looked at him and she saw the man she was determined to make a life with. A man who was angry, injured, broken beyond anything she could possibly understand.

What could she offer him?

"I am not her father in any way that counts," he responded.

"But you are," she said. "You love her. Maybe more than anyone else involved in this, because the only reason that you've never crossed that ballroom and put yourself in her life is that you love her too much to rattle her."

"No," he said, his tone fierce. "It's not love. I can't feel that way anymore. I don't."

Those words hit her like a hammer fall. "But you said... You said you loved me."

"And if it makes you happy I will say it a thousand more times."

"If it makes me *happy*. But... What about if it's not true?"

"I am who I am. What has been done to me... It is done. There is no going back. I cannot go back in time and make a different decision. I can't change what happened. Not me, not her. I can't remake that decision. Don't you understand that? And just like I can't remake that decision, I can't feel things with parts of myself that I burned away. It doesn't work that way. It can't."

"Then why did you tell me that?"

"Have you been listening?" he asked, roaring now, when she had only ever heard him speak in calm command before. There was no sense of calm about him now. It was like watching him unravel in front of her, thread by thread. "I will do anything to keep my children with me. Anything."

"I never threatened to take them. Ever. I wouldn't. I wouldn't do that to you."

"It's more than that. Samantha... She has a family. She has a mother and she has a father. How could I provide less to my children now? What is my excuse? Look what I did. I ruined my life by marrying Ashley. I will not ruin my children's lives. I was making a statement, about my unsuitability, and I nearly swept two innocent children up in that. My own children. Again. Ruined by the selfishness of the adults around them."

She could see it so clearly. The way that he did. That he was somehow building the family that he owed his children so he didn't give them less than what his first child had been given.

He had tried so hard to prove that he wasn't able. To prove that the right decision had been made, and then he had been thrust into a situation where he had to prove himself worthy.

But she had been caught in the crossfire. And understanding it didn't make her any less confused when it came to her own feelings. It didn't make it hurt less.

"You didn't have to lie to me," she said.

"I did. You made that very clear."

"Renzo…I…I gave myself to you. In a way that I don't know if I could have if…" She stopped then, because she knew it wasn't true. It had nothing to do with the way he felt, the way that she had been with him earlier. It had everything to do with the way that she felt. With how much she felt for him. But still, she was hurt, she was confused, and she wanted him to feel even a fraction of that, which wasn't really fair considering she had a feeling he had been awash in both from the moment he had found out she was carrying his children.

And she could see fear in his eyes. Stark, naked. The fear that somehow, another woman would contrive to take away what he wanted most in the world. And he might say he couldn't love, but his actions were not those of a man who couldn't love.

She knew this was all about love. Deep, unending love that hurt him every time his heart beat.

If he thought he was doing this out of a lack of love, it was only because he couldn't see another way to deal with it. And strangely, she understood that. It was easy to tell herself that she was staying with him because he said he loved her. Because she was having these babies.

Far scarier was to admit to herself that it was something

she wanted. To be with him because she cared. Because she was choosing it.

It was one thing to make a distinction between her father and Renzo in theory. And to make a case for signing herself up for something completely different from what she had imagined she would do with her life. To sign on for binding herself to a man who certainly had his own agenda and his own idea about things.

Because he had lied to her. And what if she was just walking into the same kind of thing again? To living a life dictated by somebody else. That scared her. But maybe… Maybe love was always scary.

Maybe it was a risk, and it was one that came with sacrifice, with cost.

That thought made her feel panic. She had sacrificed so much. To stay with her family as long as she had, she had ignored so much of herself that she wanted to explore. She had tried so hard to be everything her mother and father had wanted her to be.

And leaving… If leaving her siblings had been painful, just thinking about what might happen if she was forced to leave these children made her insides ache.

Renzo was a rock wall. And she was just so very soft and breakable, no matter how much she might want to fling herself against him and see if she could force a crack. Force a change.

To see if she could get to what she suspected was behind it.

But how could she do that if not even he would admit that it was there? If not even he seemed to know?

"I didn't mean to hurt you," he said. "But I'm never going to love you the way that you seem to want me to. But that doesn't mean I won't be a faithful husband. I was a faithful husband to Ashley in spite of the fact that she wasn't faithful to me. If you need a demonstration, I will even marry you here. In Italy. Where divorce will be difficult to achieve."

All of these promises, all of these things, she recognized as things that benefited him more than they did her. At the end of the day, if there was ever any genetic testing done, a judge would find that the children didn't belong to her. And then what?

Everything had changed so much in the past few weeks. Her life looked like an entirely different one from what she had imagined she would make for herself.

Had it been only four months since she had imagined that she would do the surrogacy and then walk away? That she would go on to go to school and visit exotic places, and do all of these things she had dreamed about without ever once thinking about the children she had given birth to again? Without ever once thinking of Renzo again. She knew now that none of that was possible.

She had trapped herself. Utterly and completely.

Out of the frying pan and into the fire. She couldn't even decide if she wanted out of the fire.

"You did hurt me," she said, choosing to ignore what he'd said about marriage and divorce, forcing him to discuss the lie. The lie that was, by seconds, growing bigger and bigger inside her.

Because it had been the difference. The difference between captivity and a relationship. The difference between a controlling, autocratic man and a caring, invested man.

Yes, in all of those scenarios he had done the same things, but if he did them from a position of love, if he did them out of caring for her, caring for the babies, it was different from simply wanting to make his life easier.

"That wasn't my intention. It doesn't have to change

things between us. You want me." He moved nearer to her, his fingertips brushing over her cheekbone, and much to her eternal humiliation, a shiver of need worked its way through her.

"It's not enough." She jerked away from him, shrinking back toward the headboard.

"Why not?" he asked, his tone fraying.

"I want you to be with me," she said, speaking slowly, trying to figure out a way to articulate what she was feeling, not just to him but to herself. "I want you to be with me because it makes me feel stronger. It makes me feel weaker. Because you make me want things I didn't even know a person could want. Because you make my body hum and my heart beat faster." She closed her eyes. "I thought I knew what I wanted. I thought I knew what I needed. Then I met you and I had to question all of it. I met you and looked at your eyes and found I couldn't move. Found that I didn't even want to. It's not convenient for me, Renzo. Nothing about this is. I don't want you because it makes my life easier. I don't want you because of everything you can give me, but because of all the little ways you have changed me. Because you hollowed me out and created a need that I didn't know existed before. And none of it's convenient. Not in the least. But it's that lack of convenience that makes me so sure it's real."

"But why does it matter?" he asked again. "We can be happy here. You can feel all of those things. We will be together, this whole family will be together."

"What do you feel when you touch me?"

"I want to have you."

Her throat tightened. "And when you think of me leaving you?"

He closed the space between them then, grabbing hold

of her arms and holding on to her tightly. "You won't. I want to keep you."

She reached up, brushing her fingertips over his cheek lightly. "And that's the difference. You want to keep me because it makes your life more the picture that you want. Because it's good for a man to have a wife, for his children to have a mother. But don't you understand, that's the exact reason my father wanted me to stay. The reason that he treated his children the way he did. Because he needed that picture. That perfect picture. Because it was about the way it made everyone look at him. About wanting to possess a perfect image." She swallowed hard. "I can't be someone else's trophy. I can't be the evidence of their perfect life lived. Not again. Not when it took so much strength to leave it the first time. Because if you're only telling me you love me to make me happy, then it's just more control."

"That isn't fair," he ground out. "I'm not talking about denying you anything. I'm not hiding the world from you. I have promised you an education. I have promised to show you all of life. All that the world has to offer."

"I know. I do…"

"Am I a selfish lover?"

Her cheeks heated. "No. Of course you aren't."

"How dare you compare me to the man who spent your life controlling you. It is different. It is different to come to an understanding based on mutual convenience, mutual attraction."

She lay down, letting misery overtake her, drawing her knees up to her chest and turning away from Renzo. "I need space," she said, feeling like her head was teeming with noise. She wasn't sure she'd ever be able to cut through it.

"I will see you at breakfast," he said, his tone hard.

She listened for him to leave the room. Didn't move again until she heard the door to his room close down the hall. And then she let the first sob rack her body.

She felt raw. Deceived. She felt foolish, because she had done exactly what inexperienced women did. She had believed him when he'd said he loved her, and she had used it as a shield. That lie had made her feel impenetrable. Had made her feel as though she could do anything, be anything.

And now, she just felt like a fool.

There was also something gnawing at the back of her mind. About the comparison she had made between Renzo and her father. About her life spent in the commune, and the month she had spent here.

She had known she wanted to escape that life. She had always felt like her home was a prison. She didn't feel that now, and she didn't know what that said about her. She wasn't even sure she cared.

She made a low, miserable sound and buried her face in her pillow. She didn't want to leave him. It didn't matter that he said he didn't love her. She wanted to be here. Wanted to be with him.

It had nothing to do with what he felt, and everything to do with what she felt. Her love wasn't a lie. Even his admission hadn't shaken it.

But it still confused her. Still made her feel like she had to do something, had to change something. To avoid becoming the sad, controlled creature she had once been.

"I don't want to," she said into the stillness of the room, a tear sliding down her cheek. She wanted to stay here with him. She wanted to make a life with him, and their children. She wanted him to have what he craved.

But for how long? How long would it take for her to start to feel smothered again?

What had felt like absolute freedom before felt like prison now. And regardless of her confused feelings on whether or not she wanted to leave, she felt trapped now when before she had felt liberated.

It was so easy to see the difference. Love. Love was the difference.

Knowing Renzo didn't love her, knowing that he never could, made all the difference to her.

CHAPTER FOURTEEN

RENZO SLEPT LIKE absolute hell. He felt every inch like the ass that he was. The things he had said to Esther. The way that he had hurt her. He had lied to her, it was true. Everything he had been through surrounding the loss of Samantha had done something to him. Changed him. If he had emerged from it with an edge of ruthlessness, no one could blame him.

Because he had been involved in a situation where he had allowed others to dictate things for him. But he resisted that now, more than anything. Resisted allowing anyone or anything to have the upper hand when he needed it at all times.

Still, Esther had not deserved his lies. If there was anyone truly good and sweet in the world, it was her. Anyone who had already been badly used by controlling men.

He slammed his cup of coffee down on the table and turned, seeing her standing at the bottom of the stairs. "Good morning," he said.

"Good morning," she said, shifting. And that was when he noticed her backpack.

She was back in her old clothes, too. Wearing a tight black tank top and the long flowing skirt, her stomach so much rounder than it had been when he'd first met her.

And he knew. Just what she was doing.

"You cannot leave," he said, his voice like shattered glass in the still surroundings.

"I have to," she said. "I'm not leaving town. I promise. But I can't stay here with you. Not while I'm so confused. I don't know what's going to happen between us, and I don't know…I don't know how I feel. I can't sit here where I'm comfortable, where I'm close to you, and think straight. And I owe myself the chance to think straight."

He was dimly aware of crossing the space between them, of taking her in his arms, much more roughly than he might have done if he were thinking straight. "You cannot leave me."

"I can. And I need to. Please, you have to understand."

He took hold of her wrists, backing her against the wall and pinning her there, looking deep into her eyes because she had said once that his looking at her had changed something. He needed to change it now. Needed to immobilize her now. Needed to stop her from leaving him.

"You can't go," he said again, more forcefully this time.

"Renzo," she said, "you can't keep me here. You don't want a prisoner. Mostly because you know that I've been one. You wouldn't do that to me, not again."

Desperation clawed him like an animal. In this moment, he was unsure if there was a limit to what he would do. Because he was about to watch his entire life, his future, walk out the door and away from him. "How can you do this to me?" he asked. "You know my past. You know what I have lost. I entrusted that secret to you. No one knows. My sister doesn't even know. And I told you."

"I will never take your children from you. I told you that already. I'm not going to take your chance to be a father. But…I don't believe that the two of us living together without love is going to give them a better childhood. I just don't. I grew up in a house that didn't have love. Where all of the relationships were so…unhealthy. And filled with control. It isn't going to help your children to live that way."

"Is the real issue that you want to leave? That you want to walk away? That you don't want to deal with this thing between us?"

"No."

"You feel your life will be hampered by raising children. You don't actually want the babies." That would almost make it easier. Because he would not expose children to her indifference. Though, he could not imagine Esther expressing indifference toward a puppy, much less a baby.

"This is about you and me," she said, pressing her hand to his face. She didn't struggle against his hold. She simply touched him, gently, with a kind of deep emotion he could not recall anyone ever pouring out over his skin. "About what we're supposed to be. That's all. I can't marry you. Not like this. I can't sign on to a life of being unloved."

She began to move away from him then, and he tightened his hold on her, desperation like a feral creature inside him.

"I love you," he ground out, the words coming from deep within his soul.

Suddenly, he was overcome by a sensation that all of the blood had drained from his head. That he couldn't breathe. That he might fall to the ground, black out, lose consciousness. And he was forced to come to the conclusion that it was because it was true.

That for the first time in his memory he loved a person standing in front of him more than the breath in his own body. That he loved her, in spite of his best efforts not to.

"I love you," he said again, desperation making it sharp.

"Renzo," she said, taking a step back. And he let her. "Don't do this to me. Don't lie to me. Don't use my feelings against me."

"I'm not," he said. "This is the truth."

"You already told me that you would tell me you loved me a thousand times if it would make me happy. I imagine you would say it a thousand more if you thought it would help you get your way. But I can't live that way. I won't."

"I won't live without you," he said, those words making her pause.

She turned back to face him. "When you can tell me what has changed because you love me, when you can prove to me that this isn't just another lie. When you can prove to me this isn't just you trying to keep ownership... Then you come find me. I'm going back to the bar. I'm going back to the hostel."

Then suddenly he was driven by the impulse to hurt. The wound as bad as if he was being injured. To make her bleed, because he damn sure was. "Run away, then. And tell yourself whatever story you need to tell yourself. About your bid for freedom. But this is just more of the same selfishness you showed when you left your family," he spat. "If somebody doesn't love you in exactly the way you wish them to, you don't recognize it. And you say it isn't real. Isn't that the same as your father? You accuse me of being selfish, Esther, but at least I took you at face value. You will not do the same for me."

She flinched, and he could tell that the words had hit their mark. That they had struck her in a place where her fear lived. Fear that what he said might be true.

"Maybe you're right. Except, I never lied to you. So maybe this is the one thing you'll never be able to get over, maybe this is my betrayal to you that you won't be able to let go. But yours was the first lie. How will I ever know if the words that come out of your mouth are real? How? You told me you loved me without flinching the first time. And then you told me it was all a lie, and now you ask me to believe that this is true. You ask impossible things of me, Renzo. I just wanted to see the world." She wiped at a tear that had fallen down her cheek. "I just wanted to go to a university and find myself. I didn't want to be broken. Not again. And that's what you've done. So now I have to go put myself back together again, and if you can come to me and show me, then please do. But if not... Leave me alone. I'll keep you informed about the doctor's appointments."

She moved to the door, holding on to her backpack tightly. "Goodbye, Renzo."

And then she was gone. And for the second time in his life Renzo felt like he was watching his entire future slip through his fingers. For the second time, he felt powerless to do anything about it.

When Renzo went to visit his father later that day, he was full of violent rage. Ever since Esther had walked out of his home, he had been angry, growing angrier. Ever since she had left him, the fire of rage had been burning hotter and hotter in the pit of his stomach.

It had fueled him, spurred him with a kind of restless energy that he couldn't control. And it had brought him here. His parents' home.

He walked into his father's office without knocking.

"Renzo," his father said, without looking up. "What brings you here?"

"I have something to tell you," Renzo said.

"I do hope that you've already married that woman. Because I would hate to hear that things had gone awry."

"Oh, it's gone awry. The entire thing is damn well sideways."

"Do you need me to intervene? Is that it? God knows it's what I did when your last youthful indiscretion—"

"My youthful indiscretion? You mean my daughter? My

daughter I'm not allowed to see, because you, mother and Jillian decided that it would be better that way?"

"As if you didn't believe the same. You were sixteen years old. You couldn't have raised the child. Your behavior over the last several years has proved as much."

His father said that as though it were accidental. As though it never occurred to him that Renzo had perhaps engineered his behavior around proving that very thing. But then, he supposed he couldn't blame his father for that. Not even Renzo had fully realized that until recently. Until he'd been forced to change what he was, what he wanted, so that he could seize the opportunity to be a father this time around.

"There is nothing youthful about this indiscretion," Renzo said. "I am not a child. I'm a man in his thirties. And beyond that, the situation is not as it appears."

"What is going on?"

"It's Ashley. Ashley struck up an agreement with Esther. Esther agreed to carry my children as a surrogate. Of course, I was not consulted about any of this. And then when Ashley decided that the pregnancy was not going to preserve our marriage, she contacted Esther and asked that Esther have the pregnancy terminated. She didn't want to do that. Instead, she came to me." He rubbed his hand over his face. "I lost one child, and I was bound and determined to hold on to this one. To these two," he amended, an arrow hitting him in the heart as he thought of his twins. "I was also determined to do as you said. To prevent any other scandal. Anything that might come back and hurt them. I was not going to allow my brother-in-law to get control of the company, not when it's the rightful inheritance of my children. As much as you might have hoped you were appealing to my selfishness, believe me when I say you were simply appealing to my desire to give my children everything they deserve this time around."

"I cannot believe this. It isn't true. Such a thing isn't even legal in this country."

"There are ways to circumvent legality, as I'm sure you know. But now I have ruined everything with Esther. And I have done so in part because I was letting you control things again."

"You say all of this as though you're angry about what I did back then."

"I am. I damn well am. I was sixteen, I didn't know. I didn't know what I would feel. Every time I look across the room I see her. Every time. It is like being stabbed straight through the heart. I cannot forgive myself for the decision that I made then. I cannot forgive you for the part that you played in it."

His father pounded his fist down on his desk. "That feeling that you have I have for you. Magnified with an intensity that you cannot possibly imagine. Because I raised you. Because you are the heir to everything that I have worked so hard to build. My hope is placed in you, Renzo. You are everything to me in more ways than you can know. I did what I had to do to protect you, and if I have earned your anger then I accept that. But I would not change what I did."

His father's words struck him hard. Along with the realization that while he could understand why the decision had been made, he still wished he could change it.

"Do you not think it hurts me?" his father asked, his voice rough. "Because I see her, too. She is my granddaughter. And especially since your sister had Sophia, I feel that loss. The loss of my first grandchild that I cannot acknowledge."

"But it was not as important to you as protecting the family reputation."

"The greater good," he said. "And it so happened that it also protected her mother's marriage. That entire family. You cannot claim that I am so selfish, Renzo."

"Still, you wanted me to marry Esther to preserve your reputation. I imagine you want to keep the circumstances around the conception of the babies a secret, as well."

"Do you suggest that putting all of it out in the open is for the best? What about the reputation of the Valenti family?"

"I don't know," he said, tapping the back of the chair that was placed in front of his father's desk. "I don't know. But I cannot protect the reputation of the Valentis. Not at the expense of my own life. Not at the expense of the people I love."

"And the love of your parents? Does that not figure into this at all?"

"You can protect yourself, Father. I think you're more than able. My children cannot. They are helpless. They are depending on me to make the right choice."

"And you think bringing them into the world under a cloud of scandal is the right thing to do?"

"I am tired of lies. I am tired of living a life built on a monument to the one thing I can never acknowledge. The one person I will always love that I can never acknowledge. I am tired of living in an existence that is an unholy altar to my failures. Confirmation that I had no other choice. No other choice but to give up Samantha when I did. And perhaps then it was true. But I have choices now. And perhaps I will humiliate myself. Perhaps I will humiliate our family. But if I have to do that to win back the woman I love, if I have to stop protecting myself in every way in order to prove my vulnerability, then I will do it. If the perfect reputation of our family is a casualty, then I accept it. But I will not be a slave to it." He let out a harsh breath, Esther, her lie, her story on his mind. "I can't control every-thing. I'll only end up breaking everything I care about."

"I did what I had to do," his father said. "I counseled you the way that I had to. I am the patriarch of this fam-ily, Renzo. Protecting it is my highest calling."

"Perhaps that is the problem. And where we have reached an impasse. Because I am the patriarch of my family. My family, which is Esther and the children she's carrying. I lost her. I lied to her, and I told her I could never love her. I was afraid, afraid because I could not subject myself to the kind of pain that I went through, the kind of pain I continually go through, where Samantha is con-cerned. But all I've done is made it worse. And I'm going to fix it. No matter what."

He turned, getting ready to walk out of the office. He stopped when his father spoke.

"Renzo. I might not agree with the decision you're mak-ing, but I do want you to know that I understand I can't pro-tect you now. Moreover, that you don't need me to. You're a man now, a man who has understandable anger directed at me. I only hope that someday you will forgive me."

Renzo let out a hard breath, and he thought of some-thing else Esther had said. About how she'd had to let go of the past to truly move forward.

He had one foot firmly in the past, and it had nearly ruined everything. He had to start walking forward. For-ward to Esther.

"I imagine," he said, "that will all depend on what hap-pens next."

CHAPTER FIFTEEN

ESTHER FELT DRAINED. Emotionally, physically. Going back to work at the bar was difficult now. Her stomach was bigger, her ankles were bigger, her fatigue was bigger. Plus, all she wanted to do was crawl underneath the bar and cry for the entire shift, because something inside her felt fundamentally broken since she'd walked away from Renzo.

It was oppressively humid tonight. And hot. Clouds had rolled in, and she had a feeling there was going to be a late-evening thunderstorm, the impending rain adding to the heaviness in the atmosphere. Adding to the heaviness in her heart.

She looked outside and saw drops begin to pound the cobbled sidewalk. Great. Walking home was going to be fun. All of her clothes would be stuck to her skin. Then she would spend the rest of the evening shivering, because the showers in the hostel never had enough hot water to get rid of a chill like this once it soaked into her bones.

A flash of lightning split the sky, and she jumped a little bit. "Esther?"

She turned and saw her boss, who was gesturing madly at the tables outside. She knew that he wanted her to bring in the seat covers. "Okay," she said.

She hurried outside, not bothering to put on a sweater or anything. The air was still warm, but the drops falling from the sky were big and aggressively cold. She hunched over, taking hold of the cushions, collecting them beneath her arm.

Suddenly, the back of her neck prickled and she straightened slowly. Another flash of lightning washed out the scene around her, and that was when she saw him. Renzo, standing there in a suit just as he had done that first night he had come to the bar.

He was standing in a suit, in the rain, water pouring down over him, his hands in his pockets, his dark eyes trained on her.

"What are you doing here?" she asked, the cushions suddenly tumbling from her arms. She hadn't even realized she had released her hold on them.

It was the same as it had always been. From the beginning. Those dark eyes rooting her to the spot, her entire world shifting around her, shifting around him.

Everything changed, even the air. If he had brought the thunderstorm with him, she wouldn't be surprised.

"I came to see you. You told me to come and find you when I was ready. When I was ready to prove this to you. To prove my love. And I am. Trust me, I was tempted to hold a press conference before I came to see you, but I did feel like I should talk to you first. Not for me. But for you."

"A press conference? What kind of press conference?"

"To explain. Everything. The surrogacy… Everything. Because, I thought maybe if I didn't have a reputation to protect anymore you wouldn't be able to accuse me of being motivated by it."

"I…I suppose it's easy for me to say when nobody is interested in me or my life. At least, not apart from you."

"Don't excuse yourself," he said, "not now. You were right about me. It was all about doing something that suited me, and I want to make sure that this no longer does. I want to make sure that I'm no longer doing everything with a view of creating a smooth facade over my life. All of that... It is the reason that I am the way I am now. And my dedication to it was to justify my earlier actions. But no more. I am prepared to go public with our story. To let everyone know that you are a surrogate, and that I was fooled by my ex-wife."

"But what about all the legality?"

He took a deep breath. "That's why I didn't have the press conference. I was afraid that you would be concerned I was using it to lessen your claim on the babies. That I was using it to try to make sure you didn't have a place in their life. So you see, even with the desire to enact a grand gesture, I'm somewhat hampered by the fact that I have an unequal amount of power here." He shook his head. "But only on the outside. Inside... Inside I'm trembling. Because I don't know how to make you believe me. Because I haven't earned the right to have you do it."

He moved closer to her, and she watched him come. The rain pelted her skin, her clothes completely plastered to her body. She didn't care. "My father told me that I had to make sure everything went right this time. That I had to keep the family together or he was going to take my inheritance from me. I understand that only puts another nail in the coffin of my sincerity, but please understand that in part I was motivated by the desire to keep all of the inheritance for my children."

"So, your father told you to marry me."

He nodded. "Yes, and it was the thing that pushed me to make it real. And then that first night we were together, I saw Samantha. And I knew... Whatever I had to do I would do it. Including lie to you. And that's the hardest thing, Esther. It is the hardest thing to come back from, because you know me. You know that I would do anything for my children. And I have proved to you that I'm willing to lie. But I thought for certain that I had already experienced the lowest moments life had to offer. How could I not? I watched my child grow up a stranger to me. But I was wrong. There is lower."

She hurt for him. Physically hurt. But she found that she needed to hear it. Needed to hear about the pain he'd been through, because he had hurt her so profoundly. "What was it?"

"Telling you that I loved you, knowing that it was true this time, and knowing there was nothing I could do to convince you. Knowing that I had destroyed that chance already. That I had taken something beautiful, wonderful—love and the ability to feel it—and turned it into a farce. That I had finally found that feeling and myself again, and that I wanted it, and that I had destroyed any chance of getting it in return."

She couldn't take it anymore. She couldn't hold back. She moved to him, wrapping her arms around him, letting the rain pelt them both, washing away all of the hurt that was between them. "I believe you," she said. "I do. And you haven't squandered anything. I love you. And I knew that you could love me. I did. Because the way that you rearranged your life so that you could be a father to these children, the way that you spoke about the pain you felt over Samantha, the way you continue to feel pain because you won't do anything to disturb her, that's love, Renzo. That's real love. Sacrificial love, not controlling love."

"I wanted to pretend that it wasn't there, because it was easier. Admitting that you love someone when you know you can never be with them in the way that you want to be is a terrible fate. I experienced that with Samantha. And then with you."

"I love you. I'm here. You don't have to prove anything

to me. I'm so touched that you were willing to do that, but I think it's probably for the best if we don't make our children a headline."

"Probably so," he said, sliding his hand down her back. "I love you, Esther. And what love has always meant to me has been something distant. From my father it was control. And with my daughter it was a required separation. You asked me what love was, and when it comes to loving someone and being with them, I'm not sure I know. But I want to learn. That is what I can offer you. My willingness to change. To be changed by this thing between us, in more ways than I already have been."

"I suppose that's fair," she said, sniffling. "I don't really know what it is either. All of my life it meant control, too. And I left home looking for something. Freedom. I thought that it would come with travel, with education, with no one to hold me back or tie me down. And that is a kind of freedom. But it's incomplete. I met you, I started to have feelings for you, and it made me ache. It made me want. It wasn't easy. Deciding to be a mother to twins when I had been planning on something else entirely isn't easy. But what I've learned spending these last couple of years alone is that things are easier when you don't care. The more you care the more it costs. We both know that. I would rather care. And I would rather have all of the painful things that go with that so that I can have the real, joyous things that go along with it, too. I would rather do that than drift along easily. And I would rather do it with you."

He cupped her chin, tilting her face up and kissing her, water drops rolling over their skin as he continued to taste her, as he sipped the moisture from her mouth.

"I'm going to get fired," she said.

"Well, it's a good thing you're going to marry a billionaire."

"Arrogant. I didn't say I would marry you. I just said that I loved you."

"I am arrogant. That is part of loving me, you will find."

"Well, I'll probably still eat cereal on the floor. That is part of loving me."

A smile curved his lips. "I want all the parts of loving you. From the flat shoes to the cereal, to the pain in my chest when I think of what it would mean to lose you. I want to teach you about the world, and I want you to teach me how to be a better man. How to be the man you need."

Thunder rolled through the air, through her chest, the bass note that seemed to match the intensity of the love inside her. "Renzo, don't be silly. You're already the man I need. You were, from that first moment I saw you. You're not the man I would have chosen, but you are the one I love. You are the one I needed. I wanted freedom, I wanted to see everything of the world, but believe me when I tell you I have never felt so free than when you're holding me. The world that we create between us is the most beautiful one I could have ever imagined."

"Even when I am overbearing? And impossible?"

She nodded, unable to hold back the smile that stretched her lips wide. "Even then. Because, you see, Mr. Valenti, the thing is I love you. And if you love me then everything else is just window dressing."

"I do love you, Esther. We may have had a strange beginning, but I think we're going to have the happiest ending."

"So do I, Renzo. So do I."

EPILOGUE

IT WAS AN interesting thing, to go from a family where love had been oppressive, to one where it was the very air Esther breathed.

But after five years with Renzo, their twins and two other children, plus nieces and nephews and her in-laws, Esther felt freer than she ever had. Surrounded, and yet liberated.

Renzo's parents were not the easiest people, but they loved him and their grandchildren with a very real ferocity that was irresistible to Esther.

She had become very good friends with her sister-in-law, Allegra, and her husband, Cristian. They had spent many long dinners laughing together while the children played.

The only thing that ever bothered Esther was the fact that she couldn't heal Renzo's every wound. He loved her, he loved their children. And he did it with absolutely no reservation. But still, Esther knew that he wondered about his oldest child, the one he had never gotten to know.

Until, one day a letter came in the mail. From Samantha. Somehow, she had found out about her origins and had decided to contact Renzo. Because she wanted to know her father, the man who had given her up quietly so that her family wouldn't be disturbed.

For Esther, it hadn't been a difficult thing to allow Samantha into their family. It had never even occurred to her to close the door on the daughter who meant so much to her husband. Still, one night after a visit from Samantha, Renzo pulled her into his arms and kissed her.

"Thank you," he said, "thank you so much for accepting her like you have. What we have here is so complete, and I know that adding more to it can be difficult..."

"No," she said, pressing her fingers to his lips. "It isn't difficult. Nothing about loving you has ever been difficult, and seeing you with all the pieces of your heart back in place is the most beautiful gift I could have ever been given."

Her husband's eyes were suspiciously bright when he went to kiss her again. And then he said in a husky voice, "The most beautiful gift I have ever been given was you. Without you, I would have none of this. Without you I would still be a debauched playboy who had absolutely everything except the one thing he needed."

"What's that?"

"Love, Esther. Without you, I would have no love. And with you my life is full of it."

Then he carried her upstairs and proceeded to show her just how little control he had where she was concerned, and just how much he loved her. And Esther never doubted— not once—that Renzo's love was the absolute truth.

* * * * *

Don't miss the first two stories in
Maisey Yates's HEIRS BEFORE VOWS *trilogy*

THE SPANIARD'S PREGNANT BRIDE
and
THE PRINCE'S PREGNANT MISTRESS
Available now!

**'I wouldn't lie to you, Nikolai,'
Emma said defensively, and
looked away from his dark eyes
and feigned interest in the tall
buildings clearly visible above the
newly green trees of the park.**

Maybe if she took a few shots from the carriage
he'd see she was as unaffected by him as he
appeared to be by her.

The lens of the camera clicked, but she had
no idea what she'd taken. Concentration was
impossible with his dominating presence opposite
her and the looming discussion of their baby. She
turned the camera off and looked at him, to see
he'd been watching every move she'd made.

'We need to talk about our predicament.'

Still his dark eyes watched her, assessing her
reaction to his words.

'Predicament?' she snapped, giving him her full
attention. 'Is that what this baby is to you? A
predicament? Something else you have to deal
with? Just what do you suggest, Nikolai?'

'It is a predicament.'

He said it calmly. Far too calmly. And it unnerved
her. What was coming next?

'One I never wanted, but one which now means
we must get married.'

One Night With Consequences

When one night...leads to pregnancy!

When succumbing to a night of unbridled desire
it's impossible to think past the morning after!

But, with the sheets barely settled, that little blue line
appears on the pregnancy test and it doesn't take long
to realise that one night of white-hot passion
has turned into a lifetime of consequences!

Only one question remains:

How do you tell a man you've just met
that you're about to share more than just his bed?

Find out in:

Her Nine Month Confession by Kim Lawrence

An Heir Fit for a King by Abby Green

Larenzo's Christmas Baby by Kate Hewitt

Illicit Night with the Greek by Susanna Carr

A Vow to Secure His Legacy by Annie West

Bound to the Tuscan Billionaire by Susan Stephens

The Secret that Shocked De Santis by Natalie Anderson

The Shock Cassano Baby by Andie Brock

An Heir to Make A Marriage by Abby Green

The Greek's Nine-Month Redemption by Maisey Yates

Crowned for the Prince's Heir by Sharon Kendrick

The Sheikh's Baby Scandal by Carol Marinelli

A Ring for Vincenzo's Heir by Jennie Lucas

Claiming His Christmas Consequence by Michelle Smart

The Guardian's Virgin Ward by Caitlin Crews

Look for more **One Night With Consequences**
coming soon!

A CHILD
CLAIMED BY GOLD

BY
RACHAEL THOMAS

MILLS
BOON

First Published in Great Britain 2016
By Mills & Boon, an imprint of HarperCollins*Publishers*
1 London Bridge Street, London, SE1 9GF

© 2016 Rachael Thomas

ISBN: 978-0-263-92505-0

Printed and bound in Spain
by CPI, Barcelona

Rachael Thomas has always loved reading romance, and is thrilled to be a Mills & Boon author. She lives and works on a farm in Wales—a far cry from the glamour of a Mills & Boon Modern Romance story—but that makes slipping into her characters' worlds all the more appealing. When she's not writing, or working on the farm, she enjoys photography and visiting historical castles and grand houses. Visit her at rachaelthomas.co.uk.

Books by Rachael Thomas

Mills & Boon Modern Romance

The Sheikh's Last Mistress
New Year at the Boss's Bidding
From One Night to Wife
Craving Her Enemy's Touch
Claimed by the Sheikh
A Deal Before the Altar

Brides for Billionaires

Married for the Italian's Heir

The Billionaire's Legacy

To Blackmail a Di Sione

Visit the Author Profile page at millsandboon.co.uk for more titles.

CHAPTER ONE

NIKOLAI CUNNINGHAM BRACED himself against the icy-cold winds of the homeland he'd turned his back on as he waited for Emma Sanders to arrive on the next train. The heavy grey sky held the promise of more snow and matched his anger that a complete stranger had interfered in his life, bringing him back to Russia and a family he'd long ago disowned. He and his mother had left Vladimir for New York when he was ten years old and the shadow of the events preceding that day still clung to them, threatening to unravel everything.

The train rumbled into the station and he prepared himself for what he was certain would be the worst few days imaginable. His life was in New York, and returning to Vladimir had never been part of his plans. That was until his estranged grandmother had crept from the past, offering her family story to *World in Photographs*.

He'd also been contacted, no doubt because his grandmother had very graciously provided the name he now lived under, but he'd refused. At least, until he'd learnt his grandmother was more than ready to talk and expose everything he and his mother had fled from, probably putting the blame firmly at his mother's

feet. In a bid to protect his mother from their painful
past, and prevent his name being linked to the family name of Petrushov once more, he'd had no option
but to return.

He stood back and watched the travellers climbing
down from the train, scanning them quickly, trying to
remember the image he'd seen of Miss Sanders on the
Internet and match it to one of the disembarking pas-
sengers. Then he saw her, wrapped up against the cold
in true Russian style, only her face visible between the
faux fur hat and scarf. She looked about her nervously,
clutching the handle of her small case in a gloved hand.
She could have been Russian, she blended in so well,
but her apprehension and uncertainty singled her out
as a stranger to Vladimir.

Accepting he had to do this and face whatever came
from it for his mother's sake, he pulled his coat collar
tighter against the cold and walked towards her. She
looked at him and he held her gaze as he strode along
the platform, the determination to get this over with as
fast as possible dominating all other thought.

'Miss Sanders.' He stopped in front of her, register-
ing her height, which almost matched his, something
he found strangely pleasing.

'Mr Petrushov?' Her voice was as clear and crisp
as a frosty morning, but by contrast her eyes were a
mossy green, reminding him of the depths of Russian
forests in summer. Why was he noticing such details?
She distracted him, knocked him off course, and only
now he registered how she'd addressed him.

Nikolai's anger intensified. Beautiful or not, Miss
Sanders obviously hadn't done her research well. It
had been seventeen years since he'd abandoned the

name Petrushov in favour of his stepfather's name, Cunningham.

'Nikolai Cunningham,' he corrected then, before any questions could be asked, continued, 'I trust you enjoyed your train journey from Moscow?'

'Sorry—and yes, I did, Mr Cunningham.' He saw her dark brows furrow in confusion, but refused to elaborate on why he, a Russian-born man, had a distinctly American surname. That was none of her business and he had every intention it would stay that way.

He looked down at the young woman, wrapped up against the cruel winds of winter, and although her alluring green eyes were a distraction he was unable to put aside his anger towards her. 'And you must be Miss Sanders from *World in Photographs*?' He added silently to himself, *the woman who wants to rip open my mother's past and delve into my childhood, no doubt in order to further her career.*

'Please, call me Emma,' she said and held out her gloved hand to him. He didn't take it but looked into the lustrous green of her eyes and wondered what colour her hair was beneath the fur of her hat. Her photo on the Internet hadn't done her any justice: she was stunning.

Irritation mingled with the anger. This was the last woman he wanted to stir his interests. Just being here in Vladimir meant she had the power to cause real hurt to his mother and he strongly suspected she didn't know yet just how much. It was up to him to ensure she never realised just how dramatic the true story of his family was.

He fully intended that she would be distracted by the undeniable beauty of a Russian winter and had already organised plenty of photo opportunities to keep her from the real story. A story that would destroy his mother and upend his world if it got out. All he had to do was prevent her meeting with the grandmother he hadn't seen since he was ten but he didn't yet know how to achieve that.

'We should get out of the wind,' he said firmly, trying to ignore the way the colour of her eyes reminded him of his childhood summers here in Vladimir. It was a place he hadn't thought of for a long time and certainly didn't want to think of now. 'I took the liberty of booking into the same hotel; that way, I can be of as much help to you as possible.'

His motives were much less honourable. All he intended to do was ensure she saw only what he wanted her to see and certainly not what he feared his grandmother wanted to share with her—a family torn apart by deceit.

'Thank you.' She smiled up at him and satisfaction made him return the smile. He was already winning her round. Just a few more days of this nonsense and he could head back to New York and put all this behind him. 'That's very thoughtful of you.'

'The hotel has a very comfortable lounge where I suggest we go over just what you need for your article.'

She believed he was being thoughtful. What would she say if she knew he was determined to hide all he could, despite his grandmother's attempt to ruin the family name? That was another matter he had to deal with and one thing was for certain: Miss Emma Sanders wouldn't be a witness to that particular showdown.

'That would be a good idea.' She laughed softly and, although the scarf around her face hid her lips and she drew her shoulders up against the cold, from the way her eyes sparkled he could imagine she was smiling at him. The image stirred sensations which contrasted wildly with the anger and irritation he'd been harbouring since discovering that his grandmother had agreed to be interviewed for the magazine.

'Allow me,' he said and reached for her luggage, pleased it was a small case and her photography bag. This meant she didn't have any intentions to make her stay any longer than the three days *World in Photographs* had requested from him and his family.

His family. That was a joke.

'Thank you.' This time, as she pulled her scarf a little lower with gloved hands, he could see she was smiling. It also had an unexpected effect on him. The idea of kissing those lips flashed through his mind, sending a trail of blazing lust hurtling through him. That train of thought would achieve nothing and he grimly pushed it away. This was not a time to allow lust to reign and certainly not with this woman.

'This way, Miss Sanders,' he said purposefully, ignoring her invitation to use her first name, and walked briskly away without ensuring she was following, heading for the hotel he'd booked into. He'd purposefully chosen the same hotel as the interfering Miss Sanders, enabling him to ensure she didn't meddle in the dark, hidden past of his family. Had that been the right decision?

Now that he'd met Emma Sanders he knew he'd be able to charm and distract her, making sure she learnt only the romantic ideals about his family story she was no doubt searching for. The only problem was that he suspected he himself was in danger of falling victim to her charms and distractions.

'I expect you are used to this cold, but it's a shock for me,' she said as they stepped inside, out of the wind. The warmth of the hotel, set out as if a village of cosy log cabins, gave it an intimate and even romantic feel that would no doubt help his cause. Very soon he'd have Miss Emma Sanders believing he was more than pleased to talk about his family history.

'My home is in New York, Miss Sanders.'

'Oh,' she said, pulling off her hat as they entered the lounge area of the main part of the hotel, the heat of the log fire a welcome relief from outside. 'I'm sorry; I assumed you lived here with your grandmother.'

He watched as she removed her scarf, revealing long, straight hair the colour of sable, and for a brief moment he forgot himself, forgot that this woman had the power to hurt his mother and expose him for what he really was, as that earlier trail of lust streaked through him again. Mentally he shook himself. He might have a history of brief and hot affairs with women, but this was one woman he could not want.

'Never assume anything, Miss Sanders.' Angered by his reaction at seeing beneath the layers of dark fur she wore, as if born to Russian winters, he fought to keep his tone neutral. She was a beautiful woman, and his body's reaction to her meant that his voice was anything but neutral and much harsher than it should have been.

She looked up at him, a question in her eyes, her slender dark brows furrowed into a frown of confusion. 'Life has taught me that, Mr Petrushov.'

'Cunningham,' he corrected her again, but something in the way she said those words and the look of haunted fear which had rushed across her beautiful face as she'd spoken nudged at his conscience. He shouldn't be so hard, so aggressive. Not if he wanted to steer her away from the truth of his family. Maybe playing to the attraction sizzling between them would be the way to create that distraction?

He wondered what she meant as he picked up on the inference that life hadn't been easy for her. He resisted the urge to ask, not wanting to draw her into a conversation that may turn back on him. Over the years he'd become adept at providing just enough information about himself to satisfy people, but never enough for them to know the full facts.

'Then we already understand one another.' He pulled off his coat and hat, hung them up then took hers from her, his fingers unexpectedly brushing against hers. A jolt of heat surged through him and, as she pulled her hand back, she looked up at him, her green eyes wide and startled. Her full lips, slicked with gloss, parted and he had an almost uncontrollable urge to lower his head and kiss her. Not a gentle brushing of lips but a hard, demanding kiss. The kind of kiss which led to fierce and passionate sex.

What the hell was he thinking?

She stepped back away from him as a flush of colour covered her pale face and her eyes darkened to resemble the deepest ocean. She'd felt it too, of that there was no doubt. If she had been any other woman, he wouldn't have thought twice about acting on the attraction. But she wasn't any other woman. She could tear open his past, threatening not just his mother's happiness but his reputation. He wouldn't allow it to happen—not at any cost.

'Yes, yes, we do. We—we understand each other

perfectly.' She stumbled over her words and he stifled
a smile of satisfaction. Maybe the attraction could be
used to ensure she didn't find out just who he really
was. If a touch and a brief moment of sexual chemistry could disarm her, that would be a pleasant way
to distract her from digging around too much into his
family's past.

Emma hated the way she could hardly form a sentence
as Nikolai Cunningham all but scrutinised her. He had
muddled her mind and sent her insides into turmoil
from the moment they'd met. It was as if a spark of
recognition had reached out from him, inexplicably
drawing her closer.

She thought of Richard, the man she'd always
wished could be more than just a friend, and compared him to this powerful specimen of masculinity.
Richard was attractive but safe, but this man was undeniably handsome and oozed a lethal kind of sex ap-
peal. She shivered as something arced between them.
He held her gaze and she knew she had to remember
he was also the man who held the key to her successfully completing this assignment and securing a long-
term contract with *World in Photographs*.

What happened over the next few days could launch
her career as a photographer. More importantly, it
would provide a regular income, which was badly
needed if she was to stand any chance at all of supporting her younger sister Jess as she embarked on a
lifetime dream of becoming a ballerina. They'd both
had so many knockbacks in life, going from foster
home to foster home, that she wanted her younger sister to do what made her happy. And she was good at

it—talented, in fact. After the things they'd experienced together, they both deserved happiness, and if Jess was happy then so was she.

The tall, dark-haired man who'd just sent a frisson of awareness zipping around her had been distinctly cold towards her initially, more so than the icy winds. Something had inexplicably changed in the last few moments. He'd looked at her differently, making heat surge through her in a way she'd never known before, and she wasn't sure she was able to deal with it. Thoughts of Richard had never done that to her.

'I shall accompany you to the meeting with Marya Petrushov, who is my grandmother, but first I will take you to several locations you can use for the photographs you require.' Something about the tone of his voice made it clear that to ask for more than this right now would be inadvisable, especially the way he'd said his grandmother's name. She immediately sensed unresolved issues and wondered how often he saw his grandmother with so many miles between them.

Throwing caution to the wind and quelling her curiosity for now, she looked directly at him, her chin lifted slightly, and clearly set out her terms. 'I not only need photographs of locations, Mr Petrushov, but of you and your grandmother—along with any other family members.'

Her brief was to step inside the life of the Russian family which had made its wealth only decades ago and see just how it lived. If she didn't deliver on that brief, she'd never get her contract, which would mean she'd have no way of funding Jess in one of Russia's elite ballet schools. The fact that this meeting was taking place in a town only a night-train-ride away from

where Jess had a much-coveted place at a world famous ballet school was a good sign and she'd believed
it couldn't go wrong, that it was meant to be.

Now, looking at Nikolai as he laid down his own
rules about the interview, she had serious doubts it
would ever go right. He dominated the entire room
they'd walked into; even though the residents' lounge
was large and spacious, he had taken command of
every bit of that space. He was undoubtedly in control.

He also intimidated her, not that she would ever let
him know that. It wouldn't do to let a man who was
obviously used to being in charge see subservience.
No, she would stand her ground. She sensed she would
have to be as strong as him if she wanted to get what
the brief dictated.

'There are no other family members, Miss Sanders.' He made his way towards a group of comfortable
chairs around the warmth of the fire and she followed,
determined he wasn't going to put her off so easily. She
only had a week here in Russia and she wanted to see
Jess before flying back to London.

He gestured to her to sit and then took the chair
next to hers, his long legs suddenly emphasised as he
sat. Nerves filled her and the way he watched her unsettled her more than she'd ever known. She wished
she knew what he was thinking, but those dark eyes
of his were unreadable.

'A photo of you and your grandmother...' She hadn't
even finished her suggestion when he leant forward,
bringing them close to one another in an intimate kind
of way. It was too close and her words faltered into
nothing.

'No.' That one word silenced any suggestions she

had, the anger in it reverberating around the room like a rogue firework. Then, as if he realised how hard and unyielding that sounded, he sat back and offered an explanation. 'I have not seen my grandmother for many years, so a loving family photo will not be possible, Miss Sanders.'

This wasn't going well. With each passing second, her dream of easily pulling together the article and then slipping away to Perm to see Jess for a few days was rapidly disintegrating. The wild and untamed look in his eyes as he regarded her suspiciously left her in no doubt that he meant what he said.

'Look, Mr Petrushov—sorry, Cunningham.' Now, to make matters worse, she'd called him by his family name again and, judging by the tightness of his jaw, that was not something which would endear her to him. She pressed on, not sure this whole situation could get any worse. 'I don't know what your problem is with me, but I am here to do a job. Your grandmother agreed with *World in Photographs* to be interviewed and photographed for the magazine and my job is to ensure that happens.'

She glared up at him, hoping to match his dominance with her determination, and wondered why she'd ever agreed to take on the interview role when photography was her field. The answer to that was her commitment to allowing her sister to follow her dreams.

He looked at her, his gaze slowly searching her face, lingering just a little too long on her lips. Tension crackled in the air around them and she was totally unaware of anything except the two of them. Mentally she shook herself free of it. Now was not a good time to become attracted to a man, and certainly not this man.

All through her teenage years she'd steadfastly held on to to a vow never to succumb to the temptation of a man. She'd managed that until she'd met Richard, a fellow photographer and the first man to pay her any kind of attention. She'd hoped their friendship would turn into something more, but two years down the line nothing had changed, and she watched in disillusion from the sidelines as he dated other women.

'And it is my duty to ensure my family isn't upset by your intrusion into our life, Miss Sanders.' He spoke slowly, his dark eyes hard and glittering, a very clear warning laced into every word. How could she be intruding when the old lady had agreed to be interviewed?

'I have no wish to upset anyone.' She looked up at him, into those midnight-black eyes, and knew she couldn't fight fire with fire. Her life with her mother, before she and Jess had been put into care, had taught her that. If she tried to match his strength and determination, she'd never get this assignment done. She lowered her gaze and looked down at her hands before looking back up from beneath her lashes. 'I apologise. Can we start again?'

The request completely stunned Nikolai. Moments ago she'd been brimming with fire. Passionate indignation had burned in her eyes, making his fight not to give in to the temptation to kiss her almost impossible. Now within seconds she'd become soft and compliant. Such a drastic changed filled him with suspicion. She was playing games with him.

'You want to go back into the cold and shake hands?'

He couldn't resist teasing her and was rewarded with a light flush of pink to her cheeks.

'No.' She laughed softly and her smile made her eyes shine, as if the sun was breaking through the forest and bouncing off fresh, green, spring leaves. 'I think we should start again with our conversation. Let's have a hot drink and discuss how we can both help each other out.'

Now he really was surprised. She was up to something, trying to manipulate the situation round to what she wanted. It was what the woman he should have married had always done and he'd been fool enough to let her—until he'd ended the charade that had been their engagement. She'd only wanted him for what he could provide for her.

'I don't think there is anything you can offer that will help me, Miss Sanders, but we will have a drink, and I will tell you how the next few days are going to work.'

Before she could say anything else, he signalled to a member of staff and ordered tea—something he wouldn't have requested in New York but, being back in Russia, his childhood memories were resurfacing in an unsettling way. Until he saw the flicker of interest in her eyes, he hadn't registered he'd used the first language he'd spoken as a child before his world had been torn apart by the pain of his mother's secret.

A secret that now haunted him. It was the same secret he suspected his grandmother wanted to unleash in the article and, just like her son, his cruel father, she was spiteful enough to manipulate him back to Russia to witness it all.

'Please, call me Emma,' she said, leaning back in

the chair opposite him, her jeans, tight around long, shapely legs, snagging his attention, filling his mind with thoughts he had no right to be thinking. 'And may I call you Nikolai?'

'Nikolai, yes,' he replied sharply. He had wanted to change his name to Nik when he'd left Russia as a young child—it had been his way of distancing himself from his father's family—but his mother had begged him to keep Nikolai, telling him she'd chosen the name because it was a family name and that he should keep some of his Russian roots.

'I get the distinct impression that you are not at all willing for me to talk to your grandmother, Nikolai— and yet it was her who approached *World in Photographs*, which makes me think there is something you don't want told.'

'How very shrewd.' And he'd thought he was going to turn on the charm and make her bend to his will. It seemed he'd greatly underestimated this woman. Her act of innocent shyness was exactly that. An act. Just like his ex, she was able to be whatever was necessary to get what she wanted.

'Perhaps we can come to some sort of agreement, one that will give me enough information to complete my job and afford your family enough privacy.' She sat back in her chair and looked at him, her dark brows raised in a silent show of triumph. If that was what she thought she'd achieved, he'd let her think that— for now.

'On one condition.' He picked up his tea, took a sip then met her gaze. He looked into her eyes and for the briefest of moments thought he'd seen anxiety. No, more than that—fear.

'And what is that condition?'

'That you tell me why this job is so important to you. Why come all the way from London to Vladimir for the ramblings of an old woman?' He had no idea if his grandmother rambled; he hadn't seen her for almost twenty-three years. It had been the day of his father's funeral and as a bemused ten-year-old he'd had no idea what was going on. No idea why his grandmother had turned him and his mother out. It was only six years later he'd learnt the disturbing truth and had vowed to do all he could to protect his mother from any further pain. A vow he fully intended to keep now.

'I took the job because it was a way of coming to Russia. It was as if fate was giving me the perfect opportunity. My sister, Jess, has a place at Perm Ballet School and once I've got what I need I'm going to spend a few days with her.' Her lovely green eyes filled with genuine excitement and that familiar pang of injustice almost stifled him. She'd had a happy childhood, had formed bonds with her sister, but his had been far from that thanks to one brutal act by his father, a man he had no wish to acknowledge as such.

'Your sister is here? In Russia?' This was the last thing he'd expected to discover and certainly hadn't turned up when he'd had Emma Sanders's background checked out. She had debts and she was far from well-known in the field of photography. Other than that, he'd found nothing of any significance. Nothing he could manipulate to make this situation work for him.

'Yes, ballet is her dream, and I intend to see that she can follow it.' Her face lit up and pride filled her voice and he saw an entirely different woman from the one he'd met outside just a short while ago. 'She's only sixteen and taking this job means I will be able to see her sooner than we'd planned, even if it's just a few days before I head back to London.'

At least now he could understand why she'd taken the job. Initially his suspicious mind had come to conclusions that weren't even there. She simply hadn't enough money to fly to Russia and see her sister so had taken the job. He did, however, still have doubts as to his grandmother's motives for instigating it all. Just what was she hoping to achieve? But, worse than that, how far was Emma prepared to go in order to impress *World in Photographs* in an attempt to launch her career?

'Then we can help one another, Emma. I can take you to places linked with my family's past where you can take as many photographs as you desire.' He paused, unsure why he'd used that word. Was it because of the way her body distracted him, making him want her? Colour heightened her cheeks again, making her appear shy and innocent, and he wondered if she understood the underlying sexual tension which was definitely building between them.

'And can I meet your grandmother? Ask her a few questions?' Her voice had become a little husky and she bit down on her lower lip, an action he wouldn't read into. Not if he wanted to stay in control of this nonsense and thwart his grandmother's attempt at stirring up trouble once more.

'Yes, but first we'll go to the places that are linked to my family. I have already made the arrangements for tomorrow.'

She looked happy, as if he'd just handed her a free pass. 'In that case, I will look forward to spending a few days with you.'

The irritating thing was, he also found himself looking forward to being with her. The very woman he'd wanted to despise on sight and he was undeniably attracted to her.

CHAPTER TWO

THE NEXT MORNING Emma was full of excitement and it wasn't just that, after a shaky start, this assignment, thanks to Nikolai's plans, would be done quickly and she could head off to meet Jess. She was taken aback to realise she was also excited to see Nikolai Cunningham again. After yesterday afternoon in his company, she was convinced he couldn't be as severe as he'd first appeared when she'd stepped off the train. Then he'd created such a formidable picture of power and command and she'd wished she'd been able to photograph him as he'd stood there, glaring at her.

It unnerved her to admit the excitement hadn't dissipated after they'd met and he'd shown her to his car. If anything it had increased and she had no idea why. After wasting several years worshipping Richard from afar and not being noticed, she didn't want to fall for the charms of another man—especially one as unattainable as Nikolai Cunningham.

'Where are we going now?' The large black car seemed to have glided silently through the white landscape and she'd wished many times she could stop and take photographs. Not for the magazine, but for herself. Her creative mind was working overtime and she saw images as if through the lens all over the place.

'To the place I knew as home until I was ten years old. It's just on the outskirts of Vladimir.' He looked straight ahead as he drove, his profile set into firm, determined lines. She had the distinct impression it was the last place he wanted to go and wondered at his motives for taking her there. He didn't strike her as a compliant man. Far from it.

'And who lives there now? Your grandmother?' she couldn't help but ask. The brief for the assignment and the need to be professional, to get the job done and leave on time, pushed to the forefront of her mind. She had to get this right, had to put the spin on it the magazine wanted, but everything she'd seen or been told so far was in total contrast to what she was supposed to portray. This wasn't a happy-ever-after story, unless you counted the global success of Nikolai's banking business that he'd created to complement his stepfather's exclusive real-estate business.

His silence deepened and she turned her attention to the road ahead. Moments later the car turned off onto a snow-covered lane that had no tracks on it at all, no hint that anyone had gone that way recently. Was the house empty?

Nikolai spoke harshly, in what she assumed was Russian, and most definitely sounded like a curse. She looked from him to the crumbling façade ahead of what must have once been a great house. It had rounded towers, some with turrets and others with pointed roofs, which reached into the grey sky above. The black holes, where once windows of assorted sizes had looked out over the flat landscape, seemed like watchful eyes.

Emma's heart went out to Nikolai as she pieced together the small amount she knew about him. None of it made sense, but it was obvious he hadn't expected this empty shell. She'd planned to take photographs of the place he'd grown up in, maybe even convince him to be in one, but now none of that felt right.

He got out of the car, seemingly unaware of her presence, and for a moment she sat and watched him. Then the photographer in her made that impossible for long. The image of his solitary figure, dressed in dark clothes, standing and looking at the neglected building, stark against the white landscape, was too much of a temptation. She had to take the photo.

Quietly, so as not to disturb him, she got out of the car, her camera in hand. The snow crunched under her boots as she moved a little closer. Seconds later she began taking photos. He remained oblivious to the clicks of the lens and as she looked back through the images she knew she wouldn't be using them for the article. These told a story of pain and loss and they were for her alone.

'This is where my family lived before my father died.' He didn't turn to speak to her, as if doing so would give away his emotions. Was he afraid of appearing weak? His tone had an icy edge to it, but she waited for him to continue. 'This is the first time I've seen it since I was a ten-year-old boy. My mother and I left for a new life in New York after that.'

'That must have been hard.' She moved instinctively towards him, but the cold glare in his eyes as he finally turned to face her warned against it. She just wanted him to know that she understood what it felt like to be displaced in life, not to know who you really were. Just like her and Jess, he'd been pushed from one adult to another and had known great sadness.

'Hard?' Nikolai could barely control his anger—not just at this woman, who was bringing all he'd thought he'd forgotten about his childhood back out for inspection, but also at his grandmother for instigating it. 'I don't think you could possibly know.'

He thought she'd say something, defend herself, but instead she shrugged, walked back to the car and took out her camera bag. He watched as she set up her tripod and again started to take photos of the old house. The camera clicked and, each time he heard it, it was as if it was opening yet another memory.

'Do you have any happy memories of this place?' She looked at him. Against the white snow and grey sky she looked stunning and he allowed this to distract him from the past. He didn't want to go there, not for anyone.

It was too late. A sense of terror crept over him as he saw himself, a young boy of eight, hiding beneath the antique table his father had been so proud to buy with his new-found wealth. He'd gone there seeing it as a place of safety, sure his father's temper wouldn't hurt his latest prized possession. He'd been wrong, very wrong. As his mother had begged and pleaded for his father to leave him alone, he'd been dragged out from beneath the table and lifted off his feet. He'd wriggled like mad, kicking and squealing, desperate to get away, yet knowing if he did his father would turn his attention to his mother. It was him or her and, in a bid to save her from at least one beating, he'd snarled words of hatred at his father. After that he couldn't remember what had happened.

He didn't want to.

He pushed the memories back. Analysing them wouldn't help anyone now, least of all himself.

'Not here, no,' he replied sternly and walked over to Emma, who was looking over her shoulder as she viewed the images she'd taken. The house didn't look so insidious on the screen of the camera, as if viewing it through the lens had defused the terrible memories of living there with his mother and father.

Emma's scent drifted up through the crisp air to meet him and he closed his eyes as summer flowers triggered happier memories. 'I was happiest in the summer, when we visited my mother's family.'

Why had he said that? Inwardly he berated himself for giving her information she could act on. At the thought of the country home his mother's parents had kept, he realised it was the perfect place to take her. He could hire a troika and sit back and watch as the romance of Russia unfolded. What woman wouldn't resist such a romantic story? It would be just what he needed to charm her away from the dark secrets he had to keep hidden away.

'Where was that? Close by?' Her interest was caught and she looked up at him, smiling and looking happier than he'd seen her since she'd arrived on the train. Then she looked vulnerable—beautiful and vulnerable.

'It is, yes.' He could hardly answer her as the attraction wound itself round him, drawing him ever closer to her.

'Can we go there?' she asked tentatively, her genuine smile and soft blush doing untold things to him. Why, he didn't know. He much preferred his women to be bold, dramatic and experienced at mutually beneficial affairs. Instinctively he knew Emma was not like that at all. She was the sort of woman who'd planned out a happy-ever-after, even as a small child. Definitely not for him.

'We will go tomorrow,' he said, stepping back from the temptation of this woman.

The next morning, as instructed by Nikolai, Emma waited, wearing her warmest clothes and even more excited than yesterday. Somehow they had drawn closer with each passing hour yesterday and, even though he didn't talk to her about the past and let her into his thoughts, he had shown her many wonderful places and she already had lots of images.

She also realised she liked him—perhaps a little too much. If she was honest, she was attracted to him in a way she hadn't known before, not even with Richard.

'Ready?' he said as he met her in the hotel reception.

Like a child about to be shown a Christmas tree, she couldn't stem the excitement and smiled up at him. He was clean shaven this morning, and as wrapped up as she was, but that didn't stop the pulse of attraction leaping between them. The only difference was this time his smile reached his eyes and they smouldered at her, making her pulse rate soar.

'Yes; are we going to the house you told me about yesterday?'

'We are, yes. The house I spent summers at with my mother and her parents.'

She wanted to ask if his father had gone there too, but didn't dare risk spoiling the softer mood he was in. She sensed his father was the cause of the sudden change in his mood yesterday at his childhood home, but didn't have the courage to ask. Instead she focused her attention on what was happening now. 'Is it far?'

'No, a short car ride, then something special,' he said and to her surprise took her hand and led her into the street to the same big, black car he'd driven the previous day. Her heart fluttered as she fought to control the powerful surge of attraction rushing through her; she'd never felt anything like it before.

Then the something special Nikolai had teased her with turned out to be a ride across the snow in a sleigh, pulled by three proud horses, and Emma was totally blown away by the whole experience—and by the enforced close proximity of Nikolai as they sat snuggled under a heavy throw. 'This is amazing. I can use it in the article.'

'It's called a troika; racing them is a tradition from over one hundred years ago that's enjoying a resurgence.' She could barely focus on what he was saying as his thigh pressed hard against hers and even through all their layers of clothes her skin felt scorched.

After a little while the troika driver slowed to a halt, the horses snorting into the cold air, and Emma looked at Nikolai. Again something fizzed between them, but this time he held her gaze, looking intently into her eyes just the way she would have envisaged a lover doing. 'Thank you,' she whispered softly, her breath hanging briefly in the air, mingling with his in the most intimate way, and making her blush.

'The pleasure is all mine, Emma.' The fact that he'd used her name didn't go unnoticed and a shimmer of pleasure rushed over her, making her shudder, but it wasn't from the cold. 'Are you cold?'

'No, not at all,' she said, shyness creeping over her,

and she lowered her gaze, concentrating on the throw which covered their legs, locking them into the small space together.

With a gloved hand, Nikolai lifted her chin, forcing her to look at him once more, and what she saw in the inky black depths of his eyes was as terrifying as it was exciting. 'You are very beautiful, Emma.'

She swallowed hard, unable to move away from him, trapped with her legs all but welded to his beneath the cover. 'You shouldn't say things like that.'

Was that really her voice? She had no idea she could sound so husky and so trembling at the same time. Deep within her, silly, romantic notions she always shunned sprang to life. Did he really find her attractive? Would he want to kiss her and, if he did, what would it be like?

'It's the truth.'

Her heart was thumping in her chest and she was sure he must hear it. Her breathing had become more rapid, and so had his, if their white, misty breath was anything to go by. She searched his face for any hint of teasing, any sign that he was toying with her. She didn't have any experience with men, but she knew well enough from friends how they could make a woman lose all sense of self, something Richard had never done to her.

There was nothing, not a single trace of him teasing her, and she knew she was in danger of slipping under the spell that the magic of the moment was weaving around them. If they had been in a hotel lounge, talking in front of an open fire as they had done the afternoon she arrived, would he be saying these things to her?

'I didn't come here to become mixed up with a man.'

Even as her body yearned for the unknown, her mind kept to the practical issue of keeping her feet firmly on the ground.

'Do we have to get "mixed up", as you so nicely put it?' His voice was deep and laden with a hidden agenda.

She looked away, across the vast, white expanse of the snowy landscape, and asked herself the same question. If she took the kiss she was sure he wanted to give, would that change anything between them? No, because it couldn't. She had a job to do and then it would be time to move on with her life.

She'd waited in the hope that Richard would move their friendship to something more intimate and now she wondered if that had been wrong. Or was it just Richard who was wrong?

'No, I guess we don't.' She hoped she sounded as though she knew what she was doing, as if she'd been in this very situation many times before. The reality was very different. She'd never had a man look at her with such fierce desire in his eyes, never wanted to feel his lips claim hers.

He responded by moving closer and brushing his lips over hers very gently and suddenly she wasn't cold any more as heat scorched through her. She moved her lips against his, a soft sigh of pleasure slipping from her, only to be caught by him. What was happening to her?

A jolt threw her away from him and she dragged in a long, cold breath as the restless horses shifted in their harnesses. The driver spoke to Nikolai and she blushed, burying her face deeper in her scarf to hide her embarrassment. What was happening to her?

'The driver says snow is on the way and suggests we

see what is necessary and head back.' Nikolai hadn't intended to kiss her like that; he'd just wanted to make her feel special, to give her the fairy-tale ride through the snow to a beautiful location. He'd wanted all that to distract her—at least, he had, until he'd tasted her lips, felt them welcoming him and encouraging him to take more.

'Yes, yes, of course.' She sounded flustered as she took her camera out of its protective case. 'I'll just take a few frames and then you can tell me about it on the way back. I'd rather be in the warm when the snow arrives.'

He pushed back the image of that warmth being his bed and forced himself to focus on the task at hand. He had to distract her from the truth of his family history by showing her the façade they had lived behind.

'This,' he said as he helped her from the troika, 'Is where my mother and I spent each summer until we left Russia. In the summer, though, it was much greener and warmer than now.'

He hadn't thought of those summer days for such a long time, consigning them to the past he wanted to forget, but now, as he began to talk to Emma, it wasn't nearly as hard to look back on them as he'd always feared.

'And this was your mother's family home?' she asked as she lined up the shot and took a photo of the one place he'd been happy as a child.

'It was, but I never saw it like this, all covered in snow. It was always summer when we visited and I'd run with the dogs in the orchard, enjoying the freedom.'

It hadn't been just the freedom of running free in the summer sun, it had been the freedom from the terror of his father: from not having to hide when his filthy temper struck; of not having to worry about his mother as his father's voice rose to aggressive shouts. It had been freedom from pain—for both of them. He'd realised much later on that his mother's parents must have known what was going on and it had been their way of offering sanctuary. He just couldn't understand why his mother hadn't taken it permanently.

'And is your grandmother here to talk to us now?' Hope was shining in her voice. She thought he meant the grandmother who had started this whole nonsense off.

'No, they passed away before my father. Marya Petrushov is my father's mother. The one who contacted *World in Photographs*. She lives in Vladimir.'

'So we can see her?'

She turned her attention to packing away the camera, obviously happy with the photos she'd taken, and he was glad she couldn't see his face—because right now he was sure it must be contorted with rage and contempt for the woman who had done nothing to help him or his mother. Instead she'd preferred to make excuses for her son and for that he could never forgive her.

'Tomorrow. But right now we should return to the hotel.'

Just as he couldn't put off returning to the hotel because of the impending snow, he knew he couldn't put off meeting his grandmother again any longer. Maybe facing her for the first time would be easier with someone else at his side. It might also be the worst possible decision he'd ever made.

CHAPTER THREE

NIKOLAI LOOKED OUT of the window of the hotel bar as darkness descended. The snow was falling ever harder and he couldn't help but feel relieved. At this rate they wouldn't be able to get to his grandmother's home before Emma had to return to London. He'd almost given away the secret himself when he'd taken her to his childhood home; but at least she now had something for her story, and he could relax, maybe even enjoy the evening with her.

'It's snowing really hard.' Emma's voice, soft and gentle, held a hint of anxiety as she joined him in the hotel bar.

'That is normal for these parts,' he said as she sat down, unable to drag his eyes from her. She wore a black dress which moulded to every curve of her body, but when she removed her jacket, exposing her shoulders and slender arms, that spark of attraction he'd been trying to ignore roared forward, more persistent in its need for satisfaction.

She sat down opposite him in the comfortable chairs of the lounge area and crossed her legs, affording him a tantalising view of her lower leg, now deliciously on display, and the black high heels she wore only reinforced his need to feel those legs around him. Was she doing it on purpose? Was she trying to distract him?

'Thank you,' she said firmly and he looked at her face, liking the extra make-up she wore. It accentuated the green of her eyes and he wondered how they would look filled with passion and desire. 'For what you have shown me, I mean. It can't have been easy seeing your childhood home in ruins.'

The sincerity in her voice made him curious about her childhood and he remembered what she'd said within those first moments of meeting him: *life has taught me that, Mr Petrushov*. Had life been equally unkind to her?

'What of your family home?' he asked, instantly recognising the way she tensed and the tightening of her jaw. He wasn't the only one with secrets which still hung over him.

'A family home isn't something I was lucky enough to have. My sister and I were put into care when we were young.' She looked away from him; he watched her swallow down her pain and had to fight hard against the urge to go to her and offer comfort—sure it wouldn't be comfort for long.

'I didn't intend to upset you.' He leant forward in the chair and her perfume weaved itself around him, increasing the desire for her which pumped around his body. Desire he couldn't act on, not if he wanted to keep this whole situation free of complications.

'Maybe it's only fair, after what you endured yesterday. It must have been heart-breaking, seeing your family home like that.' She turned to look at him and suddenly they were very close. He held her gaze, looking into those green eyes and seeing an array of emotions swirling within them. He watched her lips move as she spoke again. 'I feel responsible for that.'

She looked down again at her hands clasped in her lap. For a moment he followed her gaze and then something he'd never experienced before pushed him on. He needed to touch her so he reached out and with his thumb and finger lifted her chin, forcing her to look at him.

The spark of attraction that had been between them from the moment she had got off the train mutated into desire as her gaze locked with his. It arced between them, pulling them together. He pressed the pad of his thumb along her bottom lip and he knew he'd already crossed the line, already passed the point of no return. All he could hope for now was that she would stop this madness from going further. She didn't. She stayed still, her eyes wide and beautiful, and when his fingers caressed her soft skin again her eyes fluttered closed, long lashes spreading out over her pale skin.

Did she have any idea what she was doing to him?

'Maybe we should eat.' Her voice was husky as she looked back up at him, her eyes full of desire. Food was the last thing he wanted, but he couldn't give in to the hot surge of lust racing through him, not when he'd decided this woman was off limits; he'd always prized himself on control.

As she closed her eyes slowly, her lips parting slightly, he wondered how the hell he was supposed to hang on to any sense of decency. She was so alluring, so tempting. When she opened her eyes again the mossy green was swirling with the same lust-filled desire which coursed wildly through his veins and he knew it was too late. There was only one way this heated attraction could be calmed now.

'It is not food I hunger for.' He leant even closer, still holding her chin, and pressed his lips briefly against hers, leaving her in no doubt what it was he hungered for. Was he insane? He'd gone past caring. Somewhere in the recess of his mind he knew this was so wrong, but the thought of kissing her, making her his, was so very right.

Emma could hardly breathe. The message in Nikolai's eyes was so very clear she couldn't miss it. He wanted her. She had no idea how she knew that, having done nothing more than kiss a man. But on a primal level that she'd never known existed within her she recognised the hunger in those inky-black eyes.

Hunger for her.

After years of believing she was unattractive to men, this powerful, dominating man wanted her. Worse than that—she wanted him too. She wanted to taste his kiss and feel his arms around her. She was so far from home, and everything she'd hoped this trip would bring looked in doubt, but right now none of that mattered. Only the searing hot attraction between them mattered. Only the promise of being desired for the woman she was.

What was it her last foster mother had always said? *Live for the moment.* She let the advice swirl in her mind, pushing back the cruel words her father had taunted her with the one and only time she'd met him.

She looked again at Nikolai, at the intensity in his eyes. She'd never done that before, never taken the lead with a man, even though she'd always hoped she and

Richard could be something. Now she knew why. What she felt for him was purely friendship, whereas what she felt for Nikolai, and had done since the moment they'd met, was far more intense. She had no choice but to live for the moment. If she kissed him, allowed herself to step into the sanctuary of his strong arms, would that be living for the moment?

'Neither am I.' Her whisper was so soft she wondered if she'd actually said anything, but the slight rise of his brows and the deepening intensity in his eyes told her she had—and he'd understood.

In answer he lowered his head and covered her lips with his, moving them gently until hers parted, allowing him to deepen the kiss. Heat exploded through her and she knew this was far more than a kiss; this was a prelude to something she'd never done before. He deepened the kiss again, setting light to her whole body. They couldn't do this here. Anyone could see them.

She pulled back, alarmed at how her heart raced, thumping in her chest like a horse galloping across the finishing line. Except this wasn't the end. This was only the beginning. Empowered by that knowledge and the need to let go of restraint and become a real woman, one who knew desire and passion, she smiled at him. 'Let's go upstairs.'

He looked down at her, his eyes searching hers, and she hoped he wouldn't be able to tell how inexperienced she was. A man like this must have had many lovers and the last thing he'd want would be a shy virgin. Although she couldn't change the fact that she'd never done more than kiss a man lightly on the lips, she could stop herself from being shy. All she needed to do was let go and live for the moment.

'It can't be anything more than this night,' he said as he took her hand. 'I don't want a relationship and commitment. I'm not looking for love and happiness. I want to know you understand that, Emma.'

'Love and happiness,' she said, a little too sharply, if his hardening expression was any gauge. 'It doesn't exist, Nikolai. I'm not a fool. In just three days we will go our separate ways and it will be as if this night never happened.'

Where had all that come from? Had passion muddled her mind? She was actually asking to spend the night with him, just one night and nothing more. She who'd told herself she would wait for her Prince Charming, although deep down she knew he didn't exist. Her childhood might have been hard, but it had grounded her expectations of life. She knew true love didn't exist—or, if it did, it never lasted once passion had subsided.

He said nothing. Instead he took her hand in his and led her away from the hotel lounge. Her hand was small in his as she glanced down at it, but she didn't pull back. Her step didn't falter. She was emboldened by the fizz of powerful desire humming in her body, the freedom to be a very different woman and a chance to erase the ever-present doubt her father had planted within her by denying she existed.

As they walked along the corridors of the chalet-style building she wondered if anyone else could tell that she was on fire at the thought of what she was about to do. But there wasn't anyone around and finally he stopped outside his room. She leant against the wall, needing the support of something solid as her knees weakened just from the intensity in his eyes.

'Are you sure this is what you want?' His voice broke as desire turned it into a very sexy whisper. He touched his hand to her face, brushing his fingers down her cheek, but she kept her gaze firmly on him.

Did he think she was playing games? She'd never been as sure of anything in her life. Whatever had ignited between them during those first moments they had met was destined to end like this. There could be no other outcome. Even she knew that and this was exactly what she wanted.

'Yes.' The word came out as a husky whisper and boldly she placed the palms of her hands on his chest, relishing the strength beneath his shirt and cashmere sweater.

His arms wrapped around her, pulling her against him, and a startled gasp slipped from her as she felt the hardness of him pressing intimately against her, awakening her further. To hide her embarrassment she slipped her hands around his neck, her fingers sliding into the dark hair at his collar.

His mouth claimed hers in a demanding kiss, one which stoked the fire he'd lit, sending it roaring higher until she knew it would totally consume her. The dark stubble on his face burned her skin with pleasure. His tongue slid into her mouth, tasting her, teasing her. She matched his kiss, demanding as much from him as he did from her. Whatever this was, she intended to make the most of it. Just for one night she would give in to her own needs and do exactly what she wanted. For one night she was going to put herself first, believe in herself, believe that at least someone cared, someone wanted her.

His hands cupped her bottom, pulling her tighter

against him. His breathing had become as ragged as
hers and she plunged her fingers deep into his hair,
kissing him harder still. When he broke the kiss she
gasped and let her head fall back, her carefully pinned-
up hair beginning to fall apart—just as she was.

He kissed down her neck and she arched herself
harder against him. She gasped as he kissed lower still
over the swell of her breast and right along the neckline of her dress. It wasn't enough. She wanted more,
much more.

'Take me to your bed.' Horrified and excited that
she'd been bold enough to say what she felt, what she
wanted, she laughed. Who was this woman?

'That is exactly what I intend to do, Emma Sanders. You can be sure of that.' Instead of letting her go
and opening the door of his room, he kissed her again,
one hand holding her back as the other slid up her side
and to her breast.

Pleasure exploded around her as his fingers teased
her hardened nipple through the fabric of her dress.
She couldn't take much more of this. As if he read her
thoughts, he pulled back and let her go. She stood and
watched as he unlocked the room and pushed the door
open. Was she really doing this? Was she really about
to step into this man's room and give herself to him?

Embarrassment rushed over her again, but she hid it
with boldness, walking towards him with a suggestive
smile on her lips. Tonight she wasn't Emma Sanders,
responsible for everyone else, she was just a woman
drowning in desire. With a gentleness which surprised
her after the kiss that had bruised her lips, he took her
hand and led her into the room. Quietly he clicked the
door shut and they were left in almost darkness, the

only light coming from outside, creeping in through the blinds in beams of whiteness.

Nikolai looked at Emma, not wanting to turn the lights on, but wanting to see how beautiful she was. In one minute she seemed bold and seductive and then, as if a switch had been flicked, she looked innocent and shy. He had no idea which was the real Emma, but either way she was full of passion and desire. More importantly she shared his views. Love and happiness were only for the select few and they were not destined to be two of those.

'You are very beautiful,' he said as he moved towards her. Those expressive green eyes widened, pushing the desire within him higher still. He'd never wanted a woman as much as he wanted her and for that very reason he intended to savour every moment. Was it because she didn't threaten him by hinting at beyond the here and now, looking for more than just one night? Or was it because they had both known pain and hardship in their lives? Either way, he wasn't going to rush one minute of their night together, not when it was all they had.

'Nikolai…' She breathed his name, a hint of a question lingering in her whisper.

'Now is not for talking,' he said gently, pulling her to him. 'It's for pleasure like this.'

Before she could say anything else, he kissed her, resisting the urge to deepen the kiss and demand so much more. Savour the moment. Those words played in his mind as her lips parted beneath his, her tongue tentatively entwining with his.

With practised ease, his fingers found the zip at the

back of her dress and pulled it slowly down her back as she deepened the kiss. He pulled back from her, needing a moment to gather his control again. Her lips were parted and her eyes so full of desire they were almost closed.

He took the straps of her dress and slid them slowly off her shoulders and down her arms. The only movement was the rise and fall of her delectable breasts as she breathed deeply. He let the straps go as his hands lowered past her elbows and the dress slithered to the floor, leaving her in a black bra and panties.

Her eyes had widened and she looked at him, the innocent woman who'd slipped in and out of the limelight back once more. Then she smiled and the innocence was gone, the bold temptress returning as she reached behind and unfastened her bra, letting it fall away to expose full breasts, testing his control further. Then slowly, without breaking eye contact, she pulled her panties lower, wriggling with ease out of the black lace. Finally she stood and looked at him, a challenge in her mischievous smile. Was she daring him to resist her or daring him to make her his for tonight?

'You are even more beautiful now… I want to taste every part of you.' Just saying those words made his pulse leap with heated desire, but when she stepped towards him, her naked body highlighted by the pale light from outside, it was almost too much.

'I want you to.' She reached up and stroked the backs of her fingers over his stubble. It was such an erotic sensation he was glad he was still fully clothed, otherwise he would have pushed her back on the bed and plunged into her; all thought of making the pleasure last would have gone.

He caught her wrist, putting a stop to her caress before it pushed him over the edge. She looked up at him and for a second he thought he saw shock, but she recovered before he could analyse it, pressing her naked body against him wickedly. He let her wrist go and trailed his fingers down her arm and then to her breast, circling the tight bud of her nipple. She wasn't the only one who could be so wickedly teasing.

'And so I shall,' he said and lowered his head to tease her nipple with his tongue. She pushed her hands into his hair as he moved to her other breast to begin the torment again. Then he dropped to his knees and kissed down her stomach, holding her hips tightly as a spike of lust threatened his control. Gently he moved lower, teasing at the dark curls as she gasped her pleasure and gripped her hands tightly in his hair.

'I never knew,' she gasped, writhing beneath his exploration, 'that it could be so nice, so…'

'You make is sound like you've never made love.' He looked up at her, each breath she took making him want her all the more.

'Would that be so bad?' She looked at him and bit at her lower lip. He frowned in confusion, wondering if this was why one minute she was a temptress, the next an innocent. Was she telling him she was inexperienced—or even a virgin? After the moments they'd just shared, and her boldness, could that really be true?

'Why do you ask?'

'It's just that I've never…I'm a…' She blushed, unable to finish the sentence, the temptress gone.

'You are a virgin?' Shock rocked through him, followed by something else. She'd never made love and was choosing him to be her first lover.

'Yes,' she whispered and looked down at him, her eyes full of longing. 'And I want you to be the man who shows me what desire and passion is like.'

He stood up and took her hands in his, looking at her as she stood naked before him, uncertainty all over her beautiful face. He shouldn't want her, shouldn't want to be the man who showed her the pleasures of sex for the first time, but an overwhelming need to be that man flowed through him, making him want her more, testing his control beyond endurance.

'It wouldn't change anything, Emma.' He wanted her to be sure, wanted her to know that after this there wasn't anything else. 'If we have sex it will still be just tonight. I don't want a relationship. I don't intend to settle down any time soon.'

She pressed her palm against his face, her fingers running over the stubble, unleashing the same wild desire as before. 'I want nothing more than this moment in time.'

He pulled her to him, enjoying her soft skin beneath his hands and the feel of her nakedness against his clothed body. He kissed her gently, determined to make this as special as possible—for both of them.

In one swift movement he swept her up in his arms and carried her to the large bed he'd spent the last two nights alone in. As he placed her on the soft covers, he allowed his fingers to trail over her, his gaze fixed firmly on hers.

He stood before her and pulled off his clothes, enjoying the way she watched, her eyes widening when he stood before her naked and aroused. He picked up his wallet from the bedside table and pulled out the all-important foil packet. 'I assume this is the only contraception we have between us?'

The impish smile which had been on her face as she'd watched him divest himself of his clothes slipped away as he rolled the condom on. 'It is, yes.'

He moved on to the bed, bracing his arms on either side of her head, his body tantalisingly close to her as he teased her with a kiss. 'Now that we've sorted that out, we can get back to the important issue of pleasure.'

She wrapped her arms around his neck, pulling him to her, and he had to fight hard to stop himself covering that delicious body with his and thrusting into her. As she stroked her fingers down his back, returning his kiss with ever more passion, he knew he couldn't hold out much longer and he moved on top of her. She wrapped her legs around him; if he hadn't known she was a virgin, he'd never have considered it possible, as she rocked her hips teasing him mercilessly.

His control snapped and all he could think about was making her his. She gasped out and dug her fingernails into his back as he took possession of her, sliding in as gently as his burning need for her allowed. She opened her eyes and looked up at him as he moved within her.

'Nikolai...' She whispered his name and moved her hips with him, encouraging him to deepen that possession and pushing him over the edge.

He reached that edge, trying to hang on, trying to take her with him, and when she met him there he finally let go, collapsing afterwards into her embrace, their breathing hard and fast.

CHAPTER FOUR

IT WAS STILL dark when Emma awoke, her body humming from the exquisite pleasure of making love with Nikolai. Movement caught her attention and she looked towards the window where the soft light of dawn was starting to creep around the blinds. Nikolai stood looking out through the blinds, his body partially in shadow and every sculpted muscle of his torso highlighted like a black-and-white photo. He'd pulled on a pair of jeans and in her mind Emma filed the image away as if she'd pressed the button on her camera and taken it.

His forehead was close to the blinds as he stood looking out. He was completely lost in thought and didn't hear the soft rustle of the bedclothes as she sat up. His jaw was tense and his brow furrowed into a frown. What was he thinking? Was he angry that she wasn't the experienced seductress she'd tried so hard to be? Had their one night been disappointing for him?

'Is it still snowing?' she asked as she propped herself up on her elbow, needing to say something to break the heavy silence around them. She hoped it was snowing too much for them to do what he'd planned today and, if it was, would he come back to bed?

She'd never expected to find what she had discovered last night in his arms, that completeness, as if they belonged together. The romantic inside her that she always tried hard to supress wanted more, so much more, but the ever-present realist that life had made her pushed those silly notions aside. Once she left Vladimir, there could be no more. This was just a fling for him, a way to amuse himself on a cold snowy night. It could even be a way to distract her from what she'd come here to do. That thought slipped uncomfortably over her but she refused to give it any importance; after all hadn't there been an undeniable spark of attraction between them since the moment she'd arrived?

Nikolai continued to look out at the snow, as if he hadn't heard her, and just when she thought she might have to ask again he turned and looked at her, lines of worry creasing his brow. 'It is.'

The roughness of his voice made her swallow hard against the disappointment which rushed through her. What had she expected? A declaration of undying love because she'd given him her virginity? Even she knew better than that!

'Will it stop us meeting your grandmother?' She tried hard to keep her voice soft and calm, as if discussing the weather with the man she'd just had the most wonderful sex with was as normal as the snow falling over the Russian landscape in winter.

He turned to look at her, so slowly she wondered if she'd said something really wrong. With casual ease he hooked his thumb in the belt loop of his jeans and fixed her with a deep and penetrating gaze, and the unmistakable stamp of suspicion was on his handsome face.

'Would that be a problem?'

It should be but Emma realised with shock that it

wouldn't be, not if she could stay cocooned here with Nikolai and lose herself in a moment she hadn't expected at all. A moment which had unlocked a passionate woman within her she'd never known existed, a woman she wanted to be again before the coldness of daybreak brought reality back.

'No,' she whispered softly. 'Let's not think of anything else until daylight.'

Her words lifted the tension which had folded around them, but as he stepped towards her, every muscle highlighted for her pleasure by the growing light from outside, that tension was replaced with something far more powerful.

'Looking at you right now, that is exactly what I want to do.'

Emma pulled aside the tousled sheets, inviting him back into bed, and as he pulled off his jeans and slipped in beside her she was in no doubt what he wanted to do. Heat uncoiled deep within her, lighting the flame of desire once more. Never in her wildest dreams had she expected to find this when she'd boarded the plane for Moscow and she knew that it would change her life for ever.

'I want to be yours til morning breaks,' she said as she moved against the heat of his body, relishing the strength of his arms around her as he pressed her into the bed, covering her body with his, passion exploding like fireworks around them.

'Until daylight,' he said as he kissed her lips, then made a blazing trail down her throat. 'You will be mine, Emma.'

Nikolai felt his control slip away as he pushed the reality of the world aside and kissed Emma. How could she make him feel like this—so lost unless he was holding her, kissing her, as if she truly was his? Her hands moved over his body and her warm skin pressed close against his and all he could think was that she was his, totally his.

The fire of desire ripped through him as her lips claimed his, demanding so much and giving even more. It was so wild, so intense, all he could think about was making her his. Nothing else mattered but that. All he wanted was to be deep inside her.

'Nikolai!' She gasped his name and arched herself up to meet him as he claimed her once more, a powerful urge almost totally consuming him. 'Don't forget...'

A curse flew from him as he pulled back from her and the release which threatened to come far too quickly. How could one woman obliterate his control? Undo him so completely? Feeling like a fumbling teenager, he dealt with the contraception as she looked up at him, desire-darkened eyes holding his.

'This time there is nothing to stop us.' His words were smothered as her lips claimed his and her body welcomed him, taking him deep within her.

An explosion of heated emotions erupted, making him shudder as his release came hard and fast. He kissed Emma, binding them ever closer as the same wave he was riding crashed over her. The sea of desire left him swirling in exhaustion and, as her hold on him turned to a soft caress of his back, he allowed himself to slip under, to give in to the pleasure of sleeping in a woman's arms in a way he'd never done before.

When he woke several hours later, Emma's body warm against his, he didn't want to move, didn't want to give up the moment. Never before had he allowed

emotion into the bedroom. For him it had always been
about lust and acting upon an attraction. He'd thought
it would be the same with Emma when he'd taken her
to his room, but the moment he'd taken her virginity,
had become her only lover, something had changed.

Gently he kissed her hair as she lay against his chest.
Immediately she lifted her head and looked at him, a
shy smile on her face. 'You could always just tell me
about your family and then we can stay here all day
instead of going to see your grandmother.'

His mood was lighter than it had ever been and he
stroked his hands through the softness of her hair. 'If I
tell you too much, I will have to keep you here for ever.'

'Promises, promises.' She laughed, a soft, sexy
laugh which pushed him further from reality.

'You know the basics,' he said as she kissed his
chest, forcing him to close his eyes. 'I grew up in Russia and when my father died my mother and I left for
New York.'

'That must have been tough.' Her slender fingers
traced across his chest, easing the pain of the memories, the pain of telling them.

'My mother had help from a business acquaintance
of my father's and, several years later, she married
him.' The surprised rise of her brows made him think
more deeply and the hum of passion dimmed.

'Did you mind? That she married again, I mean,
replaced your father?' If there was one question sure
to kill the desire which had rampaged through him, it
was that one.

'I didn't mourn my father.' The pain from his childhood made his voice a harsh growl and Emma pulled
away from him to look up into his face. Could she

sense the tension in him just thinking about how he'd been conceived, that he had been the product of a violent rape?

'What happened?' There wasn't any disgust in her voice for his open admission, no judgement in those two words at all. Had she too known childhood heartache? Did she recognise it within him?

'It was not a happy marriage and one my grandmother, Marya Petrushov, very much wanted to continue. She made things difficult for my mother, prolonged the unhappiness.' He skirted around the truth, trying to explain without giving her any more of the sorry secret than she needed to know. She could even be storing away the information right now to put it in her damned article. He pulled away from her, broke the contact. It was the only way to be able to think straight.

'Is that why you have been distracting me from meeting her?' The bold question didn't match the soft innocence of the image she created naked in his bed and he fought hard against the urge to abandon this conversation and use the language of desire and passion. Her next words killed that thought, so instantly his body froze. 'I need the story, Nikolai, all of it. I have a job to do.'

How could she look so deliciously sexy when her words were like hail thrashing his naked body? Had he fallen for the oldest trick in the book? Had she acted innocent to ensure he took her to his bed and he was now spoiling her plans? Worse than that, had she bargained her virginity just to get the story she needed? He shouldn't be telling her the intimate secrets of his family, not when she could portray a family ripped apart by greed and power as it had risen to new heights of wealth.

It was precisely what had happened. His mother must have been an easy target for a power-hungry man whose own family had come from nothing. Bile rose in his throat at the thought of his father's mother selling the story. Did she expect it to keep her comfortable in her final years? Was she planning even now to blackmail him? It damn well wouldn't happen if he had anything to do with it.

'You'll get your story,' he growled as he stood up and stepped away from her, away from the temptation of her silky, soft skin. She was as devious as his grandmother. She'd only slept with him to get what she wanted. She'd crossed the barriers he'd long ago erected and had exposed his emotions to the light of a new day and, with it, the pain of who he was. 'But not now. Not until I know if there are consequences from your underhanded way of interviewing me.'

'Nikolai!' she gasped and reached out, the sheet slipping, giving a tantalising view of her breasts. The fact that it turned him on, sending lust hurtling through him faster than anything he'd known, disgusted him.

He turned his back on her, not trusting himself to leave her alone, and savagely pulled on the remainder of his clothes. He'd been a fool. He'd thought he'd glimpsed what life could be like if his past wasn't a permanent shadow hanging over him.

'You need to leave.' He turned to look at her, allowing the anger to sluice over him and wash away the lingering desire. She was as deceitful and scheming as his grandmother and he wouldn't allow her to expose the truth and hurt his mother. She'd suffered enough shame.

* * *

Emma blinked and recoiled at the change in Nikolai. Where had the tender lover gone? Anger rushed from him like a fierce tide crashing onto the rocky shore.

'No, we need to talk.'

'I'm not saying anything else to you.' He spat the words back at her, the dim light of the room only making his anger even clearer. What had she done to make him suddenly hate her? The questions had only been part of her job and she'd never hidden that from him.

He stepped closer to her and she became aware of her nakedness again, clutching the covers against her once more. From the hard expression set on his face, she knew their moment of intimacy was over. The connection between them they'd shared last night had been severed as surely as if he'd cut it.

He reached into his jacket pocket and seconds later tossed a business card onto the bed. 'If you want to pry into my life any more, you can contact me on that number.'

Ice shuttered around her heart, freezing the new emotions she'd allowed herself to have for this man. How had she been stupid enough to believe he was different, that like her he was hurting because of the past? She'd thought that made what they'd shared last night more intense, more powerful.

She took the card, holding it as if it might explode at any second. The bold black print in which *Nikolai Cunningham* was written was as hard as the man who stood angrily before her.

'One last thing,' she said before she could think better of it. 'Why do you no longer use your family name, Petrushov?' It was the one thing which had puzzled her since she'd been given the assignment on the Petrushov family and had been told the only grandson would meet her in Vladimir.

'I have no wish to use my father's name.' The harshness in his tone made his hatred and anger palpable. It filled the room and invaded every corner. 'And, so that you have your information correct when you use my family's sordid past to further your career, I changed my name to that of my stepfather when I was sixteen.'

'I'm not going to use any of what you've just told me, Nikolai. What kind of woman do you think I am?' She couldn't keep the shock from her voice or the hurt from cutting deep into her. Did he really think that badly of her?

'You are obviously the kind of woman who will trade her virginity to climb a career ladder.' The hardened growl of his accusation sliced painfully into her, sullying the memories of giving herself to him so completely last night.

'No,' she gasped, wishing she was wearing something so that she could go to him. How could he think that of her? 'It wasn't like that at all.'

He gave her one last frosty glare and then strode to the door. 'Now you have all you need to ruin mine and my mother's reputations, you can get the hell out of my life.'

The door slammed behind him and she was left, blinking in shock. Only hours ago they had been locked in the arms of passion. Nothing else had existed. A tear slid down her face as she threw back the covers and picked up the black dress from the floor, trying not to remember the burn of desire she'd had for him as it had slipped off her body last night. Angrily she pulled it on, not caring about her underwear. All she wanted was to get along the hotel corridor to the sanctuary of her room and lock herself in until her heart stopped breaking.

Still reeling from the shock of Nikolai walking out on her, she shut the door of her own room and made for the shower, needing the warmth of the water to soothe her. After standing there for what felt like hours, Emma finally turned the water off and wrapped herself in a towel, trying not to dwell on the accusations Nikolai had hurled at her. Did he really think she'd all but sold herself just to get information out of him?

Her phone buzzed on the cabinet next to her bed. Instantly she was on alert. What if it was Nikolai? With a slight tremor in her hands she reached for it and, as she looked at the text from her sister, she knew the day was going from bad to worse. Even with the limited words of the text Emma could sense Jess's distress, but it was the final word which really propelled her into motion:

I need you, Em, come now. Please.

Finally the overnight train arrived in Perm and Emma made her way straight to the ballet school. The tearful conversation she'd had with Jess during that long journey was still fresh in her mind, which at least had given her little time to think of the night spent with Nikolai and how it had drastically changed things, how he'd rejected her.

'I've missed you so much, Em,' Jess said, dragging her mind back from thoughts of the tall, dark-haired Russian who had lured the woman she'd always wanted to be out of the shadows.

'Is that what this is all about?' Emma kept her tone light but, for the first time ever, felt constrained by looking after her sister. If she hadn't had to rush and get a train ticket sorted, she might have seen Nikolai again. She'd at least wanted to try and explain, especially after the intimacies they'd shared. All she knew was that he'd checked out.

'You've been so far away and it's been months since I've seen you. I guess I couldn't stand the thought of you being so close.'

'Not exactly close.' Emma forced herself to forget her problems and laughed, pulling her sister into a hug, unable to be irritated by the intrusion into her life at the worst possible moment. 'It was a very long train journey from Vladimir. It took me all night.'

'I hope I didn't spoil anything for you,' said Jess, looking a little subdued suddenly, and Emma wondered if there was more to this.

'There wasn't anything to spoil.' Nikolai had already done that, accusing her of all but seducing the story out of him. Well, she'd show him. Nothing he'd said to her in his room would find its way into her article, although it did go some way to explaining his shock at seeing his family home again.

'That's all right, then,' began Jess, sounding brighter already. 'I only have the rest of today off class, then it's back to it.'

'Then we need to do something really good.'

Later that night, lying alone in a different hotel room, having spent the entire day with Jess, Emma's doubts crept back in. She remembered Nikolai standing at the window, the light shadowing his body, and wished she could turn back time. The only thing she wanted to change was the doubt on his face, the worry in his eyes.

Several times this evening she'd wanted to call him, wanted to reassure him that all he'd told her about his childhood would stay with her. She knew what it was to feel unloved and out of place. Was that why he'd gone to great lengths to put off the meeting with his grandmother? Was there another side to the story? Had she been fooled by his heart-wrenching admission of his past?

She had spent time on the train drafting out what she wanted to write and none of it would include the torture of the man who'd shown her what being loved could be like, even for a few brief hours. If she told him that, would he believe her? She relived the moment he'd accused her of seducing him for information and knew he would never believe her.

Tomorrow she would be taking the train back to Moscow and from there a flight home to London. There wouldn't be an opportunity to see him; maybe fate was trying to tell her that what she'd shared with Nikolai that night was nothing more than a moment out of time.

CHAPTER FIVE

NIKOLAI STOOD AT a window of his apartment, looking at, but not seeing, Central Park bathed in spring
sunshine. All he could think about was Emma. It had
been almost two months since that night but the only
communication had been from *World in Photographs*,
thanking him, although he was yet to see a copy of
what Emma had submitted. That, however, was the
least of his worries.

He'd replayed their night together many times in his
mind and, once the anger that she'd slept with him to
get her story had cooled, a new worry grew from an
inkling of doubt. The more he thought of it, the more
his gut was telling him they might have had an acci-
dent after she'd coaxed him back to bed…the hurried
and last-minute use of the condom playing heavily on
his mind.

As he stood looking out of the window early that
morning, he kept telling himself that no news from
Emma was good, that their night of passion hadn't
had the consequences he'd dreaded despite the ever-
increasing doubt in his mind.

It had been many weeks since he'd marched from
the hotel room and braced the snow to cool his mind

and body with a walk. When he'd returned to the room, Emma had gone, and that had told him all he needed to know: he'd been used. The only good thing to come out of the night was that he hadn't had to face his grandmother.

Angry that he'd put himself in such a position, he'd checked out and headed straight back to New York, but he hadn't stopped thinking about Emma. She had haunted his every waking hour and made sleep almost impossible. Something had happened to him that night, maybe even from the first moment he'd met her. She had changed him, made him think of things he couldn't have.

He'd done what he always did where emotions were concerned and avoided them. He still couldn't believe he'd almost told her all about his childhood. Those hours spent in bed with her must have muddled his mind. It should have just been a night of passion to divert her from the horrible truth of who he really was, but he'd almost told her exactly what he'd wanted to remain a secret.

He'd gone to Vladimir and confronted the ghosts of his past in order to save his mother the heartache of seeing her story all over the newspapers, exactly where it would end up once it was published by *World in Photographs*. What he'd found in Vladimir with Emma was something different.

Yes, he had been guilty of wanting to distract her from the truth, but somewhere along the way things had changed. She'd reached into the cold darkness of his heart and unlocked emotions he'd thought impossible to feel. Even the woman he'd once proposed to had failed to do that, but Emma had been different.

'What the hell were you thinking?' He snarled angrily at himself. One of the only times he'd let a woman close and she'd cheated him, used him for her own gain. He'd even begun to question if Emma was as innocent as she'd claimed. Had that too been part of the plan—to make him think he was the first man she'd ever slept with—in order to get the real story?

The fact that she'd run out on him only added fuel to the fire. Not only that, there hadn't been a word from her since that night when he'd stood there and looked at her, clutching the sheet against her. He'd had had to fight hard not to pull the damn thing from her and get back into bed. His body had been on fire with need for her and, despite having spent all night having sex, he'd allowed the anger he felt at himself for being used to have precedence. It had been a far more reliable emotion to feel, one which had propelled him from the hotel room without a backward glance.

Driven by that anger, he'd left quickly, tossing her a card as an afterthought. Or was it because even then, deep down, he knew things might have gone wrong? If their night together did have consequences, then he knew he would face up to them and be the father he'd always longed for in place of the cruel man who had filled his childhood with fear.

The fact that he knew what he would do didn't make Emma's silence any easier. It irritated him. Did it mean she wasn't pregnant? That the condom failure about which he'd since convinced himself hadn't had any drastic consequences?

He looked at his watch. Ten in the morning here meant late afternoon in London. He could ring her. It would be easy enough to get her number through *World in Photographs*, but what would he say?

He'd replayed again the scene in the hotel room early that morning. He'd woken to find her sleeping soundly next to him and had watched her for a while. Then, as the ghosts of the past had crowded in, he'd had to get up. For what had felt like hours, he'd stood watching the dark and empty street outside the window as if it held the answer or truth about his past.

Emma had stirred, her glorious naked body doing things to his, and he'd had to hold on to his self-control, wanting only to lose himself in her once more instead of facing the truth. That truth was not only the fact that she'd lured him to tell her things he'd wanted to keep well hidden.

His phone bleeped, alerting him to a text, and he ignored it, wanting to focus on what to do next. Call her? Go to London and demand to see her? He'd have to find out where she lived.

Insistently the alert sounded again and he swore in Russian, something he hadn't done for a long time before he'd returned to Vladimir. When he picked up the phone and read the text, he almost dropped it as if it were red-hot.

We need to meet. I'm in New York. E

He inhaled deeply. This could only mean one thing—the very worst thing. There was no way she'd come here, all the way to New York, to tell him the article had been accepted, or show him a copy. An email would be sufficient for that. She needed to talk. His suspicions about their night together must be right—she was pregnant with his child—and that changed everything.

He pressed his thumb and finger against his eyelids in an effort to think, but there was only one answer. The same answer that had come up each and every time he'd thought of Emma and that night together. The very thing he'd never wanted to happen. He just knew it: he'd fathered a child. Now he had to face his fears from childhood and prove to himself he wasn't his father's son…that he could bring up his child with love and kindness. The very idea terrified him.

Emma was late. She'd arrived at Central Park early and wandered around taking photographs until midday, the time specified by Nikolai in his reply to her text. She'd tried to put her reason for being in New York to the back of her mind and had almost succeeded when she had become engrossed in taking shots of the park. Now the impending meeting with him loomed large but she couldn't recall which way she'd come. She looked around at the tall buildings surrounding the park and wondered if she'd be able to find her way back out. She was tired from travelling and early pregnancy was not being so kind to her. Panic rose up. She'd have to ask someone for directions.

'Excuse me, is it this way to The Boathouse?' she asked a mother pushing a pram, trying hard not to look down at the child. It would be too much like looking into her future and she wondered how she was ever going to cope on her own. Nikolai had made it more than clear that what they'd shared was just one night. He'd been so adamant about it she began to question her reasons for telling him personally. It would have been much easier just to call him, tell him he was going to be a father. It was her conscience and knowing what it felt like to be rejected by her father that had made her come.

All through the flight one question kept going round in her head: would her own father have wanted to be part of her life if he'd been given the choice like this? The day she'd first met him, after she'd begged her mother to tell her who he was, rushed back at her, as did his icy words. *It's too late. I don't need or want you in my life.*

'Keep walking and you'll see it.' The mother's voice dragged her back to the present. She smiled at Emma before heading on in the other direction. With unease in her heart Emma watched her walk out of sight. That would be her by the end of the year, but she was certain she wouldn't be here in New York, looking happy with life.

She shook the thought away and looked at her watch again. She was fifteen minutes late. Would Nikolai still be there? With the pain of her father's rejection stinging her heart, the need to see Nikolai, to tell him and give him the chance to be part of his child's life, deepened. She quickened her step but within a few strides they faltered. He was standing where the path turned through the trees and, despite the distance, she knew it was him, as if her body had registered his, known he was close.

She could also tell from his stance that he was not happy about being kept waiting. She breathed in deeply, then let the breath out in a bid to calm her nerves and quell the nausea which threatened to rear its head yet again. Within days of returning to London she had woken each morning feeling ill and had at first put it down to all that had happened between her and Nikolai. After all, losing your virginity to a man, only to have him walk out in anger, was not the best experience in the world. Not once had she considered there was a lasting legacy of that night.

As days had turned into a week, she'd known she couldn't ignore the encroaching doubt any longer and had purchased a pregnancy test. The fact that it had taken several more days before she'd been brave enough to use it only served to increase the weight of dread which filled her from the moment she woke each day. When she'd finally had enough courage to use the test, her worry had increased as the ominous blue lines appeared, confirming that the hours spent with Nikolai had most definitely had consequences— for her, at least.

She walked towards him now and with purpose pushed those long, lonely weeks aside in her mind, focusing instead on what had to be done. She kept her chin lifted and her eyes on him all the time. Anything else would be to show uncertainty or, at worst, fear. She wasn't scared of her future any more and, although it was going to be a struggle, she was looking forward to giving her child all she'd never had. What she did fear was telling Nikolai and, from the rigid set of his shoulders, she'd been right to fear this moment.

He made no move towards her, not even one step, and she hated him for doing that. He could have made the moment easier for her. Was he punishing her for contacting him? For making their one night something more? Each step she took must have shown her anxiety a little bit more. She should have called him as soon as she'd taken the pregnancy test, but shock had set in. She hadn't even been ready to accept it herself, let alone blithely call him up and tell him their one night had created a child which would join them for ever.

How did you tell a man who'd made it blatantly clear he didn't want any kind of commitment that he was a father? Her mother obviously hadn't done it right, but could she? She was about to find out.

As she drew level with him, the inky black of his eyes held accusation, just as they had done in the hotel room the morning after they'd spent the night together, the night she'd lost her virginity to him. The firm line of his lips looked harder than they had that morning but she refused to be intimidated, just as she refused to acknowledge the hum of attraction rushing through her just from seeing him, being near him again.

She couldn't still want him; she just couldn't.

'You are late.' He snapped the words out and stood his ground. Six foot plus of brooding male towered over her, sending her heartbeat racing in a way that had nothing to do with nerves at what she had to say. She hated the way she still wanted him, her body in complete denial of the numbness in her mind. How could she still want a man who'd rejected her so coldly after she'd given him her most precious gift?

'I couldn't find my way through the park...' she began, trying to instil firmness into her voice, but he cruelly cut her off.

'Why are you here, Emma?' The hard glint in his eye sparked with anger but she wouldn't allow him to make her feel like a guilty child. What right did he have to stand there and dictate to her what she should have done and when? He was the one who'd strode from the hotel room in Vladimir without a word to her after tossing her his card. He was the one who hadn't handled this right.

'Did you think throwing a business card onto the bed was a nice way to end our night together?' Her words spiked the spring air around them, but he didn't flinch. His handsome face didn't show a single trace of any other emotion beyond controlled annoyance. This just prodded at her anger, firing her up. 'We need to talk, Nikolai. That's why I'm here.'

'About the consequences of our night together?' He'd guessed. Guilt and shock mixed together and she looked up at him, not yet able to say anything.

He moved towards her, dominating the spring air around them, and while she heard people walking past she couldn't do anything other than focus on him. If she looked away, even for just a second, all her strength would slip away.

'By consequences, you mean pregnancy.' Finally she found her voice. Her sharp words didn't make a dent in his assured superiority, but saying them aloud filled her with panic.

'Yes, exactly that. I assume you haven't flown halfway around the world to tell me about the article. You're here to tell me you are expecting my child.' He looked straight into her eyes, the fierce question in them mixing with accusation. Was he blaming her?

Emma looked away from the impenetrable hardness in his eyes and wished it could be different, but no amount of wishing was going to change those two bold lines on the pregnancy test she'd finally had the courage to use. She was pregnant with Nikolai's child and, judging by his response to her arrival in New

York, he did not like that particular revelation. It didn't matter what he said now, she had to face the truth: she was very much alone.

She let out a soft breath, trying to come to terms with what she'd known all along, finally accepting why she'd wanted to tell him in person. She'd had the faint hope that he would come around to the idea, be different from her father. But no. If the fierce glint in his cold black eyes was anything to go by, he didn't want to be a father at any price. She would do this herself. She didn't need him—or anyone. 'Your powers of deduction are enviable, Nikolai. Yes, I'm pregnant.'

Nikolai braced himself against the worst possible news he could ever be told. He couldn't be a father, not when the example he'd seen of fatherly love still haunted his dreams, turning them into nightmares if he allowed it.

He looked at Emma, the one woman who'd captured a part of his heart. Ever since she'd left he'd tried to tell himself it was because he'd shared a bit of himself with her, shared secrets he hadn't wanted anyone to know. He still couldn't comprehend why he'd done that when she'd had the power to make it completely public, shatter his mother's peaceful life and destroy his hard-won business reputation. He was thankful he'd stopped at the unhappy marriage bit, glad he hadn't told her the full horror of how that marriage had come about. How he'd come about. If she knew the truth she wouldn't want him to have anything to do with his child, of that he was sure. But, although he had shared some secrets, he would now do anything he could to ensure those she didn't know about stayed hidden away.

'And did you leave Vladimir in such a hurry because

you thought you'd discovered extra facts for the story? Perhaps you rushed off to get it in?'

The anger he'd felt when he'd realised she'd left not only his room and the hotel but Vladimir itself still coursed through him. He'd had to leave her in the hotel room because of the desire coursing through him. He'd needed the cool air to dull the heavy lust she evoked in him with every look. He hadn't intended it to be the last time he saw her. He'd intended to go back and talk calmly with her, hear what she would want if the worst had indeed happened.

'No.' She looked down, as he quickly realised she always did when confronted with something difficult, as if she too was hiding from past hurt—or was it guilt for throwing herself at him just to get a few snippets of inside information? When she looked back up at him, her eyes were shining with threatening tears. 'I had a call from my sister and left soon after you did.'

'A call from your sister? So, after we'd worked together on the article, you thought spending time with her was more important?' Her face paled at his icy tone and a rush of guilt sliced briefly through him before he pushed it aside. She'd run out on him to play happy families with her sister.

'She was upset.' Emma looked up at him as if imploring him to understand. 'We only have each other. I left her to go back to Moscow but there wasn't any time to contact you again. It's not as if I knew there were such consequences then.'

'When did you first discover these consequences?' The fact that she must have known for at least a few weeks infuriated him more than the fact that she'd used him, seduced him into taking her to bed and spilling secrets.

'I've only fairly recently had it confirmed...' He moved even closer to her, dominating the very air she breathed and halting her words in mid-flow.

'And now we have to deal with it.' His attention was caught by passers-by, happy in the spring sunshine when he now had the weight of guilt pressing down on him, all but rooting him to the spot like one of the large trees of the park.

This was his fault. He should have been more careful, more in control, but if he was honest with himself he should never have given in to the attraction in the first place. Not with the woman who had the power to destroy his and his mother's happiness. What the hell had he been thinking? What had happened to his usual self-control? Emma had happened. She'd completely disarmed him, which he strongly suspected had been her intention all along.

'Deal with it?' He heard the panic in her voice and turned his attention back to her, to see she'd paled even more dramatically. She needed to sit down. He did too, but the restaurant would be busy, far too busy to discuss an unplanned pregnancy and the ramifications of such news.

'This way,' he said as he took her arm, ensuring she came with him. He strode towards the edge of the park where he knew the horse-drawn carriages would be waiting for customers. They could talk as they toured the park and, more importantly, she wouldn't be able to run out on him this time. She would have to face their situation, just as he'd had to as he'd gone over this very moment in his mind during recent weeks. In the carriage she would have no choice but to listen to him and accept that his solution was their only option.

'Where are we going?' She pulled back against him as if she was on the verge of bolting again, backing up his reasoning for taking a carriage ride like a tourist.

'Somewhere we can talk. Somewhere you'll have no choice but to sit and hear what I have to say, how we are going to deal with this.' Still she resisted and he turned to face her, sliding his hand down her arm to take her hand in his. As he did so, that fizz of energy filled him once more and he could see her face again, full of desire the night she'd taken his hand in Vladimir. The night they'd conceived a new life. His child. His heir. 'You are not going to slip away so easily this time, Emma, not now you carry my child.'

The determination and bravado slipped from Emma and her body became numb. She was too tired to fight any more, too tired to worry and fret over the future, and Nikolai's suggestion of sitting down seemed the best option. She walked hand in hand with him through the park. To onlookers they would have appeared like any other couple, walking together in the sunshine, but inside dread had begun to fill her, taking over the sizzle of attraction from just being with him again. Exactly how did he intend to deal with it?

'We'll take a ride round the park,' Nikolai said as he stopped beside a horse-drawn carriage and she blinked in shock. Was this just another of his romantic pastimes to distract her? Then the truth of that thought hit her. That was exactly what he'd done in Vladimir. He'd gone out of his way to distract her and had even successfully managed to keep her from meeting his grandmother.

He'd been keeping her from knowing more about his family and, thinking back to the moment they'd met, she could see he'd been evasive about the story of rags to riches she was supposed to cover. Why, then, had he said the things he had that morning after they'd made love, giving her a deeper insight into the childhood which had shaped the man he now was?

She still couldn't shake off the sensation that he'd wanted to say more but had guarded against it. Had he really believed she would put all those details in the article? She'd just wanted to create a fairy-tale story to go with the amazing photographs she'd taken, but he'd accused her of manipulating everything to get what she wanted.

'Trying to make me all soft again, are you?' The words were out before she had time to think of the implications. If she'd been clever she would have never let him know she'd guessed his motives.

'There is nothing to go soft about. I need to know exactly what you submitted to *World in Photographs* about my family and then we can discuss what happens next.' He opened the door of the carriage and, with a flourish of manners she knew he was displaying for the purpose of getting what he wanted, waited for her to climb in.

Emma looked from his eyes to the park around her and beyond that to the tall buildings of New York, a place she'd never been to before. What choice did she have? She was alone in a city she didn't know and pregnant with this man's baby.

'I have my laptop at the hotel, I can show you exactly what will be in it.' The painful knowledge that he'd rather discuss an article she'd written than talk about their baby cut into her. She sat in the seat, wishing she hadn't got in the carriage. The idea of playing the tourist with him again brought back heated memories of that first kiss in the sleigh.

'Did you use anything to do with what we talked about after our night together?' His voice was deep and firm, quashing those memories instantly as he snapped out the question.

'No,' she said and looked directly at him, into the depths of eyes that were shuttered, keeping her out and his thoughts locked away. 'I never wanted to pry into your family history, more to show an insight into your country. It was what Richard had suggested in the first place.'

'Who is Richard?'

'A photographer I met while on my course. He works for *World in Photographs* and helped me get the contract to write the article about your family.' She had nothing to hide, so why shouldn't she tell him about how she'd got the contract in the first place? If he chose to see it in the wrong light, that was his problem.

'What do you owe this Richard for getting you the contract?' The sharpness of his voice made her look at him quickly, but the coldness of his eyes was almost as bitter as the wind in Vladimir had been.

'Nothing. All I wanted was to take the best photographs I could and showcase your country, weaving in some of your family stories, which I have achieved without adding in anything you told me in your hotel room.'

'Then for now I trust you,' he said as the carriage

pulled away, the sudden movement making her grab the seat to steady herself. Instantly his hands reached out to hold her and from the seat opposite she felt that heated attraction connect them once more. Their eyes met; she looked into the inky blackness and swallowed as she saw the glint of steely hardness had given way to something more dangerous—desire. She couldn't allow herself to fall for his seductive charms again; she just needed to deal with the consequences of their night together and leave before she fell even further and deeper for him. Irritated by the direction of her thoughts, she pulled away and sat back in the carriage seat, desperate to avoid his scrutiny.

If he didn't trust her with his secrets then why had he told them to her? Had that also been a way of manipulating her to do what he wanted, make her think what he wanted her to think? It had not occurred to her until now that what he'd said might not have been the complete truth.

'I wouldn't lie to you, Nikolai,' she said defensively, and looked away from the dark eyes, feigning an interest in the tall buildings clearly visible above the newly green trees of the park. Maybe if she took a few shots from the carriage he'd see she was as unaffected by him as he appeared to be by her.

The lens of the camera clicked but she had no idea what she'd taken. Concentration was impossible with his dominating presence opposite her and the looming discussion of their baby. She turned the camera off and looked at him to see he'd been watching every move she'd made.

'We need to talk about our predicament.' Still his

dark eyes watched her, assessing her reaction to his words.

'Predicament?' she snapped, giving him her full attention. 'Is that what this baby is to you? A predicament? Something else you have to deal with? Just what do you suggest, Nikolai?'

'It is a predicament,' he said calmly, far too calmly, and it unnerved her. What was coming next? 'One I never wanted but one which now means we must get married.'

'Married?' she said loudly, then looked around to see if anyone had heard her. From the satisfied expression on Nikolai's face, that was exactly the reaction he had been hoping for. 'We can't get married.'

'Give me one good reason why not.' He sat back and regarded her sternly.

'We live on different continents to start with.' She grasped at the first thing she could think of and, from the amused look which crossed his face, he knew it. Why did he have to look so handsome, so incredibly sexy? And why was she still so attracted to him?

'That can easily be sorted. I have a home in London if New York isn't to your liking.' His instant response unsettled her. Had he worked it all out already?

'It's not easy for me,' she said quickly, angry that everything seemed so cut and dried with him. 'I have my sister to consider and my job. I've only just been offered a job with *World in Photographs*.'

'Your sister is in Perm for the next few years and your job could be done from anywhere, could it not?' The tone of his voice confirmed her suspicion of moments ago. He did have it all worked out—completely to suit him.

None of what he was suggesting suited her. She needed to be in London, especially now she had a job with *World in Photographs*, a job she needed for financial security, now more than ever. Not only did she have Jess to help through the ballet school, she had a baby on the way, but deep down it was more than that. His so-called deal tapped into her deepest insecurities after growing up knowing that out there in the world was her father, a man who didn't want to know her.

Overwhelmed by the panic of her situation, she glared at Nikolai. 'I need to be in London if I'm to keep the job as a photographer with *World in Photographs* and I need that job to support Jess.'

'That is easily sorted.'

She frowned, not sure what he was getting at. 'For you, maybe.'

'Jess will have all the financial help she needs to ensure she can—what was it you said in Vladimir?— chase her dream.' The look on his handsome face was as severe as she'd ever seen it, not a hint of pleasure from the generous gift he'd just offered. Or was it a gift? Was it not dangling temptation in front of her?

No, it was more than that. It was a bribe and all she had to do was marry him. The thought filled her with dread. She'd dreamed of the day a man would propose to her, dreamed of it being a loving and romantic moment. Nikolai was being neither as he sat watching her; even the ride in the carriage couldn't lend a romantic mood to the moment.

'I can't accept that,' she said, still unable to believe what was happening. He was making a deal with her for their child: marry him and she, the baby and Jess would be financially secure. It hurt that she had very little chance of ever matching that, especially now her pregnancy would affect her ability to work. If she turned him down, said no, as instinct was urging her to do, she would be turning down so much more than just a marriage proposal. She would be saying no to something which would help Jess but, more importantly, give her baby what she'd never had: a father.

Turmoil raged inside her as he watched her, the motion of the carriage making her feel slightly ill, and the steady rhythm of the horses' hooves sounding like drums in her head. How could this be happening? How could all this come from one desire-laden moment in time? How could those few blissful hours have such an impact on her life?

'No,' she said again, more firmly. 'I can't accept that.'

For a moment he looked at her and the tension between them intensified, but she refused to look away. She wanted to challenge him, wanted to push him in the same way he was pushing her.

Finally he spoke. 'Just as I will not tolerate being pushed out of my child's life, and the only way to ensure that is marriage.'

He leant forward in the carriage and she looked away, not daring to look into his dark eyes a moment longer. He had touched a raw and open wound. She was here because she'd hoped he'd want something to do with his child, that he wouldn't turn his back on either her or his baby. She'd never expected this from a man who'd declared one night was all he could give. If she turned him down, didn't that make her worse than her mother?

She couldn't help herself and looked deep into his

eyes, seeing what she'd seen that night in Vladimir, and tried to plead with him again. 'But marriage—'

'Is the only option.' He cut across her once more. 'We will be married, Emma. I will not take no for an answer, not now you are carrying my child.'

CHAPTER SIX

THE REST OF the carriage ride had blurred into a shocked haze and now, as she stood in one of New York's most renowned jeweller's, that haze was beginning to lift. She couldn't marry Nikolai. What was she thinking, allowing him to bring her here to buy an engagement ring? It wouldn't change the fact that this wasn't what he wanted. Turmoil erupted inside her. She didn't want to make the same mistakes as her mother, not when she knew what it felt like to be the child whose existence a father denied.

Could she really do this—sacrifice everything to do the right thing by her son or daughter? If she walked away now would her child blame her later, as she blamed her mother for depriving her of a father?

She looked anxiously at the door but had to steel herself against the reaction Nikolai provoked in her as he stood right behind her, so very close she could feel the heat of his body. It reminded her of the night they'd shared in Vladimir. The passion had been so intense, so powerful. Didn't the undeniable attraction count for something?

'Not thinking of running out on me, are you?' The whispered question sent a tremor of awareness down her spine, which deepened as he held the tops of her arms, pulling her back against the latent power of his body.

She shook her head in denial, unable to put a sentence together as his touch scorched through her, reminding her of the passion they'd shared the night their child had been conceived. That thought chilled the fire he'd unwittingly stirred to life just by being near her. She had to remember the cruel way he'd bargained not only with Jess's future, but her past, exploiting the one thing which had been a constant shadow in her life. Because of that, whatever she did, she had to control the desire he evoked within her from just a touch.

'No, you have made it perfectly clear what has to be done.' She turned to face him, wishing she didn't feel the rush of desire which flooded her as she looked into his eyes. They were dark and heavy with passion, just as they had been that night in Vladimir. Would she ever stop seeing images in her mind of him like that? He'd become imprinted there and he invaded every thought. Had it been because he was the only man to have touched her intimately, the only man she'd made love with or simply the worry of facing him to tell him about the baby?

A heaviness settled over her as an ominous clarity finally allowed her to see that night for what it really was. It had just been a seduction, a way to keep her from whatever it was he was hiding, and for him it most definitely hadn't been about making love. For him it would have been purely lust.

'Then I suggest we select the ring that will seal the deal.' His voice sounded firm and in control. Yet again he was manipulating her, forcing her to accept his terms.

Panic filled Emma. This wasn't how she'd envisaged the moment she would get engaged. It had been very much more romantic than this demand that she choose a ring. But what choice did she have now? Not only would he provide the funds for Jess, he would be in his child's life. It was exactly how she'd always envisaged being a mother—supported by the child's father. The only difference was that in her dreams that man had been there for her too—out of love, not duty to his child.

'You're right,' she said calmly, reluctantly acknowledging this was the only way forward.

Further doubts crowded in on her, solidifying the need to accept Nikolai's deal, no matter what she felt. What if she couldn't cope, just as her mother hadn't been able to do? Would her baby be taken from her, as she and Jess had been? That wouldn't happen if she was married to the child's father.

'So, are we agreed?' he asked in a calm voice.

'Yes,' she replied, seeing no other option but this deal he'd given her. 'This is the best way.'

Before she could back out of the marriage she'd agreed to, with a man she'd never expected to see again after he'd left her at the hotel, she gave her full attention to the rings displayed before her. The sparkling stones blurred for a moment and she blinked to try and refocus them, horrified to realise it was tears filling her eyes that were distorting the almost endless display of expensive rings.

Once she'd selected one of the rings and was wearing it the deal would be sealed. She would have accepted his terms. She blinked quickly once more, trying to stop the threatening tears from falling. She couldn't cry. Not yet. She had to be as strong and detached as he was being.

'I think an emerald.' He moved to her side and put his arm around her, his hand holding her waist as he pulled her tighter against his body. 'To match your eyes.'

He'd noticed she had green eyes? That snippet of information shocked her, because it meant he had taken an interest in her beyond the seduction he'd obviously been planning since the ride in the troika. The memory of that day was now tarnished by the reality of the fact that he'd engineered it all—and she'd fallen for it. Had that wonderfully gentle yet powerfully seductive kiss been part of the plan too?

Of course it had and you fell for it.

'How about this one?' she asked, tiredness washing over her, brought on no doubt by the stress of everything, combined with the time difference and pregnancy. All she wanted to do right now was get back to her hotel room and rest, but she held the ring up by the delicate diamond-encrusted band, the emerald sparkling in the bright lights of the store.

'Are you sure you wouldn't prefer one of the larger ones?' He moved away from her and sat in a distinctly antique-looking chair to the side of the table. She tried hard not to look at his long legs as he stretched them out before him. He looked far too relaxed when she was as tense as she'd ever been.

'No,' she said and looked boldly into his eyes, not missing the way his gaze slid down her body before meeting hers. The tingle of awareness was disconcerting and she pushed it aside, determined to be in control of this moment at the very least. 'No, this is much more my style.'

He stood up and came back to her. He took the ring from her, looking at it, then, to her astonishment, took her left hand in his, raising it up. With deliberate slowness he slipped the ring onto her finger and she was amazed to see it was a perfect fit, as if it had been made for her. 'In that case, will you do me the honour of becoming my wife?'

It was the last thing she'd expected him to do after having all but put a deal to her and she stumbled over her words, aware of the store staff watching the exchange. Was this all for their benefit or his? She looked at him, wondering if she'd be able to speak, but finally the words came out in a soft whisper. 'Yes, Nikolai, I will.'

He kept hold of her hand for far too long and she watched as he looked down at the square emerald now sat neatly on her finger. Would he keep his side of this strange bargain? Would he provide the funds for Jess to continue on her chosen course in life and, more importantly, be there for his child?

If he doesn't you only have to walk away; you have nothing to lose by agreeing.

As that rebellious thought rocked through her he stepped closer and lowered his head; she knew, with every nerve in her body, that he was going to kiss her. Right there in the store.

When his lips met hers fire shot through her and her knees weakened and, as her eyes fluttered closed, she forced them open again. He moved slightly and she could see his lips lifting into a smile that was full of self-satisfaction. Then he spoke so softly only she could hear. 'A very sensible answer.'

Nikolai opened the door of the car he'd ordered while he'd completed his purchase for the engagement ring—an item he'd never envisaged buying again. But what choice did he have? He couldn't turn his back on his child. This was his chance to prove to himself he was a better man than his father. His child had not been conceived in the underhand way he himself had been, so didn't that already make him a better man? But it wasn't enough. He needed to prove to himself he was not like his father.

He watched as Emma slid into the back of the car, looking weary, and a pang of guilt briefly touched him. He had nothing to feel guilty about, he reassured himself. Emma was here to secure her and her child's future and, now that he'd also added her sister's into the bargain, she had everything she'd come for—and more.

She would become his fiancée and, as soon as possible, his wife. He wanted this particular deal sealed long before news of their baby broke. He wanted his mother to think he'd found love and happiness. It was all she'd ever wanted for him and now, due to one night when he'd been less than in control, he was able to give her that.

'Where are you staying?' he demanded as he joined her in the back of the car.

'A hotel on West Forty-Seventh Street,' she said without looking at him, provoking that twinge of guilt once more as he gave the driver instructions.

'This is the right thing to do,' he said as he took her hand from where it lay in her lap. She turned to look at him, her sable hair moving invitingly, reminding him of how soft it had been between his fingers.

'What if you meet someone you really want to marry?' The doubt laced in her voice did little to soften the emotions running through him. As far as he was concerned, that would never be an issue. The example of married life his father had set him was one which had stayed with him long after his mother had found happiness. He might have seen her marry for love when he was almost twelve years old but inside he knew he had his father's genes. The way to avoid testing that theory had been to avoid any kind of emotional commitment. By the time he'd become a successful businessman in his own right, he'd also become cold and cynical and knew he would never think of marrying—at least, not for love.

'That won't be an issue. I could, of course, ask the same of you.'

'Oh, I always dreamed of the fairy-tale wedding. You know—big white dress, flower girls and bridesmaids, fancy location and a honeymoon in a tropical paradise.' At first he was taken aback by her soft, wistful voice, but the hard glint in those green eyes warned him it was just a cover-up. He knew all about hiding emotions, only he was better at it than she was; but he'd play the game her way. For now, at least.

'And now?'

'Now?' She pulled her hand free of his and glared up at him, defiance adding to the sparks in her eyes. 'Now I know better.'

'So you won't be looking for love and happy-ever-afters?'

'Never.' That one word was said with so much conviction he didn't doubt it for one minute.

'Then we agree on that too. You see, already we have a good base for our marriage. A child who needs us both and an obvious dislike of anything remotely romantic.'

She looked at him, questions racing across her beautiful face, and all he wanted to do was taste her lips once more. The memory of that kiss in the snow had lingered in his mind for the best part of two months, just as the hours spent making her truly his had filled his dreams night after night. It had been those memories which had made kissing her in the store impossible to resist, that and the smouldering anger, defused by an undeniable attraction in her alluring eyes.

'We're here,' she said quickly, the relief in her voice more than evident.

'I'll come with you whilst you check out,' he said as he got out of the car into the bustle of New York's streets.

'I'm not checking out,' she said sternly as she joined him, defiantly glaring up at him.

'We are now engaged—you will not stay here alone; besides, we have a party to plan.' Did she really expect him to leave her here after the news she'd given him today? He wasn't going to give her any opportunity to run out on him again, which he suspected was exactly what she wanted to do.

'What party?' The shock in her voice angered him more than he was comfortable with. It seemed everything today was out of his comfort zone.

'Our engagement party. I'll call the planner as soon as we get back to my apartment. I think the weekend would be best.' Before she could say anything, he took her arm and propelled her into the sleek interior of the hotel. 'But first you need to collect your luggage and check out.'

Emma couldn't believe how things were going. She'd had no idea what to expect when she'd made the journey to New York, but it wasn't this. She walked across the spacious apartment which gave stunning views over Central Park and that feeling of disbelief that he'd insisted she check out of the hotel intensified. 'There was no need for me to leave the hotel.'

'There is every need, Emma. Apart from the engagement party, which is scheduled for the weekend, I want you to rest.' The authority in his voice was unmistakable. She wanted to rebel against it but, just as she had done when she and Jess had moved from one foster family to another, she held it back. It was a skill she'd become adept at over the years.

Nikolai strode across the polished wooden floor to stand looking out of the large floor-to-ceiling windows and seeing his solitary figure reminded her of the photo she'd taken at his family home. He'd looked desolate and alone then. Now the firm set of his shoulders warned her he was far from desolate and very much in control of the situation and his emotions.

She wished she had her camera in her hands right now but instead walked softly across the floor to join him, her footsteps light. Just remembering him like that had calmed her emotions, made her want to find again the companionship they had experienced in Vladimir before they'd spent the night together. Maybe, if they could find that, then this marriage she was about to make had a chance of success.

She was fully aware the attraction was still there, the chemistry that sparked to life from just a single touch. His kiss as they were buying the ring had proved that, but if they were to make this work they needed to be friends; they needed to be able to hold a simple conversation without being on guard.

'That's quite a view,' she said as she stood next to him, hoping to make light conversation about something neutral. He didn't look at her and she glanced at his strong profile. 'I'd like to take some photographs, perhaps as the sun sets.'

'So that you can sell them?' Harshness had crept back into his voice and he turned to face her. 'Is that what this is all about? Extracting yet more from me and my family? Exposing even more details to bargain for money?'

As his words sank in she realised with shock what he was asking. 'It's not about that at all, Nikolai, I just wanted to take the photographs for my own enjoyment. I've never been to New York, let alone in a swanky apartment with views over Central Park.'

'I haven't yet seen what you submitted to *World in Photographs*.' He turned to look at her, his dark eyes black with veiled anger.

'That is easily sorted,' she said as she headed to the room he'd had her small amount of luggage delivered to. She'd been relieved to discover that he had no intention of spending the night in the same bed as her, but to her dismay that relief had been tinged with disappointment.

When she returned to the large open-plan living

space of the apartment, he was still looking out of the window, his shoulders more tense than ever. What was he so worried about? What could a few photographs and a small piece about his family really do?

She put her laptop down on the table and fired it up, the question as to what he was so worried about going round in her mind. All families had troubles they kept hidden from the world. She knew that more than most. She opened the piece she'd written for *World in Photographs* to go with the stunning images she'd taken and stepped away from the table.

'It's there for you. Richard liked it,' she said softly and sat down on the large cream sofa which dominated one corner of the apartment.

'Richard has seen it?' From across the room, Nikolai glared at her.

'He's been very helpful, and I wouldn't have got that contract without his help.' She fixed her gaze on the view of the park, not daring to look at him as he walked towards her laptop and began reading.

After five minutes of heavy silence he turned to look at her, his handsome face set in a forbidding frown. 'This is what you submitted?'

'Yes; what did you expect, Nikolai?'

'Not this light-hearted, romantic stuff about life in Russia. You have turned what I told you into something quite different.'

He walked towards her, his footsteps hard on the polished wooden floor, and she wished she hadn't chosen to sit down. He was too imposing, too dominating. 'You told me very little, Nikolai, and as I didn't get to meet with your grandmother I had to come up with something.'

'None of it true.'

'What is the truth, Nikolai? Why were you so worried I would meet your grandmother?'

He sighed and sat down next to her on the sofa, the air around them suddenly charged with something she couldn't yet fathom out. 'My family's story is complicated.'

'I know all about complicated, Nikolai. Jess and I have experienced it first-hand.' Why had she said that? She wanted to find out about him, not spill out her own sorry story. Would he still want her as his wife if he knew what kind of upbringing she'd had?

'Then we have that in common at least.' Sadness tinged his voice and her heart constricted, just as it had done when she'd taken the photo of him outside the ruins of what had once been his family home. She wanted to reach out to him, but kept her hands firmly together in her lap.

'Do you want to talk about it?' she asked, knowing full well he didn't, that he wanted to keep it all hidden safely away. It was what she'd done all through her childhood, mostly to protect Jess, who didn't know half of it.

'No but, as you are soon to marry into my family, then you should know.'

Her mouth went dry with fear. Would that mean he too would want to know about her childhood, her family? 'You don't have to tell me anything you don't want to.'

'You should know something of how I came to be living in New York and why I no longer use Petrushov, the surname I was born with.'

She looked at him, unable to stop herself from

reaching out to touch him. She placed her hand on his arm, trying to ignore the jolt of something wild which sparked between them from that innocent touch. 'We don't have to do this now.'

He ignored her and continued, his face a firm mask of composure. 'My mother's marriage to my father was not happy, neither was my childhood, and when he died it was a release for both my mother and I.'

'I'm sorry,' she said softly but her words didn't seem to reach him. Instead they only brought forward her own painful childhood memories—and she wasn't ready to share them yet.

'My mother was helped by a business acquaintance of my father and I guess it was one of those rare moments when love conquered all.' He looked down at her hand, still on his arm, and frowned, as if he'd only just realised she was touching him. Obviously her touch didn't do to him what his did to her.

'You say that as if you don't believe in such a concept.' She pulled her hand back and kept it firmly in her lap.

'I thought we'd already established that love is something neither of us believe in.' His dark eyes bored into hers, accusation and suspicion filling them, and she recalled their conversation in Vladimir. She remembered being blasé about looking for a fairy-tale wedding and happy-ever-after. She knew no such thing would ever happen to her, but from the way he was looking at her now he thought she wanted such things.

'We did; you just threw me when you said it was one of "those rare moments". As if you really believe they happen.' She smiled at him, injecting lightness into her voice. It was far better he thought she didn't believe in love in any shape or form. The last thing he needed to know right now was that she did believe in love and happy-ever-afters; she just didn't believe it would ever happen to her. It never would now she'd agreed to marry him as part of a deal.

'Well, whatever you believe, it happened for my mother. She changed from the constantly scared woman who lingered in the shadows of her marriage and blossomed into someone very different—and it's all thanks to Roger Cunningham. Even in my early teens I could see that, and at sixteen I changed my surname legally to his, although I'd already spent all my years here in New York as Nikolai Cunningham.'

'I did wonder,' she said, remembering his insistence that his name wasn't Petrushov when she'd first met him, and the card he'd tossed on the bed just before walking out on her. She pushed the pain of that moment aside and focused on the present. 'And now your child will take that name too.'

'As will you when we are married.' He looked at her hand, at the emerald ring on her finger, and she wondered if he was regretting what had seemed an impulsive move, telling her they would be married.

'We don't have to get married, Nikolai. I would never keep you from your child, not after having grown up without a father myself.' She swallowed down the nerves as she waited for his response. He looked into her eyes, as if he was trying to read her thoughts, and as much as she wanted to look away she held his gaze.

'Is the idea of being my wife that abhorrent to you?' His voice had deepened and a hint of an accent she'd never noticed before came through. The idea of being married was terrifying, but the idea of being this man's wife was less so. Was that because he was the only man she had truly known?

She shook her head, not able to speak.

He lifted his hand and pushed her hair back from her face. 'I will never do anything to hurt you, Emma; you do know that, don't you?'

The words were so tender she had to swallow down the urge to cry. His fingers brushed her cheek, bringing their night together vividly back to her mind. 'Yes, I know that.'

He leant towards her, his hand sliding round beneath her hair, holding her head gently, and before she could say or do anything his lips were on hers, the same gentle, teasing kiss as in the store. Her resistance melted like ice-cream on a hot day and she kissed him back. He deepened the kiss, sending a fury of fireworks around her body, reviving all the desire she'd felt for him and, if the truth were told, still felt even though she'd supressed it well.

She still wanted him, still yearned for him.

'We still have the passion we found in Vladimir,' he said as he broke the kiss and moved away from her, leaving her almost shuddering from the heat coursing through her. 'And that at least will make our marriage more bearable.'

She blinked in shock at his words. He'd been toying with her, proving his point. He obviously would never have chosen her to be his wife if it wasn't for the baby, but he'd told her he'd never wanted to be married when he'd first met her. She'd already accepted it was what she had to do for Jess as much as the baby. 'It will, yes.'

He smiled at her, but the warmth didn't reach those black eyes. 'Then we shall marry in three weeks. But first, there is the small matter of an engagement party.'

CHAPTER SEVEN

THE WEEK HAD flown by in a whirl of party arrangements and now it was time to face not only Nikolai's friends as his fiancée but his mother and stepfather. Emma's nerves jangled as she waited and she thought back to those two kisses on the day they'd become engaged. She had thought they were a positive sign, that he did at least feel something for her, but for the last week he'd withdrawn into his work and she had spent much of the time out with her camera.

Just this morning she'd been shopping in a store Nikolai had instructed her to visit for a dress suitable for the glamorous event the engagement party had turned into; now she stood looking out over a city which never slept, wearing the kind of dress she'd never imagined possible and feeling more like Cinderella every minute. The only thing she needed was Prince Charming to declare his undying love and sweep her away for a happy-ever-after but she doubted Nikolai would be willing to play that role.

She'd been in the beauty salon for the early part of the afternoon, nerves building with each passing hour. The cream dress, encrusted with beads, fitted to perfection and when she'd looked in the mirror before leaving her room she hadn't recognised herself. The woman Nikolai had met in Vladimir had gone, replaced by someone who looked much more polished and refined. What would Nikolai think of that? Or had it been his intention all along to mould her into the woman he wanted her to be?

She heard Nikolai's footsteps and nerves filled her so quickly she didn't want to turn round, but knew she would have to. When she did her breath caught in her throat. She'd seen him in a suit, but never a tuxedo, and the image he created stirred more than just her creative mind.

The fine black cloth hugged his broad shoulders, caressed his biceps and followed his lean frame downwards. The crisp white shirt set off the black tie to perfection, but it was his face which drew her attention far more. Stubble which had been tamed to look effortlessly sexy covered his jawline, emphasising the firm set of his lips. Dark hair was styled into conformity but a few locks were already breaking free and forming curls at his temples.

'You look…' he said softly as he stood and fastened his cufflinks, the movement showing off his wrists and designer watch. His dark eyes were full of controlled anger as he sought the words he was looking for.

'Very different.' She didn't want to hear what he thought and finished the sentence for him. All she wanted was to get his charade over with. She hated the pretence of it all.

He stepped a little closer, dropping his arms by his side, making the cloth of the tuxedo cling even more provocatively to him. 'I was going to say very beautiful.'

'I'm not so sure about that.' She blushed beneath his scrutiny and clutched her bag ever tighter.

She was about to walk past him when he caught her arm, the look in his eyes heavy with desire; as much as she wanted to look away, to avoid the way her body sizzled with pleasure, she boldly met his gaze. She stood there, locked in time, waiting for him to say something. He didn't and finally he let go of her, the connection gone, snuffed out like a candle, leaving a lingering scent in the air.

'We should go. My mother will be expecting us.' He turned away from her, as if he'd made a mistake even touching her, and she wasn't sure what worried her the most: the thought of meeting his mother and stepfather or that he couldn't bear to look at her.

'I'm looking forward to meeting her,' she said as she fiddled with her bag, anything other than witness his obvious discomfort at being around her.

'There is one thing I need to ask from you.' He stopped at the door of the apartment and looked down at her. 'My mother knows nothing of the baby and I'd like to keep it that way. For now, at least.'

He was ashamed of her, ashamed of the child she carried. That hurt her more than anything, but it also showcased the fact that this marriage was nothing more than a deal and she must never fall into the trap of thinking it was anything else.

She frowned and tried to smile, but she couldn't help but ask, 'Why?'

'She believes I am in love. We are in love. I want to keep it that way. I want her to believe we are marrying simply because we fell in love.' Each time he said the word 'love', his voice became harsher, as if he couldn't bear even naming such an emotion.

So he was ashamed he was to be a father. Was that why he wanted to get married as soon as possible— so that he could make it look like something they'd planned or at least wanted?

She shrugged, trying to hide her hurt at what he'd just said. 'If that's what you want.'

Nikolai watched as his mother hugged Emma, then held her hands and stood back to look at her, as if shocked that he'd finally brought a woman home to meet her. His gaze lingered a little too long on Emma's glorious body, encased in a gown which caressed her figure in a way that evoked memories of kissing her all over before making her his—truly his.

'I am so pleased to meet you.' His mother's words dragged his mind back from the erotic path they had taken, forcing him to concentrate on the present. 'I never really believed I'd see this day; and such a gorgeous ring.'

'A gorgeous ring for a very beautiful woman.' Nikolai spoke his thoughts aloud before he had time to evaluate them, but when Emma blushed and his mother smiled he knew they had been exactly what was needed.

'You must of course stay here tonight,' his mother offered Emma, just as she had done with him earlier in the week, but he'd refused, claiming a need to work the next day.

'Emma and I will be travelling back tonight,' he said sternly and felt Emma's gaze on him. Was she pleading with him to extricate them both from the invitation?

'I won't hear of it. How can you enjoy your engagement party if you have to travel back tonight? Besides, I've already had a room prepared, so there is no excuse.'

'I need to be at the office first thing in the morning.' Nikolai knew his voice sounded abrupt and, if the curious glance Emma cast his way was anything to go by, his mother would know he was making excuses.

'Nonsense. You work far too hard, and besides, it's the weekend and you should be spending it with your fiancée. Isn't that right, Emma?' His mother smiled at him, using her charm and tactics as she always did to get what she wanted, but he didn't want Emma pushed into a situation that she clearly didn't want. Also, staying here at his mother's house in The Hamptons would almost certainly mean sharing not only a room with Emma, but a bed. The fact that his mother had made a room ready suggested she'd already planned it all out.

'I don't have anything with me, Mrs Cunningham.' Emma's soft voice caught him unawares, as did the way it sent a tingle of awareness down his spine. He looked at her, at the worried expression on her face, and something twisted inside him, as if his heart was being squeezed.

He couldn't be falling for her. He didn't want that kind of complication, especially when she was here to celebrate their engagement only because he'd made a deal which would secure not only her baby's future but her sister's. A deal she'd been more than happy to agree on once he'd made her see that refusal would leave her child without a father. Something he knew she was all too familiar with.

'Well, if that's the only reason, I can soon sort that

out. My stepdaughter is here with her husband and between us both we can loan you anything you need.'

Nikolai's control on the situation was slipping through his fingers and he was torn between saving Emma from being forced to spend a night in the same room as him and allowing his mother to continue with the illusion that he'd finally succumbed to love.

'I couldn't do that...' Emma began, but before she could finish he spoke over her.

'Then we shall stay.' He pulled Emma against him, the fine fabric of her dress no barrier to the heat from her body as it seared through his suit, setting him alight with a desire he had no intention of acting on. Diversion was what he needed. 'We should mingle.'

At the extravagantly laid tables all around them were friends and members of his family, or rather his stepfamily. Everyone was enjoying themselves and their laughter mixed with the music from the live performers. He and Emma were the centre of attention, and that was something he hadn't thought of when he'd put the party planners in touch with his mother and let them loose together. A big mistake.

'I'm sorry,' he said as he took Emma's hand and led her to a table where they could sit and try and keep out of the limelight, for a while at least.

'For what?' She sat elegantly beside him and again that strange sensation washed over him.

'There isn't anyone here you know.'

'That's okay,' she answered as she looked around the marquee, hardly recognisable beneath its lavish decorations. 'It's not as if it's a real engagement.'

'It's very real, Emma.' Anger surfaced, smothering the simmering desire which brewed deep inside him.

She turned in her seat to give him her full attention and all he could do was look at her lips, red with lipstick, and imagine kissing them until she sighed with pleasure. He couldn't let her do this to him. He had to get back his control and fast. 'We are engaged and will be married by the end of the month.'

'But it's not for real, Nikolai, despite what you want your mother to believe. None of it is real—and I can't do this again.' A look of fear flitted across her face and he frowned in confusion.

'Do what?' He took her hands from her lap, where she'd clutched them tightly together. She looked at him, directly into his eyes, and he saw the anguish in hers.

'Be paraded around like this. When we get married, I want it to be with as little fuss as possible. I don't want to be the subject of everyone's scrutiny.' Her green eyes pleaded with him and the slight waver in her voice unsettled him. Was she having second thoughts about their deal?

'That suits me perfectly.' He snapped the words out and let her hands go, angered by the thought that she was at this very moment looking for a way out of their planned marriage—and the deal.

Emma didn't want the party to end. It was so lavish she could hardly have dreamed it up if she'd tried, and if she and Nikolai had truly been in love it would have been the perfect start to their life together. But they weren't in love. Nikolai's stern words as they'd sat talking at the beginning of the evening had been more than enough proof for her.

'Emma, Nikolai.' His mother came up to them, excitement all over her face. 'It's time for the finale, and

I want you to be in the prime spot when it happens. Come with me.'

'What have you done now?' Nikolai's deep voice demanded of his mother, but she wasn't listening, and she headed off through the crowds, leaving them no choice but to follow her out and across the lawns. Emma could hear the water in the darkness which surrounded the extensive garden, now lit up with hundreds of lights, and it was a relief to be away from the many people who had attended the party, none of whom she knew.

'I have no idea what this is about,' Nikolai said sternly, his irritation at such a public display of them as a newly engaged couple all too obvious.

'We should at least see,' she said to Nikolai, unable to supress a smile. How nice it must be to have a mother who would arrange surprises for you; it was exactly the kind of mother she wanted to be herself.

Nikolai didn't say anything, but took her hand and made his way to where his mother was talking to a group of people. His annoyance at the arrangement was very clear.

'Stand here, with the party as a backdrop. I want an engagement photo of you both.' The excitement in his mother's voice was contagious and Emma couldn't help but laugh softly. Nikolai didn't share her appreciation and wasn't in the least amused by it.

'That's not necessary.' Nikolai's brusque tone didn't make a dent on his mother's enthusiasm.

At point Emma realised this wasn't just a snapshot for a family album, as a party photographer joined them and set about making them stand just where he wanted them to. Instantly she was uncomfortable. She hated being on what she considered the wrong side of the lens.

'Now, embrace each other,' the photographer said as he stepped back and started clicking, his assistants altering lights to get the best result. 'Kiss each other.'

Kiss.

Emma looked at Nikolai and wondered just what he was going to say about being forced to kiss her. The same kind of boldness which had come over her in Vladimir rushed through her again.

'We'd better do as we're told,' she whispered with a smile on her lips, amused at his hard expression. He wasn't doing a very good job of acting the part of a man in love, which was what he'd wanted his mother to think he was. 'We're in love, remember?'

His eyes darkened until they were so black and full of desire that she caught her breath as anticipation rushed through her. Her heart thumped harder and she was sure he'd see the pulse at her throat, but his gaze didn't waver. He pulled her closer against him and she could feel his thighs touch hers, his chest press against her breasts.

He moved slowly but with intent purpose until his lips met hers and, acting on instinct, her eyes closed and her body melted into his. His arms held her tighter still and she wrapped hers around his neck as he deepened the kiss. She didn't want to respond, didn't want to acknowledge the power of the passion racing through her, but she couldn't help herself. She opened her lips and tasted his with her tongue as fireworks seemed to explode around them.

'Perfect,' the photographer directed. 'Keep kissing her.'

Nikolai's hand slid down to the small of her back, pressing her against him, and the fire of desire raged through her. If she didn't stop him now she'd be in danger of giving herself away, of allowing him to see just what he did to her.

She let her arms fall from his neck and pushed against his chest, wanting to continue, yet not wanting him to know that just a kiss could make her his again. 'That's pretty powerful acting,' she said, alarmed at how husky her voice sounded.

A large bang sounded behind them and, startled, she looked towards the party. Fireworks filled the night sky behind the marquee and relief washed over her. She thought she had heard fireworks as he'd kissed her, ones created by this man's kiss. The relief at discovering that they had been real made her laugh and, still in Nikolai's embrace, she looked up at him.

'The same can be said of you.' Desire filled his voice as he responded.

Nikolai let her go as his mother walked towards them, a big smile on her face. 'That was perfect. I will see you both in the morning.'

Emma watched her leave, an ultra-glamorous woman who believed her son had found the love of his life. What would she say if she knew the truth, and why was it so important to Nikolai that she thought that? Questions burned in her mind.

'Shall we return to the party or retire to bed?' The question shocked her and she didn't know which was more preferable. She didn't want to continue to be the centre of speculation but neither did she want to go to their room.

'Perhaps we should just go back to your apartment.'

The suggestion came from her before she had time to think.

'I can see that my presence in your room is not going to be welcome, but I can assure you, nothing will happen. The pretence of being in love can be dropped once we close the bedroom door.'

'In that case, we should retire,' she said, trying to keep the despondency from her voice. He didn't want her, didn't find her attractive. The kiss of moments ago had been just an act. Pretence at attraction and love, purely to keep his mother happy.

Nikolai saw the expression of horror cross Emma's face, and wished he'd been firmer with his mother, but she'd looked so happy he just couldn't destroy that for her. This whole sham of an engagement was to make his mother happy and now he was guilty of making Emma unhappy. Strangely, that was worse, but it was too late to back out now. They would spend the night in this room and leave as soon as they could in the morning.

Emma crossed the room to the only bed and looked at the items his mother had instructed to be left for them. She held up a cream silk nightdress which would do little to conceal her figure and he closed his eyes against the image of her in it—and, worse, next to him in that very bed.

'It appears your mother has thought of everything,' she said as she looked up at him. 'It's almost as if she was planning on us having to stay.'

Emma had just echoed his own thoughts, but he brushed them away in an attempt to put her at ease. 'Whatever it was my mother had planned, she believes we are in love and, as I said earlier, I want to keep it that way. I also promised that nothing would happen between us, so I will sleep in the chair.'

He gestured to an easy chair which would be perfect for relaxing in during the day, but not so great to sleep in for a night. She looked from him to the chair and sighed, as if in resignation.

'I hardly think that will be conducive to a good night's sleep.' He was about to argue the point when a smile tugged at the corners of her mouth. 'We'll just have to manage together in the bed. We are, after all, both adults and have agreed that nothing is going to happen.'

He might have agreed, but he seriously doubted if he could carry through that promise. She stood before him now in the dress which shimmered in the lights of the room, and he wanted her more than he'd ever wanted any woman.

Maybe one more night in her arms would be enough to suppress the desire-laden thoughts he constantly had about her? That question sent a rush of lust sparking around him, but as he looked at her worried expression he knew it couldn't happen. Not after he'd been the one to set the time limit—just one night in Vladimir.

'In that case, I suggest we get some sleep.' He pulled off his tie and tossed it onto the chair he'd planned to sleep in, determined to prove to himself he was able to exercise firm control where this woman was concerned. Emma didn't move. 'Is there a problem?'

'Can you unzip me?'

She blushed and looked more beautiful and innocent than she'd ever done, but there was a hint of humour in her voice. Did she know just how much she was torturing him?

'I had help this afternoon, but I don't have a stylist to hand at present. Thanks for arranging all that; it was very thoughtful.'

He walked towards her, wondering if he trusted himself to be so close to her, undoing the dress he'd wanted to remove from her sexy body all night. She was testing him, pushing him to the limits of his endurance, whether she knew it or not.

'I wanted you to look the part,' he said, then added more gently as her perfume weaved around him, drawing him ever closer like a ship lured to the rocks by a raging storm, 'And you looked beautiful—so very beautiful.'

'I felt beautiful,' she whispered, as if letting him hear her thoughts. 'It was a fairy-tale night.'

'My mother believes in that fairy tale, at least,' he said firmly, desperate to remind himself why he was even here like this with her. 'You played your part well.'

She looked up at him as he stood in front of her, boldly locking her gaze with his in a fleeting gesture of defiance before lowering her lashes and looking away. She turned her back to him and lifted up her hair, which hung in a glossy veil down her back, exposing the silky, smooth skin he remembered from their night together.

His hand lingered on the zip. He couldn't let go, couldn't step away from the temptation she was creating. He could see her spine and curled his fingers tight against the need to trail them up it and then all the way down. He wanted to kiss her back, to take every last piece of clothing from her sexy body and kiss her everywhere, before claiming her as his once more.

He bit down on a powerful rush of desire which surged through him. Not only had she made it clear she didn't want him, he didn't want the complications of sex becoming something more. He had to ignore the lust which was rapidly engulfing him, if only to prove to himself he didn't want her, didn't feel anything for her.

He reached out and gently pulled the zip downwards, inwardly groaning as her back became visible. The heat of passion was rushing straight to his groin. If this was any other woman, or any other moment in time, he would be kissing that wonderfully bare back and sliding the dress from her, exposing her near nakedness to his hungry gaze. But this wasn't any other woman. This was the woman who was to become his wife and everything was so very complicated.

'Thank you.' She stepped away from him and he clenched his fingers tightly to prevent himself from doing anything else.

Passion pounded in his body, begging for release as she turned to face him. Her hardened nipples were clearly visible through the fine material and he wondered how he'd never noticed until now she was braless. The thought shifted the demanding desire inside him up several notches, ever closer to breaking point.

The air hummed with heavy desire as she picked up the nightdress his mother had magically found from somewhere and walked into the adjoining bathroom and closed the door. For a moment, relief washed over him until he realised that when she returned she'd be wearing even less. The cream nightdress would offer even less protection from him.

With an angry growl he took off his jacket and slung it over the back of the chair. What the hell was wrong with him? He'd never been a slave to desire. He was always in control. *Except with this woman.*

As the bathroom door opened he crossed the room, not daring to look at her, not wanting to see her wearing the silky nightdress which would reveal far more of her body than he could tolerate. He kept his back to her as he heard the bedcovers being moved and then headed for the bathroom. Once inside, he shut the door firmly and turned on the shower, selecting the coldest setting.

When he returned to the bedroom, invigorated from the icy cold jets of water, Emma was lying in the bed, as far to one edge of it as was possible, and either asleep or pretending to be. Wearing only his underwear, he slid beneath the cool covers, turned off the light and lay on his back, looking up at the ceiling through the darkness. Anger boiled up in him, thankfully dimming the throb of desire, allowing his usual stern control to return.

Emma sighed softly next to him and turned over, moving closer to him. He lay rigid in the bed as her breathing settled into the soft rhythm of sleep again. He could feel the warmth of her body, and in his mind all he could see was her naked in his bed in Vladimir. Nothing had changed. He couldn't relax. Damn it, he'd never sleep.

He closed his eyes, willing his body to relax, and, just when he thought he might achieve that elusive state, Emma stirred and moved again. Closer to him. Far too close. She put her arm across his chest and pulled herself closer, pressing her body against the side of his, and instantly his body was ready for her. He clenched his jaw tightly, fighting the throb of desire and the urge to turn to her, to wrap her in his arms and kiss her awake before making her his once more.

A feral curse slipped from his lips as she sighed once more, pressing herself tighter against him so that he could feel the swell of her breast against his arm. He couldn't move. He didn't trust himself to. He had to prove he was stronger than the desire he had for her, something he'd never had a problem with before.

How could he want her so much? What had she done to him? Questions raced through his mind and he focused on them instead of the heady warmth of Emma's sleeping body next to his.

Never in his life had he spent a night with a woman without having sex. How had it come to this? He tried again to sleep, to ignore the heat of her body, and it was more than torture as he lay rigid next to the one woman who threatened everything, from his sanity to his family. How the hell could he want her so badly?

CHAPTER EIGHT

EMMA BLUSHED AGAIN as memories from the few hours they'd spent in bed together came rushing back to her. She still couldn't believe that she'd been wrapped around Nikolai when she'd woken. She'd opened her eyes as spring sunshine had streamed into the unfamiliar room, wondering at first where she was. Then she'd realised they were entwined, as if they were lovers. Slowly she'd moved away from Nikolai as he slept, taking the chance to steal a glance at his handsome features before slipping away to put on a dress left for her last night.

Had anything happened? Had she embarrassed herself by saying or doing something stupid in a sleepy state? She hoped she hadn't let her growing feelings for him show—especially as he'd been adamant that nothing would happen between them. So many questions had raced around her mind as they'd left the beautiful house and started the drive back to his apartment in New York. A tense silence had enveloped them in the car and she hadn't been about to break it, especially not by asking about last night.

Now they were back in his apartment and she was lying in her bed alone, replaying the events of the party.

The kiss for their engagement photo had been so powerful, so very evocative, she'd thought it was real, but then he'd pulled away from her, the hardness of his eyes warning her against such thoughts. But it was when he'd helped her out of her dress that things really had changed. She'd seen raw desire in his eyes as he'd looked at her, and when he'd touched her she'd clamped her mouth tightly closed, worried she might say something and give herself away—because she'd wanted him to touch her.

She should be grateful he hadn't said a word about the previous night other than to make small talk about the party itself, but she wasn't. It didn't feel right, ignoring whatever it was that sizzled between them. With a huff of irritation, she flung back the covers. There was no way she could sleep now. Her mind was alive with questions and her body still yearned for a man who didn't want her.

Silently she left her room and padded across the polished wooden floor to the kitchen as the sounds of a city which never seemed to sleep played out in the background. Was this what her life would be like from now on? Would she be hiding an ever-deepening affection for the father of her child for ever? Could she live like that?

She poured some water and went to sit by the windows, needing the peaceful view of the park to soothe her tortured emotions. She just couldn't be falling for Nikolai, not when all she'd wanted was that happy-ever-after with a man who loved her. But she'd never get that happiness now, even by marrying Nikolai. He didn't love her and had made it clear their marriage was to be nothing more than a deal.

'Are you unwell?' Nikolai's voice startled her, but when she looked up she was even more startled. Just as he'd done that night in Vladimir, he'd pulled on a pair of jeans, and looked so incredibly sexy she had to stop herself from taking in a deep and shuddering breath.

'I couldn't sleep.' She tried hard to avert her gaze from his bare chest, but couldn't. All she could think about was lying with her arms across it last night. She could still feel the muscles beneath her palm and distinctly remembered the scent of his aftershave invading her sleep. What else was she going to remember?

'But you are feeling quite well?' The concern in his voice was touching and she smiled at him.

'I'm fine, just not sleepy.' She didn't have much chance of feeling sleepy now after seeing him like that. All her senses were on high alert, her body all but tuned into his.

His gaze travelled down her bare legs and she realised how she must look, sat on the sofa wearing only a vest top and skimpy shorts, but there wasn't anything she could do about it now, not without alerting him to the fact that she was far from comfortable having a discussion with him when they were both half-undressed. It was much too intimate.

'Is it because you are alone tonight? Nobody to curl up with?' The seductive huskiness of his voice held a hint of laughter. Was he making fun of her?

She looked up at him and knew that wasn't true. He moved closer and stood over her, his dark eyes seeming to penetrate deep inside her, searching for something. 'About—about last night…' she managed to say, but hated the way she stumbled over the words. 'What I mean is, did we…? Did anything happen between us?'

The air heated around them, laden with explosive sexual tension, but she couldn't look away, couldn't break the connection which was becoming more intense by the second.

'Trust me, Emma, you'd remember if it had.' A smile lifted his lips and a hint of mischief sparked in his eyes.

He was making fun of her.

'Oh,' she said softly, heat infusing her cheeks.

'You sound as if you're disappointed to discover that we slept in the same bed without having sex.' Like a brooding presence, he towered over her, suffocating the very air she breathed, making her pulse leap wildly. 'It can of course be rectified.'

This time she wasn't able to stop the ragged intake of breath or the shudder of desire. He wanted her. Just as she wanted him. It was like the night in Vladimir all over again. Then she had believed she was giving in to the allure of a powerful sexual attraction for just one night; even though they were to be married, she knew this was exactly that again. He didn't love her. This was nothing more than sex.

Her heart thumped hard, and warnings echoed in her mind, but she didn't want to heed them. She wanted Nikolai, wanted him to desire her, and the allure of that was more powerful than the prophecy of a broken heart.

The seconds ticked by and the power of the sexual chemistry between them increased as surely as if he'd touched her. Her body yearned for his touch, her lips craved his kiss, but most of all she wanted his possession. She wanted to be his.

Nikolai stood over Emma as she sat and looked up at him. Did she have any idea just how damn sexy she looked in that white vest top, her nipples straining against the fabric? As for the white shorts, well, he couldn't go there or he'd drag her off to his room like a Neanderthal.

'We could rectify it now—tonight.' The lust coursing through him had got the better of him, and he spoke the words before he had time to think, but, judging by the sexy, impish smile, it wasn't something she was horrified by.

'Could we?' Her voice was husky, teasing him and testing him. Damn it. What was the point in denying the attraction which fizzed around them? He wanted her and, unless he was very much mistaken, she wanted him too.

'I want you, Emma,' he said and held out his hand to her, more emotionally exposed than he'd ever been in his life. He had no idea how, but this woman was dismantling every barrier he'd erected to shut himself away, to prevent himself from ever having to feel anything for anyone.

The silky softness of her throat moved as she swallowed, her gaze fixed on his. Then she parted her lips, the small movement so sexy he almost groaned out loud. Finally she took his hand, placing hers in his, and he pulled her gently to her feet and towards him.

Shock rocked through him as her body collided with his and he wrapped his arms around her, pulling her against him. Her body seemed to beg his for more, but he wanted to hear it from her lips, needed to know this was what she wanted. 'Is this what you want?'

She slipped from his embrace and he drew in a sharp breath as she crossed her arms in front of her and, taking hold of her vest top and pulling it over her head, threw it carelessly to the floor. His gaze devoured her slender figure, her full breasts, and he clenched his hands into tight fists as he fought to hold on to control. But when she slithered the white shorts down her legs, kicking them aside, he knew that control was fading fast.

It was like Vladimir all over again. Except this time he didn't have to worry about consequences. This time he could make her his totally.

'Yes.' That one word was a husky whisper that sent fire all over him at the knowledge this woman was his, and the fact that she'd given him her virginity only increased the power of that idea.

He closed his eyes briefly against the need to take her quickly, to thrust into her and possess her more completely than he had ever taken a woman before. She'd only ever known his touch and because of that he had to take it slowly, make this a night of pure pleasure for both of them.

Slowly he undid his jeans, maintaining eye contact with her as he removed them to stand before her as naked as she was. A dart of satisfied pleasure zipped through him as she lowered her gaze to look at him, arousing him still further.

She moved back to him, looking into his eyes and taking on the role of seductress, just as she had in Vladimir; she wrapped her fingers around him, pushing him to a new level of control. He actually trembled with the pleasure of her touch and groaned as her lips pressed against his, her hand still working the magic.

When she let go of him and kissed down his neck, over his chest, he groaned in pleasure, but when she lowered herself down to continue the torture her touch had started it was nearly his undoing. He pushed his fingers deep into her hair but, as his control began to slip, he pulled her back and she looked up at him, her green eyes dark and full of question.

'My turn.' The gravelly growl of his voice was almost unrecognisable as he pulled her to her feet then pushed her back onto the sofa. With predatory instinct he knelt up before her and, leaning on her, pressed his lips to hers, taking in her gasp of pleasure.

'Nikolai,' she breathed as he kissed down her neck rapidly. She arched herself towards him as he took one nipple between his teeth, nipping, teasing, before caressing it with his tongue.

Again enforced restraint made him shake and he braced his arms tighter to hold himself over her. She writhed in pleasure beneath him as he turned his attention to the other nipple, her hands roaming hungrily over his body.

As he moved lower still, kissing over her stomach, she clutched at his shoulders, her nails digging in, the spike of pain so erotic he could hardly hang on to his control any longer. But he wasn't finished with her yet.

He moved his head between her legs, tasting her as she lifted her hips upwards, all but begging him for more. He teased her with his tongue, pushing her to the edge, but stopping as he felt her begin to tremble, not ready to let her go over just yet.

'Let's go to the bedroom,' he said between kisses as he moved back up over her stomach, over the hardened peak of her nipple and up her throat.

'No,' she gasped as she clung to him, wrapping her legs around him, the heat of her touching him; he knew that he was lost, that all control was gone.

In one swift move he filled her, thrusting deep into her and making her his once more. She gasped as she gripped harder onto his back, her hips lifting to take him deeper inside her. It was wild. Passionate.

Her body was hot and damp against his, but still it wasn't enough. He wanted more, much more. With a growl he thrust harder, striking up a fierce rhythm she matched. Her cries of pleasure pushed him further until he forgot everything except her. With one final thrust, he took her over the edge with him.

Darkness still filled the room as Emma lay contentedly against Nikolai after the hours of making love. They had moved from the sofa to the shower and then finally to his bed. She should be exhausted, but she'd never been so alive, so vibrant. It was almost too good to be true.

The doubts she'd had about accepting his so-called proposal had been blown away by the hot sex they'd shared. If things were that good between them, wasn't there hope he might one day feel something deeper for her? She certainly wanted that to be true because her feelings were definitely growing for him. They had become deep and meaningful. Did that mean she was falling in love with him?

As the question reared up before her, Nikolai stirred and she braced herself, remembering how she'd woken to find him staring out of the window in Vladimir. Had he regretted that night? A night which had changed both of their lives beyond recognition. More questions stirred in her mind as Nikolai propped himself up on his elbow and looked at her, his eyes filling with desire once more.

'I'm going to see some sights today,' she said, trying to fight the rise of a fresh wave of desire. She didn't want their time together to be all about sex. She wanted to get to know him better, but while he kept the barrier raised around himself that was going to be difficult. Did he ever let anyone get close?

'We'll go together.' He pulled her against him and kissed her and she almost gave in.

'That would be nice,' she said with a teasing smile and moved away from him. 'It will be a nice way to get to know each other better.'

'How much better do we need to know each other?' He was smiling but there was a hint of caution in his voice.

'There's so much we don't know about each other.'

'Such as?' The hard tone of his voice had become guarded and it was like being back in Vladimir that first night with him. The impenetrable wall was right round him, shutting her out.

'What we really want from this marriage.' She let the words fall softly between them.

'I know what you want. You want financial security. Why else would you come all this way? You also want for your child what you never had—a father figure.'

Did he have any idea he'd got it so right? Was he really that cruel he'd manipulate her insecurities so coldly?

'My offer of marriage is exactly what you wanted.' He spoke again and all she could do was take it, knowing it was all true. 'Even though you held out for a bit more, marriage is what you came here for, wasn't it, Emma?'

'What?' She couldn't believe what he was saying,

but neither could she move. All she could do was stay there and look at him.

'Is tonight part of a bigger plan?'

How could a night so perfect turn into a one so terrible? Emma shivered in the shadow of the gulf which had opened up between them at the mention of the deal they'd struck. 'Is that what you really think?'

'You have given me no reason to think otherwise.' He threw back the sheets and strode across the room to pull on his jeans, totally uncaring about his nakedness. He was running again.

'Nikolai.' She said his name more sharply than she intended. 'Don't go. Not again.'

He stood at the end of the bed in the semi-darkness of the room and glared at her. 'What exactly is it you want to know, Emma? And, more to the point, who is asking—the woman I am to marry, the one who is carrying my child or the woman who wants to get to the truth just for an article in a magazine?'

Emma recoiled at his fierce tone, but it proved he was hiding the truth, that whatever it was he'd gone to great lengths to conceal from her in Vladimir was still there, creating a barrier around him as physical as a wall of bricks and mortar.

'I'm asking, Nikolai—as your fiancée—because I care, because if we don't deal with this, whatever it is that's keeping you emotionally shut away, making you so cold, it will fester between us, always dominating, always threatening. Do you want your child to grow up under that cloud?' Her passionate plea didn't dent his armour.

'What do you want? My life story? I gave you that in Vladimir.'

'You gave me the version you wanted me to know, but things have changed. We are having a baby and, if we're to marry, then I want that marriage to be a success. I don't want our child to grow up knowing any kind of insecurities.'

'What do you know of insecurities, Emma?' His voice had softened, taken on a more resigned tone.

'Much more than you might think.' Her own childhood, the unhappiness of continuously moving to new foster homes, crept back to the fore, as did her father's rejection. She pushed it away. Nikolai must never know what sort of mother she'd been raised by. If he did, he might think she wasn't fit to be a mother herself, and she couldn't risk her baby being taken away, like she and Jess had been.

'Do you really think that's possible?' He glared at her and she knew he was angry that she was not only challenging him but being evasive herself.

'Tell me, Nikolai. I know some of your story but, as your fiancée, I want to hear it from you.' She spoke softly and held her breath as he paced the room and ran his fingers quickly through his hair.

Nikolai didn't know where to start. He was angry, at himself and Emma. She knew the basic facts so why did she want more? He looked down into her eyes and realised it didn't matter any more what he tried to keep from her; she knew half the story and he was sure that it would only be a matter of time before she'd know every sordid detail. Better it came from him—now.

'Why exactly do you feel it is necessary to know?' Why the hell was he doing this? It was far too deep, too emotionally exposing, and he just didn't do emotion. He'd learnt long ago how to keep fear, anger and even love out of whatever he was doing. Each time he'd come to his mother's rescue as his father had used his fists, he'd acted calmly and without emotion. It hadn't mattered whether he was wiping her bleeding nose or merely standing between them, he'd been devoid of any emotion. It had been the only way—and still was.

'You said before, in Vladimir, that your parents were forced to marry.' She nudged his memory with the start of the story he'd told her that night they'd first slept together. Then, just as now, being with her had threatened to unleash his emotions.

'Yes, they were, but only because she was pregnant with his child.' He watched her face pale and had the urge to kiss her, to forget the past and lose himself in her wonderful body once more. It surged through him like a madness. Thankfully, sense prevailed. Despite the fact that she looked so sexy sitting there naked in his bed, her hair no longer sleek but ruffled from sex, he was sufficiently in control to acknowledge things were already complicated enough without giving her hope of having a normal, loving marriage.

'That's hardly the crime of the century,' she said, sympathy in her voice and a smile lingering tentatively on her lips as he sat on the bed and looked at her.

He knew what she meant. She was pregnant with his child and they were going to be married; that fact only compounded his misgivings, making him ever more determined to keep emotions out of this deal they'd struck, because that was how he had to think of it: as a deal for his child. Just as his father had forced his mother into marriage, he was forcing her.

Now the one thing he didn't want to happen was

happening. Emotions were clamouring from his child-hood, demanding to be felt, and he hated it. Memories rushed back at him and he fought for control. What would she think of him if she knew the truth?

He should just say it. However he tried to dress it up, those words would be painful; knowing how he'd come into the world, how it had forced his mother into something she hadn't wanted, made him feel worthless. It was that sense of worthlessness which had driven him hard, making everything he did a success.

He looked at Emma and knew she had to know just who he was.

'He'd raped her.'

There, he'd said it. Finally said the words aloud. He was the unwanted product of a rape which had devastated his mother's life, forcing her into a violent marriage.

'Rape?' Her voice was hardly more than a whisper, and it helped to be near the warmth of her body as the cold admission finally came out, but strangely just saying those words wasn't enough. He wanted to tell it all now he'd finally started, as if he'd opened a door he could never close.

'My father was a family friend and had asked to marry my mother. He'd wanted the connections our family name and wealth would bring him.'

Emma didn't say anything but moved a little closer to him, heat from her body infusing him. He wanted to hold her, to feel the goodness within her cleanse the badness from him, but he couldn't, not yet, not until she knew it all. 'Did she refuse him?'

He gritted his teeth as he recalled the time he'd first found out what had happened, how his gentle and loving mother had become the wife of a vicious brute of a man just because of him. He had no idea why, but now he wanted to talk, to tell Emma everything, even knowing she could use it all and destroy him. He wanted to prevent it all coming out as a headline story in the press. That was why he'd flown from New York to a country he barely remembered to ensure a grandmother he'd come to hate didn't tell her the damned story. Now here he was, spilling it all out to the very woman who wanted to know his family story for that very reason.

'She did. And because of that he attacked and raped her.' He bit down on the anger which raged in him now, just as it had done the day he'd realised he'd been the reason his mother had married a violent man. Surely their life would have been better without a man like that in it? He'd never questioned his mother, never asked her about it. She didn't even know he'd overheard her and his stepfather talking. That would break her heart as much as the story being leaked to the world would.

'I don't understand. Why did she marry him after that?' Incredulity filled her voice as she once again looked up at him.

'That is something I have never understood.' Despite the warmth of her body his mind drifted back in time, to the many occasions when he'd cowered in a corner, hiding from his father's wrath. 'When my mother and I left Russia I was ten and I never wanted to go there again. I did all I could to fit in with our new life, to please my new father. It was like being given a new chance.'

'Why did your mother marry your father if he'd done that?' It was a question he'd asked himself so many times.

'Maybe she saw marriage to that brute as her only chance. She was from a well-known family and wouldn't have wanted to bring such a scandal out into the open.'

Emma moved and wrapped her arms around him, pressing her lips to his forehead. It was strangely comforting to be held by her, to feel her compassion wrapping around him. 'I'm sorry,' she whispered. 'For making you go there again.'

'Maybe I should have faced my father's mother when I had the chance, asked her why she helped to hide such horrible things from the world. From the outside we must have appeared a normal family. I want to know if she realises that by doing that she trapped my mother and I with an angry bully. Only his sudden death freed us.'

'It doesn't mean we shall be the same,' she said, homing in on the worry he'd had since the moment she'd arrived in New York with the news of her pregnancy. He wasn't fit to be a father with a past like that, but that just made him more determined to be a part of his child's life, to be a better father.

'How can you say that when you only agreed to marriage for the child's sake?' He began to build his barriers back again, using all the ammunition he had to push her away. As he spoke he looked into her eyes and saw the flash of pain within them, but buried it deep inside him.

'Our child was not conceived through violence,' she said firmly as she touched his face with the palm of her hand, a gesture he wanted to enjoy, but he couldn't allow himself that luxury.

'But it most definitely wasn't conceived out of love.' He threw the harsh truth at her and her hand stilled.

'No, it wasn't.' The softness of her voice, mixed with sadness, slashed at him harshly. What the hell had he been thinking of, talking about this with her?

She moved away from him, looking like a hurt and wounded animal, and that strange sensation squeezed his chest again. This was getting far too deep for him and he had to put a stop to it right now.

'I never want to talk of this again.' Anger boiled over inside him, threatening to spill out everywhere, turn him into a copy of the man who'd terrified him as a child, and she'd done that to him.

Emma looked up at him and he watched her bare shoulders go back as she sat a little taller, her chin lifting in that sexily defiant way of hers. 'I understand, and we won't.'

She understood? How could she understand? He wanted to ask her about her childhood, just what it was in her past that qualified her even to say that, but he couldn't deal with any more emotion. He needed space, time on his own. He strode from the bedroom as the light of dawn filled the apartment, thankful that she hadn't attempted to follow or ask anything else.

CHAPTER NINE

THE GENUINE CONCERN Nikolai had been showing her all week, taking time out from the office and going sightseeing with her, had definitely brought them closer in many ways. After the disastrous way last weekend had ended she felt a glimmer of hope and the uneasy sensation that she was doing the wrong thing marrying him melted into the background.

Today he'd chosen a trip on the Hudson River to see the Statue of Liberty. He'd hired a private boat and it was so romantic it reinstated the flailing hope. It was a perfect spring day but, even so, the motion of the boat was making her queasy. Just as she had done every day this week, she tried to hide it from him but, as if he'd become tuned into her feelings, he guessed she was unwell.

'This wasn't such a good idea,' he said as he stood behind her and pulled her close against him. She closed her eyes, enjoying the sensation of being cared for, being protected. Deep down it was all she'd ever wanted. Love and protection had been so lacking in her childhood it had become the elusive dream. A dream which right at this moment felt tantalisingly close.

'It's fine,' she said as she snuggled closer. The spring

wind not yet carrying any warmth didn't help, but, against the man she was most definitely falling in love with, she really didn't care about anything. Being here in his arms like this was so right, so natural, she didn't want anything to spoil it. 'I just don't think I can take photos today.'

'Then don't.' He kissed the top of her head and she smiled. Was he falling in love with her too? Could she be on the brink of her happy-ever-after? 'You should stop working and just enjoy the moment. Photographs can wait.'

'Can I ask you something?' She started speaking while watching the buildings of New York become ever taller and more modern as they made their way down the river towards downtown Manhattan. Before he had a chance to reply, she spoke again. 'Have you ever been in love?'

She needed to ask, needed to know if he'd ever let a woman into his heart before, but the tension in his arms as he held her warned her she'd gone too far.

'No.' The sharply spoken word told her more than she needed to know. 'You know what happened when I was a child. You even told me yourself that you didn't believe in such nonsense as love.'

'I didn't,' she said softly and swallowed down the disappointment. If his mother had found happiness after such a terrible marriage, then love must exist. Her heart was opening to the idea, but could his?

'I hope that doesn't mean you've changed your mind.' The sharpness of his words cut the air around them and she shivered, as if winter had returned.

Her heart went into freefall and she focused hard on the New York skyline, determined not to allow his

throwaway comments to hurt her, but the truth was she
had changed her mind. She'd changed it because of her
deepening feelings for him, feelings that she knew for
sure could only be love.

'Of course I haven't,' she said quickly, sensing that
to tell him now wouldn't be sensible. She had to remember why she was here as his fiancée at all. She
was carrying his child and he'd made a deal with her,
a deal which gave her baby all she'd missed out on as
a child, and she wasn't about to jeopardise that. 'We
are doing this for our child.'

'And your sister.' His stern reminder left her in no
doubt he considered his offer the deal clincher. It was
nothing more than a deal for him, but his next words
cut her heart in two, making her feel shallow. 'Funds
for her "dream", as you called it, were the sealing factor in the deal, were they not?'

He let her go and moved to stand next to her, feigning an interest in the city's skyline, and she knew she'd
got too close to the barriers erected around him, barriers to prevent him from being affected by any kind
of sentimental feelings. Deep inside her that newly
discovered well of hope dried up. She had thought he
might be able to find it in his heart to feel something
for her, as she was beginning to for him.

They'd created a child together in a night of passion,
a child that would bind them together for evermore,
but she wanted more than that. She wanted to be loved
and love in return. Every night this week, since they'd
returned from their engagement party, the hours of
darkness had been filled with passion and her love had
grown, but for him it had been nothing more than sex.

She'd let herself down, done the one thing he'd

warned her not to do. She wanted more; it hurt to admit it, but she loved him. She tried to distract herself with thoughts of her sister but they made her lonelier than she'd ever been. The last few times she'd called her, Jess hadn't been able to take the call, and she'd just received brief texts in reply.

'I'd like to see if Jess can make it to New York for our wedding.' She tried tentatively to steer the discussion away from the subject of love. Maybe it was a safer thing to talk about. 'Do we have a date yet?'

He laughed softly and looked at her, almost frazzling her resolve not to feel anything for him. 'Are you that keen to become my wife or are you just changing the subject?'

'There's nothing to be gained by waiting now we have agreed our terms.' It might be the truth, but her voice had a tart edge to it as she tried to stem the hurt and rejection growing within her.

He looked at her, studying her face for a few seconds, and all she could hear was the sound of the boat engine and the wash of water. The spring sunshine was warm on her face, but not as searing as his gaze. 'Then you'll be pleased to know it has all been arranged for this Saturday.'

'Saturday?' She whirled round to face him, not caring that she was missing the spectacular views he'd brought her here to see. Saturday was too soon. She'd never be able to organise Jess flying in from Moscow by then. Was he deliberately trying to cut her off from everything she held dear? 'Jess will never be able to get here by Saturday—and she's all I have, Nikolai.'

Before he could answer, her phone rang and she snatched at the chance of avoiding his scrutiny. She'd left so many messages for Jess, it had to be her, and she needed to speak to her now more than ever. She looked at the screen, but it wasn't her sister. It was Richard. Nikolai looked down at the screen while she thought of not answering. She didn't need to talk to Richard of all people right at this moment, no matter how much he'd helped her get her contract with *World in Photographs*.

'You had better answer that.' His voice was harsh, each word clipped with anger. She looked up at him in confusion but he turned from her and walked away a few paces.

'Richard,' she said as she answered the call. 'How lovely to hear from you.'

Nikolai didn't like the way Emma smiled as she spoke to Richard or the way she'd turned her back on him to take the call. He recalled he was the photographer who'd helped her get her career off the ground, but now he was beginning to question exactly what she thought of him.

'The article is out?' Emma's voice carried across the deck as she continued her call. 'That's brilliant. Thanks for calling to tell me—and, Richard, thanks for your help.'

Nikolai clenched his jaw against the irrational anger which bubbled up just from hearing her talk to this other man. Was it really possible that he was jealous? The thought was ludicrous. To be jealous of another man he'd have to have feelings for Emma—deep feelings he just didn't want.

He turned to watch her as she spoke on the phone. Her long silky hair was in a ponytail down her back, but the wind kept playing with it, reminding him how it felt against his skin while she slept. For the last week, since the night they had returned from their engagement party, she had spent every night in his bed. Each of those nights of passion had claimed them in its frenzied dance; afterwards she'd always slept wrapped around him and he'd enjoyed the closeness.

Her laughter as she responded to something Richard said only served to send his irritation levels higher and he turned from her, determined he wasn't going to be affected by it. Their marriage was to be one of convenience for the sake of his child and all he had to do was remind himself how easily she'd been talked into the marriage once he'd used the lure of funds for her sister.

Before Richard had called, he'd been about to tell her that he'd made arrangements for Jess to come to New York for the wedding. He'd put things in motion after the engagement party, which had been all about his family and friends, because he'd wanted her to have someone there for her. He'd also insisted that the wedding itself was limited strictly to close family, which had been a battle with his mother, but now the urge to tell her these details had gone.

'That was Richard,' she said as she joined him and he certainly couldn't miss the smile on her face. Irritation surged deeper through him at the happiness in her voice. 'The article is out and he said it's really good.'

'If it's what I have already read, then I am pleased for you.' He kept his voice neutral, not wanting a trace of any kind of emotion to be heard, especially the new and strange one he suddenly had to deal with.

'Why would it be any different?' She frowned up at him. 'You don't trust me, do you, Nikolai?'

Of course he didn't trust her and now, thanks to a

moment of weakness, she knew everything. She still had the ability to shatter his mother's happiness. That was something he wasn't going to allow to happen at any price and precisely why he'd flown to Russia in the first place.

'Is Richard a close friend of yours?' he asked, unable to keep his curiosity under control any longer, or the anger at the way the idea of Richard and Emma being close filled him with such strong emotions.

'Why do you ask?' Her cautious question was just what he'd expected—and feared. She was hiding something; of that he was certain.

Despite his suspicions, there was no way he was going to let her know how he felt, so he assumed an air of indifference he definitely didn't feel. 'I have limited the wedding guests to immediate family and close friends. I just wanted to know if he was a close friend.'

She looked down, not able to meet his gaze, and when she looked up again disappointment and sadness were in her eyes, but he refused to be made to feel guilty. 'He's helped me a lot and, yes, once I hoped we could be more than friends. I'm sure there are women like that in your past.'

He hadn't anticipated such honesty and it threw him off balance for a moment as he realised the truth of what she'd said. 'There was someone once, yes.'

Why had he said that? Why had he brought his ex-fiancée into this?

'Someone you loved?' she asked cautiously.

'No, someone I couldn't love, someone who needed that from me and I couldn't give it to her—or maybe it was because I didn't want to give it. Either way, the engagement ended.'

'You were engaged?' Her brows lifted in surprise and he regretted saying anything, but then maybe it would back up all he'd already told her, convince her that love was not something he could do.

'I was, yes.' He didn't want to have this conversation with her. It was something he never spoke of.

She clutched at her hair and looked away from him, as if she sensed his reluctance to talk. 'I've always wanted to see the Statue of Liberty. Thanks for this.'

Shocked by her change of subject, he looked up, and sure enough they were close to the statue as it reached up into the spring sky. He'd been so absorbed in her and the way he was thinking about her, feeling about her, that he hadn't even registered they'd got this far.

Emma turned and looked at him, her expression serious. What was it about this woman that muddled his senses so much? Every time he was with her he lost all clarity on what it was he wanted from her and from life.

'I don't expect love from you, Nikolai.' Her voice was as clear as a mountain stream but it didn't settle the unease he felt.

'What do you expect?'

'Nothing, Nikolai. You've made that perfectly clear from the very beginning. Our marriage is purely for the baby's sake.' She laid her hand lightly on his arm and, just as he had done before, he pulled back from her touch, not wanting such intimacy.

'We each have things to gain from the marriage, Emma.'

Emma looked at Nikolai and her heart began to break. She knew the whole thing was a deal, that their marriage was nothing more than a convenience, but always there had been a spark of hope fuelled by the heady passion they'd shared. Now that spark had gone, extinguished by his cold words.

'All I want is to be able to bring up my child, Nikolai. Do you promise me my ability to do that will never be questioned, even if we are apart?' She didn't want to tell him the truth behind her demands, but if it made him realise just how much she wanted this then it would have to be done.

She wanted her child to know who she was, not to think of her as a distant shadow in the background, as her own mother had become. It still hurt that a woman could turn her back so easily on the two children she'd given birth to, but she'd always told herself and Jess that their mother had been sick and didn't know what she was doing. Now, with her own baby on the way, she seriously doubted this. Her mother just hadn't wanted either her or Jess.

Nikolai's dark eyes searched hers but she couldn't look into them for fear he'd see the pain she felt about her mother and she looked beyond him to the passing city as the boat headed back along the river to the pier they'd left earlier.

'Why would I ever question that?' He moved a little closer, as if sensing there was much more to her demand.

She looked back at him, feeling the cooling wind in her face. 'I have already told you my sister and I were in care as children.'

He frowned and looked down at her, his mouth set in a firm line of annoyance. She was well aware now that he hated personal conversations, anything that meant he might have to connect emotionally. Did he think she was trying to make him feel sorry for her?

Before he could say anything which might stop the flow of words from her, she continued. Whatever he thought, this was something that had to be told. She couldn't spend the rest of her life, whether living with Nikolai or not, worried that she might be classed as an unfit mother and her child taken from her. She knew what it felt like to be that child.

'We were taken into care because my mother couldn't look after us. She'd rather have cuddled a bottle of something strong and alcoholic than hold my sister, and certainly hadn't worried about me.'

She looked directly at the passing buildings, into the mass of stone and windows that created a maze that ordinarily she'd long to explore. Now it was just something to look at. She couldn't look at Nikolai, didn't want to see the disapproval on his face. All she wanted was the promise that, no matter what happened between them, she could be a mother to her child.

'Do you really think I would keep a mother and child apart?' The stinging anger in his voice forced her to turn and look at him, and his dark eyes sparked with annoyance, heightening her own sense of anxiety.

'You made it virtually impossible for me to refuse the marriage deal.' Had he forgotten how he'd dominated that discussion?

'You were the one who quickly accepted the suggestion of funds for your sister.'

'It wasn't exactly a suggestion, Nikolai. It was more of a demand. It probably even comes much closer to blackmail.' She should tell him about her father, about the fear and rejection she'd grown up with.

Darkness clouded his eyes, as if the spring sun had slipped behind a cloud. 'It was not a demand and most certainly not blackmail. What kind of man do you think I am that I need to use such underhanded tactics?'

Defiantly she looked up into the icy blackness of his eyes. Her heart was pounding in her chest but she knew this had to be dealt with before they married. She didn't want to enter into a marriage, even a loveless one, with unresolved issues such as these. She couldn't live with that uncertainty hanging over her.

'I don't know, Nikolai. You have made it clear marriage isn't something you want to enter into freely, and yet you insist your mother lives under the illusion that we are in love. What kind of man does that make you?'

'I want only the best for my child. That's what kind of man I am.'

The boat bumped against the pier and Nikolai looked at Emma, wondering just what kind of monster she thought he was. Did she really believe he would separate her and their child, after all he'd told her about his childhood? Anger rushed through him and he couldn't look at her any more, couldn't take the accusation in her eyes.

Had he made a mistake, insisting on marriage? He couldn't walk away from his child, but none of this felt right.

No, it had to be this way. It was the only way he could prove he was not like his father, that despite the genes inside him he had his mother's goodness, he could be a good father. He wanted his son or daughter's childhood to be very different from what he'd known—and from what Emma had known, if what she'd told him was anything to go by.

'Do you really believe a loveless marriage is the way to achieve that?' she demanded hotly.

Her question caught him off guard and neither of them moved, despite the need to leave the boat. That word again. Why did love have to come into everything?

'Our marriage will achieve that precisely because it won't be swallowed up by nonsense such as love.' The hardness of his tone shocked her; he could see it in her eyes, feel it radiating off her.

'And what if one of us falls in love?' Her bold question challenged him from every side. Nikolai's suspicion about the ever-helpful Richard increased.

'If what you told me before is true, that will not happen. Neither of us believe in love—unless of course you are already in love with another man?' Again that irrational jealousy seeped into him as he thought of how happy she'd been talking to Richard on the phone. How she'd smiled and laughed.

'How can I love another man when I have known only you?' The hurt in her voice was clear, but his rational sense had jumped ship, replacing it with intense jealousy for a man he hadn't even met. A man who could make *his* fiancée smile so brightly that happiness danced in her eyes.

'Do you love Richard?' He couldn't think clearly, and didn't even register her words properly, but fired the question at her. She gasped in shock and stepped back from him.

'You think I am in love with Richard?'

'Why is that so implausible?' Impatience filled him at her act of innocence. She'd used that act once before.

'Because he's a friend. But I'll be honest with you—

it hurts like hell to feel anything for someone who feels nothing for you. But you wouldn't know what that's like, would you, Nikolai?'

Before he had a chance to ask more, she left him standing on the deck and he watched as she disembarked and strode away from him. What the hell had all that meant?

CHAPTER TEN

EMMA HAD TRIED to keep alive the flicker of hope that things had changed between them after returning from their engagement party. Nikolai had avoided the painful discussion they'd had that night, but had played to perfection the role of adoring fiancé. Yesterday on the boat had doused that hope and now the ever-increasing nausea was making everything so much more difficult to deal with.

'I've cleared the diary for today,' he said as he strode across the room to stand looking, brooding, out over the park and the vastness of New York beyond. His withdrawal from her made her feel insignificant and rejected, feeding into her childhood insecurities which were growing by the day.

'You did that yesterday; please don't feel you have to do it again.' A wave of nausea washed over her. She pressed her hand against her forehead, her elbow on her lap, and curled over as a sharp pain shot through her. She didn't feel well enough to do anything this morning, least of all play happy bride-to-be with Nikolai.

Was it the strain of everything: the way he'd manipulated the whole marriage deal, using the one thing she wouldn't wish upon any child, least of all her own?

Another cramp caused her to take in a sharp breath and she bit down against the pain. There was something wrong. Very wrong. Panic rushed through her like a river breaking over a waterfall. She wanted this baby so much, with or without Nikolai's support, but what was happening to her? What had she done wrong?

'Nikolai,' she said, her voice shaky. 'The baby. Something's wrong.'

She closed her eyes against another wave of nausea and tried to fight back the tears—not just tears of pain, but tears of fear for her baby. She couldn't take it if something happened. What if she lost her baby? In the back of her mind, as the fog of pain increased, the thought that it was exactly what Nikolai would want rampaged round like a wild animal, making her angry and more panicked.

'Emma.' Nikolai's stern voice snapped her back from that fog and she looked up at him as he stood over her, phone in hand. His brows were snapped together in worry and his face set hard in stern lines. 'I'm taking you to the hospital.'

A tear slid down her cheek as relief washed over her. He was in control. But could he stop what was happening, what she feared was the worst thing possible? As another pain stabbed at her stomach she closed her eyes and the need to give in to the blackness rushing around her was too much. Would that be the best thing to do for the baby? Further questions were silenced as she let go and did exactly that.

When she opened her eyes again she knew she was in hospital and panic charged over her like a herd of wild, stampeding horses. She tried to sit up, but Nikolai's hand pressed into her shoulder, preventing her from doing so. 'It's okay. Lie still.'

His voice was soothing and commanding without any of the panic she felt, but still she tried to get up. She wanted answers, wanted to know what was happening to her and her baby.

'My baby?'

He leant over her, forcing her to look into his face, his eyes. She smelt his aftershave, felt the warmth of his hand on her shoulder, and relished the calm control he had. 'The baby is fine. You are fine. So please, just relax. Stress won't help you or the baby at all.'

'Thank goodness.' She breathed and closed her eyes as relief washed over her.

What would she have done if she had lost the baby? A terrible thought entered her mind, slipping in like an unwanted viper. If this had happened just a week later, and it had had the most unthinkable consequences, she and Nikolai would have been married. What would he have done then, married to a woman who no longer carried the child he'd made a deal for?

'You have been doing too much,' he said sternly. 'Rest is what you need.'

'Maybe we should call off the wedding.' She couldn't look at him, couldn't bear to see the truth in his eyes. She'd been rejected by her father before he'd even seen her and then again as a teenager. For him marriage and fatherhood wasn't what he'd wanted in life and she knew it was the same for Nikolai; he'd made that more than clear. She couldn't trap him into something he didn't want but neither could she deny her baby the chance of knowing its father. A heart-wrenching decision, born out of the panic of the moment, grew in her mind. Who should she be true to—her child or herself?

'If the doctor agrees you are well and can come home, that will not happen.' There wasn't a drop of gentleness in his voice. The man who'd become more gentle and loving each night had gone and the cold, hard man who'd walked out on her in Vladimir was back.

'But this isn't what you want.' She hated the pain that sounded in her voice, hated the way she still clung to the hope he could one day love her.

'What we want is irrelevant.' He looked down at her, his dark eyes narrowed with irritation. 'It's what is best for the child, Emma. We will be married.'

Nikolai fought hard against the invading emotions as he helped Emma to sit up. This was more than the physical pull of sexual attraction that had surrounded them since the day they'd first met in Vladimir. This was something he'd never known before. Something he'd been running from since the night he'd made her his.

He cared, really cared, not just about the child who was his heir but about the woman he'd created that child with. When had that happened? When had lust and sexual desire crossed the divide and become something deeper, something much more powerful than passion?

He had no idea when, but all he knew was that it had happened. He looked down at Emma, her face full of uncertainty, and knew without doubt that he cared for her. And it scared the hell out of him. Caring caused pain.

'We will take Emma for a scan now.' The nurse's

voice snapped him back from that daunting revelation. A scan? Would he be able to see his child? Now?

'Is there something wrong?' The quiver in Emma's
voice reached into his heart and pulled at it, making
him want to hold her hand, give her reassurance. Making him want to love her. But how could he do that
when he didn't know how to deal with the emotions
that were taking over? Or even exactly what they were?

'Is there?' he demanded of the nurse.

'Everything is fine,' she said with the kind of smile
meant to dispel any doubts. 'We just want to reassure
both of you.'

'Thank you.' Emma's reply called his attention back
to her and he looked down at her, noticing, as he had
done several times in recent days, how pale she was.
Should he have done something sooner? Guilt ploughed
into him. He'd pushed her too hard, not taken enough
interest to see how tired she'd become. He'd risked
his baby.

His baby.

Those two words crashed into him and for a moment
he couldn't draw a breath. Then he felt Emma's hand
on his arm, the sympathetic touch almost too much.
He didn't deserve that from her.

A short time later, and with no recollection of how
he'd got there, he was in a small room with Emma. She
lay on the bed, the soft skin of her stomach exposed
as the nurse pressed the scanner probe against her. He
noticed her hand was clenched as it held her top out of
the way, as if she feared the worst. He watched as the
nurse moved the probe, trying to get a clear image on
the screen. He wouldn't have been able to tell Emma
was pregnant with his child, her stomach was flat, but

the first image filled the screen and he knew the machine didn't lie.

In his mind he tried to add up how many weeks' pregnant she was. How many weeks was it since they'd had the most amazing night which had had such far-reaching consequences. Before he could work it out, the nurse's voice broke through his thoughts.

'There we are. Baby at ten weeks.'

He looked at the screen, not able to take his eyes from it. The fuzzy image had a dark centre and in that darkness was his baby. Small, but unmistakable. He couldn't move, couldn't do anything but stare at it.

A tense silence filled the room as the nurse continued to move the scanner around, losing the image briefly. He couldn't look at Emma, couldn't take his attention away from the screen that showed him the secret of his baby.

'And everything appears normal,' the nurse added as she paused once more, showing an even clearer image. 'See it moving and its heart beating?'

Fierce protectiveness rose up in him like a rearing horse and he knew in that tension-filled moment he would do absolutely anything for his baby. He would go to the ends of the earth for him or her. It would want for nothing and he would love it unconditionally.

Love.

Could he love it? Could he give it the one thing his father had never given him? The one thing which terrified him?

Finally he looked at Emma as she watched the screen, a small tear slipping down her cheek. Did he love her? What was the powerful sensation of crushing around his chest and the lightness in his stomach each

time he saw her or thought of her? Was it love? Had
he fallen in love with a woman who could never love
him? A woman whose heart was already elsewhere?

Emma looked at the screen and tears began to slide
down her cheeks. They were in part tears of happiness:
her baby was well. She'd seen it move, seen its little
heart beating. But those tears of happiness mingled
with tears of pain. Nikolai had been silent throughout.
He hadn't uttered a word, had barely moved, and she
could no longer look at him. Was he now seeing the
reality of the deal he'd made?

She glanced up at him now as the nurse completed
the scan and then left them alone. No doubt she thought
she was giving them private time to be happy together,
but then she didn't know the truth.

The truth was that Nikolai didn't want this baby.
He'd stood stiffly by her side, his hard gaze fixed
rigidly on the screen as the first images of their child
had appeared. Now he couldn't move, couldn't look
her in the eye.

The elation that filled her from seeing the baby,
from knowing it was well, cooled as the tension in the
room grew to ominous levels and she wished the nurse
hadn't left. At least then she might have been able to
avoid the truth.

'You must rest,' Nikolai said, his voice deeper and
more commanding than she'd ever known it. Was he
blaming her? Was he even now thinking she was as
uncaring as her mother had been?

'I—I think we should at least postpone the wedding.' She stumbled over her words as his fiercely intense gaze locked with hers. If she could get him to

agree to postpone it then it would give them both time to decide if it really was the right thing to do. She loved him but couldn't marry him, tie him to her, if there was never going to be a chance that he would one day feel the same for her.

'No, but you won't need to worry about anything. I will arrange for your final dress fittings to be at the apartment.'

He moved away as she sat up and slipped off the bed, but she felt more exposed than she had that morning she'd first woken in his bed. It was as if he knew everything about her. She knew he didn't, knew that she still guarded her fear of rejection—his rejection. Her father had rejected her. Richard had too, just by refusing to see her as anything other than a friend, and the last thing she wanted was to be rejected by the father of her baby, the man she'd fallen in love with.

'I'm not sure marriage is the right thing for us at the moment.' It was like standing on the shore, allowing the waves to wash over her toes, each wave taking her deeper into the conversation until it was swim or allow the depths to swallow her up.

His eyes narrowed. 'Why?'

'It doesn't feel right, Nikolai.'

'We made a deal, Emma.' The uncompromising hardness of his voice shocked her.

'It's almost as if you've bought me, bought the baby.'

'You agreed to the deal, Emma, and if my memory serves me right held out for just that little bit more. Not content with securing yours and the baby's future, you also wanted to secure your sister's.'

'But this isn't right. We don't love each other.' The plea in her voice must have reached him somehow because he moved closer to her and she waited with bated breath to see what he was going to do or say.

'Love isn't always needed, Emma.' He touched her cheek, brushing his fingers across her skin so softly she could almost imagine he cared. 'Sometimes passion and desire is a better base on which to build a marriage and we've proved many times that exists between us.'

'But that's not love, Nikolai.' She drew in a shuddering breath as he moved even closer. Why couldn't he just admit he didn't love her, that he would never feel that for her?

'I don't care what it is, we made our deal with it.'

'But will it be enough?' She stepped away from him, wanting to get out of this dimly lit room and away from the sudden intensity in his eyes.

Nikolai looked at Emma as she tried to evade him. Was she that desperate to get away from him? Was he doing the right thing, insisting the marriage deal went ahead?

'For me, yes.' There was no way he was going to reveal the depths of the emotions seeing his baby had unlocked. He wanted to protect his child, always be there for it. He also wanted to do the same for Emma, but after the call from Richard he doubted Emma felt the same way.

She'd come to New York to secure her and her child's futures. She must have done her homework on him because she'd then held out for more than that when all he'd wanted was to keep his child in his life.

Fatherhood might not be something he'd looked for, or even wanted, but now that it had happened he wasn't about to let any man or woman stand in the way and prevent him from being a father. He had to prove to himself he had not inherited his father's mean streak.

'And what if one day that changes?' She challenged him further, deepening his resolve to make it work, to be the father he'd never had.

'It will not change, Emma. We have created a child together and that will bind us for all eternity; nothing can change that now.' The truth of his words sounded round in his head and he knew he couldn't let her walk away from their marriage, their deal.

'So there's no going back?' An obstinate strength sounded in her voice, as if sparring with him was making her stronger.

'Never.'

CHAPTER ELEVEN

THERE WERE JUST two more days until she married Nikolai and Emma was restless. She'd been taking it easy since returning from the hospital but today felt different. She'd had lots of time to think and, although Emma knew brides had nerves, she didn't think they had the serious doubts she was being plagued with.

She still cringed with embarrassment at how close she'd come to revealing she loved him whilst they were on the boat, but those tense few minutes in the hospital had highlighted how bad the idea of marrying him was.

His reaction at the scan emphasised clearly that marriage was the wrong thing to do. She could feel him pulling away from her emotionally, locking down those barriers again, and she braced herself for his rejection.

It didn't matter how many times she let the question wage a battle in her mind, she still came back to the same answer: how could she marry a man who didn't love her? Each and every day she had fallen deeper in love. If only they hadn't spent that night together after they'd returned from the party. If only he hadn't stirred her emotions up and awakened her love for him, then maybe she could have merely acted the part of adoring and caring fiancée. Such thoughts were useless when each night spent with him filled her heart with more love.

Her phone bleeped on the table and she abandoned the view of the park she often contemplated and opened the usual daily text from Jess, missing her more than she thought possible. If Jess were here, sharing this moment with her, she might be able to deal with it better.

With a sigh she picked up the phone and read the text from Jess. As she read the words, her heart leapt with excitement.

Surprise! Be with you in five minutes.

Jess was here? In New York? How had that happened? She recalled the lighter conversations with Nikolai when they'd taken the boat along the river. He must have arranged for Jess to come over for their wedding. Why had he done that? He confused her. Such actions made him look nice, as if he did have some feelings for her, making everything even harder. She couldn't back out of the marriage now if Jess was here, knowing that by doing so she'd be letting Jess's chance of a worry-free future slip away as well as depriving her child of its father.

Ignoring the inner churning of her heart, she sent a text back to Jess. Excitement almost took over the nauseating worry that filled her. She wondered again about Nikolai's motives for organising it. With a huff of frustration, she sent a text to Nikolai to say thank you. Two could play at the relationship game.

Before Emma had a chance to do anything else, the apartment door opened and Jess stood there, a big smile on her face. Disbelief kept Emma rooted to the spot for a moment and emotions overwhelmed her. Jess let go of her case and walked towards her and, as she'd always done, Emma enveloped her in a hug, not able to believe she was actually here.

'How did you get here?' she asked when they'd finally let each other go.

'Your wonderful fiancé.' Jess's excitement was palpable and Emma couldn't even think straight. Of course she would think he was so wonderful; it was exactly what she'd wanted her to think. She couldn't let Jess know the real reason she'd accepted the marriage.

'Nikolai?' she asked and Jess laughed.

'How many do you have? Of course Nikolai.' Jess walked around the apartment, taking in the luxury of it all, something neither of them were used to. 'He arranged everything, right down to the key to get in. He's amazing, Em, you're so lucky. He must love you so much.'

Jess's enthusiasm for her soon-to-be brother-in-law was so zealous it almost brought Emma's world crashing down. Despite the miles that had separated them, he'd charmed Jess, made her see what he wanted the rest of the world to see. She'd never felt more trapped in her life.

'He didn't tell me, though,' she said, quickly pushing away the doubts, not wanting them to creep in and spoil this time with Jess.

'Because he wanted to surprise you. He made me promise not to say a word. Have you any idea how hard that's been the last few weeks, keeping it a secret from you?'

Last few weeks? He'd organised this long before they had the discussion about Jess attending the wedding? Had he done it even before their engagement party? Was that why he'd been so concerned that she had nobody there for her that night?

'Well, he's certainly done that,' she said as she took Jess off to her room, determined not to let Nikolai's motives spoil this unexpected moment with her sister.

Nikolai arrived back at his apartment to the sound of women's voices drifting through the open plan living area from the bedroom Emma had used on her arrival, which her sister would now use. For a moment he was taken aback and stood listening to them, grateful that Jess had managed to keep her arrival a secret. The lack of anyone for Emma at their engagement party had made such a surprise important, but the visit to the hospital had reinforced it.

'You're having his baby?' Jess's unfamiliar voice was filled with shock and he remained silent and still, waiting to hear Emma's reply, but none came. Was she smiling and nodding her confirmation to her sister or giving away the truth of it all? Would she let Jess know this was nothing more than a marriage of convenience?

Silence echoed around the apartment for what seemed like hours, but he knew it was merely seconds. He stood still, not daring to move, not wanting them to hear his footsteps on the polished wooden floor. Finally the silence was broken by Jess's voice.

'But you love him, right?' Jess asked, concern in her voice, and Nikolai held his breath, hoping Emma would act the same part she'd acted for his mother, that of a woman in love.

'He's a good man.' Emma's subdued answer was not at all what he'd expected her to say. It seemed her

acting skills were not on form today and disappointment flooded through him. The last thing he wanted
was Emma's younger sister letting slip to his mother
that the marriage was not a love match. That would
make his mother feel guilty for what had happened in
his childhood. The only thing she'd ever wanted was
for him to find the real love she had.

'I thought you wanted true love.' Jess's voice lowered so he was hardly able to hear it and right now he
certainly didn't want to hear Emma's answer. He recalled her light-hearted view on love when they'd first
met and knew it must have been true and not the throwaway comment she'd allowed him to think it was. She
did believe in love, and was looking for it, but love was
something he couldn't give her.

He strode across the room, his footsteps loud on the
polished floor, and perfect for blocking out the answer
he didn't want to hear. He poured himself a much-
needed glass of brandy. The voices had gone silent
and now he wished he had waited to find out what she
thought. Would it be so bad to be loved by the woman
who was carrying his child, his heir? Somewhere deep
inside him the idea stirred those emotions from the day
at the hospital and for a brief moment of madness he
wanted exactly that.

'I didn't hear you come in.' Emma's voice sounded
cautiously behind him and he turned his back on the
view to face her. She looked pale and he wondered if
she was well enough to have Jess here.

'I've only just arrived,' he said grimly, wishing she
didn't have such an effect on him. With just one questioning look she cracked the defensive shield around

him, made him feel emotions, which as far as he was concerned was dangerous.

She walked closer to him and, for the first time since they'd arrived back from their engagement party, she looked shy and unable to meet his gaze. She'd had the same look in her eyes as she'd met him in the hotel lounge the night after the sleigh ride. That shyness hadn't lasted long. It had soon been replaced by the temptation of a seductress. Had it been that which had pushed his limits of control beyond endurance?

'Thank you,' she said softly.

'For what?' She looked at him with big green eyes and to see the emotion within them was too much. He didn't want the complication of emotion in his life. Never. It was why he hadn't looked at her as they'd seen their baby on the scan.

She smiled shyly. 'For getting Jess here. You have no idea how much that means to me—and Jess.'

As she said the words a young, dark-haired girl came into the room and smiled, the similarities between the sisters striking. 'And you must be Jess?'

Emma turned round as he spoke and held out her hand to her sister. 'We are both grateful for everything, but this is such a surprise. Getting married will be easier with Jess at my side.'

Irritation surged through him. She thought getting married to him was going to be difficult? From what she'd just said, it was obvious Jess was in full possession of the facts; no pretence at love for her sister's benefit was needed now. Didn't that show she was as cold and calculating as he was? It certainly proved she was only marrying him because of the baby.

'You helped me with my mother. It was only fair you got something out of our deal too.' He then turned his attention to Jess, needing to put some barriers back up between him and Emma, uncomfortable at the effect she was having on him. 'Did you have a good flight?'

'I did, thanks. I've never flown first class before,' Jess replied, grinning enthusiastically. He felt Emma's curious gaze on him, but ignored it, and the way his body warmed just from her nearness. He had to get out of here now.

'I'll leave you two girls to it, then. You have dress fittings later.' Before Emma could say or do anything, he left them alone. It was more than obvious to him now that he had to leave and check into a hotel until his wedding day. His wedding day. After ending his first engagement, he'd never thought he'd ever get married, let alone be a father.

He turned at the door. 'I've booked into a hotel until after the wedding, so you will not be disturbed by my presence.'

'You don't have to do that,' Emma said, alarm in her voice.

'Of course he does,' Jess chipped in. 'It's bad luck to see each other before the wedding.'

'In that case, I will go now.'

Emma watched Nikolai leave, angry that after all she'd done for the benefit of his mother he'd made no attempt to act the part of loving fiancé in front of Jess. He'd looked angry and irritated by her presence and their thanks, and she worried how that would look to Jess.

Especially when she'd made every effort to make it appear they were in love when she'd met his family at their engagement party.

Why had he chosen that precise moment to drop the caring façade he'd hidden behind all week? She'd only just told Jess she loved him and that she was happy to be his wife as well as a mother. Then he'd arrived back at the apartment like an angry lion whose authority had been challenged and made it obvious that the marriage was a deal that was going to unite them and definitely not love.

'I'm not stupid, Em, I know what's going on.' Jess's voice broke through her thoughts.

Emma whirled round to look at her sister and saw a frown of worry creasing her brow. What did she know? That the pregnancy was a mistake and that she'd abandoned her dreams of love and happiness to do what was right for the baby?

'Nothing's going on. Every bride and groom is nervous before the big day.' She bluffed her way out of the corner Jess was backing her into. But it was too late. Emma's fragile faith in her love for Nikolai was fading fast. Was she really doing the right thing by her child, marrying a man who didn't want her around, much less love her?

'Tell me, Em, please.' Her sister's pleas showed wisdom beyond her years, wisdom born out of the hardships they'd faced growing up.

Emma sighed heavily. 'I can't marry him, Jess. I can't marry a man who doesn't want love in his life. But, more than that, I can't live each day waiting for him to reject me and his baby.'

Any further attempt at spilling out her sorry story

was halted as the dress fitters arrived. Emma let them in, amazed at the quantity of dresses that hung wrapped up on the rail they were quickly setting up. The fact that they were here also made what she was doing seem even more real. She was actually going to marry a man who didn't want love in his life, who could never give her what she'd always dreamed of finding.

But he can give Jess a chance to be something.

Emma tried to shrug off those thoughts and walked over to stand by the tall windows. She looked but didn't see the view which usually captivated her so easily as she battled to halt the doubts which were growing by the second. She heard Jess come to stand beside her.

'What makes you say that?' Jess asked, shock obvious in her voice.

'He's never told me how he feels,' Emma said quietly, not quite able to add that he'd already told her he didn't want love, that the deal they'd struck was one which would benefit Jess.

'I don't think it's something men say,' replied Jess confidently, and Emma turned to look at her, finding it odd that she could even smile at such a remark. 'What?'

'Do you actually know what you are saying?' Emma laughed, trying to lighten things up. She shouldn't be talking to Jess like this. Not if she wanted to prevent her ever finding out the exact terms of the deal.

'Of course I do—I watch films, listen to people talk.' Now Jess laughed, but it was edged with relief. Guilt rushed over Emma. She must have worried Jess for a moment.

Emma pushed all her doubts to the back of her mind.

She was doing this for Jess as well as her baby, which meant she couldn't let on how much she doubted her sanity for accepting the terms of the deal.

'What colour do you think?' She strolled over to the rail of bridesmaid dresses and touched a pink one.

'Blue.' Jess joined her. 'You always said blue was your lucky colour.'

'But I thought you liked pink?' Emma was touched by her sister's acknowledgement that it was her day.

'I do, but I want you to have all the luck in the world, so I want blue.'

As Jess spoke, the dress fitters pulled out several dresses, but a pale-blue strapless gown caught hers and Jess's attention at the same time. Moments later, Jess was twirling round the apartment. 'It's a perfect fit. This has to be the one.'

'You look gorgeous, Jess. All grown up.'

'And I am, so you can go off into the sunset with your very own Prince Charming and not worry about me.' The reproach in Jess's voice brought a mixture of tears to Emma's eyes and a soft giggle of happiness.

'I guess I'd better decide on my dress,' said Emma. 'This is so last minute, I can't possibly find one to fit.'

Cream silks blended with white on the rail and Emma didn't know which one to look at first. Should she even have a full-length gown? What about cream? Or should it be white?

'This is the one,' said Jess as she pulled the skirt of a beautiful white gown towards her and grinned. 'Try it on.'

Helped by the fitter, Emma tried on the white lace gown with a strapless bodice that matched Jess's perfectly; it was almost too good to be true. As she was zipped into it, she looked at herself in the mirror and saw, not plain Emma, but a beautiful bride. The dress was simple yet elegant with a small train; she'd never imagined herself in such a dress.

'It's all meant to be,' Jess gushed. 'First my dress, now this one. You and Nikolai are going to make the perfect couple.'

CHAPTER TWELVE

EMMA WOKE EARLY with a start, the big bed cold and empty, just as it had been since the day Jess had arrived and Nikolai had moved into a hotel. He was stepping back from her as if he too had doubts. Why hadn't she tried harder to sort things when they'd been at the hospital?

She looked around her. The early-morning sun shined with wicked brightness into her bedroom, seeming to highlight the wedding dress hanging in readiness for that afternoon, when she would step into it and seal the hardest deal of her life.

Could she do it? Could she put on the white gown of lace and become Nikolai's wife, knowing he would never love her?

She pulled on her jeans and jumper and put on a pair of flat pumps. She couldn't stay and look at the wedding dress any longer. She had to get away, get out of the apartment and think. The sensation that she was doing the wrong thing had taken over, blocking out everything else.

'Where are you going?' Jess asked, quickly taking in her casual clothes as she went into the bedroom.

'I need to go for a walk. I need to think, Jess. I need

to think really hard before I make a terrible mistake.'
Emma looked at the long pale-blue dress she and Jess
had selected the day she'd arrived. It hung in readiness,
mocking, from the wardrobe door. During those few
hours when she'd tried her own dress on for the final
time, Jess had enjoyed herself so much selecting styles
and colours that her enthusiasm had become infectious
and for a while Emma had believed everything was
going to be all right.

But it could never be all right. Nikolai could never
love her as she loved him. If she married him it would
be the worst mistake of her life.

'What's the matter, Em?' Jess crossed the room
quickly and Emma wondered how she was ever going
to tell her. How did you look your sister in the eye and
tell her you were throwing away her chance of fulfill-
ing her dream, of being what she wanted to be, and
worse, subjecting a child to a life without a father?

'I'm not sure I can do this.' Emma felt ill at the concern on her sister's face and wished she hadn't said
anything, but she had to. In about six hours she would
have to put the wedding dress on. What if she couldn't?
What if she couldn't unite herself with Nikolai in marriage? She had to tell Jess something, had to give her
some warning that things weren't as they should be.

'I thought you were happy, that you loved him,' Jess
said, a hint of panic in her voice, and that was the
last thing Emma wanted her sister to do. They'd had
enough panic and upset in their lives. How had this
turned into such a mess?

'I was,' she said with a sigh as she looked past her
sister and to the view of the green trees of the park beyond. 'And I do love him.'

I love him too much and I can't face his rejection.

'So what's wrong, then?' Jess touched her gently on the arm, pulling her back from her thoughts, back to what she had to do.

She closed her eyes against the pain of knowing she'd fallen in love with Nikolai even after he'd readily confessed he couldn't love anyone. She couldn't stop the words any longer, couldn't hold them back. 'He doesn't love me.'

She felt Jess's hand slip from her arm, but she couldn't look at her and tell her what it was all about, why they were really getting married, so pulled away. Even when Jess spoke again she couldn't look at her. She'd failed her. If she ran out on Nikolai now, she'd be throwing away the chance for her baby to know a different life. 'I think you are wrong about that.'

'Don't, Jess, you don't know the half of it.' Emma's hot retort left her lips before she had time to consider what she wanted to say.

'Last night he looked as if he'd wanted to eat you alive.' Jess's bold words, so out of character for her little sister, didn't ease the doubt; instead, it increased it. Lust had been responsible for that look on Nikolai's face. Nothing other than desire-fuelled lust.

'That's not love, Jess, and it's not something to build your future on. Don't ever fall for that.' But wasn't that what she herself had done—fallen for the power of raw lust?

'You're wrong, Em. What I saw in his eyes last night was love. Anyone can see that.'

'Don't be so silly. You're not even seventeen. How can you know what love looks like?' Emma was becoming irritated with this conversation. All she wanted to do was leave the confines of the apartment. She needed time to think what to do next—after she'd told Nikolai they wouldn't be getting married.

'I know it was love, Em, I just know it. He loves you.' Jess pleaded with her, but it was too late. She'd made up her mind. 'Don't let your past stand in the way of your future. You are not Mother and he's not your father.'

That was so painfully close to the truth, she didn't want to hear it. 'I have to get out of here.'

For nearly an hour Emma all but marched around the park but none of it gave her any joy, any release from the feeling of impending doom which loomed over her. All she could think about was that she had to tell Nikolai it was over. She stopped walking and found a bench and, sitting down, took out her phone. Her hands shook and, even though her heart was breaking, it was what she had to do. This sham of an engagement had gone on long enough. It was time to end it.

She pressed Nikolai's number and listened to the ringing tone, part of her wanting him to pick up, part of her wishing he wouldn't, that she could hang up and walk away. The message system took over, and for a moment she nearly ended the call without leaving a message, but if she didn't do this now, didn't say what she needed to, it would be too late. He'd be waiting for her to arrive at the church he'd booked for the small, intimate ceremony with only his family and Jess as guests. They might have struck a cold deal for their child's sake, but she couldn't marry him knowing he'd never love her.

'It's me, Emma,' she said, not liking the quiver in

her voice, and she tried to sound much sterner. The message she left had to be decisive and firm. 'I can't do this, Nikolai. It was wrong of me to accept your deal. I can't marry you. I'm going back to London with Jess—tonight.'

She ended the call and stared at the phone as if it might explode, but inside she knew she'd done the right thing. She couldn't marry a man who didn't love her, not when her love for him grew deeper and stronger each day. All along she'd thought she was doing the right thing, but now she couldn't see any happiness for her or the baby in a loveless marriage.

She looked at the time on her phone: almost ten. The wedding was due to take place at three. Nikolai had plenty of time to sort things out and make all the necessary cancellations, just as she had time to get a flight back to London booked for her and Jess. She hoped he wouldn't come and try and persuade her to go through with the wedding. Would he really do that when marriage and fatherhood were the very things he'd admitted not wanting? She wanted to be able to leave in peace. Of course, they'd have to settle things to do with the baby, but that could wait until she was more in control of her emotions, more able to be strong and hold back her love.

It was what she had to do, but she couldn't move, as if by doing so it would make it worse. But how much worse could it get? She was pregnant with the child of the man she'd lost her heart to and all he wanted was a loveless marriage, a convenient deal. The spark of sexual attraction wouldn't keep the marriage alive for ever, and once it dwindled to nothing she didn't think she could continue to live the lie—or hide her love.

She turned off her phone and as she sat in the peace of the park, letting the birdsong soothe her, she wished she could turn off her emotions as easily. All she needed was a few minutes to compose herself and then she'd go back to the apartment, book the flights and leave New York. She could explain to Jess on the long flight home, admit it had been a mistake to come here, and an even bigger mistake to accept Nikolai's deal, whatever extras he'd thrown her way.

Nikolai tried to get Emma on the phone again as he strode through the park. Jess had told him to try there after he'd called at the apartment. Anger boiled up inside him as he heard her message going round and round in his head. She didn't want to get married. *I can't do this, Nikolai:* that was what she'd said.

Each time he replayed the words in his mind anger sizzled deep inside him. Anger and rejection. He should have seen it coming. What she'd said at the hospital after the scan suddenly made sense. While he'd been bonding with his child and liking the idea of fatherhood, of settling down with Emma, she'd been thinking of ending the engagement and calling off the wedding.

Anger simmered, pushing him to walk hard and fast through the park. He had no idea where to begin looking and savagely pulled out his phone and tried to call her again. Nothing. She'd turned it off. If she thought a switched-off phone would be enough to deter him, she was very much mistaken. He wasn't used to people backing out of a deal and he certainly wasn't accustomed to being denied what he wanted—and he wanted Emma.

The thought trickled through him like a mountain

stream thawing after a long, hard winter. He wanted her, really wanted her. Not just with the hot lust that had driven him mad, but with something much deeper. It wasn't anything to do with the baby. He wanted Emma.

The park was full of morning joggers and dog walkers wrestling with groups of dogs as he stopped and looked around for Emma. She'd been so enamoured with the park since her arrival; she could be anywhere. A strong curse left his lips as he marched on towards the lake; then, as he rounded a corner, he could see her through the trees. She was sitting on a bench, looking away into the distance, totally absorbed in thought.

He reined in the instinct to rush over to her and demand to know just what the message had been all about, and instead walked slowly towards her, taking advantage of the fact that she was looking the other way. Her long hair gleamed in the morning sunshine as he got closer and he rubbed the pads of his thumb and finger together, remembering the silky softness of her hair. Would he ever feel it again?

Emma turned to look his way and he stopped walking, frozen to the spot with something that seemed horribly like fear, but fear of what? He saw the moment she realised it was him, saw the tension make her body stiffen, and the realisation that he did that to her hurt more than he knew. She was either afraid of him or hated him for what he'd done to her.

She didn't move, but she did look down, as she always did when something was difficult to do. Was her reluctance to leave an invitation for him to join her? He didn't care what the hell it was. He was going to sit with her regardless.

I can't let the woman I love walk out on me.

That thought crashed into him and he stopped again, his heart pounding as he realised exactly what that thought meant. He'd felt the same at the hospital. Why hadn't he seen it then?

He looked at her, sitting on the bench in the morning sunshine only a short distance away, yet it was like a chasm had opened up right there in the park. It yawned between them, becoming greater with each passing second.

He couldn't move, couldn't cross it.

He'd pushed her to the other side of it right from the very beginning and she'd been more than happy to be there. She'd agreed with everything he'd said about commitment and love, accepted the cold terms of his marriage deal. She scorned love or happy-ever-after just as much as he had, but now, as if he'd finally opened his eyes and seen what was real, he had to accept that he did want all that. He did want Emma in his life, as his wife and the mother of his baby, but not out of any obligation—out of love.

Did he risk everything and tell her how he felt, that he loved her after all he'd said to her? Or did he try and persuade her to keep the deal in the hope he'd got it wrong? Maybe panic had filled his head with such nonsense as love.

But he didn't just feel that desolate distance in his head. He felt it in his chest—in his heart. That sensation he'd experienced since the moment he'd first met Emma was back, squeezing tighter than ever, as if trying to get him to acknowledge the truth, acknowledge it as love.

She looked at him, apprehension clear on her face, and finally he managed to move towards her. Each step was harder than the previous one. How could he tell her what he really felt when he'd only just realised the truth of it himself?

'Did you think a quick phone message would be enough to extricate you from our deal?' That wasn't what he wanted to say at all, but the protective barrier around his heart wasn't just keeping her out, it was locking the truth inside him, preventing him from saying what he had to say, what he wanted to say.

She looked up at him as he came to stand in front of her, those gorgeous green eyes narrowing against the sun. Or was it the harshness in his voice? 'I didn't expect you not to answer.'

'I was in the shower,' he said quickly, banishing the memories of the time they had spent in the shower together not so many days ago.

She looked down and away from him again. Was she recalling the same thing, the same heated passion? He sat down next to her and once again her gaze met his. 'It doesn't matter, Nikolai, because I can't marry you.'

'Not even for the baby?' He flung the question at her as he clenched his teeth against the panic which flowed through him like a river in flood. He couldn't let her go, let her just walk out of his life, not now he knew what he really felt for her. How long had he loved her? The thought barely materialised before he knew the answer. He'd loved her from the first night they'd spent together in Vladimir, maybe even the first moment he'd seen her.

'No.' She shook her head and looked directly ahead of her, as if distracted by the surroundings, but he sensed she was holding back on him. But why? And what?

* * *

Emma looked at the pain in his eyes and knew he was blaming his past, his father's mistakes. Her heart wrenched and she desperately wanted to reach out to him, to reassure him it was nothing to do with that. But, if she did, she'd weaken and the last thing she wanted to blurt out was that she couldn't marry anyone who didn't love her as she loved them, that she couldn't put herself in the path of such rejection.

'No. I know it sounds very clichéd, but it's me.' She looked into his eyes, seeing their darkness harder than they'd ever been.

'So you are quite happy to back out of our deal.' His voice was deceptively calm and that unsettled her even more. Was he just going through the motions of asking her to reconsider when he'd rather book flights back to London for Jess and her himself?

'For our child's sake, yes.' She skirted around the truth, her heart pounding harder than ever, and despite the warm spring sun she shivered as skitters of apprehension slithered down her spine.

'Our child will benefit from the marriage, but will it benefit from being brought up by you alone, while I am on the other side of the world?' The scorn in that question was almost too much for her. Was he deliberately trying to make it harder for her or was he finding a way to make her worst nightmare come true and take her baby from her?

Whatever he was doing, this had to be sorted now. She couldn't go on for the rest of her pregnancy wondering what he would do next. 'Our baby will be better off with two parents who are apart and happy than two living under the same roof that are unhappy.'

'And will you be happy?' The question threw her off guard, as did the change of his tone. He sounded defeated. She'd never heard Nikolai sound like that.

'All I want is for my child to grow up happy, to never feel the sting of rejection from its father.' She wanted to say more, to make him aware just how anxious she was, but stopped the words and the pain from flowing out.

'And you think I will reject my son or daughter?' Hurt resounded in his voice, but his eyes narrowed with annoyance. 'After all I saw and witnessed as a child, do you really think I want to hurt my own child?'

She looked down, knowing her words had been taken the wrong way, and she hated herself for hurting him. He'd done all a young boy could to protect his mother and even now, as a grown man, was doing the same. That was why he'd insisted on the pretence of love at the engagement party and why he'd gone to Vladimir in the first instance.

Instinctively she reached out to him, placing her hand on his arm. 'No, Nikolai, that's not what I thought. I don't want my child to know what I've known. I can't stand by and let you reject them when they are no longer any use in your life.'

He took her hand in his, the warmth of it briefly chasing the apprehension away 'I would never do that, Emma, never.'

She looked at him as his eyes softened and she almost lost her resolve, but his next words brought it hurtling back to her.

'I'm not about to let you walk away. I want to see my child grow up and, just as I never want to be like my father, I promise I will never do what yours has done to you.'

'It doesn't mean we should marry, though.'

'We will marry as planned, Emma.' He looked at his watch. 'In less than four hours, you will be my wife.'

CHAPTER THIRTEEN

'I'm sorry, Nikolai.' Emma jumped up away from him, breaking the tenuous connection he'd just forged. Her hard words hit him like a speeding truck. 'It's too late.'

He watched as she stood up and looked down at him and, when he couldn't respond, couldn't say what he wanted her to hear, she turned and began to walk away. It seemed as if he was watching each step she took happen in slow motion, but each one took her further from him.

He couldn't let that happen. She couldn't walk away from him until he'd told her what he'd only just realised himself. Nerves sparked through him, briefly making it impossible to say or do anything except watch her begin to walk away.

'Emma, wait.' The demand in his voice rang clearly through the morning air but she didn't slow, didn't turn. She was leaving him, walking out of his life. He had to make her see reason, had to make her understand, and there was only one way to do that.

He walked briskly after her, catching up with her as she began to cross Bow Bridge. 'I need you, Emma.'

Had he said that aloud? He stood still at the end of the bridge and watched as her steps faltered, then she stood, her back to him in the middle of the bridge. Seconds ticked by but it felt like hours as he waited for her to turn to look at him. When she did, he could see she was upset, see she was on the verge of tears, and he hated himself for it. He'd handled this all wrong, right from the moment he'd woken after that first night they'd spent together. The night that had changed not only their lives but him.

'Don't say what you don't mean, Nikolai.'

'I mean it, Emma, I need you.' Inside his head a voice was warning him that that wasn't enough, that he had to say more, he had to put himself on the line and tell her he loved her. He couldn't do that, not knowing she loved another man, but it was his baby she was carrying and he'd been the only man who'd made love to her. Surely that meant something?

'It's not enough,' she said firmly, her chin lifting in defiance. 'I want more than that, Nikolai. I want to be needed for who I am, not for the baby I carry. But more than that I need love.'

His stomach plummeted as she said those final words. Was she going back to London to be with Richard? Did she love him that much?

'I always thought love was nothing more than a word.' He took a step towards her. That chasm he'd felt earlier now had the thinnest of wires across it, but could he use it? Did he have the courage to reveal his emotions when they were still shockingly new to him?

'You made that more than clear from the very beginning.' Still she stood there in the middle of the bridge, looking at him with fierce determination. She didn't even notice a couple walking across the bridge towards him. Her gaze didn't leave his face for one second.

He had done exactly that; there was no denying he'd made it absolutely clear he didn't want love. Such a denial was what had kept him safe. It meant he'd never have to give a piece of himself to someone who could use it and destroy him emotionally—something Emma had had the power to do from the moment they'd first met. As a teenager he'd spoken just once about his father to his mother and she had confessed she'd loved him when they'd first met, before he'd shown his true self. From that moment on he'd vowed to keep such destructive emotions as love locked away.

He couldn't do that any longer. He had to acknowledge them and set them free, even if Emma did have the power to destroy him. If she didn't feel the same burning love for him, then he would be nothing, but he couldn't just tell her, not when he wanted her to be happy—with or without him. If she truly loved someone else, then he would have to let her go. It shook him to the core to realise he loved her enough to do that, enough to set her free into the arms of another man.

He thought back to their discussion on love, to the day she'd laughed at such a notion existing. It had been that denial of what she'd truly wanted that had forged the path forward for them.

'You made a joke out of love and happiness. You scorned it as much as I did, Emma.' He took several tentative steps closer, encouraged when she didn't move, didn't turn and walk away. Inside, his heart was breaking. He was a mess, but he kept his stern control, retaining that ever-present defensive shield.

'I can understand why you want to shut love out of your life, Nikolai, but the things I experienced as a child made me want that kind of happiness even more.'

She took a step towards him and hope soared inside him. 'We want different things. You want to be free of commitment and emotion, but I want love, Nikolai.'

Those last words goaded him harder than he could have imagined, pushing him to ask just what he needed to know, even though the answer would be like a knife in his newly revealed heart. 'And does Richard give you that love?'

'Richard?' Emma's mind whirled in shock. Why did Richard have anything to do with this? She struggled to think, struggled to work out how he'd come to that conclusion, and then it hit her as she remembered their afternoon on the river trip. She'd taken a call from Richard and had been so happy the article was out and that he liked it, approved of what she'd done, but Nikolai's mood had darkened the instant she'd told him who was on the phone. She'd thought he was angry with her, but was it something more? Had he felt threatened by Richard, even though he'd been on the phone?

That wretched flicker of hope flared to life within her once more and kept her where she was. She looked at Nikolai, standing now at the end of Bow Bridge, as if to continue to walk towards her was something he couldn't do.

'Do you love him, Emma? Is he the man you are leaving to go back to?' Nikolai's voice was hoarse with heavy emotion in a way she'd never heard before.

She blinked at him in total shock. He seriously thought she was in love with Richard? *You used to, before he rejected that young love and adoration.* The taunt echoed in her head and she saw it from Nikolai's perspective. She saw the easy friendship she and Richard had established over the last few years, saw how it might look to someone on the outside. But, like Nikolai, Richard had made it more than clear he didn't want anything serious, squashing that first crush until it withered and died, leaving nothing but friendship— a working friendship.

'Richard and I are just friends. Always have been.' She frowned at the scowl which crossed his face. Did such a reaction really mean he saw Richard as a threat? But to what—their marriage born out of a deal or something more?

'But that isn't what you want, is it, Emma? You told me as much on the boat.'

'I did?'

'"It hurts like hell to feel anything for someone who feels nothing for you". Those were your exact words, Emma.' He calmly repeated what she'd told him, his dark eyes watching every move she made, every breath she took.

Emma's knees almost buckled beneath her and she moved to the side of the bridge, clutching at the ornate balustrades for support. She'd been talking about him, not Richard, but he'd interpreted it as something quite different. No wonder he'd become distant to the point of coldness since that day. The closeness they'd begun to share, which she'd hoped would give rise to love, had vanished—because of what she'd said.

Waves of nausea rushed over her and her head swam. She couldn't think any more, could barely stand. She hadn't eaten anything yet, too anxious earlier to face anything, and now it was all too much. She couldn't do this now.

She felt as though she was falling then strong arms folded around her as Nikolai wrapped her in the safety of his embrace. To feel his arms around her, holding her against his body, was almost unbearable. It was like coming home—and it broke her heart a little bit more.

'You're not well.' The deep, seductive timbre of his voice radiated through her and she closed her eyes, allowing herself a brief moment in the haven of his embrace.

'Maybe we can talk later.' She clutched at the lifeline the moment had given her, not wanting to have this discussion any more. It was bad enough that he didn't love her, that he was about to reject her, but to accuse her of loving Richard was too much.

'No, we talk now—or not at all.' She looked up into his dark eyes and saw myriad emotions swirling in them, emotions she'd never seen in them before. 'It's your choice, Emma.'

She didn't want to talk now, didn't feel well enough to think, let alone talk, but she couldn't walk away and say nothing. Not when he held her so gently and looked at her so longingly. Was it possible he did feel something for her? Could it ever be love?

She needed to make herself clear, to let him know how wrong he'd got it all. She looked up at his handsome face, fighting the urge to reach up and touch his cheek, feel the smoothness of his freshly shaven face. 'It wasn't Richard I was talking about that day.'

Nikolai had moved quickly, taking Emma in his arms, holding her against him before she'd slithered completely to the floor. He'd inhaled her sweet scent, felt the warmth of her body, and his senses had exploded despite the worry he had for her health. How had he not seen it before? How could he not have known he loved her?

Because you shut your heart away.

She leant against the balustrade and looked up at him, as if waiting for him to say something, expectation mingling with desperation in her eyes. She'd just spoken, as his mind had whirled and his body had gone into overdrive just from holding her. Whatever it was she'd said, she obviously expected a response, but his ability to think rationally had left him the moment he'd held her.

'What did you just say?' he asked gently, unable to resist the urge to brush her hair from her face and then stroke the silky length of it down her back.

She looked up at him, tears beginning to brim in her eyes. 'I said that it wasn't Richard. When I said that on the boat, it wasn't him I was talking about.'

His hand stilled at her back and he held his breath, willing her to say more, but she looked down, her head dipping against his chest. If it wasn't Richard, who was it that didn't love her in the way she loved him? Had she been referring to him? Was it possible she loved him?

'Emma,' he said and lifted her chin forcing her look up at him. 'Have you ever told that person you love them?'

Still he couldn't say that he loved her, couldn't admit his deepest emotion. She searched his face, her gaze flicking over every part of him, as if committing him to her memory in the same way a camera did at the touch of a button.

She shook her head. 'It's not what he wants to hear. He doesn't believe love exists—at least, not for him. I could never tell him. I just can't.'

There was nothing else to do. He had to prove he loved her by telling her right now just how much. He had to risk having got it wrong, risk making a fool of himself. If he didn't tell her he loved her now, he'd lose her for ever.

'Maybe he just has to tell you,' he said as he looked deep into her eyes, the tears now dissolved and hope glowing from them. 'Maybe he needs to be bold and admit something he'd never thought possible.'

'Maybe he does,' she said as she watched his lips, as if willing him to say it, and his heart began to thump hard with trepidation.

He took a deep breath and swallowed, trying to instil calm into his body. This was the one thing he thought he'd never say. 'I love you, Emma Sanders. Completely and utterly.'

She closed her eyes, her body relaxed in his embrace and he couldn't resist her any longer. The temptation to kiss her was too much and he lowered his head and pressed his lips against hers. The soft sigh which escaped her did untold things to his body, but passion and desire could wait. This was a kiss of love.

Emma sighed as Nikolai kissed her, so tenderly it almost made her cry. He loved her. It wasn't only that he'd told her, but it was the way he was kissing her which proved it more than anything else. This kiss was different. It wasn't hot and filled with lustful desire that stoked the fire of passion within her. This kiss was very different. It was gentle and, more importantly, it was loving.

She wrapped her arms around his neck and kissed him back, finally allowing all the love she felt to pour from her. He stopped kissing her and pressed his fore-head to hers, the gesture so unguarded emotionally she couldn't say what she wanted to say for a moment.

'I thought you didn't want love.' She smiled, her voice teasing and light.

'That was before I met you. Everything changed the moment you stepped off that train in Vladimir.' His eyes were so tender, so filled with love, it was heart-rending and his voice broke with intense huskiness that sent a wave of pleasure breaking over her.

She closed her eyes and revisited the memory of the day they'd met, but even more importantly the knowledge that he had felt something for her from the moment they had met seeped into her. It had been no different for her. There had been something between them from that very first moment at the station in Vladimir, and he'd admitted that had turned to love even before she'd been carrying his child. That could mean only one thing.

'So our child was conceived out of love, Nikolai.' She breathed the words against his lips as he once more claimed them in a deep and meaningful kiss, his hands holding her face as if he couldn't bear not to kiss her.

Around her life went on: voices of people in the park, the ripple of the water beneath them and birds singing their joy of spring all blended into the most perfect backdrop for the moment the man she loved with all her heart confessed his love for her.

As he pulled back from her, she let her palms slide down to his chest, feeling the beat of his heart beneath her right palm, a heart which was filled with love for her. He'd had the courage to admit his love even though he'd been convinced she was going to walk away from him. How had she got it all so wrong?

'I love you, Nikolai Cunningham—with all my heart.' She smiled up at him as he smiled back at her, then kissed her tenderly, his lips gentle and loving. She wanted to melt into the moment, enjoy the kiss, but she needed him to know how much his words meant to her. She pushed against his body and pulled away from him, away from the temptation to deepen the kiss.

'You have no idea how relieved I am to hear that. The thought that you were in love with another man has been eating me up for days.' His deep, sexy voice held a hint of seriousness and she knew it had been hard for him to talk about his feelings, no matter what they were.

'Is that why you really moved out of the apartment?' she asked as shyness crept over her. 'I thought you wanted me out of your life.'

'Like your father? No, Emma, that will never happen. I figured I needed all the luck I could get after what Jess had said, so didn't want to tempt fate by flouting tradition. I knew even then I couldn't risk losing you, but I was too blinded by my past to realise why—that I'd fallen in love with you.'

'Really?' She looked up at him to see amusement sparkling in his eyes, mixing with the newly acknowledged love.

'Yes, but I also wanted you and Jess to have time to catch up and have girl chats about me.' The laughter in his voice was contagious; she laughed softly and when he stroked her hair back from her face she almost melted all over again.

Then what he'd said finally registered and embarrassment flooded her. 'You heard us talking?'

How much had he heard? She recalled telling Jess she loved him with all her heart, and she'd meant it, but they wouldn't be here like this, with the worry of the last few days behind them, if he had truly heard what she and Jess had spoken about.

'Only a little bit,' he said and his brows rose, his eyes filling with that sexy amusement that had captured her heart in the first place.

'Well, you obviously didn't hear the part where I told Jess I loved you so much that it almost hurt; that marrying you was what I wanted to do,' she said with an impish smile on her lips, taunting him mercilessly.

The humour left his face. 'No, I didn't hear that, but it could have saved me a lot of heartache if I had.'

She laughed softly, wanting to lighten the mood. 'I'd much rather just tell you myself.'

'In that case, don't let me stop you.' He pulled her against him once more and pressed his lips briefly to hers.

'I love you, Nikolai, so very much, I just want to marry you. Today.'

'Is that so?' he teased. 'In that case, you are in luck; I have everything planned for a perfect wedding for the woman I love.'

She looked at her watch and let out a shocked gasp. 'I have to go now. The man I love with all my heart is going to make me his wife and the happiest woman alive. I just hope he'll be there waiting for me.'

'I have every faith that he will be, because he's madly in love with you.'

EPILOGUE

EMMA PULLED ON an elegant black gown and looked at her reflection. The last time she'd studied herself so intensely had been the day she'd tried on her wedding dress. Now, over a year later, she was a mother to a beautiful little boy and so happy the doubts she'd had in the days before her wedding seemed like a bad dream.

'As ever, you look amazing, Mrs Cunningham.' Nikolai kissed the back of her neck and looked into the mirror at her. The usual flood of love for him filled her and she smiled back at him as he continued to compliment her. 'It will be an honour to escort you to the ballet tonight.'

A quiver of apprehension ran through her as she thought of Jess being given a chance to dance as the lead ballerina so early in her career. 'I hope Jess isn't too nervous. This is her first leading role.'

'And what better place than here in Russia, at its greatest school? She is the rising star of the company. She will have a wonderful life.' Nikolai's reassurance helped to quell the nerves she had for Jess and she knew he was right.

Emma still couldn't believe that Jess was now halfway through her training and already other ballet companies were interested in offering her a place. She had the world at her feet. It was more than she could ever have hoped for her baby sister.

'I do wish we could have brought Nathan.' Emma turned to Nikolai, wrapping herself into his embrace.

'He is just fine with his grandma.' Nikolai kissed her gently—stirring sensations she couldn't allow to take over moments before they were due to leave the hotel. She blamed it on how amazingly sexy Nikolai was in a tuxedo.

'But it's the first time we've left New York without him.' She smiled as his brows rose in a suggestive way, hinting at the plans he had to fill that time without a six-month-old baby making demands on their attention.

'Which is precisely why I intend to take full advantage of the fact. Once we've seen Jess in her starring role, I intend to bring you back to this room and that very large bed. I want to make love to you all night, just to make sure you know exactly how much and how completely I love you.'

'Is that wise?' Emma teased as she kissed his freshly shaven cheek, not daring to press her lips to his.

'What makes you ask that?' His eyes darkened with desire and an answering heat scorched inside her.

She shrugged nonchalantly. 'You know what happened last time we made love in Russia…'

'This time will be different,' he said as he kissed the back of her neck. She watched him in the mirror until she had to close her eyes against the pleasure.

'In what way?' she asked in a teasing voice.

'This time you will know how much I love you with each and every kiss.'

She turned in his arms and looked up into his handsome face, hardly able to believe how happy she was. 'Everything you do for me, Nikolai, shows me that—from bringing me here to see Jess dance, to supporting me with my photography. I couldn't be happier.'

'But I'd still like to show you,' he said softly.

'Then who am I to argue?' She laughed up at him.

Nikolai looked down at her, a seriousness brushing away the humour of moments ago. 'You are my wife, the mother of my son and the woman I love with all my heart.'

* * * * *

If you enjoyed this story, check out these other great reads from Rachael Thomas
MARRIED FOR THE ITALIAN'S HEIR
TO BLACKMAIL A DI SIONE
THE SHEIKH'S LAST MISTRESS

And don't miss these other
ONE NIGHT WITH CONSEQUENCES
themed stories

THE GUARDIAN'S VIRGIN WARD
by Caitlin Crews

CLAIMING HIS CHRISTMAS CONSEQUENCE
by Michelle Smart

Available now!

MILLS & BOON®

MODERN™

POWER, PASSION AND IRRESISTIBLE TEMPTATION

A sneak peek at next month's titles...

In stores from 12th January 2017:

- **The Last Di Sione Claims His Prize** – Maisey Yates
- **The Desert King's Blackmailed Bride** – Lynne Graham
- **The Consequence of His Vengeance** – Jennie Lucas
- **Acquired by Her Greek Boss** – Chantelle Shaw

In stores from 26th January 2017:

- **Bought to Wear the Billionaire's Ring** – Cathy Williams
- **Bride by Royal Decree** – Caitlin Crews
- **The Sheikh's Secret Son** – Maggie Cox
- **Vows They Can't Escape** – Heidi Rice

Just can't wait?
Buy our books online a month before they hit the shops!
www.millsandboon.co.uk

Also available as eBooks.

MILLS & BOON®

EXCLUSIVE EXTRACT

Even unsentimental Alessandro Di Sione can't deny
his grandfather's dream of retrieving a scandalous
painting. Yet its return depends on outspoken Princess
Gabriella. Travelling together to locate the painting,
Gabby is drawn to this guilt-ridden man.
Could their passion be his salvation?

Read on for a sneak preview of
THE LAST DI SIONE CLAIMS HIS PRIZE

Alessandro was so different than she was. Gabby had
never truly fully appreciated just how different men and
women were. In a million ways, big and small.

Yes, there was the obvious, but it was more than that.
And it was those differences that suddenly caused her to
glory in who she was, what she was. To feel, if only for
a moment, that she completely understood herself both
body and soul, and that they were united in one desire.

"Kiss me, Princess," he said, his voice low, strained.

He was affected.

So she had won.

She had been the one to make him burn.

But she'd made a mistake if she'd thought this game
had one winner and one loser. She was right down there
with him. And she didn't care about winning anymore.

She couldn't deny him, not now. Not when he was
looking at her like she was a woman and not a girl, or
an owl. Not when he was looking at her like she was

the sun, moon and all the stars combined. Bright, brilliant and something that held the power to hold him transfixed.

Something more than what she was. Because Gabriella D'Oro had never transfixed anyone. Not her parents. Not a man.

But he was looking at her like she mattered. She didn't feel like shrinking into a wall, or melting into the scenery. She wanted him to keep looking.

She didn't want to hide from this. She wanted all of it.

Slowly, so slowly, so that she could savor the feel of him, relish the sensations of his body beneath her touch, she slid her hand up his throat, feeling the heat of his skin, the faint scratch of whiskers.

Then she moved to cup his jaw, his cheek.

"I've never touched a man like this before," she confessed.

And she wasn't even embarrassed by the confession, because he was still looking at her like he wanted her.

He moved closer, covering her hand with his. She could feel his heart pounding heavily, could sense the tension running through his frame. "I've touched a great many women," he said, his tone grave. "But at the moment it doesn't seem to matter."

That was when she kissed him.

Don't miss
THE LAST DI SIONE CLAIMS HIS PRIZE
By Maisey Yates

Available February 2017
www.millsandboon.co.uk

MILLS & BOON®

Why shop at millsandboon.co.uk?

Each year, thousands of romance readers find their perfect read at millsandboon.co.uk. That's because we're passionate about bringing you the very best romantic fiction. Here are some of the advantages of shopping at www.millsandboon.co.uk:

* **Get new books first**—you'll be able to buy your favourite books one month before they hit the shops

* **Get exclusive discounts**—you'll also be able to buy our specially created monthly collections, with up to 50% off the RRP

* **Find your favourite authors**—latest news, interviews and new releases for all your favourite authors and series on our website, plus ideas for what to try next

* **Join in**—once you've bought your favourite books, don't forget to register with us to rate, review and join in the discussions

Visit **www.millsandboon.co.uk**
for all this and more today!